See You Again

Rachel O'ROURKE

MM ROMANCE AUTHOR

Content Warning

For further information, please scan the QR code for a list of possible content triggers.

By reading further, you, as the reader, are continuing with the understanding that not all possible triggers may have been mentioned. The author and any who contributed to this work cannot and will not be held accountable for a reader's actions, reactions, or state of mind after reading this book.

See You Again

Rachel O'Rourke

Everyone is born with a soulmate.

Whether yours is in the form of a best friend or a lover, the universe has made the decision to give you the version of a soulmate they know you'll need most in life.

You might have met your soulmate early in life, or maybe you're still on a journey to find them. Regardless, you are always connected.

Never stop searching, when the universe says you're ready, you'll meet.

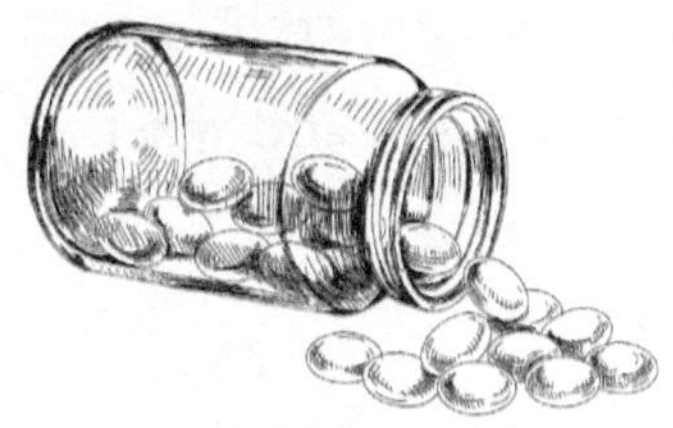

Chapter 1

"So, Riley." Hearing Dr Clara Bech address him has Riley turning his attention from the picture frames on the wall to the psychologist before him. "Can you tell me what brought you into my office today?"

Riley draws his bottom lip into his mouth, gnawing at it as his eyes avert back to the certificates hanging on the pastel blue wall.

"Why blue?" he asks, well aware he has ignored her original question.

"Excuse me?"

"The walls. You could've picked any colour and you go with blue. Why? Figured white would've been a more standard, good way of lettin' ya patients know that they could end up in a white padded cell."

"Is that what you think? That if you don't talk to me, you'll end up in a psychiatric ward?"

He shrugs. His lip ends up back between his teeth, and he's biting hard enough to draw blood if he isn't careful.

"If it's any consolation, I would have to complete a detailed assessment to determine if you needed to be admitted, get an understanding of what you may be struggling with, and whether you were in danger of harming yourself or others."

"Who says I'm struggling?" Riley bites back.

"I wouldn't know since you've not yet told me why you're here. But what I do know is that your sister called to help set up an appointment. She mentioned…" Dr Bech stops talking, but Riley isn't stupid enough to fall for her tricks; he knows what she is trying to do.

"Tell me why you chose blue," he demands. A test to see how much control he has.

"It's soothing. Peaceful. Studies found that most shades of blue are considered calming due to their likeness to the sky and the ocean."

"I hate it." He doesn't really. He's trying to fight against science to show authority.

"I'll take that into consideration." The psychologist makes a note and Riley is back to reading the certificates on the wall.

The sound of the ticking clock fills the silence between them. He knows it's impossible, but after sitting on the couch that feels as though it is trying to swallow him whole, Riley could swear black and blue that his heartbeat begins to beat in time with the ticks.

Tick. Boom

Tick. Boom

Tick. Boom

His mind wanders from the certificates and moves on to count how many plants are in the room; twelve, which, in one way, sounds like a ridiculous amount of foliage and yet in another, doesn't seem like it's enough for the space. Riley exhales and begins to count how many books are on the corner shelf. It's only then, once he's double-checked that there are thirty-nine books, that he finally answers the psychologist's question.

"Like you said, sister made me come."

Twelve Months Ago

It was like any other day. Riley woke to the sound of his phone alarm playing the Imperial March from Star Wars, his body already sweating from the August heat. He found it was the only tune that helped get his ass out of bed to turn it off; its excessive use of the trumpet and trombone would otherwise screech in his ear, the volume purposely set to max. He stumbled out of his room and rubbed the sleep from his eyes, not surprised to see his twin sister was already in the kitchen making breakfast for him and their father, who was catatonic in front of the TV, no doubt high as a kite thanks to his self-medicating.

"Hey, eggs are almost ready, bacon is on the table," Noelle explained to him.

Riley gave her a nod in thanks, his body unable to produce a single word before caffeine entered his bloodstream.

He took a sip. "Ah, thanks." The words fell from his mouth with ease. He sat at the table, the same place he had sat for the last twenty-five years of his life, his chair changing from a highchair to a booster seat, then to the rickety wooden one he was sitting in now.

"He alive?" Riley motioned at their father, Malcolm, who was reclined in a stained singlet, what looked to be soiled boxers—but thankfully weren't—and white ankle socks that appeared more yellowy brown.

"Unfortunately," Noelle confirmed. "Had to put my hand in front of his nose to check if he was breathing since he hasn't stirred from a single noise I've made," Noelle explained as she took a seat at the table across from Riley.

"That'll be the day." He grabbed his cutlery and dug in.

"Riley!" Noelle chastised him.

"What? You were thinkin' it," he bit back.

"But you said it."

"Oh, so now I'm the asshole because I believe our lives will be better if our deadbeat drug addict of a father kicked the bucket?"

Noelle shrugged. "You know it's not his fault."

"Please. You and I know it's his fault and the last thing he needs is sympathy. He'd only see it as an encouragement to continue." Riley had lost his appetite. His sister knew how sensitive he was when it came to the cause of their father's habit. He threw his food in the trash, took a gulp of his coffee and went back to his room to quickly change for work.

"You home for dinner?" Noelle called out.

"Not like I got anywhere else to be," he yelled back at her.

"You could call—"

"No!" Riley stepped out from his bedroom, head poking around the corner so he could look his sister in the eye. "Stop tryin' to set me up with one of your work buddies. They're all weird, self-absorbed assholes. I ain't interested," he explained to her for what felt like the hundredth time.

"Hey, real estate is a hard business. They need to be confident in what they do to beat the competition."

"Whatever. Deal with your own love life and leave mine alone."

His sister worked in the rental department at Realty 1 Maryland and yet, between Noelle's wage and his—he worked as a full-time mechanic at Rising Sun Motors—they couldn't scrape together enough to find their own place, cover the bills, and leave the dump that they used to love calling home.

Like everything, the housing costs went up around the same time Riley's mother died. Ten years ago, he and his sister would have been able to find a small two-bedroom, one-bathroom, and have a small amount left over for expenses. But that's not the case now, which is why he put up with his piece-of-shit father, looked out for his twin, and put every spare dollar to his name aside to help them escape at the first chance they got.

"Yo, Charlie. I'm here," Riley called out as he entered the garage. It was still early, the shop was not officially open to the public for another thirty minutes, but his boss and mentor, Charlie, always insisted on a chat and a coffee in peace before the day began.

"Back here," Charlie called back. Riley followed the voice and found his boss under a 1977 Ford F-250. Riley recognised it instantly.

"Jesus. Again?" Riley questioned.

His boss slid out from under the car as he wiped his hands with a cloth.

"I told Tommy it would be cheaper for 'im to sell her parts and buy somethin' a little newer, but you know how he is, sentimental bastard," Charlie explained.

Riley chuckled, knowing how emotional Tommy got when he had to drop his baby off after it once again died and needed towing to their shop. A small part of him suspected that Tommy saw his car as something more than a vehicle on four wheels. The way that man would eye off the exhaust, Tommy seemed to be more than a simple car enthusiast.

"Anyway," Charlie continued. "Clint is running an errand for me. Junkyard said they had some parts I could use, still in good condition, and were offering to sell 'em to me cheap. Means he won't be in until this afternoon. Think you can manage?"

"You askin' if I can handle the Chevy that Clint was meant to have ready for the owner by tomorrow?" Riley smirked.

"Yes. But don't go tellin' that little twerp that he's fallin' behind or his father will be down here with my balls in a vice grip."

Riley chuckled, rolling the sleeves of his coveralls up so he could get to work. "I swear," Riley began. "Big Jim has everyone in this town shaking in their fucking boots and yet I've never seen that guy so much as squish a spider."

"Kid, you don't get the name Big Jim just because you're taller than the rest of the class," Charlie offered, though Riley still felt like further detail was needed.

Charlie took care of opening the garage, turning on the radio to some classic rock station that Riley always appreciated, and he set out to work, getting lost in the car's engine.

When he got home, Riley's blond hair, which had a hint of red when under a certain light, had enough grease in it to get an idea of what he'd look like if he ever wanted to dye it black. His hands were not much better and his back was stiff after spending hours leaning over the bonnet of the Chevrolet Silverado.

The screen door banged against the doorframe after he unlocked it and walked inside.

"That you, Noelle?" A voice called out from the living room.

"Nah, Pops. It's me," Riley answered. He received a grunt in return.

He made his way into the kitchen, opened the fridge and smiled when he saw dinner on a plate, a note from his sister sat on top.

Gone out for dinner with Joel. Enjoy eating alone, loser. xx

The words made Riley smile; he could hear his sister's teasing voice so clearly in his mind it was as though she had said it out loud.

"Where the fuck is she? 'm starvin'," Malcolm called out from the same place Riley had left him ten hours ago.

"Out with Joel." He wondered to himself if this boyfriend would last longer than three months, which seemed to be the length of time that Noelle kept them around before kicking them to the curb.

"Good. Quicker she gets hitched the quicker she can stop freeloading off'a me."

"Like you'd survive if we left," Riley whispered under his breath, though it seemed not to have been soft enough.

"The fuck you say to me, kid?" The sound of the chair recliner being pushed down and locked in was what put Riley on alert. His father was suddenly stumbling over toward him, the look on Malcolm's face dared Riley to speak out of line.

"Nothin' Pops. Was just grabbing dinner from the fridge for ya." Riley went to open the refrigerator but a heavy palm slammed it closed. He cringed, instantly regretting the sign of weakness that his father would have soaked up.

"You know better than to talk back to me, boy. Show your father some goddamn respect."

Riley gritted his teeth and bit his tongue while the voice in his head told him not to fight back and make things worse.

"Sorry, Pops. I'll get you dinner. Was planning to meet up with Billy 'n Jackson anyway." He wasn't really, but it might be something he should consider since the energy in the house had become more than unpleasant.

"Still hanging around that faggot, are ya?" his father questioned. Malcolm was a few inches taller than him, but his father had this power that caused Riley to feel as though Malcolm were towering over him, especially when in a rage, which had recently become a new addition to his father's behaviour.

This time, Riley didn't hold his tongue.

"Gee, Pops. Real nice considering your gay son is standing right fucking here."

"God damn it, Riley!" His father swiped the dinner plate out of his hand. The food Noelle had cooked crashed to the floor along with the broken ceramic plate. "Your mother would be rollin' in her grave if she knew what perverted lifestyle you had chosen to live."

Riley clenched his fist. It was one thing to have his father spit venomous words at him a few times a week, but it was a whole other story when he brought up their mother. He used her death to make Riley feel guilty for the person he was, even though Riley knew in his heart that she would have loved him regardless.

"Please. The only thing makin' her roll in her grave is seeing the man she married turn into a low-life addict who spends all his time treating his kids like shit, like slaves who he can boss around." Riley fought back.

He saw the fist coming towards his head and swiftly ducked out of the way. Quick reflexes, one. Drug-induced fog brain, zero. His father's knuckles connected with the glass cabinet above the kitchen sink. Glass shattered, cutting into the skin of his attacker.

"Motherfucker!" Malcolm screeched; his fist held close to his chest as blood dripped down his knuckles. "Look what you made me do."

Riley ignored Malcolm's commentary and made his way towards the bathroom for the first aid kit. He came back to the kitchen to find his father sitting at the dining table. He paused for a second to take in the scene. The smashed plate was shattered on the floor, the food now smeared into the tiles from where his father had stood on it, either not aware or not caring. The cabinet had blood on the white wooden frame that had dripped from the shattered glass. And yet, his father sat at the head of the table, the same spot he had sat in since Riley could remember, his hand somewhat forgotten as he pulled out the bottle of pills from his ratty bathrobe and swallowed two of them dry.

He dropped the first aid kit in front of his father and decided that he could take care of himself while Riley cleaned up the mess. He didn't want Noelle to come home and see it, though the cabinet might be hard to explain come morning.

It was as though the encounter had been forgotten. Riley was sweeping the mess into the garbage bag when his father stood, his hand merely wrapped in gauze, not bothering to clean or check for shards of glass. Malcolm made his way back to the single-seat recliner where the TV was waiting for him, not a single word was exchanged between them.

It took an hour to clean everything up. By then, Riley was too exhausted to try to make himself something to eat, opting for a glass of milk and a couple of pop tarts. He showered, used Fast Orange and hand soap; and mixed the two to remove all evidence of grease from his body, a trick Charlie had taught him day one on the job. He made sure to run his fingers through his hair before using his shampoo to bring himself back to his natural hair colour.

Once dressed, Riley checked that the front door was locked and was not surprised to see his father passed out in his chair. Riley couldn't even remember the last time he saw Malcolm spend a night in his bedroom.

Cautiously, Riley walked toward the man he used to have respect for. He reached for the remote and switched the TV off. The house was silent. It was eerie. What used to be a home full of laughter and joy was now more like a haunted house, his father a ghost amongst the echoes of infomercials and sitcoms on repeat.

Riley placed the TV remote back on the small table beside his father's chair. His eyes caught sight of the pill bottle poking out of the bathrobe pocket, which was barely a pocket due to the loose stitching.

Riley felt like a kid again as he slowly, carefully, approached his father's listless form, like when he used to steal change from his mother's purse so he could go down to the corner store and buy lollies for himself and his sister. He held his breath as he grabbed the bottle, instantly stepping back and standing frozen in place till he was sure his father had not woken.

A minute. That's how long he stood silent before he knew it was safe to walk into the bathroom where he opened the bottle of street-bought fentanyl and tipped the round white pills down the toilet. The flush felt like a relief, though deep down, Riley knew it wasn't permanent.

Riley wasn't surprised to find he was awake before Noelle. His sister still hadn't returned home by the time he had gone to bed, and she had this weird rule about not staying at Joel's house during the week, which she claimed was because of work.

As he waited for his toast to pop, he sipped his coffee and scrolled through his phone, not really one for social media but interested in what the rest of the world was curious about. The agonizing groan of a person who had drunk too much and slept too little caused him to look up. A chuckle fell from his mouth as his sister shuffled into the kitchen with her makeup still on from the night before, smudged from sleep. She rubbed her temples.

"Had fun, sis?" He may have raised his voice a little more than usual, simply to be a dick.

"Shhh." Noelle's own voice caused her to wince.

"Serves you right. I don't know why you don't just crash at his place." He took his toast, freshly popped, and tossed it from each hand as the heat burned his fingers, before dropping it onto his plate.

"Because, unlike my relationships in the past, if I want this one to work, I need to set some boundaries."

"So, fucking in his car and being dropped back home seems classier than waking up in his bed and going to work from his apartment?" He placed a finger on his chin, acting deep in thought.

The stale muffin that hit his head had him laughing at his sister's expense.

"Whatever. Come to me when you've been in a committed relationship. Then you can question my motives."

"Sure, since it's so easy to date when the leader of every anti-gay rally never leaves the house." Riley nodded over at Malcolm, who was drooling in his chair.

Noelle took a seat at the table, coffee in one hand, and yogurt in the other.

"First, how can he lead the rallies if he doesn't leave the house? Second, all you have to do is not bring them home."

"Who knew my big sister could make back alleys sound so sexy?"

"Please, I have more class than that. Use a bathroom stall. Or, go back to their place but come home like I do."

It's not that Riley hadn't thought about it, but perhaps he was old-fashioned. He was the type that liked to get to know the person he was sleeping with. The whole three-date rule before he bent over and let a guy pound him five ways to Sunday.

"Think about it. You're only getting older and your big sister knows what's best." Noelle stood.

"You're older by twenty minutes." Riley rolled his eyes.

"Technically. But according to our birth certificates, I'm a whole day older than you and that counts as something."

"Yeah, yeah."

He took a bite of his toast and watched as his sister analysed the kitchen. He waited for her to 'spot the difference' from how she had left it the night before.

"The glass cabinet is broken," Noelle pointed out.

Ding, ding, ding!

Perhaps his sister wasn't as hungover as he thought, simply sex drunk.

"It was either the glass cabinet or my face. Personally, I'm glad the cabinet lost." He should have felt something at that moment. Sorrow. Mournfulness. Anger. Fear.

Instead, like the silent conversations he and his sister learned to share from an early age, he offered her a shrug, and in return, she gave him a closed-lip smile. With their bond, Riley knew that his sister got the message that he was okay, and he had received her apology on their father's behalf.

Noelle shuffled back towards the bathroom to ready herself for work. He had fifteen minutes to finish getting dressed, pack his food and head out the door for the thirty-minute drive ahead of him.

"Ey, Riley. Thanks, man, for helping out with that Chevy. I would have had it but, ya know, Charlie needed me to run that errand for him." Clint leant on the counter, his dark blond hair fell on either side of his face, the length cut just below his chin. Riley tried to prevent the eye roll that threatened to escape whenever he saw Clint tie it into a bun before he got to work on a car.

"It's whatever, Clint," Riley stated. "We all gotta help each other out, right?"

"Exactly. So, ya know, if you want some help with that Charger—"

"Not gonna happen." Riley looked up from the computer where he'd been placing an order for parts. Tommy's Ford used most of what they had on hand.

"Oh, come on, man. How am I going to learn if I'm always working on older models?"

"How do you think newer car models are made?" Riley shouldn't have been surprised to see the blank look on Clint's face. "Through the evolution of older cars. Once you know how an older car works, then you can start working on the newer stuff. Simple as that." Riley wasn't sure how accurate that statement was, but he did remember Charlie using that exact phrase when he first started working at the garage straight out of high school.

Riley shook his head in amusement as he watched Clint huff his way toward the Honda that reminded Riley of the first car he ever owned. He went back to placing the order, lost in the task before him to the point where he hadn't heard the bell above the door chime.

"Excuse me, I'm looking for Shane."

He looked up and the sight before him had Riley stuck for words. The guy was tall, clean cut, and his smile glowed against his auburn hair, though as the late afternoon sun shone through the shop window, it proved to have more of a red tinge than brown.

The guy was dressed in a simple forest green T-shirt, which matched his eyes accordingly. Riley could see the guy's toned physique thanks to how his clothes were sticking to his body, perhaps a size too small for his frame.

"Ah…" Riley shook his head in the hopes of clearing the daydream that had caused him to freeze mentally and physically. "Shane. Right. No, she ah, she left a month or so ago."

"Shit. Okay." The guy rapped his knuckles on the counter and looked around the garage as though he was lost.

"Something I can help you with?" Riley offered, hoping to be in this man's company a little while longer.

"It's my car," the Disney Prince explained.

"Well, you're already at the right place." He offered a smirk that seemed to ease the tension in the man before him.

"Ha, true. My, um, my work colleague told me to speak with Shane. Said she could help me out."

Riley bit his bottom lip. He had no idea the situation this guy's car was in, but it was obvious he was sniffing for a family-friend discount.

"What's the issue?" Riley questioned.

"Honestly, it's just due for a service. It runs fine but the last place I went to, they told me I had all these issues, ended up paying a thousand dollars, which was most of my savings, and then I got home and my dad told me none of those issues were even a real thing."

"Shit, let me guess, the place down on Franklin?"

"Yes!" The man before him bellowed with more enthusiasm than Riley expected.

"That garage is the reason us mechanics are getting a bad rep. The assholes smell virgin blood and use it as a scare tactic."

"Strange since my virginity sailed a long time ago."

Riley was taken aback, surprised that out of everything he said, that was the part of his story that the customer commented on. Perhaps this guy didn't have a filter.

Even though his mind was trying to process the reason for the comment, Riley's body betrayed him as his cheeks felt warm, a sign that they were turning a dusty pink colour, and his mouth had lifted into somewhat of a smirk.

"Well." Riley scratched the back of his neck, a nervous habit of his. "Shane met some guy online and has run off to the other side of the fuckin' world to be with him. So, best I can do is look your car over myself and promise to call with a quote before I go fixing anything. That way, you feel like I'm rippin' you off, you can go elsewhere for another quote."

"I don't know whether to take your honesty as a good sign or listen to the voice in my head that's telling me it's all a ruse to lure me in."

This guy was a fucking dork, and Riley was eating it up.

"Why would I lie? You said it yourself, not a virgin, which means my sacrifice to the motor gods will only end in my demise for lying."

"It is impressively scary how accurate that sentence is," the redhead stated.

"I mean, Clint's about to finish his break, so I could always get him to look at it if you don't trust me. But heads up, he once put gas in a diesel car and broke a gearbox when he told us he could drive stick and, well, couldn't."

Riley watched the sea-green eyes flick down his body before they locked back onto his eyes. For the first time in his career, Riley suddenly felt exposed with his overalls unbuttoned down to the waist, the sleeves tied around his hips with his white tank top on display.

"I'd rather take my chances with the sacrifice, thanks."

Riley swallowed.

He nodded his head, his body once again betraying him as he smiled from ear to ear, unsure of why. "Good choice. Lead the way." Riley walked out from behind the desk and watched the man, who looked roughly five-eleven, walk confidently before him, the view something Riley thoroughly enjoyed.

Outside the garage was an emerald green Jeep Wrangler parked along the curb. From the look of the rounded headlights, Riley guessed it was dated back to the late 1990s.

He whistled at the beauty of it.

"Not bad. Had it long?" He squinted against the sunlight that was shining over the redhead, which changed his hair once again to mimic the colour of a phoenix's feathers.

"Three years. Had a little over a hundred thousand miles on it when I bought it. No issues. Service was due six months after I got it, took it to those devil worshippers and since then, I haven't had it checked out. Figured it was time."

"Shit. You know Wranglers are meant to be serviced every ten thousand miles, right?"

The guy before him shook his head. "No."

"Alright. It's officially my duty of care to make sure this car is safe for you to continue driving. Give me the keys."

Without question, the redhead threw the keys in the air. Riley caught it with no issue, then signalled for the guy to follow him back inside to grab some details.

Ten minutes later, Callum Reed, according to the form, had provided a contact number, email address, keys to his Jeep, and a mental image that Riley was going to store away and use multiple times in the not-so-distant future.

"How long do you think it will be? Don't really have any other way to get around."

"Should only take me a day to look it over, though today's Friday and we're only open on Saturday for drop-offs." He found it fascinating how intently Callum was listening to him, something he wasn't used to. "From there, guess we'll see."

"Guess we'll see," Callum repeated.

They both stood there for a moment or two until eventually, Callum broke the bubble.

"I suppose I'll be seeing you."

Then he was gone and Riley was left standing in his place of work, feeling as though he had met someone who was going to change his life.

However, what Riley wasn't taking into account was how change was not always favourable.

Chapter 2

It has been a month and Riley still isn't used to the ceiling above his bed. The paint is too perfect. The lights are warm rather than cool and now he has four. For as long as he can remember, his bedroom has only had a single globe in the centre.

Riley's phone is buzzing on the nightstand. Has been for some time, but he's lost in the fact that his ceiling no longer has a texture. He used to be able to stand on his bed, the low ceiling making it possible for him to barely touch the roof with his fingertips, the coarse texture reminding him of goosebumps. As a kid, he'd laugh with his mum that the house was always cold. He wonders if by saying such a thing, he put it out into the universe, who then decided to take his mother away and create the cold house he always joked about.

The constant buzzing causes his phone to dance off the bedside table and crash to the floor. Riley eventually reaches over the edge of his bed to retrieve it. He swipes the screen to answer the phone but doesn't say anything.

"Thank Christ! I've been calling for the last five minutes! Was about to get into the car and drive my ass down there to make sure you were okay!" Noelle screams through the phone, but he keeps it close to his ear, the pain a welcome reminder that he is still present.

There's a sigh. "Did you get much sleep?" his sister asks in a softer tone.

"Couldn't." His voice is void of any emotion.

"Nightmares?" Noelle asks.

Yes.

"No," he answers quickly, in the hopes that she believes him. "My ceiling is different."

"I mean, that's what happens when you move houses, Ry."

"No. I mean, I couldn't sleep because it's not the same. It's, it's too smooth. Where are the cracks and the rendered texture and the, the—"

"Riley…"

Noelle's voice puts an end to the panic he can sense building inside of him.

"Are you seeing Dr Bech today?"

Riley pulls the phone away from his ear and checks the date to confirm that it is, in fact, Tuesday. He wasn't entirely sure. He places the phone back against his ear before answering.

"Yeah. Appointment's at two."

"I'll pick you up. Drive you over."

"You don't—"

"I know. But I want to, okay?"

Fighting Noelle involves energy he doesn't have. Besides, with his lack of sleep, it's probably safer if his sister drives. Shame, though. Falling asleep at the wheel seems like a pretty easy thing to do.

Riley stares out the passenger seat window. The office building looks cold from the outside, a contrast to the multiple rooms inside, all offering different services. There's only one of them that has any value to him.

"I know it's hard, but I'm proud of you for going. For getting help." Noelle reaches over, going to place her hand on his but he pulls away before she makes contact.

"You didn't give me much choice." The time on the car dash reads 1.55. He opens the car door without offering a thank you or a goodbye.

"I'll be back at three to get you. We can go out for din—"

Riley slams the car door closed before his sister finishes her sentence.

He stands out the front of Dr Bech's office door trying to convince himself to knock rather than flee the scene like his body is itching to do. He raises his hand, his fist trembles as his body and mind argue. However, the decision is made for him as the door opens, his arm still frozen in mid-air while he stands face-to-face with Dr Bech.

"Riley, hi. I'm sorry, I didn't hear you knock. Have you been waiting long?" Dr Bech steps to the side, holding the door open for him so he can walk through.

He shakes his head in response, allowing a few more moments before he steps over the threshold and takes his seat on the couch.

Nothing looks different. He didn't expect it to. He's sure psychologists keep their environment the same so their patients don't feel unsettled by any sudden changes. But still, he expected maybe a book to be out of place, or even a layer of dust on the window sill, something to suggest that the doctor herself wasn't so perfect, sitting in her pristine room, judging everyone for not having their life in order.

"So," Dr Bech starts, smiling kindly, sitting in the armchair across from him. "I'm glad you decided to come back. After our last appointment, I wasn't too sure."

He studies his hands, his nails bitten down, cuticles gnawed.

"How have you been sleeping?" Dr Bech asks.

A shrug is the only answer Riley can muster up.

Why does he bother?

It's a waste of his time and the doctor's.

"Let's try this. Rather than talking about what brought you here, let's talk about something else."

Riley looks up, an eyebrow cocked, waiting for further instructions to understand why they would talk about anything besides the one thing he doesn't want to talk about.

"Like what?" he questions.

"Tell me about your sister. Tell me what it's like having a twin."

Eleven Months Ago

"I was banging this chick," Billy explained in far too graphic detail for Riley's liking. He passed the joint back to Jackson, hoping the puff would take the edge off of his friend's story. "And then in walks her boyfriend."

"Oh, shit." Jackson coughed the words out as the inhale of smoke clashed with the exhale of his response.

"No fucking way," Riley interjected.

"Swear to God. The guy was big too, looked like The Rock. I was lucky to make it out with my pants still around my ankles," Billy continued.

"Then what's she doing with a Michael Cera look-a-like?" Riley clicked his fingers for the joint. Jackson passed it to Billy first before it returned to Riley's hand.

"Guess she realised big muscles equals a small dick." Billy grabbed the front of his jeans and shook himself. Both men grumbled at their friend's bullshit while dick-size jokes broke out between them.

The laughter settled, the joint down to the nub as the three of them sat on the back porch of Jackson's house.

"What about you, Ry? You getting any?" Jackson passed the beer bottle to him, which he took a pull from before answering.

"Would I be spending my Saturday with you losers if I were?" He took another gulp.

Jackson placed his hand over his chest, faking a wounded heart. "Ouch. And here I thought best friends come before dick."

"Easy for you to say, you got a revolving door of dicks to choose from." Riley finished off his beer and passed the bottle to Billy so he could put it in the bin beside him.

"That I do. And my mumma's sleeping pills keep her knocked out for all of it."

Again, laughter broke out between them.

"What the hell you tellin' the guys you bring home? Don't go in that room, my mumma is down for the count?" Riley sat back in the porch chair, the night air still warm for fall, but not unpleasant enough that he was sweating his ass off.

"As far as they know, I live alone." Jackson shrugged like it was a no-brainer.

"At your age? Yeah right, you couldn't afford a place like this." Riley motioned his hand in a jerk-off manner.

"Maybe I inherited it. Anyway, the fuck it matters? They get a warm bed to dick me down in, that's all they need to know." Jackson picked up the baseball from the porch floor and began to play a game of catch with Billy from their seats.

"Wait, is this why you two never hooked up? You're both bottoms?" Billy asked for the first time in their ten years of friendship.

"Jesus. Not all gays have to sleep together, Billy. We can just be friends, ya know." Riley leapt off his chair to intercept the ball, the game now a three-way toss around.

"Exactly. Besides, screwing Riley would feel incestuous. Dude's like my brother," Jackson elaborated.

It seemed the answer was to Billy's satisfaction because he shrugged and moved on from the conversation.

"Alright, jerkoffs. I gotta head home." Riley belched; beer breath made his nose scrunch up as he caught a whiff.

They all called out their goodbyes, everyone too tired or relaxed to bother with a high-five or a hug farewell. When Riley turned the car engine on, he knew he was sober enough to drive, never having more than one when he had to get behind the wheel, and only a puff or two if they decided to smoke up. But after the long week and the end-of-summer weather, he wound the windows down and blasted the music to be on the safe side.

He was a mechanic. Car safety was his priority, especially after seeing the multitude of crumbled-up vehicles that sat at the wreckers.

The drive was short, he could see the road ahead of him clearly and when he pulled into the driveway, he was surprised to see his sister was already home.

When he turned off the ignition, that's when Riley heard the yelling. He ran inside and the first thing he noticed was how the house was torn apart, appearing as if a tornado had swept through it in his absence.

"Where the fuck are they, Noelle?" His father was screaming in Noelle's face, his sister cowering against the wall Malcolm had her trapped against.

"I told yo-you. I don-don't know." Noelle stuttered through the tears that streamed down her face. The fear in her voice caused Riley to rush over and pull his father away.

"Get the fuck off her!" Riley yelled. His rage matched that of his father's.

"My pills. Where the fuck are they, huh?" His father lunged towards him, the crazed look in his eyes had Riley on alert. He pushed Noelle out of the way. His back slammed into the wall, the impact causing the last family photo ever taken to fall and shatter onto the floor. His father's forearm pressed against his throat, the pressure enough to restrict his breathing.

"Where. Are. They?" His father spat out each word. Riley didn't blink when the saliva landed on his face, it would only show weakness.

Between gritted teeth and what would no doubt be a bruised oesophagus, Riley got what he needed out.

"Flushed." He smiled as his father's face dropped at the realisation.

"You little shit." Unfortunately, this time, Riley was unable to dodge the fist that Malcolm threw his way. The impact of firm knuckles landing on his cheekbone was enough to have him buckle forward and hold his face in his hands.

"You got no right goin' through my things. This is *my* goddamn house!"

It was Noelle who came running toward him, checking to see if he was okay. Checking if anything was broken. It was his sister who helped him stand as he tried to open his eye before it swelled shut. His father did nothing but pace back and forth, the first sign that he was having withdrawals.

"Look at you," Riley barked at his father. "You took what was prescribed for your pain as a way to cover the real pain, the one you're hiding from while Noelle and I try to live our lives and move on."

He was sure none of the words were registering with his father but he said them anyway.

"She's gone. And while Noelle and I work our asses off to try and keep us afloat, you spend whatever money you have on pills that are turning you into a person she'd be disgusted to see."

Riley watched as his father got down on his hands and knees and began to search the couch cushions for any remnants of dropped pills. There was no use trying to get through to him and honestly, he had given up years ago. Riley took his sister's hand and walked into the kitchen for a bag of frozen peas before he pulled her into his bedroom. Closing the door, he used the desk chair in his room to wedge under the handle to give himself and his sister an extra sense of protection.

Noelle was already lying on his mattress when he turned back around. His face was aching. The adrenaline had faded and the pain was setting in. He collapsed beside her, the peas finding their place on his face where they'd stay until thawed.

"Do you ever think about what it would be like if she were still alive?" His sister's voice sounded so innocent in the quiet of his bedroom.

"All the time." He exhaled.

"He never used to hit you before she died," Noelle voiced into the comfort of the pillow.

"It's the drugs, Noelle. It's not him. You know that, right?" It's not that he wanted to defend his father after what happened, but he didn't want his sister's memory of the man he was to be tarnished. Malcolm wasn't perfect back when their mother was alive, but he was at least a father.

"I dream about her still. About family road trips and seeing her face when I walk down the aisle. Her excitement at being a grandmother."

"You tryin' to tell me something, sis?" Riley turned his head just enough to see his older sister lying peacefully on his pillow.

"No, dickhead. I'm just saying…it's sad that she won't be here when those things happen." He stretched an arm out. It was an offer for his sister to lay her head on his chest, which she took, and both of them snuggled into one another.

"She might not be there for all of that, but I will be. Always." He planted a kiss on his sister's forehead.

Noelle huffed. That was code for "Gee, thanks."

He wrapped his other arm around her. Although Noelle was older, when it came to size, they were the same height and both somewhat small, which they say is normal for twins. Riley, however, had muscle, but he wasn't beefy. His work was his daily exercise and his sister looked as though she never ate. Her superpower was being able to constantly consume food while looking starved. It allowed them to fit together perfectly.

"Mum used to say we could never sleep unless we were holding each other like this." Noelle broke the comfortable silence.

"That's because you'd scream bloody murder without me beside you," Riley corrected her.

"Whaddya expect? You were practically glued to me in the womb."

"If I recall, you'd kick me away so you could have your space." They bantered over secondhand memories that their mother used to share with them. But regardless of their bickering, when either of them needed comfort and didn't have the strength to ask, they reverted to the stories that reminded them why their bond was not only strong but important. Finding solace in what they shared.

Riley had no doubt in his mind that the twin bond was real. He had felt it, numerous times. A sudden need to be close to his sister, a voice in his head telling him to call her so she knew he was thinking of her. They sometimes craved the same food or gave the same snarky response. Their hair was the same shade of blonde, though when Riley spent time in the sun it took on a gingery gold colour, while Noelle had a habit of dying her hair bleach blonde. His eyes, were an electric blue whereas his sister's eyes were softer, with speckles of green.

They stuck up for one another, helped each other get out of trouble by lying or finished the other's homework when it was too difficult. They had their own friend groups growing up but refused to be separated in class, which unfortunately didn't always work out.

But there was no denying that he would do anything for his sister. Be there for her no matter the time or day. Protect her, love her, encourage her and let her know when she was making a mistake. He could have stayed with his friends for another drink and told them about the stunning redhead that caught his eye at the garage, but he chose to come home and with that, he made it back in time to stop his father.

Coincidence? Perhaps.

Luck? Maybe so. Their bond telling him it was time to get home? That seemed more accurate.

He removed the thawed-out peas from his face. The swelling would hopefully be gone by Monday, but the graze against his cheek would take a little longer. In the safety of his bedroom and the comfort of his bed, Riley held his sister tight and drifted off to sleep while the sound of their father crashing around faded into the night.

"Well, shit," Riley exhaled. He wiped his hands on his overalls as he stood from the creeper.

"What seems to be the matter this time?" Charlie questioned as he walked by.

"Three years too late for a service," he mumbled.

Charlie whistled. It's not as though Riley didn't understand the reason behind Callum's hesitancy in getting his car looked over, but if money were an issue, this guy was not going to like his options.

"All you can do is tell 'em the truth, son. What they do with that information is up to them," Charlie offered as he walked toward Tommy's Ford, which was getting picked up the following morning.

It seemed as though Charlie was hovering. Riley suspected it had to do with the shiner he was sporting, though neither man offered to mention it, even after Clint walked into the garage that morning and blatantly asked who was lucky enough to get a swing in.

Read the fucking room, Clint.

Riley allowed him to hover. The guy had no one outside of work, no kids, though Charlie said he always wanted them. Unfortunately, his late wife was never able to conceive. Riley began working for Charlie shortly after his wife passed. The man had a heart of gold and knew almost everyone in town. Riley was aware that Charlie worried about him, even if there was nothing to worry about, most of the time. But still, Riley wasn't about to cause a fuss where it wasn't needed.

"Clint, tyre check on the Hyundai. I'm goin' to make a call," Riley called out as he went in search of Callum's papers.

As Riley looked at the number, a small part of him became nervous. His palms began to sweat, and the rhythm of his heart was a few beats faster than normal, but Riley pushed past it. He dialled the number into the work phone and placed the receiver to his ear. By the third ring, he hoped that it was going to go to voicemail, but the line connected and the sound of Callum's voice instantly caused Riley to smile.

"This is Callum."

"Ah, yeah, Callum, it's ah—it's Riley. From the garage. Rising Sun Motors." He fumbled over his words.

"Oh, hey!"

He swore he was only imagining the higher pitch in Callum's voice after Riley confirmed it was him.

"I had a look over your car and I wish I was calling with better news but—"

The sound of a pained groan cut Riley off.

"How much?" Callum straight out asked.

"Huh?"

"How much is it going to cost?" Callum elaborated.

"Ballpark, two grand, worst case, four."

"Je-sus." Callum dragged out the word.

"I know. Oil changes can make or break your car, man," Riley stated

"But I was checking the oil, it's probably the only thing I know about cars. That and tyres."

"So, then you know there is engine oil and transmission oil?"

The silence on the other end answered Riley's question.

"Transmission oil was filled with so much dirt that it contaminated the gears, caused the transmission to break down and honestly, I'm surprised your Jeep hadn't stalled on you with how it's lookin'. Not to mention the thing is leaking like a bitch. Didn't you ever notice reddish, brown-type patches on the ground?"

"Was always in too much of a hurry to look. And, I mean…it may have, sorta, kinda stalled on me once or twice. Might'av surged when I shifted gears."

Riley pinched the bridge of his nose. Typical. Customers always came out with information that would have been useful after the fact. It's as though they don't want to admit anything is wrong for fear of being charged unnecessary costs.

"How long can I hold out?" Callum's voice broke through Riley's mental whining.

"What?" He heard the question, but he needed to clarify that Callum asked him such a stupid question.

"The transmission. It's going to cost me the same now as it will when it blows, so, how long can I hold out?"

"Not exactly, man. You push that thing anymore and you'd be causing further damage, possibly a whole new transmission. That, plus labour on top of, and you could be looking at close to five grand."

"I don't have much of a choice," Callum voiced. "I've recently moved into my own place and I've started a new job. Whatever expendable cash I have available, it's nowhere near that amount."

Riley had started to tap away on the desk calculator, dividing, multiplying and then subtracting the numbers before he got a final figure.

"Eighteen hundred," Riley let out.

"What?" This time it was Callum who was confused.

"Look man, I can't let you take that car out of here without it gettin' fixed. Where it's at now, it'll need a filter change and a complete rebuild. Holding out will result in a whole new transmission and whatever other damage it could do to the engine. I need my conscience clear so you don't end up as roadkill when you break down on the highway and some truck smashes into you." Although the statement was true, what he was about to offer was the first time he'd ever made such a deal.

"Eighteen is the lowest I can do and my boss will probably still have my ass, but I'd rather that than have you on my mind all night." He realised the double meaning of his words only after they were out of his mouth.

"You saying I'm on your mind?" The flirtatious tone came and went like a snap of a finger.

"You want the discount or not?" Riley let out, wanting to move past the hiccup quickly enough to alleviate the pink hue he could feel warming his cheeks.

"Right," Callum coughed. "Sorry. Ahem, yes. Please. That would, that would really help."

"I'll start on it tomorrow. Should be ready by the end of the week."

"Thanks, Riley."

"Don't mention it. Like, literally. Don't want word getting around town."

"Of course. Scout's honour."

Riley could picture Callum holding his index, middle and ring fingers up, saluting the air as though Callum were in front of him.

He chuckled. "Friggen knew you were a boy scout." The comment had Callum chuckling along with him. It broke some of the awkwardness from the serious part of their conversation.

"Alright. I'll keep you posted on when you can collect." Riley didn't wait for any response. He hung up the phone, only to jump out of his skin when he caught sight of Charlie standing before him.

"We handing out discounts now, I see," Charlie stated.

"Used my staff discount on the parts. I'll work on the car when we're closed. Take it out of my own time so he doesn't have to pay for labour."

"My, my. In all the years you've been working here, not once have I seen you offer up your time free of charge," Charlie pointed out.

"It was either that or see him on the five o'clock news."

"Wouldn't be the first or last I'm afraid." Charlie leaned his arms on the counter. "This behaviour have anything to do with that black eye of yours?"

"It's nothing. Let it go." Riley checked the system, making sure the part he needed for Callum's car was in stock.

"He was a good man, Malcolm. Town folk loved him. But grief, grief can change a person." Charlie knocked his knuckles twice against the countertop. "You know where I live if you need a place to cool off." And with that, Charlie turned and walked away.

He was so hungry that the engine parts began to look like baked goods. The clock on the wall read quarter past seven. The garage had been closed for two hours and Riley had used his lunch hour on Callum's car rather than feeding his stomach.

There was a pizza shop down the road, close enough to walk, and the second that thought popped into Riley's mind, he already knew there was no other option than to walk down and order a pepperoni with extra cheese.

He locked up and made his way towards the restaurant. Riley swore the smell of pizza dough and garlic was leading him to his destination. He pulled his phone out and sent a quick text to Noelle to let her know he'd be home late, again. Her reply was instant, stating she had plans to see Joel.

Good. After what happened, their father needed time to cool down, or more accurately, detox, before Riley felt comfortable with Noelle being alone in the house with him. Riley's eye had mostly healed; the evidence of what happened was a mere smudge of yellow and green, which he hoped most would mistake for grease. It seemed as his bruise faded, so too did his father's memory of what happened between them.

That's when a body crashed into him. Riley's phone tumbled out of his hand and onto the pavement. A rush of hands bent down to retrieve it, only for their heads to bump into one another, which caused Riley to lose his balance and land on his ass.

"Oh my god. I am so, so sorry."

Riley heard the apology, but the bump to the head must have given him a concussion because he swore the voice sounded like Callum's.

"Riley?"

He looked up.

He blinked once. Twice. On the third blink, a smile spread across Callum's face. The restaurant's lights offered an aura over Callum's head, as though his hair was shooting off sunbeams.

"Callum? Hey."

Riley went to stand, and noticed the hand in front of him, offering to help him up. He accepted, and the ache in his head faded the second he was level with the green-eyed Adonis. Callum was still smiling at him. He swallowed; his mouth was awfully dry.

"You planning to give me my hand back or...?" Callum questioned.

The realisation that their hands were linked hit him harder than when his head collided with Callum's. He let go. His palm felt sweaty with an afterburn sensation he couldn't understand.

His mouth opened, an apology or explanation had formed on his tongue, but he was greeted with silence. Words seemed to have been knocked out of his head as he watched the way Callum was waiting for him to say something. Anything.

What the fuck was happening?

The eye contact broke as Callum looked down and bent forward. Riley could only stand there and watch as Callum straightened and held out a hand to offer what looked to be his phone.

"You dropped this in the crash," Callum stated.

He licked his lips. "Thanks." *Well, that's a start.* Riley reached out to take his phone back, pleased to see the screen hadn't cracked.

"You grabbing something to eat?" The question seemed to jolt Riley's brain and kickstart his system.

"Eat. Yes. Right." *One syllable words; bravo, Riley.*

It's not as though this was the first time he had communicated with Callum; however, did it count if it was during work hours and revolved remotely around Callum's car?

Snap the fuck out of it.

Riley shook his head. He envisioned the cartoon birds flying around his head magically vanishing like a poof of smoke. It seemed to have worked.

"I was working late. Figured I'd grab something to eat before I mistook the muffler for a choc-chip muffin." He cringed the second the lame-ass joke left his mouth, but that feeling he had where he wanted to face-palm himself and walk away evaporated when Callum began to laugh.

The sound was captivating.

"How long have you been waiting to use the joke?" Callum's question had Riley chuckling. He shrugged.

"I heard plenty of sexual jokes about mufflers from Clint, figured it was time to switch it up a bit, relate it to pastries."

"It was so bad that it was kinda good."

The comment made him preen. The jingle of a door opening, and the sight of a person exiting the restaurant, set Riley's mind back on track.

"I ah, I better get in and order," he explained.

"Or we could share?" Callum offered. "I no doubt ordered way too much, but after getting off a twelve-hour shift I figured, why not?"

"What ya order?" Riley nodded at the pizza box stuffed under Callum's arm. The need for food outweighed the implication of what Callum meant by asking him to share.

"Hawaiian, of course."

"Are you shitting me? Pineapple does not belong on a pizza," he argued, but there was no heat to his words.

"Excuse me, it's the pinnacle of pizza toppings."

"No, pepperoni and cheese. End of discussion. When I bite into my pizza, I ain't meant to taste something sweet," Riley continued.

"Oh, no?" Callum fought back.

"No."

"Pancakes and bacon."

"What about it?" Riley questioned.

"Do you not enjoy them together?"

"Yeah, who doesn't?"

"Does your bacon not get covered in maple syrup making it a sweet and salty dish?" Callum was smirking. "What about chocolate-covered pretzels? Or—"

"Alright, alright. You made your point," Riley chuckled.

"Then I think you should have no issues trying my Hawaiian pizza." Callum sounded so smug that Riley was determined to eat his pizza just to prove him wrong.

"Fine. But when I hate it, you're coming back to get my pepperoni."

"Deal."

Turning on his heels, Riley walked back in the direction he came from, Callum in step beside him, as they made their way towards the garage.

Honestly, he should have been embarrassed. The sounds that were escaping his mouth were sinful, but in all of his years, he had never tried a Hawaiian pizza and fuck, he was missing out.

"I told you. The sweet and salty mix—there's nothing better." Callum bit into another slice. A string of cheese landed on his chin, and both of them laughed at the mess it made.

"Guess I gotta learn to step out of my comfort zone." Riley reached for his beer. The back fridge was always stocked for those Friday nights he might stay and share one with Charlie. "My parents always ordered the same pizza. It's what I grew up having, ya know, and by the time I could order my own, guess I figured why waste money on trying something new when I knew what I liked?" He took a sip, wondering if it was the alcohol that was making him open up or the company.

They were sitting in the break room; the ceiling fan offering them a slight breeze to help with the warmth in the small space.

"They never asked you what you wanted as you got older?" Callum questioned.

"Nope. Would come home or walk out of my room and there it was, waiting for me and my sister." He took another gulp.

"Ah, there it is."

Riley cocked an eyebrow.

"Your sister," Callum offered.

Riley simply waited; further explanation was needed.

"I'm an only child so my parents would always ask me what pizza I wanted and then we'd share two pizzas between the three of us, whereas if your parents had asked you and your sister, the next thing you know, there'd be fights about who wants what, extra food ordered to make everyone happy. It was probably easier to stick to the one type that everyone could share." Callum chewed on his crust, acting as though he had solved the mystery.

"You think you know everything, don't ya?" Riley teased.

Callum shrugged; a coy smirk appeared on his face.

"See, the thing is, your little theory is missing one important detail." Riley leaned forward to pretend his information was top secret. "My sister is my twin, so when it comes to food, we never disagree." He sat back, a smug smirk on his face.

"Twins?" Callum clarified.

"Yep," he confirmed.

"Who's older?"

"She is, and fuck if she ever lets me forget it." They both chuckled.

"That's ah," Callum's laughter died down so he could speak. "That's actually kinda cool. Must be special to have something like that with your sibling."

Riley smiled instantly. It was unavoidable when talking about his sister. "Yeah, man. She's like my family within my family. It's us and then it's my parents." Riley moved his hand to demonstrate two separate groups. 'We're a team."

"Wow," Callum let out. "Can you, like, I don't know, if I touch your arm will she feel it?"

Riley rolled his eyes and downed the last of his beer. "Jesus, the twin questions growing up in school were enough to drive a person insane, and *that* right there was one of them."

"Hey," Callum held his hands up in surrender, "not every day you meet a twin. Us boring folk simply want to know if all the legends are true."

"Legends?" Riley scoffed. "We ain't the Loch Ness monster."

"Okay, fine. Tell me the most annoying things about being a twin. You make it sound special so, what about it is shit?"

"Seriously?" Riley wondered how much time Callum had, especially since they had finished the pizza.

"Seriously. I don't want to be that asshole if I ever meet another twin, so, lay it on me."

"Alright." He sat up in his chair. "First," he pointed to his index finger as he began to count them off, "I had a constant bruise just above my right elbow from where every kid would walk past and pinch me to see if not only my sister felt it, but if she too would bruise." He pointed at his middle finger. "Our gym teacher would put us on opposite teams so he could see, and I quote, which twin was stronger. And, because we're not identical, he always assumed she was weaker because she was a girl."

"Jesus," said Callum.

"We'd get called Twin One and Twin Two. Our grades would get compared, like, why can't you do it if your brother can? That kinda shit. Oh, and the worst, was when we were asked to prove we were twins."

"Prove it?"

"Yep. Some kids and teachers swore we were lying, using it as a con or somethin'," Riley explained.

"So, how'd you prove it?"

"We played a game." The frustration he had felt while relaying his childhood slowly vanished as he began to retell one of his favourite memories.

"We made up a code. Square. Thirteen. The symbol for pie. Sixteen. Sun. House. Car." He loved the confused look on Callum's face. "One of us would take a piece of paper, draw these things in that exact order while the other turned away, and then when finished, we'd hold it up, and back still turned, the other would recite what was drawn as though we had read each other's minds."

Callum burst out laughing. A hand on the stomach, head tilted back, genuine laugh. Riley never believed he was this funny. Perhaps Callum was the kind of guy that found humour in everything. Regardless, Riley found it infectious.

"And did it work?" Callum questioned between taking in gulps of air.

"Every time. We made sure to think of a new code if we had been asked a few times, even if it were the same symbols in a different order, but everyone fell for it."

"Okay. Okay. So, to recap; I should never compare twins, cause them physical pain in the hopes the other would feel it, pit them against one another or believe they have psychic abilities."

"I mean…doesn't mean there haven't been cases where that stuff is true, but if you want to stay on our good side, best you treat us like plain old boring folk, as you said."

A comfortable silence settled between them. The hum of the fridge was a relaxing white noise as they sat gazing at one another.

Riley was the first to break the spell. He coughed to clear his throat and looked down at the mess he had made from the picked-off beer label.

"I should probably get back to work."

"Shit. Right. Sorry." Callum stood, busying himself by collecting the rubbish.

"Thanks," Riley let out. "For the pizza."

Callum had stopped rushing, his hands now full, with four beer bottles and an empty pizza box. "Better than eating alone. Besides, the least I could do considering how you're helping me out."

"It's fine." He pointed to the bin so Callum could discard the mess, then began to walk out onto the shop floor, heading toward the door so he could let Callum out. With his hand on the handle, he froze, not yet ready to unlock it and say goodbye.

"You guys must be busy if you're having to work after hours." Perhaps Callum didn't want the night to end either if he was opening another line of communication.

"Not overly," Riley stated. He sighed before offering up the truth. "It's how I'm able to give you the discount. Working off the clock. No labour fees, just parts."

"What? Riley, no. I can't let y—"

He held his hand up. "What's done is done, man. Paperwork is signed and the invoice has been made. Just…I get it, okay. Shit's expensive. But safety comes at a cost." With that, he turned the lock on the door and held it open, a clear indication that it was time for Callum to leave.

"Thank you. Really." Callum stepped outside and walked back toward the pizza restaurant.

He closed the door and locked it before leaning against it and letting out a deep breath to help calm the racing beat of his heart.

The late nights were catching up to him. Although Riley wasn't the kind of guy who would go to bed at ten o'clock every night to make sure he got a solid eight hours, he found himself coming home and falling into bed around that time voluntarily. The difference was that his body was working longer hours, not getting that additional downtime to relax, debrief and tend to his aching muscles.

He had hit snooze on his alarm twice, Noelle's banging at his door being the final warning to get out of bed or risk being late. Perhaps what was keeping him from wanting to get up wasn't so much how tired he was, but the delicious dream he was having that involved feeding pineapple to a certain redhead. The juice dripped down his hands, lips around his fingers, tongue lapping up the mess.

Riley adjusted himself before he walked out to greet his sister. He didn't have time to take care of himself before work, so he made a note to schedule a little self-care that evening.

His tardiness meant toast or cereal for breakfast, neither of which he was in the mood for. Taking a sip of coffee, he stood against the kitchen counter, the glass cabinet above still broken, though all the shattered glass had now been removed, leaving an empty frame.

"What's with all the late nights?" Noelle asked him as she took her bowl to the sink.

"Car I'm working on has to be done after hours." Riley didn't have to look up from his mug to know his sister was giving him a cocked eyebrow as she waited for more detail. *God, they really were twins.*

"Guy couldn't afford the labour so I offered to do it for free."

"Wait, you what? Why would you do that?"

With his thumb and index finger, Riley rubbed his eyes to help wake him up. "His car was one moment away from breaking down."

"And how is that different from all the other people that come to you?"

The best answer he could provide was a shrug.

"Oh, my god. He's hot, isn't he?" Noelle accused.

"Sure…I gave up my hard-earned money because some guy looked like an eleven out of ten." Sarcasm in his voice.

"You pimped yourself out," his sister teased him.

He moved his hand in a jerking motion. "Believe what you want. I, for one, didn't want to read his obituary in the paper."

"Mhm, whatever makes you sleep better at night, or, you know, not sleep." Noelle winked and laughed at her own joke as Riley shoved her shoulder in the hopes it would shut her up.

The time on the oven caught his attention. If he didn't get a move on, he was going to be late. Breakfast on the road was his only option at this point. Of course, that's when his father decided to step out of the bathroom, belching loud enough to wake the neighbours while he scratched his crotch. Riley had been trying to avoid any further confrontation, which was a benefit to working as late as he was.

He nodded his head in the direction of his father.

"How's he been?" He directed the question at his sister.

"Caught him with another pill bottle. Not sure if he found an old stash or went out and bought more."

Riley scoffed. "Fucker was always arguing about having to work, now he's got his wish and he's blowing through whatever money he has left." He sulked off to his bedroom, put on a fresh tank top, and a clean pair of overalls and walked out the door before his father could catch him.

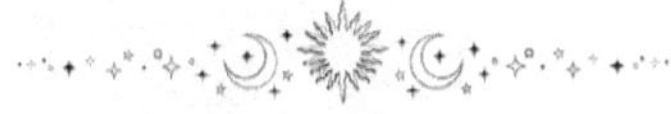

It had taken longer than Riley had expected to fix Callum's car, but only by an extra two days. The weekend went against him, and Charlie refused to let him stay back, which would have allowed the car to be ready by Monday.

So, by Wednesday, a week and a half after Riley had called with the quoted cost, he was finally dialling Callum's number with good news.

"Hey, Riley," Callum answered when the line connected, pep in his voice.

"Hey. How'd you know it's me?" he questioned.

"Saved the number. Figured the only person at the garage that'd be calling me is you."

He wasn't sure what to do with that piece of information, so he moved on. "Good news, car's ready to be picked up. It's officially roadworthy."

"Finally." Riley could hear the relief in Callum's voice. "I was getting tired of having to ask Deja to drive me to work. Those extra fifteen minutes of sleep make a difference to her mood for the remainder of the day."

Riley smiled even though he knew Callum couldn't see it.

"I'll get her to drop me off after my shift," Callum explained.

"Sure, man. I'll see you then." Riley hung up the phone only to wish he had asked what time that was going to be so he wouldn't spend all day watching the clock.

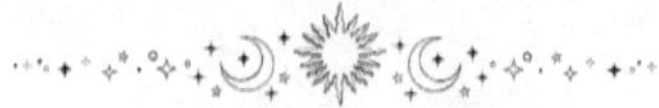

"Riley!" Clint bellowed from the shop counter. "Some guy here to see you."

He sat up instantly, regretting it when his head collided with the undercarriage. "Ah, fuck." Riley was forced to lie back on the creeper, his hand rubbed at his forehead as he wheeled himself out from under the car.

His head sure was taking a beating this month.

As he approached the counter, the pain eased the second he saw Callum waiting for him in slacks and a button-up shirt, both dark navy, tucked in, with short sleeves that had some kind of patch on the arm.

"You're meant to wheel out from under a car before you try and sit up, you know. Even *I* know that one," Clint stated.

Riley gave him a deadpan look, but the kid still hadn't got the hint.

"I'll try and remember that for next time." He wanted to hit himself in the head again when Clint patted his shoulder, acting as though he taught Riley something for a change.

"Clinton, get over here, boy, and finish pumping these tyres," Charlie called out, which had him dashing off like Roadrunner. The only thing missing was the cloud of smoke.

"You ah, you got a little something." Callum pointed at his head.

On instinct, his hand wiped across his forehead, but then Callum let out a chuckle which meant only one thing, he missed it.

"Here." Callum reached out before Riley could piece together what was happening. A thumb began to drag against the top of his left eyebrow, skin trailing against skin. The area felt a sizzling heat compared to the remainder of his body.

"There," Callum stated when he pulled his hand away and placed it back into his pocket.

Breathe, Riley.

And for the love of God, say something.

"Th-thanks."

Smooth.

His eyes finally read the patch on Callum's arm as he took in the uniform.

"Holy shit, you're an EMT," Riley pointed out.

Callum smiled as he looked down at his uniform. "'m still a rookie. Only graduated a few months back."

This explained the issue of limited funds to spend on the car.

"Nice to know that if I have an emergency, I'll be in good hands." Riley groaned internally.

He did not just say that!

The warmth on his cheeks was enough to confirm he was blushing harder than his sister when their parents tried to give them the 'what is happening to your body' talk at twelve, together. He broke eye contact and looked at the desk for the paperwork he had prepared earlier.

"Okay." He cleared his throat, eyes focused on the document. "So, this is your invoice stating what I checked during the service, the issue, and then what was fixed." His finger moved down the page as he pointed at each section. "Your total, as agreed to, is one thousand, eight hundred. Tax included."

Riley had to make eye contact when a credit card was placed in front of his face.

"You sure? Won't this put you in more debt or something?" Why Riley thought he had the right to ask such a question, he didn't know.

"It's new. Comes with no interest or repayments for the first three months," Callum explained, a smile still plastered on his face.

Guess the question hadn't upset him, Riley thought.

He charged the card, got Callum to put in his pin and then stapled a receipt to the invoice. The keys were waiting on a hook under the counter, which Riley retrieved and passed over.

"Car is round back, in the parking lot connected to the garage."

Should he offer to walk him?

"You have no idea how much I appreciate what you've done, Riley. Really. I just…maybe we could grab a drink sometime, you know, as a thank you."

"Yeah. Sure, man."

The words 'as a thank you' played through his mind as Riley accepted Callum's phone. He entered his number as a new contact on autopilot, not even taking in the repercussions of what this could mean. He handed the phone back, a polite smile on his face.

"Guess I'll be seeing you," Callum said.

"Guess so."

Riley watched the GQ model walk away.

'As a thank you,' echoed in his ear.

Was he just friend-zoned?

Was Callum even gay?

He couldn't wait for the day to be over so he could grab a beer and crash into his bed.

Chapter 3

Riley wipes the bathroom mirror. He isn't sure what he expected to see once he removes the condensation from the glass but when his eyes lock onto his face, a part of him wishes he had left the dripping water to cover his reflection.

He has work today. He likes his new job, but that's all it is, a job. A way to make money that he needs to survive, which, in theory, seems pointless.

Survive.

What does that even mean?

If he pays his bills on time. If he drives his car without having an accident. If he eats a meal and doesn't get food poisoning, is that what it means to survive? To have these everyday experiences that could go wrong, but don't—is that what he's supposed to call a victory? Does a means of survival equal skirting by in life knowing he hasn't drawn the short straw, yet?

His phone is sitting on the bathroom countertop. It lights up, and the vibration from being on silent has it moving against the porcelain. Jackson's name flashes back at him. He knows what the call will be about, some friendly chit-chat before being asked to join him on a night out which Riley honestly doesn't have the energy for.

The phone stops vibrating and a minute later, an alert for a new voice message appears on the screen. He applies deodorant, brushes his teeth and then looks down to see his phone once again dancing along the bathroom countertop, Billy's name staring up at him.

It says a lot about his friends that they continue to reach out, even if he avoids their calls and, more often than not, doesn't call them back. The thought of having to socialise has his heart pumping a little too fast. The need to smile and make conversation has his body breaking out into a sweat.

His hands grip the bathroom sink. He hates this feeling. It comes from nowhere and he can never understand why, but he can recognise the signs. He's hot, as though his blood is boiling, cooking him from the inside out. It's so hard to breathe that he's convinced hands are gripping his throat, cutting off his air supply. A nauseous tingling sensation has him believing ants are crawling under his skin and as he tries to think of anything else apart from these sensations, they painstakingly begin to simmer down.

Riley draws oxygen back into his lungs and he wants to scream from how much it hurts. He's dizzy, but with his hands still gripping the sink, it steadies him. As quickly as it came on, it disappeared. Riley considers calling in sick for work. He has an appointment with Dr Bech later today, unfortunately, but perhaps she can help get him the approved time off.

She's got to be useful for something, right?

No.

He can do this.

Because if he doesn't, Noelle will be down his throat and that's the last thing he needs. He's already doing this for her, and *only* her. He doesn't need Dr Bech. He doesn't need to talk about something that can't be changed. He needs…he needs…*fuck,* he knows what he needs.

When the vibration of his phone penetrates the silence of his bathroom for the third time, he's ready to pick it up and smash it against the wall, only he doesn't. Slowly exhaling and going to grab the phone with a shaky hand, Riley swipes across the screen, connecting with the call.

"Hey…wasn't sure you'd pick up."

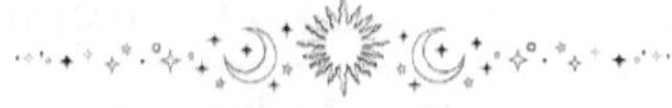

"Is everything okay, Riley? You seem a little nervous," Dr Bech asks.

The room feels different today. He does a quick sweep of the area; nothing is out of place or missing. No new plants or books or furniture have been added to the room.

So why does it feel unfamiliar?

"I ah, I'm fine. Long day at work is all." He lies, sort of.

"Work was good?" Dr Bech asks.

He shrugs. "Pays the bills."

It's not the garage, but it's work.

His fingers begin to drum on his knees. His eyes are still darting around the office space, trying to decipher why the room seems…foreign.

"Riley, I'd like to ask if you've ever experienced a panic attack before."

His fingers stop drumming.

"Why you askin' me that?"

"It's merely a question. I'm trying to understand you. Understand why your sister insisted on you seeing me."

His hands feel sweaty.

"This is our third session and yet I still don't know what brought you to my office besides the brief conversation I had with Noelle."

"I mean, if I'm wasting your time, I'm happy to leave." He goes to stand but Dr Bech holds her hand up to stop him and even though it's only a hand gesture, it seems to have the desired effect on him because his body freezes, keeping his ass firmly on the couch.

"I didn't say that, Riley." Dr Bech takes her pen and notepad, placing them on the table beside her.

"I've been observing your body language, your behaviour when certain topics are brought up. My question was simply put forward because your answer could help me distinguish what may be troubling you."

"Troubling me?" The psychologist makes it sound like he's had a fight with his best friend and regrets what he said during the argument.

Dr Bech picks up her pen and notepad. "Do you know what a panic attack is, Riley?"

Great. Back to this.

"I'm sure you're going to tell me." His knee begins to bounce as though he is hitting the pedal of a bass drum.

"A panic attack is a brief moment of intense anxiety, which can mimic sensations similar to fear. Have you experienced a racing heartbeat? Perhaps shortness of breath? Maybe dizziness, trembling, muscle tension?" Dr Bech explains.

Riley swallows.

Is that what was happening this morning?

"Panic attacks can occur frequently," Dr Bech continues, "or unexpectedly, and more times than not, they aren't related to any external threat."

His heart is in his throat. The fabric of his denim jeans is damp.

"S–so what if I have?" His voice betrays him by breaking.

"That's perfectly okay." Dr Bech leans forward, one elbow resting on her knee. "Can you remember what was happening the last time you might have been having a panic attack?"

If he tells her, it doesn't mean he's admitting that he's broken, right? That's not why he's here. To be fixed or put back together. Like the doc said, it's a moment of fear. People feel fear all the time. At a haunted house, on a rollercoaster. Starting a new job or relationship.

Relationships. Friendships. Panic attacks.

I don't need to be fixed.

"I got phone calls from my best friends."

Ten Months Ago

It had been two weeks.

Two weeks of Riley wondering if Callum was ever going to ask him out for that drink.

Two weeks where Riley questioned whether the offer was genuine or said only out of politeness after the large discount he had given.

He kept checking his phone in case it had died or was on silent. He tried to remember if he had written his number down wrong but then realised if he had, Callum had the shop number, knowing he worked every single day.

When his phone finally rang, he answered without checking the name on the screen.

"Yeah. Hi. Hello?" He stood behind the Mitsubishi Ute; using its size as a protective shield.

"Yo, what's got you all flustered?" Riley slumped at the sound of Jackson's voice.

"Nothing, man. What's up?"

"Ouch, don't sound so disappointed. A guy could take that to heart."

Riley chuckled at the clear picture in his head of his best friend's face, feigning hurt. "As if you have a heart."

"True. I only seem to break them," Jackson stated. Riley couldn't fathom how his friend sounded proud at the fact.

Better them than him, he supposed.

"In case you forgot. Some of us are working, so talk quickly or fuck off."

"Fine." Riley could practically see the eye roll in the tone of his friend's voice. "Tonight. You, me, Billy, and a few others. Burgers on the grill. Drinks and some good music."

It had been a few weeks since he had seen his friends. Having to work the extra hours to finish Callum's car, and then catching up on the sleep he missed, meant any form of a social life was off-limits.

It did sound enticing. A night to unwind, forget about the fact that Callum had probably ghosted him.

"Fuck it. Fine. Whaddya need me to bring?" He chuckled at the sound of his friend whooping on the other end of the line.

"I'll text it to ya. Better not flake on me, man. All work and no play makes Riley a dull boy."

"Whatever." He laughed. "Fuck off and let me get back to work." He pocketed his phone, feeling the vibration against his leg a minute later, which he suspected was a list that covered everything Jackson would need to host a barbecue.

The days were still comfortable enough to walk around in jeans and a T-shirt, but as the sun set, the cool air began to set in, bringing with it the perfect vibe for Halloween, a holiday the town loved almost as much as Independence Day. He considered removing his phone to text Jackson a reminder about getting wood for the fire pit when his phone began to ring again.

Riley figured it was Billy, inviting him to Jackson's. He got the sense that his friends had missed him, which was a comforting thought. With one hand on a vacuum hose that had a tear in it, his other reached for his phone and swiped it to answer before he placed it between his ear and shoulder.

"Yeah?"

"For a second I thought you wouldn't pick up since it took me so long to call." Riley froze. The sound of Callum's voice seemed to have that effect on him. It would stun him to the point of forgetting what it was he was doing or even how to formulate words into a sentence.

"Hello? Riley?" Callum questioned.

He coughed to clear away the lump in his throat. "Yeah, sorry, man. Had my hands on a hose when you called." Riley yanked his hands out of the ute so he'd have a firm grip on his phone. Heat rushed to his cheeks from his poor choice of wording. "A vacuum hose. In a Mitsubishi. It has a tear in it and I was—" The word vomit stopped the second he could hear Callum chuckle on the other end.

"No, no. Please continue. I'm sure the hose is more important." He could picture Callum's face so clearly at that exact moment, unsure if that was a good thing or not. The way Callum would be smiling through his laugh, a soft wrinkle at the corner of his eyes.

"Nice to see you're finally taking car care seriously." He said it as a joke, but it was enough to settle Callum down.

"You must have magic hands because my Jeep's been running like a dream thanks to you."

Was Callum flirting?

It was getting hard for Riley to spot the difference, that's how out of the game he was.

"This time, remember to bring it back for a service before it's fallin' apart, 'aight?"

There was a moment of silence where all Riley could hear was Callum's soft breathing on the other end of the line.

"I'm sorry it took so long to call. They put me on night shift, and even though I spent the whole time reminding myself to call you the second I finished work, I ended up crashing in my bed and sleeping until I was due back at the station."

Relief. That's what he felt as all the racing thoughts in his mind about being used, lied to, or played vanished.

"I wanna say it's fine, but two weeks, man…you're gonna have to do more than say a few words." He could feel his confidence returning.

"How bout that drink, then? Tonight."

And once again, the universe was out to get him.

"Ah, shit. No can do. If you had called ten minutes sooner, you could have locked me in first."

"You got someone else wanting your attention?" Callum's tone was playful. Riley couldn't help but bite his lip to hold back his smile.

"Oh, at least once a week I have suitors asking for my hand in marriage. Though I'm sure it's only so they can get the family discount."

"That so? I'm not afraid of a little competition." There was a cockiness to Callum's voice.

He wanted to see Callum. He wanted to keep talking.

"You could always join me." Shit, he shouldn't have said that.

"The answer's yes. But I should probably know what I have agreed to."

The panic subsided the second Callum agreed. "Some, ah, some friends are throwing a little get-together at their place. Low key."

"Wow, feeding me to the wolves already?" Callum chuckled.

"You want the wolves, I can get my sister involved. These guys, I'm sure this will hurt me more than it will hurt you."

"Oh, and why's that?"

"Cos they've never met a guy I was interested in before." At that stage, he had no filter. Everything he was thinking and feeling was coming out like a spy being fed truth serum.

It might have been too much too soon, but on the contrary, the last two weeks of not knowing had been torture. No way was he going to last a whole night around Jackson and Billy, unsure whether Callum was there with him so he could meet new friends or because he was interested in something more, specifically with him.

"Guess I better bring my A-game so I get their tick of approval then."

He exhaled; unaware he had been holding his breath.

Guess they were on the same page after all.

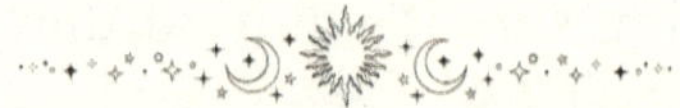

Riley offered to pick Callum up. He used the excuse that his apartment was on the way, but the truth was, he didn't want Callum anywhere near his house, or more specifically, anywhere near his father.

When Malcolm was mid-trip, he was tolerable. When he passed out, he was a dream. But when he woke, needing that next hit, or was coming down from a large dose, that's when he became someone Riley couldn't recognise. That's when he wanted to yell and fight and take himself and Noelle far away. That's the version of his father he was scared Callum might see if he came to his house, so he didn't risk it.

They weren't exactly close. There was a twenty-minute drive between them, but when Riley arrived at the address, he could see the appeal. The complex was large, at least five stories, though Callum was on the first floor. He buzzed the intercom, and Callum answered quickly, letting Riley know that he was coming out.

The door opened and Riley soaked in the view. Callum was dressed in dark grey jeans that hugged all the right places and a thin white sweatshirt with two thick black lines across the chest and biceps.

Callum's hair had changed since he saw him last. What were once soft curls, Callum now had a slight fade on either side with the top styled to look spiked in a fluffy, natural kind of way. Riley had the urge to run his fingers through it to test if it was as pillowy-soft as it looked. To top it off, facial hair had set in, and a neatly trimmed beard—that was more scruff—hugged Callum's face. It made him look even more like a Greek god that Riley wanted to kneel in front of and worship.

"Casual enough?" Callum asked with a smirk, evidence that he had caught Riley staring.

Riley was wearing black chinos and a soft, grey Henley that had a few buttons to help emphasize the V-neck. His sleeves were already pulled up mid-arm, and he wore a simple pair of black leather sneakers with a white sole.

All he could do was offer a nod in reply to Callum's question, his thumb pointed over his shoulder to indicate where he had parked his car. It took Callum to start walking towards him for Riley to finally find his voice.

"Looks good." His eyes cast down, so Callum couldn't see his blush from the compliment he so openly offered.

They walked back to his car, and it wasn't until Riley was on the road towards Jackson's house that the conversation picked up.

"I don't know why, but this is not the car I envisioned you in." Callum looked around as Riley glanced from the corner of his eye, his focus on the road.

"No? What'd ya picture?"

"I don't know, but not a beat-up Toyota Corolla." Callum started to laugh.

"Ey, I'll have you know this car has lasted me longer than some of the new shit those car factories are spitting out with all their fancy gadgets and whatnot. Old school was made to last." His voice was stern but there was a smile behind the heat. A quick look in Callum's direction proved that he was smiling back at him.

"I'll take your word for it." He held his hands up in surrender.

Riley relaxed his shoulders and settled back into his seat. There was a moment of silence before Callum spoke up.

"I bet you service this car so good."

They both broke out laughing. Riley was thankful that he had stopped at a red traffic light.

"You're a dick," he said through his chuckles. He loved that Callum took no offence, that the joking and name-calling back and forth already felt easy and natural between them. He liked that in a guy. Life was serious enough.

Callum shrugged. "Only child syndrome, remember?"

"Of course. Totally explains it then." The light turned green.

"What's with the scruff? Tryin' to stay warm for winter?"

At another set of lights, he caught the way Callum's hand came up to rub over his cheek and chin.

"Got lazy during night shift and then decided to stick with it. The barbershop cleaned it up for me and I don't know, figured I'd give it a go. Why? Not your thing?"

Riley gulped as he tried not to envision how it would feel rubbing up the inside of his thigh.

"Don't put words in my mouth. Making conversation."

"Or a backhanded compliment."

"Nah, I'll tell it to your face if I don't like it." He winked.

"So, you approve?"

"Depends."

"On?"

"On how it feels, I guess." His cheeks burned, but from the looks of things, so were Callum's. Riley kept his eyes on the road for the remainder of the drive.

He opened the gate and walked into the backyard, acting as though this was his own home while Callum followed beside him. Jackson's mother had an open-door policy to every one of her son's friends. Thankfully, Jackson liked to keep a tight group of friends.

The music was good, which meant Billy hadn't taken over and switched it to his reggae playlist yet. The smell of grease and charcoal filled the air. Riley had dropped off Jackson's list of supplies earlier that day.

The sight of his friends had him smiling. He turned towards Callum and offered him a reassuring smile. Maybe he should have checked during the ride over if this was still something Callum wanted to do. But it was too late now—his friends had spotted them.

"Riley! Finally!" Jackson opened his arms, offered a hand out to be grabbed and pulled in for a bro hug. Riley did it out of habit, the familiar gesture calmed his nervous energy knowing any second now one of them would ask—

"Yo, who's this?" Billy bounded up the stairs to greet them on the porch.

"Goddamn it, Billy. Don't scare him away. Not every day our boy brings a plus one." Jackson nudged Billy in the ribs while jutting his chin out toward Callum.

"Jesus Christ, told you this would be worse for me," Riley mumbled at Callum.

"Alright, alright. Calm your tits, you two." His thumb scratched the end of his nose even though it wasn't itchy.

"Billy, Jackson, this is Callum." He pointed to everyone as he said their names. "Callum, this is Beavis and Butthead."

"I'm assuming you're Butthead since you're into ass." Billy pointed at Jackson.

"Naturally," Jackson agreed. "Though technically so are you."

"I mean, who doesn't love grabbing ass, gay or straight? But the sphincter spelunking is your department. I'll stick with muff diving."

"It's ass-eating, not cave diving," Jackson debated.

"Same same, if you ask me." And just like that, Riley knew his friends were already helping to ease the tension on his behalf, even if he wanted to face-palm and groan in embarrassment.

"Ignore Billy. We mostly do." Jackson's attention was now on Callum. "Grab a beer, man, cooler is by the door." Jackson held his hand out, which Callum happily shook. "Any friend of Riley's is a friend of ours."

Riley didn't miss the wink Jackson sent his way. He made sure to ignore it by walking over and grabbing two beers, cracking them open and giving one to Callum.

"Come say hi to the others," Billy offered as he walked back down onto the grass, leaving Jackson to finish cooking.

"This customer was a total Karen. And when she asked to speak to my manager, I had to hold back my laugh as he walked out and said that I was the one in charge, he was only the owner." The group laughed at Kimberley's story. Riley had no idea who the girl was, but from what he gathered, she was someone Billy was trying to impress.

"Food's up. Let's eat!" Jackson called out. Everyone made their way up to the back porch. The group consisted of some guy Jackson was currently beneficial with, Liza, who was Kimberley's friend, and then there was Rihanna who was in the same circle as Riley, Jackson and Billy during high school.

"I know this probably isn't what you had in mind for tonight," Riley admitted as he hung back, hoping he could have a moment with Callum.

"Actually, it couldn't be more perfect," Callum offered.

"Well, now I think something is wrong with you if you call this a perfect first date." He hadn't meant to use those words. First date. It was only meant to be a drink, which turned into a social group gathering. None of which could classify as a date, could it?

"Shit, I didn't mean—this isn't exactly—I mean it can be, but if you don't—"

"Are you always this nervous? Or only around me?" Callum asked, a gentle smile on his face.

"Both." Riley rubbed his bottom lip with his thumb as he looked around to make sure the others were busy collecting their food. "Look, let's just say it's been a while for me. Dating or otherwise."

"We'll go slow." Callum wasn't denying that they were classing this as a date. "This, tonight, these people are a part of your life. It's another glimpse of who you are, and that's what I wanted, to get to know who you are."

"Ay, hurry the fuck up before the food gets cold," Jackson called out, breaking the moment but not the connection that was building between them.

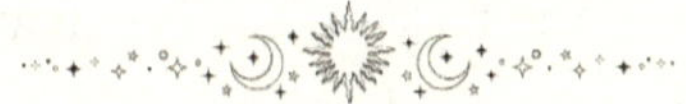

"Are you serious?" Callum asked Riley after Jackson had finished his story.

"Yep. For a year, I watched the cafeteria chick give Jackson and Billy less food because, and I quote, 'They don't need as much food as everyone else. If anything, they could lose a few pounds.' So, one day—"

"Loud enough for the whole cafeteria to hear him," Jackson cut in, "Riley called out—"

"How bout you give these two their fair share and stop hoarding it so your fat ass can eat it at the end of the day?" Billy, Jackson, and Riley said simultaneously.

The group broke out laughing around the table.

"Joke was on her. The next year, puberty hit, and we both shot up. The weight fell off, and poor Riley here got left behind." Jackson playfully shoved at his shoulder.

"Man, fuck off. I'm five foot seven," Riley bit back.

"And in the summer, you stand next to me for the shade," Jackson joked.

"Guess he has a thing for taller guys," Billy added, and Riley gave his friend the finger.

"Wait, you two?" Callum motioned between Riley and Jackson.

Was that jealousy Riley detected?

He was quick to shut it down. "Hell no. He's the brother I never had. That'd be way too fuckin' weird," Riley explained.

"Besides, two gay dudes growing up, that shit came in handy when we needed someone to vent to. No way were we going to ruin that with sex," Jackson added.

"Never know, could have led to a strong bond, maybe a deep connection," Callum stated.

"Nah, dude," Billy mumbled through a mouthful of his third burger. "I already asked. They're both catchers, never would have worked."

Riley groaned. He wanted to bury his head and hide away. He snuck a glance at Callum, whose cheeks were a little flushed, but the redhead was still smiling and hadn't faked a family emergency yet.

Thankfully, Kimberley slapped the back of Billy's head, since Riley was too far away to do it himself. The look on Kimberley's face showed that she was trying to get Billy to understand his mistake, that Riley's preferences weren't his friend's business to share. However, he had known Billy half his life, and unless someone verbalised what the guy did wrong, his best friend would have no clue why everyone was suddenly annoyed at him.

He reached for his beer and chugged everything that was left in the bottle. He wanted another, but figured leaving the table at that exact moment would result in Callum thinking that he was embarrassed or felt awkward. Neither of which was true, however, he would have preferred to have waited longer than their first date to let Callum know his position in the bedroom.

"So, what's the story with you two? How'd you meet?" Kimberley asked, perhaps as a way to clear the air.

"Oh, ah, through Riley's work. He helped fix my car," Callum offered.

"Aww, that's so cute," said Rhianna.

Riley rubbed the back of his neck. He wasn't used to so much attention.

"Alright, you vultures," Jackson interrupted. "Help me clean or my mumma is gonna whoop all'ya asses."

"Jesus. Now I know why Mumma is always exhausted after hosting holiday events." Jackson crashed on the seat beside Riley, where he was sitting alone and watching Callum socialise with Rhianna, being polite. Laughing, smiling and looking as though he was tentatively listening to what Riley assumed were embarrassing high school stories that involved him.

"We used paper plates, what are you moaning about?" He gulped his beer. His second and last one for the evening since he had to drive.

"I still had to empty the trash and clean the grill."

Riley found humour in the way Jackson would exaggerate everything he did, as though daily chores that he completed once in a blue moon earned him a medal because they were ten times harder when he had to do them.

"So, we gonna talk about it?" Jackson questioned.

"Nope." He popped the *p* for emphasis.

"I think we should."

"Nothin' to talk about."

"No? You tellin' me, the first time in ten years you bring a plus one and we're meant to act like it's no big deal?"

"That's exactly what you're meant to do." He ran his fingers up and down the neck of his bottle. "Because this *is* a big fuckin' deal, Jack, and if you make it a big deal, I'm gonna get all in my head, freak the fuck out, and sabotage something good before it even gets to become something better. So, we're going to act like it's not a big deal. Deal?"

"Fuck…" Jackson slumped back in his chair. "You really like this guy."

"What did I just say?!"

"No. No. I'm not making it a big deal, I'm just…taking it all in."

Riley wished he could down another beer, or three. The small fire pit that Callum was standing near gave the air a comforting smell.

"Why'd you bring him here?" Jackson asked.

"Whaddya mean?"

"I mean, ya could have told me you had a date and then bailed. But ya didn't. You threw him in the deep end to see how well he could swim."

He shrugged, but Riley knew Jackson better than that, which meant his friend wasn't going to give up till he gave an acceptable answer.

"It feels different with this guy. I don't know. One night when I was workin', we bumped into each other, talked, shared a pizza.

Fucker even got me eating pineapple on my pizza." Riley chuckled at the memory.

"Hold up. He did what? Call the priest y'all, I think my boy's possessed," Jackson teased.

"Shut the fuck up, man." Riley laughed at his friend's exaggerated reaction. "Anyway, I didn't even know if he was gay until…well until he finally called me two weeks later to ask me out for a drink."

"Two weeks? Damn!"

"Shift work. He's an EMT." Riley made sure his mannerisms proved that he hadn't minded the wait, once he understood why it happened of course. Jackson would have gladly called Callum out on his behaviour if Riley made it seem like being ghosted for two weeks had upset him.

"Ah, there it is. Boys in uniform, they win every time."

This was why Jackson was his best friend. Riley could sit and have a deep discussion with him, and Jackson would find a way to joke and lighten the mood while doing so, but eventually, he'd lay down the hard-hitting truth.

"Look, man." And there it was, the truth, right on cue. "All I know is, you've only ever told us about the guys you were seeing. We never met 'em. So, if you're telling me this guy is different, even though all you did was share a pizza with 'im, then I believe ya."

He leaned forward, resting his elbows on his knees. He caught the way Callum tilted his head back to laugh at whatever Rhianna had said. It was captivating.

"That's the thing. I don't get *why* this is different. I barely know him."

"Isn't that why you date someone, to get to know 'em?" Jackson sounded like he wanted to add 'duh' to the end of his sentence. "Riley, come on, man. I ain't saying this is love at first sight b—"

"God, no. I—" He was quick to agree.

"BUT!" Jackson cut him off by raising his voice. "*Sometimes* our hearts know things before our heads do." Riley looked away from his friend and found his date staring back at him. Callum had a soft smile on his face, eyes warm and welcoming. The fire crackled and sparked. Its hue enhanced Callum's hair. It felt as though no one else was there besides the two of them.

"Mumma used to say that when we're born, our hearts are already tethered to someone, and when we finally meet that person, the tether will tighten, causing an ache in our hearts whenever we're too far apart."

Riley bit his lip.

"Maybe I wanted your approval before things got serious. Make sure what I was seeing in him…I wasn't imagining, ya know?"

Jackson clapped his shoulder and gave it a reassuring squeeze.

"He ate my charcoal burger with no complaints. He listened to Billy try to convince him that the earth is flat and right now, he's invested in hearing childhood stories about you when you were an awkward dweeb."

Hearing it laid out for him was helping.

"Safe to say, whatever you're feeling, this guy is feeling it too." Jackson stood up to join the others on the grass. Riley was glad. The conversation was getting a little too heavy for a casual barbecue with friends, but as always, the words of wisdom, as Jackson liked to call it, seemed to be on the money.

"You have a great group of friends," Callum said the second they were in the car and Riley was driving away from the curb.

"Yeah, I guess I do." He hadn't meant to say it in a way that sounded cocky or showy, but after the night they just had, Riley felt this sense of pride in who his friends were and how supportive they have been throughout their friendship.

"I used to spend a lot of my time at Jackson's. Billy and I would go over after school and stay until we were due home for dinner. We'd have horror movie marathons and gaming nights. But then—" Riley squeezed the steering wheel a little too tight when the memory came back to him. "Well, then things changed and I was needed at home more often. But ah, they ah, they still stuck by me. Still checked in. Made sure I was doing okay."

He waited a moment, relieved that Callum hadn't pushed on what that moment in Riley's life was. He'd eventually tell him. He'd have to, but not yet. "I could be MIA due to work but I can guarantee Jackson would still be blowing up my phone to see if I wanted to hang or make sure I was still alive."

"They care about you," Callum offered. "I even got *the speech* when you went off to use the bathroom."

Riley quickly looked at Callum, but the darkness of the night prevented him from seeing if Callum was joking or serious. "Bullshit."

Callum chuckled. "I bullshit you not. I believe it went something like, 'You fuck with his heart, I fuck with your face, and not in a homo sexy way.'"

That sounded exactly like something Jackson would say.

He groaned. "Well, I *did* say that tonight would be more painful for me than for you."

Before Riley knew it, he was parking out the front of Callum's apartment building, the drive back seemed to go by quicker than it did driving to Jackson's.

He didn't know what to do, whether he should turn off the ignition or put the car in park. Should he walk Callum to his apartment building or his front door?

"Thank you. For tonight." Callum interrupted his internal panic. "I meant what I said, it was perfect."

The uncertainty of what to do from here caused him to keep his hands firmly on the steering wheel.

"I'd, ah, I'd like to see you again…" Callum offered.

"Yeah…me too. But don't leave me hanging for two weeks this time," he said as a joke, but with some truth behind it.

"Wouldn't dream of it." And with that, Callum opened the passenger side door and Riley was left to sit in his car, collecting himself after Callum walked inside.

Callum

I dreamt about you last night.

That so. Gonna share or just tease me?

Jackson was Willy Wonka and you were his Oompa Loompa.

LMAO

WTF

You Series?

Not what I was expecting when you sent that message.

I think it was the height jokes.

And Jackson said something about the guys loving his chocolate dipping sauce. (°_°)

He has no filter.

I did expect more hard-hitting questions or death stares.

You'll get them. If you meet my sister.

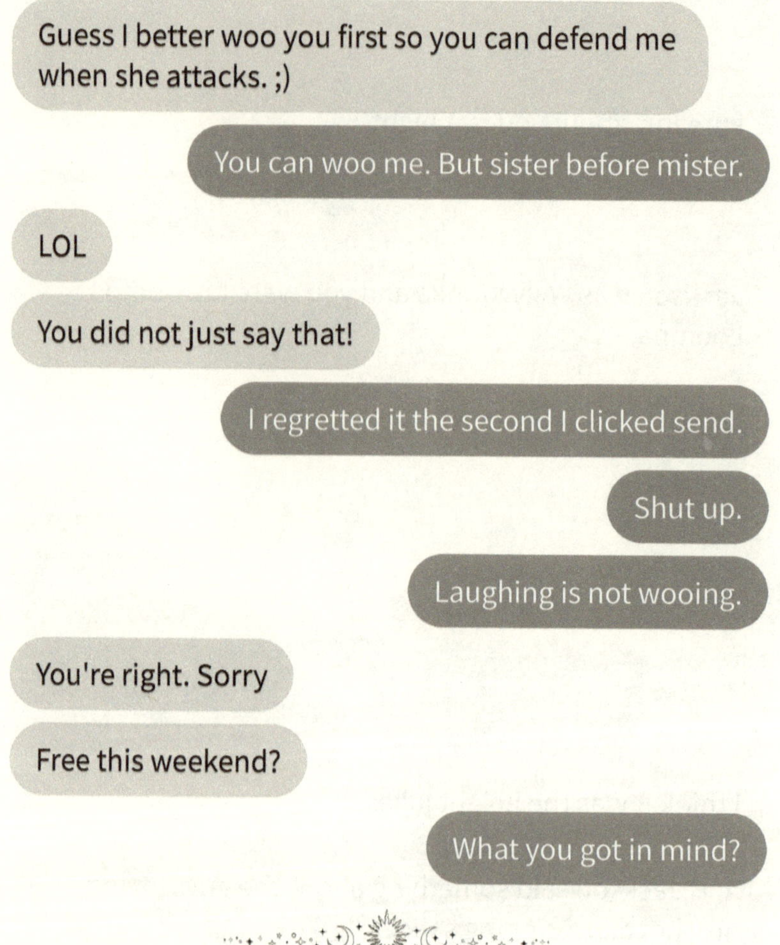

It was the annual Maryland Halloween Fall Festival. For as long as Riley could remember, his parents would take him and his sister each year so they could carve a pumpkin, get lost in the corn maze, and shove their faces in a barrel of bobbing apples.

The first year after their mother died, Riley brought Noelle, and the two of them spent the day walking around, more so reminiscing than getting involved. They decided that it wasn't the same without her there with them.

But there he was, stepping outside his comfort zone, something he told Callum he needed to do more often the night they shared a pizza in the garage. And to his surprise, when Callum had texted him that this was the idea he had for their date, Riley smiled, thinking that perhaps this was the perfect chance to come back and make new memories.

"Hey, you." The words ghosted against his ear. If anyone asked, Riley would have said it was the fall breeze that gave him goosebumps, not the warmth of Callum's breath or the serenade of his voice.

He spun around, his breath catching as he took in Callum's attire. Black chinos, a knitted sweater that was tightly fitted. It looked warm, made from an array of black, white and grey tones with high-top black boots to tie it all together. It was perfect, especially against Callum's striking red hair and the short scruffy beard he still had.

A smile instantly appeared on his face when he locked eyes with Callum, who smiled in return, green eyes roaming up and down Riley's body. He was glad he decided to go with his black skinny-leg jeans, a baby blue V-neck, and his black cardigan. He knew it accentuated all his best features.

"Hey. Find a parking space okay?" He started with a light, casual, yet genuine question since the Fall Festival was an event the whole town loved, making it damn near impossible to get access via a car.

"My partner, Deja, lives not too far. She told me to use her driveway to park my car," Callum explained.

"Good thing it won't leak all over the concrete then." Riley poked his tongue into his cheek. He smirked and chuckled as Callum playfully pushed his shoulder.

"I'm never gonna live that down, am I?"

"Hmm, probably not."

Together, they casually began to walk, both still chuckling, with no destination in mind.

They strolled through the corn maze. Children giggled around them as they looked for the exit, though neither of them was trying very hard. To make it a little more interesting, each time they faced a dead end, they took a turn telling two truths and one lie about themselves.

"Okay, this time I'll start," Callum offered after they'd each already had two turns. "When I thought I might have been gay, I asked this girl in school who was known for being, well, to say it bluntly, a slut, to blow me. Justin Timberlake was my gay awakening, and I quit my first job because my boss tried to fuck me."

Riley's hand stopped halfway to his mouth; the candy corn forgotten as he processed Callum's comment.

"Jesus, please tell me the third one is the lie. Though the first makes you sound like a dick."

"Unfortunately, the first one happened, wasn't my proudest moment. After twenty minutes, she complained that her jaw hurt and I was still as soft as a wet noodle."

The visual had Riley laughing and grossed out simultaneously.

"So, your boss didn't hit on you?" Riley was relieved that was the lie, knowing almost every gay kid had a thing for Justin Timberlake.

"Yes and no. He did hit on me, but the lie is that I didn't quit, he fired me when I refused to sleep with him."

"Fuck…how young were you?"

"Too young. I didn't tell my parents. I just looked for a new job and made sure I never went back to that store."

"Did you tell them later, you know, like, when you were older?" Riley asked because he was curious why Callum was telling him.

"Eventually. Once they knew I was gay and had started to date, I told them what happened. I don't know why I'm telling you this." Callum seemed embarrassed, as though it was his fault. "Suppose a part of me wanted you to know that's something I had to deal with, I guess."

"You say that like it happened more than once?"

Callum had his hands in his pockets while they walked, and he kept them there as he shrugged off his reply. "The red hair kinda made me stand out…attract attention. Sometimes unwanted attention."

"Fuck, man. I'm sorry."

"Thanks. I promise I'm okay. It was this weird reoccurrence that I had to deal with growing up, but it helped me see the world clearer."

They kept walking, squeals and pounding feet on gravel filled their ears.

It was Riley's turn when they came face to face with another dead end.

"I've never been interested in one-night stands. Noelle and I both lost our virginity on the same night and Jackson was my first gay kiss."

"The last one has to be the lie."

Riley cocked an eyebrow. "You sure?"

"Wha—I mean—you said—"

Callum's fumbling was cute. "I said we never hooked up. But that was because we kissed and it wigged us out so much that we knew nothing sexual would ever happen between us."

"That bad, huh?"

"The worst. I don't know how to describe it, but nothing was there. No attraction, no lust. It was the weirdest, funniest thing ever."

"I guess that means the lie is…" Callum scrunched up his face in thought.

Riley waited, curious.

"You and Noelle?"

"Correct. I lost it first and she was so annoyed that she went to her boyfriend's house the day I told her and asked him why they hadn't slept together yet."

"Oh wow. How did he take that?"

"The guy said it was because he was gay and trying to get close to me."

Callum erupted into a fit of laughter. "You're kidding?"

"Swear to God. I had to let him know I wasn't interested, so he got dumped and rejected on the same day. Noelle was so annoyed that she wasted three months with the guy."

"You're her brother. She honestly didn't see the signs that her boyfriend was team dick?"

"I didn't even know. She got all pissy that my gaydar didn't pick it up and save her the time."

Suddenly they found themselves at the exit. The large crowds and overly heightened sounds of chatter and music made Riley want to go back into the maze.

"So…no one-night stands, huh?" Callum asked.

Riley looked down as he scuffed his shoe along the gravelled ground, the bag of candy corn long forgotten in his hands.

"That scene isn't really for me…"

A hand brushed against his empty one; long, slender, lightly freckled fingers tugged at his palm.

"Hey," Callum said.

His hand relaxed and slid into Callum's grasp. Riley looked up.

"That's not what I'm looking for either." Callum squeezed his hand. "C'mon, let's grab some apple cider." Callum pulled at his arm and Riley followed on instinct. His hesitation faded, especially when it dawned on Riley that he was walking around the Halloween Fall Festival, holding hands with a guy he couldn't believe was interested in him.

Food was devoured. Drinks were consumed. They argued over who would pay for what until they decided to take turns with each new purchase. Callum attempted to carve a pumpkin, confiding that he had never done it, but had always found the idea appealing.

It ended in disaster when Callum's carving utensil got stuck. He put a little extra force into pushing down the double-sided saw, which resulted in his pumpkin getting cut wide open.

Some of the kids around them giggled and Riley watched as Callum owned his mistake, letting the children prove that they were better at pumpkin carving than he was. But Riley was a sucker for helping people, which is why he took over and turned Callum's pumpkin into a face that had a scar across his eye, one that he told the children the pumpkin head got in battle. The kids loved it and Riley felt pride over how impressed Callum seemed.

As the sun began to set, Callum insisted they take a hay ride around the parkland.

"A hay ride? Seriously?" Riley had to admit, out of all the festivities they had partaken in that evening, this one seemed the most childish.

"Come on. Unless you're afraid of horses?" Callum asked sincerely.

Riley rolled his eyes at the stupidity of the question. "No. I'm not afraid of a horse."

Callum smiled. "Guess you don't have a reason not to get on then, huh?"

And with that, Callum reached out, took his hand, and pulled him along as they ran toward the line for hay rides, which only had another couple ahead of them and two horses being led to the starting point.

"See, perfect timing. We didn't even have to wait," Callum said excitedly as they watched the children and their parents get assistance to hop down and the couple before them get on the back of a small wagon. It was lined with hay, and pulled along by two horses.

The first wagon took off and the second trotted up, already empty. Callum stepped up first and turned to extend an arm for Riley to take, which he hated to admit he needed.

"You make a short joke and I'll push you off this wagon." Riley raised his eyebrows to emphasise that he wasn't joking.

"It was one dream. You can't hold it against me. I had no control over what my brain was doing while I slept."

"Ready, boys?" the voice from the front called back.

Riley knew that voice. He turned and peeked from behind the wooden paling to see none other than Tommy, one of their most frequent customers.

"Tommy?"

"Ey kid, fancy seein' you here. It's been a while," Tommy called out.

"Yeah well, someone asked me and I couldn't very well say no." Tommy turned further to take a look at who he was referring to as Riley turned to the side to give Callum a warm smile.

"Ah, say no more. How 'bout we take the scenic route? You lot would 'av been my last ride anywho, seeing how it's almost dark out." Tommy turned back around. Riley moved a little further down the wagon and took a seat on the wooden floor so his legs could dangle over the edge.

With his head, he motioned for Callum to join him.

"Trust me, it's more comfortable than that itchy shit." He moved over to make room for Callum, whose legs thankfully didn't reach the ground once they joined his over the edge of the wagon.

"He a friend of yours?" Callum asked. His voice had dropped, whether it be to match the quietness around them or so Tommy couldn't eavesdrop. It made him feel as though it was only the two of them. The sound of the horse's hooves trotting along was the only other noise that they had to compete with.

"Loyal customer. Brings his Ford in at least once a month," Riley replied.

"Jesus. Wouldn't seem worth it at that point," Callum offered.

Riley shrugged. "The sentimental value is what makes it worth it," he explained. "To some, cars are just a piece of machinery. A vehicle to help get you from A to B. But for others, well…" He looked out toward the landscape, taking in the orange leaves on the trees, dropping slowly as they rode past.

"Cars can hold memories and sometimes those memories are too precious let go." He faced Callum, surprised to see him staring with interest and not boredom, so he continued. "Your first child could have been born in the backseat, or even conceived." Riley smiled as Callum chuckled. "It could have been someone's home when they couldn't afford rent or it could have been the most unreliable piece of shit, yet every time you were in a jam, it always started on the first go and got you to where you needed to be." He thought back to the few special memories he had of his own car. "You treat a car right, it could last you a lifetime. It could even save your life."

The wagon went over a pothole. The bump caused them both to lose balance. He found himself in Callum's arms, who was holding him securely while Riley had one hand out, gripping onto the wooden railing of the wagon.

"Sorry, lads. Didn't see that one. Best I be heading back before we're stuck in complete darkness," Tommy called back to them.

His head was resting against Callum's shoulder, whose left arm was wrapped around his neck, his palm firmly grasping Riley's chest.

"Sorry, I can—" Callum went to let go, but Riley released his grip on the wagon and placed his hand above the one Callum had on his chest.

"No, it's…it's okay." He wanted to say it was nice, but the smile Callum gave was enough for Riley to figure he already knew.

The sun had virtually set. The sky was painted a hue of reds, oranges, and yellows, but if they looked out in front of them, they could barely see beyond their outstretched hands.

"It reminds me of you," Riley blurted out, the darkness helped to mask his vulnerability. "The sky."

"Let me guess, because of my hair," Callum said in a teasing manner, as though he had heard the joke before.

"No. Well, obviously yes but, that's not why I said it," Riley confirmed. "It's soothing, the way the sun can paint the sky a different colour each morning and each night. It's this force that comes back every day, no matter what happened in between.

Shining down, warming us." That's how he felt about Callum, and after speaking so truthfully, Riley was worried he went too far, admitted something too deep and personal this early on in their…whatever this was. This force that he knew would always be there, shining a light, warming him in darkness—that was Callum.

"If I'm the sun, does that make you the moon?" Callum gently asked.

"Is this you getting back at me for the hair joke?" Riley questioned with a chuckle in his voice.

"The moon is white; your hair is a blond colour with light ginger tones," Callum spoke matter-of-factly.

"God, we sound so gay." Riley was glad to see his comment only led to laughter from Callum and not a snobby eye-roll or scoff.

"You know, I thought you were pure blond the first time we met." Callum continued their prior discussion. "That was until you stepped outside and the red tones outshined the blond. I think I was mostly distracted with how the sun made you as transparent as Casper, though." It was an insult, in a joking manner, which was why Riley found himself laughing. "Never thought I'd date another ginger." Callum laughed.

They played around, pretending to push one another back and forth but it wasn't long before they settled into the position they were in, holding one another close.

"So, is that what we're doing…dating?" Riley asked.

"Is that okay with you?" Callum asked back.

He pretended to ponder over the question. "Guess we could give it a go." They began to laugh as Tommy brought the wagon to a stop, neither of them aware that they were back at the festival. The night sky had created an atmosphere for the event that was entirely different to how it started.

They both jumped down from the wagon, their hands automatically finding one another as they entwined their fingers, and took in their surroundings. The pumpkins that had been carved throughout the day were now lit, along with hanging lanterns that were stationed around the stalls.

A few fire pits had been ignited to help mask the cold, fall night air, and a guitarist had begun to play acoustic versions of well-known songs throughout the ages.

Although they had already spent hours together, it didn't seem like it was enough.

"If you have to go, that's fine. I'm sure you got work tomorrow or something," Riley offered an out. It was hard to put an end time on a date when an event goes well into the night.

"I'm in no rush."

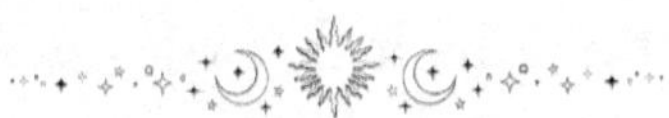

It was close to midnight when Riley parked his car out the front of his house with a smile that hadn't left his face all night. He took the keys from the ignition and collected his phone and wallet from the console when he noticed a notification from Callum.

He opened the message.

Callum

> I know we just parted ways, but I already want to see you again.

> Are you free Thursday night?

> Pick me up at six from the garage.

> I'll be there at 5.55!

The reply was instantaneous.

It had Riley feeling warm and giddy. He had never felt this before. He'd dated, and had a boyfriend or two, but never had they made him feel as though they needed to see him to live. That the time between seeing one another was not only cruel but torturous.

It reminded him of the literature they taught in school of fated love, and souls destined for one another. It made him feel alive and invincible, something he hadn't felt since the day his mother passed.

Callum truly was the sun. A beacon of light awakening him from a life that he felt doomed to live in the shadows.

Chapter 4

"Clean up on aisle four." Renee's voice sounds as exhausted as Riley feels, and he's only an hour into his shift. Today he isn't on clean-up duty or bagging duty. No, he's been tasked with restocking the fresh produce, his least favourite job.

When he's bagging groceries, he's aware of what's around him. The customers can only approach him from one direction and his back is guarded by a wall that stocks items customers specifically have to ask for.

But out on the floor, he's on guard. The slightest brush of a person walking behind him makes him nervous. The sound of someone politely asking him to move causes him to jump. On the off chance that they are out of stock of a product and he's been asked to check out back, Riley takes the moment to stand against the wall in the back room and remind himself where he is.

When this happens, he tends to forget to check for the item he was asked for, so he politely lies and tells the customer they are currently sold out.

Thankfully, it's rare that he gets floor duty. When he took the job, they specified that it would mostly be check-out duty. They weren't too concerned about his lack of experience. His age allowed him to work the shifts opposite the kids who were only available after school or on weekends.

It's tolerable, but it's nothing like working at the garage and some days, he misses it. He misses the way his hands used to get covered in grease and how he could work in relative silence with nothing but the hum of the shop radio playing in the background.

He misses the fact that he could go a whole day without a single person stopping by, whereas now, the ding of the shop doorbell going off every time someone walks through is enough to give him tinnitus.

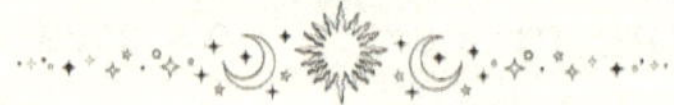

Riley's in the process of preparing dinner when Noelle's name appears on his phone. He sighs. He doesn't have the energy to talk to her. He barely has the energy to eat, but he knows he should, it's why he opted for a steak with a side of sauteed butter and garlic vegetables.

He's about to let the call go to voicemail when a sense of guilt washes over him. After all, she is his sister. His twin. And all he's been doing lately is finding an excuse to not talk to her.

Swiping the screen, the call connects and he puts the phone to his ear.

"Hey, you answered." Noelle sounds surprised.

"Yep."

"No, I mean, I wasn't sure if you were still working."

"Well, I'm not." He turns the steak over and waits.

"How've you been?"

Great. Small talk.

"Fine. Just like every other time you call." He takes a swig of his beer, it's not uncommon for him to have one or two, especially after work.

"I was hoping to visit this weekend. Maybe we could hang out, watch a movie?"

Taking a quick sweep around the apartment, his eyes track the lack of furniture and bare walls. He's had no desire to make it feel homey and welcoming.

"Yeah, maybe. I'll have to make sure I'm not working." He knows that excuse won't get past his sister. "I was thinking of catching up with Jackson and Billy."

"Oh?" Noelle sounds shocked.

"Mhm," he lies. He hasn't spoken to them since he moved in.

"That's—that's great, Ry. Those sessions must be working, then."

"What do you mean, workin'?" There is heat behind his words.

"I meant that talking to someone about everything can be helpful, ya know? Might make things better."

"Make things better." He grinds each word out between his clenched teeth.

"Ry, that's not…shit. See, this is what happens when you don't answer the phone. I stumble over my words and screw everything up."

"Oh, so this is my fault now?" He knew he should have ignored her call. "Those sessions were your idea, not mine, Noelle. I'm doing this for you."

"You should be doing it for yourself."

"Why?" he bites back, but he doesn't leave time for her to reply. "What did Mum always say, hmm? We shouldn't force ourselves to do something we don't want to do just because someone else doesn't like who we are."

"Well, Mum's dead."

Silence.

Riley's knuckles are white from how tightly he is clenching the phone.

"Ry," Noelle's voice is cautious, "I'm sor—"

"No. You're right." His voice sounds cold. "She is dead, and we can't change the past, Noelle. But you need to remember that the past can change us. So, if you don't like that, then maybe you should stop calling me." He hangs up the phone.

Blue eyes are glaring back at him on the black screen, daring his phone to light up with his sister's name.

Does he want her to call back?

Would he answer if she did?

Riley doesn't have the chance to think over his questions due to the loud beeping of his smoke alarm. His eyes avert to the cause, his steak now a charcoal rock, his vegetables void of any colour, and the smoke is so thick his small overhead fan above the stove can't keep up.

He grips the handle of the pan, and his brain sends a signal to his hand to let go. The hot metal burns his hand before the pan crashes onto the stove, metal hitting metal. He jumps back as he drops it. Curses fly from his mouth as he looks at his hand and rushes over toward the sink so he can run cold water over his soon-to-be blistered skin.

The constant beeping is deafening. He keeps his right hand under the water as he uses his other hand to wave a towel in the air to clear the smoke. Eventually, it stops, but the sound still echoes in his ears.

Looking around, he knows he has a first-aid kit somewhere, but he'll have to leave the sink to look for it. He runs the towel under the cold water, soaking it enough so he can wrap it around his hand while he goes on the hunt.

Eventually, he finds it stashed away in a box. He opens the windows, the cool breeze airing out the smell of smoke as he looks for the burn cream.

Of course, that's when his phone rings. The last call he took led to this mess in the first place. But as he glances at the screen, his breath hitches and relief washes over him as he swipes the screen and puts the call on speaker.

"Hey, is now a bad time?"

Riley feels like he could cry. "God, you have no idea how good it is to hear your voice right now."

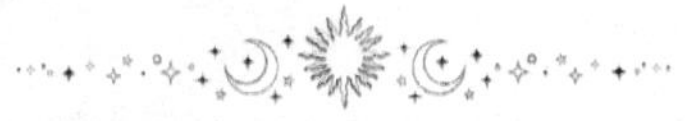

Riley knows Dr Bech is going to ask, so he decides to come right out and tell her.

"I had an accident while cooking the other night." He holds up his bandaged hand, the burn cream freshly applied underneath.

Dr Bech looks concerned. "Oh my. Are you okay?"

He waves her off. "I've had worse." From the look on Dr Bech's face, he's assuming that isn't an answer she's comfortable with.

"May I ask what happened?"

Is she asking out of politeness or to analyse him and take more notes?

"Had an argument with Noelle."

"Did it get physical?"

"What? No. We were on the phone."

"Oh." Dr Bech sounds somewhat relieved. "Then how did an argument cause the…"

"Burn," he clarifies. "Was cooking dinner when it happened. Argument had me forgetting about the food until my apartment was smoking up, reached for the pan and now here we are."

"You seem unfazed by this event."

"As I said, I've had worse."

"Yes, but I'm referring more to the argument than the injury." Dr Bech crosses her legs. "For you to be so engrossed in this discussion with your sister that you not only burnt your dinner but forgot entirely that you were cooking, then it must have been quite troubling."

Troubling. There's that word again.

"Look, siblings fight. Hell, twins probably more so, since we're born to almost be an exact copy of each other."

"Are you saying you fight with your sister a lot?"

"Wha—That's not what I—" He slumps further into the couch, getting more frustrated by the second, reminding himself why he refuses to participate.

"Did my question upset you?"

"You goin' to let me answer that or you goin' to throw another question at me?"

Dr Bech waits.

Riley breathes, his irritation evident.

"You really want to do this?" He takes control by asking the questions.

"Excuse me?" Dr Bech seems thrown by his question.

"You really want to sit here and listen to whatever I have to say?"

"Is that not what you're paying me for, Riley? To listen and to help you understand what's going on."

"Nothing is going on!" he yells back. "My sister brought up our dead mother, I got upset and burnt my hand. Big fucking deal."

"Okay, okay. Let's take a minute," Dr Bech instructs.

Within that minute, Riley steadies the pounding in his chest by counting the books on the shelf. Only after he has counted them twice, confirming there is still the same amount since the first time he sat in this room, does he give his attention back to Dr Bech.

"Riley," Dr Bech says, "how about you tell me what your mother was like?"

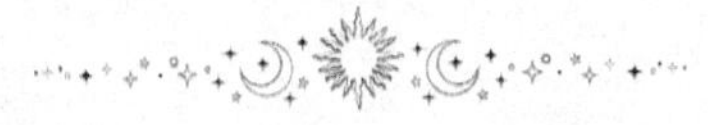

Nine Months Ago

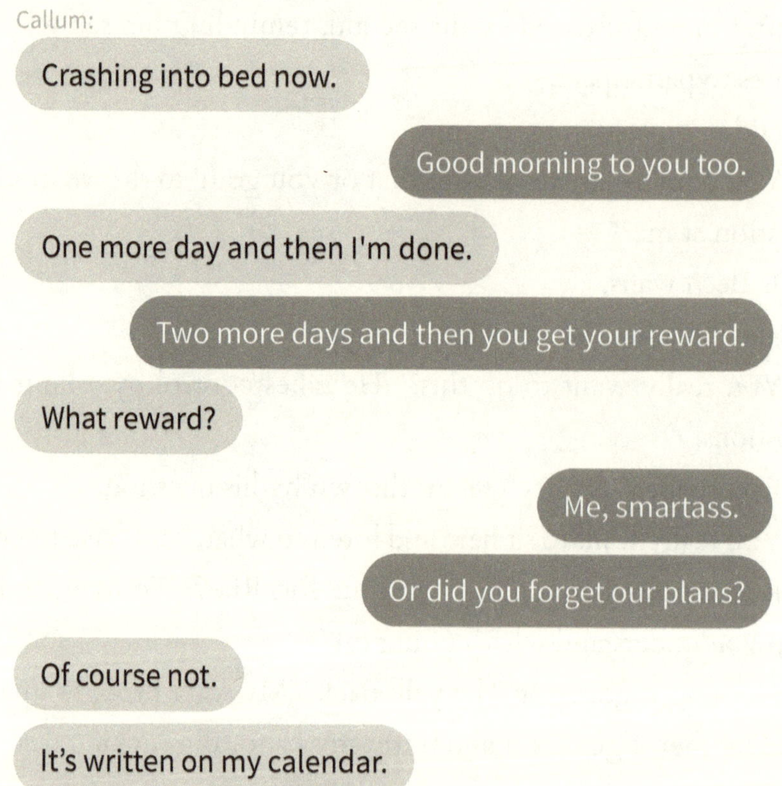

A picture came through of a wall calendar that had 'DATE WITH RILEY' written in capital letters for that coming Saturday. It made Riley smile and then realise he was going to be late for work if he sat in bed any longer. But that hadn't stopped him from replying.

Was free from work.

Sexy firefighters, how could I say no? ;)

Guess I'm not the only one who loves a uniform ;p

I'm meant to be going to sleep but I can put the uniform back on if you want ;)

Go to sleep. I gotta get to work.

Night Cal.

Mmm, Cal.

I like that.

Riley knew he was smiling at his phone like a doe-eyed idiot but he couldn't help it. He was happy.

"Took you long enough," Noelle complained as he stepped out of the bathroom, freshly showered and dressed in clean, yet stained overalls. "Hope you didn't use all the hot water rubbing one out."

He threw his sister the finger, a bright smile plastered on his face as he walked backwards toward the kitchen to grab coffee and a doughnut to go. Like he did every morning, Riley began to scroll his phone as he ate, only this time he went back and looked over old messages between him and Callum.

"Okay, seriously. You're like, attached to that thing," Noelle complained as she walked back into the kitchen.

"Am not." He pocketed his phone.

"You goin' to tell me why you're all sunshine and rainbows or am I gonna have to steal your phone while you're asleep?"

"You don't know my code."

"Mum's birthday." Noelle took a bite of an apple. He was about to tell his sister she was wrong until she cut him off, mouth full of the chewed fruit. "Backwards."

His twin's smirk was enough for Riley to know he shouldn't try and deny it.

"Speaking of. We still going tomorrow?"

It was the anniversary of their mother's death and each year, he and his sister would go to the cemetery, sit on a blanket in warm winter coats and spend hours talking, whether it be to each other or to her. They had done it every year since she passed.

"Course. Can you pick up the flowers?"

His sister gave him a nod, and with that, Riley knew he had to leave for work.

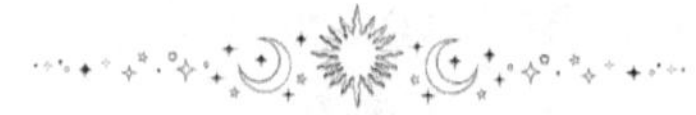

Callum

I had a dream about you.

If you dreamt I was another Oompa Loompa I'm blocking your number.

Riley groaned as he pocketed his phone, glad he had spent extra time in the shower that morning. Work was constant, each of them tinkering on their own car. Instead of his typical hum along to the radio, Riley was getting his hands dirty while blushing over the thought of Callum dreaming about him. Over the idea that he meant enough to someone that he was infiltrating their mind even when asleep. For the first time, he felt special. Wanted. And he was thankful the undercarriage of the car was hiding him from Clint and Charlie as the revelation of that showed on his face.

At this stage of his life, Riley figured nothing could surprise him, but perhaps that line of thinking was his undoing.

When he returned home from work, he was surprised to find the front door unlocked, which should have been the first red flag. The second was how uncannily quiet the house was.

"Yo, Pops." Had his father been asleep and woken by him calling out, no doubt Riley would have been reprimanded for waking him. But as he walked through the house, throwing mail onto the kitchen table, his eyes landed on his father, lifeless on the floor, with a needle stuck in his arm.

"DAD!" He screamed the word so loud he was sure it would have been enough to wake his father.

Skidding onto the carpet, Riley wasn't sure where to begin. He placed his hand over his father's mouth to assess whether he was breathing, the faint heat a welcomed relief.

He didn't touch the needle, but he did call for help.

"911. What's your emergency?" a female voice answered.

"My father. He's had an overdose."

"Is he breathing?"

"Barely."

"Okay, sir. What's your address?"

Riley gave the information while his eyes roamed over his father's body, eventually noticing the slight shade of blue at his father's fingertips.

"We have a response team in the area. Their ETA is five minutes. What's your father's name, sir?"

"Malcolm. Malcolm Maddox."

"And your name, sir?"

"Riley." He sniffed; his emotional state surprised him.

"Riley. Has he responded to you at all?"

Riley shook his head, only to remember he couldn't be seen.

"I haven't—I—"

"Can you try to get your father's attention, Riley?"

He looked down.

"Dad?"

Nothing.

"Pops!"

Zilch.

"Malcolm!" he screamed. The fear and anxiety of the situation had finally hit him.

"Riley." The calm voice in his ear brought him back to the present. "I need you to vigorously grind your knuckles against your father's sternum, okay? That's the breastbone in the middle of his chest."

Riley looked at his father. For a split second, he feared touching him.

"Riley. Speak to me. How are we doing?" The operator's voice broke through and Riley set to work. Whether he was following orders for seconds or minutes, he never stopped. Not when his hand was getting sore. Not when the skin on his knuckles began to feel raw. And not when the banging on the front door told him that the ambulance had arrived.

"It's open," Riley called out, hanging up the phone, which he had stopped talking into long ago.

"Sir." A body knelt beside him. "My name is Deja, and this is my partner—"

"Riley?"

At the sound of his name, he looked up. Callum's soft, green eyes looked down at him, concern written across his face.

"Wait, *this* is Riley?" Deja interjected.

"Are you okay?" Callum sat on the floor beside him as Deja began to gently move his hand away from his father's chest.

"Reed. Focus. I need your help over here." Deja's voice boomed through the silence.

"Sit back, okay?" Callum moved Riley away from his father. "We've got this. I promise."

"Do you know what he took?" Deja called out.

"Fentanyl. But it's always pills. I've never…I—" Riley's mouth felt dry. He watched as the needle was removed.

"He has a prescription?" Deja asked.

"He did." Deja turned her head toward him. "He buys 'em off the street."

"Parkes." Callum had spoken and although it wasn't directed at Riley, it had caught his attention and helped him focus on what was going on.

He was confused as he watched Callum retrieve a bag full of purple pills from his father's pocket.

"Shit. Down." Deja's words had his head spinning.

Down?

"Wait," Riley tried to cut in. "No. They aren't—My dad's pills are whi—"

"Riley, hey. Look at me, okay?" His eyes instantly focused on Callum's. "Deja is going to give your dad a shot of naloxone. We'll get him in the rig and take him to White Oak Medical Center."

He nodded his head, but no part of him took in the information.

"Riley…call Noelle. I don't want you driving like this." He could feel Callum's hand on his cheek, and even though it was covered with a latex glove, the warmth emanating beneath the plastic was still soothing.

"Reed. Need you over here," Deja called back, breaking the contact with Callum.

With shaking hands, he watched as his father was placed on a gurney and wheeled out to the ambulance while his fingers struggled to dial his sister's number.

"Hey Ry," Noelle's cheerful voice came through the speaker. "I'm almost home if that's what you're wondering." It had felt cruel to ruin the happy mood she was in.

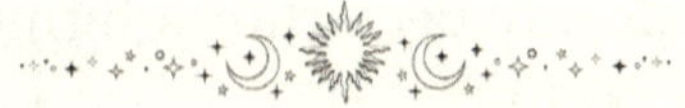

"You said your father was self-medicating?"

Riley was holding his sister's hand, whatever energy he had left was split between dealing with the doctors and being her rock.

"Yes. He was prescribed some pills ten years ago and when the doctors stopped writing the scripts, he fuckin' went out and found some himself, okay?" He was frustrated. The repeated questions and the fact that they had yet to see their father since they arrived were getting on his nerves.

"Ten years ago, when…?"

"When he had the accident." He squeezed Noelle's hand. "Look, will you just—" He exhaled before he did something he would regret. "Will you just tell us if he's okay?"

The doctor continued writing notes, avoiding their eyes and questions. It felt like ten minutes had passed before the doctor paid them any attention.

"He's stable. No major issues. He had to be restrained temporarily, the effects of the naloxone can cause aggression once a patient wakes. But besides that, he's okay." Riley finally felt as though he could breathe. "You found him early," the doctor continued, "and the three doses of naloxone saved his life."

Riley wasn't sure if he was relieved or disappointed. His emotions were confusing, his heart and mind not syncing up.

"You said your father was taking fentanyl?" The doctor asked, again.

He nodded. "That's what he was prescribed and he...stuck with it." Riley had already been through this.

"You're lucky, Mr Maddox. Fentanyl is highly addictive and lethal if the dosage is taken incorrectly. Generally speaking, most of our patients who die of an overdose are a result of opioid abuse. For this to be the first time in ten years that your father has had an overdose, someone up above must be looking out for him."

Did they have a guardian angel? Or it could have been as simple as his father's dealer cutting him a weaker batch.

"His blood work also indicated that there were traces of heroin in his system," the doctor explained.

"I'm sorry, did you say heroin?" Noelle spoke up.

"It's called down. It's a street drug that's been circulating recently. Fentanyl cut with heroin. The EMTs on the scene mentioned purple pills, which is how it's sold. Based on the track marks on your father's arm, it seems he chose the injection method over the oral."

It didn't make sense.

His father had issues, but heroin?

The white pills Malcolm swallowed daily were to numb the pain and mask the depression that hit after their mother died. The effects of the comedown caused Malcolm's agitation, which at times led to his anger, but he'd never seen his father go into a full withdrawal. There had been instances where Riley had seen what that anger may be like. The comedown of Malcolm's high, when he hadn't popped a pill quick enough to balance himself out. That was when the violence struck and Malcolm spat hateful remarks. He would be lying if he didn't admit that those moments of anger generated fear within him, and knowing this new information caused Riley's skin to crawl. The unwanted future scenario of what could one day be a battle he'd have to face. A battle that may be arriving sooner than Riley could be prepared for. He was now being told that the buzz his father had been chasing for ten years was no longer sufficient for his pain. That the highs, lows and withdrawals could soon be a hundred times worse if his father decided to continue on the path of this new drug.

The doctor handed him a few pamphlets. Riley had no recollection of the white-coated Ivy League schmuck even retrieving them.

"It's never too late to get help. I also suggest getting a naloxone kit to keep on hand." The doctor tried to smile, but it came across as condescending more than sincere. "Thankfully, it sounds like down is a fairly new substance for your father, so he does have that working for him."

Doctors, they're like shooting stars. Blink and suddenly you miss them. Or in this case, lost all faith in them.

Riley took the pamphlets, blinked, and was then faced with the back of a doctor who seemed not much older than he was, clearly done with the discussion, and them.

"Riley?" His name echoed through the hall.

For the second time that day, the voice that could lull him to sleep spoke his name. He spun around, Callum was panting as he jogged closer. He was still in uniform, though it looked more worn than when he saw him back at the house.

How long had he been at the hospital?

"I wasn't sure if you'd still be here." Callum stopped in front of him, slightly out of breath. "I came straight from work to check in on your father…was hoping to catch you. Wanted to see if you were okay."

"Ah…" He didn't know where to look. How to start. "He's um. They said that—"

That soothing warmth reappeared when Callum placed his hand on his bicep, a gentle squeeze letting Riley know he could take his time.

"I'm sorry. Who are you?" Noelle interrupted, and although Riley was struggling to form a sentence, the reminder that his sister was standing right beside him reconnected his brain-to-mouth motor functions, that were otherwise short-circuiting.

"Shit. Right." He pointed to Callum. "Noelle, this is Callum, he was the EMT on the scene today." *And the guy he's been dating.* "Cal," he pointed at his sister, "this is Noelle."

He didn't miss the side-eye both Callum and Noelle gave him. But it was not the time nor place to discuss his relationship.

"Thank you for helping him," Noelle offered.

"Of course. I'm glad our rig was close by when the call came in." Callum spoke to Noelle but his eyes were focused on Riley.

"They said it was a heroin overdose. That I found him in time before any serious damage could set in," Riley explained, knowing that had Callum not shown up, he still would have turned to the man for support.

"Down has been hitting the streets hard the last couple of months."

Riley wanted to defend his father. Explain that he wasn't an addict, at least not in the sense that Callum was no doubt judging him for being.

"He's awake. They said he'll be discharged in the next hour or two." Riley couldn't wrap his head around that fact.

"Each hospital is different. But now with naloxone, some patients can leave within an hour of being administered the drug, others they hold for hours."

"Ya know, I've been hearing that word all day and yet not a single person has told me what the fuck it is." Riley hadn't meant for his voice to rise enough for the nurses at the desk to look over and see where the commotion was coming from.

"It's a drug that can temporarily reverse opioid overdoses," Callum began to explain. "It works by blocking opioid drugs from attaching to opioid receptors in the brain. So, being that we administered the first dose so early…" Callum stopped talking, no need to continue as Riley now understood.

"You do this often? Check up on your patients?" Noelle asked.

"Ah, no." Callum huffed a laugh as though he were nervous. "No, not really. Once I drop them off, I don't hear back, just gotta hope for the best."

"Okay, so then—"

"Noelle." Riley cut her short. He didn't want to get into it here. Especially now. But it seemed one look from his twin sister was all it took for her to piece it all together.

"Oh my god. The reason for all the stupid smiling at your phone. He's the reason, isn't he?"

"Jesus, could you not?" Riley didn't have the energy for this discussion.

"Fine."

Riley was suspicious of how easily Noelle conceded. "I'll go check on Dad. Give you two a moment. But when we get home, you're not getting out of this."

There it was.

He took in a deep breath, probably the first since he stepped foot in the house that evening. With Noelle's hand no longer in his, Riley found himself twisting his hand around his fingers, ringing them tightly to settle nerves he couldn't understand as he focused on Callum.

"Don't," Callum spoke first.

"Don't what?"

"Don't act like this is an out for me."

"*Callum…*" It scared Riley how easily the redhead could read him.

"You think your dad being an addict is going to scare me?" Callum's voice didn't sound cruel or judgemental. If anything, Riley could hear the surprise in his voice, as though it would take a lot more for the handsome man in uniform to be pushed away.

"H–he's never done anything like this before..." Riley kept his eyes downcast. "Never...taken anything this..." He couldn't explain it because he couldn't understand it.

The skin of his right hand was red raw from how tightly he was twisting his fingers. But then the pressure faded and instead, he felt the familiarity of long slender fingers intertwined with his left hand.

"I've finished work if you want to go somewhere and talk about it."

That was the moment when Riley finally realised how long he'd been waiting at the hospital. "You're finished?"

"Nightshift roaster is now complete. I should be sleeping, getting my body back into routine and ready for..."

"Ready for Saturday. Shit. Right." It was as though all sense of life outside of the hospital had been forgotten.

"Hey, no. It's fine. I wouldn't expect you to after everything that's happened."

Call him selfish. Call him a bad son. Either way, Riley wasn't going to change his plans because his father decided that his high was no longer sufficient.

"I wouldn't want to miss it." He even offered a smile to prove that he meant it. "I better go check on Noelle."

Funny how his sister came to mind before his father.

"I'll call or text or…whatever." He extracted his hand from Callum's, albeit with more force than he intended. "Work out the plans…I'll be there" He was already walking backward towards his father's room. "Promise." And even though his body language was saying otherwise, he never broke a promise.

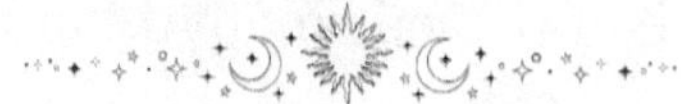

Around the time when Riley was due to wake up and get ready for work was when he, Noelle and their father finally got back home. He sat Malcolm down on the recliner he practically lived in, walked toward his bedroom and went to sleep. No words were exchanged with either his sister or father. He crawled into bed, closed his eyes and allowed sleep to overcome him.

It was the raised voices that woke him hours later, the sun still in the sky. The soft rays filtering through his window shutters brought images of Callum to mind. His scruffy beard and soft hair. Riley sat on the edge of the bed, eyes closed as though the rays were heating his body, or perhaps it was the mere thought of Callum that was creating those warm tingly feelings from the inside out.

The voices grew louder and Riley left the calmness. His body instantly ran cold the second he walked away from the halo of light.

"What were you thinking?" Noelle shouted. Riley rubbed his eyes as he shuffled into the living room where it seemed World War Three was in the works.

"Heroin, Dad? Really? It's bad enough you're stoned out of your mind on the painkillers you pop like candy. But now this! And how the hell do you even know how to use heroin? Your dealer show you?"

Riley stood back, the fire in his sister resembled the few times he had caught their mother screaming at their father, and although his mother was unaware that he had been a witness, the memory was one of the few that stuck with him the most.

It wasn't because he looked back at it to remember the trouble his parents had in their marriage or because it was a side of her he saw often, far from it. No, the reason Riley kept holding onto those memories was because it proved how strong his mother was. How she never allowed 'the man of the house' to walk all over her or push her to the side. When times were tough, she was the one who told their father to pull his head out of his ass and step up.

And here Noelle was, doing the same thing.

"Don't act like you give a shit. Like either of you do." Malcolm's eyes locked onto Riley's, which meant he could no longer stand in the background while his sister took charge. Noelle whipped her head around, her face pleased to see he was there to take part in the 'discussion'.

"I hear you two whispering about me. Just cos it looks like 'm asleep don't mean I fuckin' am."

"Look, Pops. The pills were one thing." He stepped deeper into the room. "You were high as a fuckin kite and an aggressive asshole when itching for your next hit but we figured you had a small chance of killing yourself. You took one hit of this new drug and OD'd in the living room." For years, he ignored their father's addiction, assuming it was a simple high that acted a little stronger than weed. Riley now knew how wrong they were after the doctor explained how lethal fentanyl was.

"I wasn't—Jesus Christ, I wasn't trying to off myself. Ya, think I would have waited this long if that's what I wanted?"

"Honestly, who fuckin' knows? We don't. You never talk to us anymore and when you do, it's to bark orders or to bring us down." Riley felt himself standing taller. "Do you even know that Noelle has a chance at being promoted?" He lifted his eyebrows to emphasise that it was a rhetorical question. "Or that I've been dating someone? Or how about the fact that today is the anniversary of Mum's death? Do you even remember that?"

"Of course, I fucking know!" His father spat the words; saliva flying through the air as he did so. "Why do you think I went to the dealer? Because I knew. I knew what was coming…what today would mean." For the first time in years, the emotion in his father's voice was something besides anger.

"She was the love of my life. The *only* person I ever loved." His father's fist clenched the top of the couch cushion he was standing behind. It reminded Riley of the Great Wall of China, built up to protect its territory. "I had her for eighteen years and then she was taken from me." Malcolm's voice wobbled at the words 'taken from me'.

"From us, Dad. She was taken from us," Riley corrected. "And *you know* it's your fault she isn't here." He pointed an accusing finger at him. "You know goddamn well that this 'pain' you're feeling, this everlasting heartache…that's nothing more than fucking guilt."

"Riley…" His father tried to plead.

"No." He held his hands up and took a step back. "Don't you fuckin' dare. You want to shoot up, get numb? Be my fuckin' guest. At least next time I'll know not to save you when I find you gasping for air." He turned.

"Don't you walk away from me!" The dominance in his father's voice was back.

"Or what?" He was no longer afraid of his father. "You'll hit me? Kick me out? You. Need. Us. A lot more than we need you." He went to grab his sister so they could leave.

"So, you're just gonna leave like some pussy?"

Riley took his car keys and his coat, and motioned for Noelle to do the same so they could get the hell out of there. Right before they went to leave, Riley turned back to his father and looked him dead in the eye.

"I'd like to think you're not stupid enough to keep taking that down shit. But if you do, keep it in the bedroom. Noelle doesn't need to see you getting fucked up like that." And with that, he slammed the door closed.

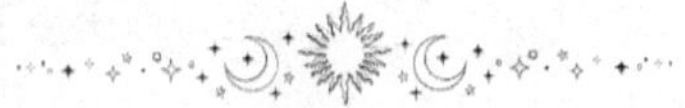

A blanket on the damp ground covered the last of the fall leaves. Riley and Noelle sat facing their mother's tombstone. Neither one of them offered to speak, the mere silence a peaceful welcome after their morning chaos.

Sunflowers lay atop the tombstone. They were hard to come by this time of year, but a local florist ordered the flowers specifically for Riley and Noelle, making sure they arrived by the anniversary.

"I could never understand why she loved that sunflower festival so much." Noelle broke the silence, but the reminder of one of the activities their mother loved to do made Riley smile.

"I know why." He looked over at his sister. "First weekend of August, she'd have us in the car driving to Fulton so she could stand in the middle of the sunflower field." He shook his head in delight at the memory. "We were nine and I was holding her hand as she looked up toward the sun and I remembered wondering the same thing, what's so special about a festival for one flower…so I asked her."

He picked up a dried leaf, only for it to crumble the second his fingers held it. "She said that every year, all she wanted was to take a moment to feel the positivity and hope that radiated off a sunflower."

The look his sister gave him was enough for Riley to know she was confused, much like he was when his mother first said it. "It's what a sunflower symbolises. You know, like how each flower has its own meaning?" Again, a blank stare from his sister. "Well, they do. And I had to look it up to know that's what she was talking about." He shuffled so both his knees were against his chest, his arms wrapped around his legs to keep them in place.

"Anyway. She said what she said, and then looked down at me, smiling away, and said the sunflower has the ability to turn toward the sun. That they chase the light so it can get back everything the darkness stole…and ah, then she squeezed my hand and that was it. We went back to find you and Pops near the bathrooms because you almost pissed your pants on the car ride there."

"That's right." A shove to the shoulder broke the trance Riley was in. "It's because you dared me to drink a whole bottle of Sunny D before we left."

They both began to chuckle at the memory until the silence naturally washed over them.

"You think she was talking about Dad?" Noelle asked. "Ya know, the whole, hope and darkness thing?"

He was shaking his head, telling her no before the question was even finished. "They had their issues but their love was…I mean, this whole town speaks of them like they were the couple everyone wanted to be. Their devotion to one another is the reason Dad is destroying himself from the inside out."

And it's why Riley had spent years looking for someone who could live up to what they had. To find a love that was as deep and meaningful as the one his parents shared. It was their example of true love that made Riley not want to settle for anything less. What caused him to stop wasting time with meaningless flings so that he was open to meeting someone he wanted to share his life with.

He never knew what darkness his mother was referring to, perhaps it was a reference to the evils of this world. But no darkness tainted the love between her and his father.

"You going to tell me about sunshine now?" Noelle gave him a devilish look.

"Who?"

"Sunshine and rainbows." Riley still had no idea who Noelle was referring to and his face indicated that. "The guy who made you stare at your phone like a love-sick puppy and turned out to be this smoking hot EMT."

Riley rolled his eyes, now aware of the connection.

"Calm down. Things are still new." Though he couldn't help the smile that spread across his face at the mere thought of Callum.

"Can't be that new. The guy came to the hospital to check on you and Dad, though mostly you."

"Don't be jealous," he teased.

"Jealous? If Joel knew what had happened, he would have been there."

"You didn't tell him?"

His sister shrugged. "He doesn't need to know. Besides, Dad's fine. And stop changing the subject."

There was more to that statement than Noelle was letting on, but he chose to let it pass. They had been through enough in the last twenty-four hours. If she wanted to discuss something, she would have brought it up.

"God, you're annoying," he said with love. Noelle poked her tongue out and the sight caused him to chuckle.

"His name's Callum."

"Oh, totally looked like a Callum."

Riley ignored his sister's comment, bringing his thumb up to scratch the corner of his eyebrow. "He was a customer at the shop. Brought his Jeep in for a service."

"Boys and their toys. I'll never understand."

"More like boy's lack of getting a car service in the last three years." Riley felt a twinge in his heart after he said the words.

"So, you're…boyfriends? A couple?"

"It's been a month." Riley was counting it from the barbecue at Jackson's house. "We're…dating."

"You haven't had the exclusive talk, have you?"

The talk was one of the main reasons why dating was so hard for his generation. Back when their parents were his age, hell, even younger, it was simple. Dating meant a couple. Exclusive. No ifs or buts. But now, there was a label for everything and everyone, and with it came that awkward discussion about exclusivity. The talk about whether they would be seeing only each other, that they were committed, or whether they were just having fun while keeping an eye out for 'the one'.

"Ry?" Unaware he had zoned out, Riley blinked a few times till his sister was back in focus.

"You like him. Like, *really* like him."

He averted his eyes to his mother's tombstone.

Marlene Maddox

"Gone too soon from this world,
but never will she leave our hearts."

1970-2004

"He's always on my mind, one way or another," he began to explain. "A song comes on and it'll remind me of him. I'll order a pizza and I'll consider getting a Hawaiian."

"Ew, what?" Noelle cut in.

Riley chuckled. "Long story." The smile stayed on his face as he continued.

"Weirdly enough, every time I've looked at the sun, all it does is make me think of him." It wasn't lost on Riley how they had only just discussed their mother's love for sunflowers and their connection to the sun, and there he was, explaining to Noelle that Callum had become this beacon in his life, and he was now the one turning to face the sun rays.

"I don't think that's weird, Ry," Noelle offered. "Look, you're probably the only guy I know who isn't into fooling around and having fun. Enjoying our youth as we're now told to do." Noelle bumped into him playfully. "But whatever the reason, it's allowed you to keep a look out for Mr Right rather than Mr Right Now. So, if you're feeling this strongly about Callum, I'd say trust your gut."

"You don't think it's my way of trying to convince myself that Callum is…" He didn't want to say 'the one' because he honestly had no clue himself. Everyone goes through those honeymoon stages in a relationship where the first few months are centred around one another, thoughts consumed by each other. It's that fine line between wanting to spend every second together and coming across as clingy.

"I think you can sometimes overthink things, Ry. Take it slow. He obviously cares, otherwise, he wouldn't have come to the hospital after he finished work."

"Fuck. I said I'd message him." Riley retrieved his phone and began to message Callum regarding their plans for tomorrow.

"While you're at it, call Charlie. He called the house wondering where you were this morning."

Right.

Work.

Callum first, though.

"Hey, right on time." Callum opened his apartment door after Riley had buzzed to be let in.

"I may have been sitting in my car for thirty minutes." Riley walked inside while Callum held the door open.

"You could have come in. I had the apartment ready an hour ago." Callum had a glint in his eyes that made Riley smile with a blushing glow to his cheeks. He chose to look past how eager they both were for tonight.

The minute the door closed behind him, Riley was transfixed by his surroundings. It was a studio. The only doors in the apartment were connected to the bathroom or the one Riley had walked through. It had a warm artist's feel, with its dark wooden beams that split the room into four distinct areas. The flooring was soft timber and the main wall was exposed brick, which featured Callum's king-size bed that had small lights hanging above the headboard.

"Are they…?" Riley cocked an eyebrow and asked to be sure.

"Christmas lights." Callum looked down, bashful. "I know Thanksgiving is next week but," the redhead shrugged, "it's kinda my favourite time of year. Figured why wait till December to decorate?" Green eyes looked up at him and with the warm glow of the hanging lightbulbs within the apartment, Callum was more gorgeous than ever before.

"Are you gonna give me the tour?"

"Hmm, I thought I'd pretend to go to the bathroom and let you snoop around for a few minutes," Callum joked.

"A few minutes? Wow, you underestimate my detective skills." He licked his suddenly dry lips.

"It's bigger than it looks." Callum took a step closer.

He didn't miss the innuendo, but he played it off. "Hmm, not really though." Riley began to point to the four corners of the room. "Bed. Kitchen. Dining table for four, and a couch big enough for two to watch whatever streaming service you're subscribed to."

"Thought you needed a tour?" Callum cocked a well-groomed ginger eyebrow.

Riley took a step closer. "What can I say? I adapt quickly to new surroundings."

If Riley was reading the situation correctly, he was sure that Callum was about to—

Repetitive beeping broke the spell between them. Callum looked towards the kitchen, walking off to stop the sound that Riley could only assume was the timer on the oven.

He cleared his throat, trying to shake off the tension they had built.

"Hope you're hungry." Riley watched Callum place a large baking dish on top of the stove. "It's a family recipe and the only way it tastes good is if it's cooked in a large batch."

He took a seat on the stool that was parked under the raised countertop, which gave him a front-row seat to the show.

"Wait, you actually cooked for me?"

"Did I not invite you over for dinner?" The sarcasm in Callum's voice only made him sexier.

"You did, but I figured we'd order in or something."

"So, what I'm hearing is, you don't have faith in my cooking." Using the base of his foot, Callum kicked his oven door closed, but threw a wink in for good measure.

"What if I have allergies?" Callum froze, his eyes widening at the realisation that it was a factor he didn't take into account. It was enough to make Riley forget everything that'd happened over the last few days.

He chuckled, unable to let the man before him stew any longer. "Relax man, 'm kidding. I'm good with everything."

"Except pineapple on pizza."

"Well, that one is now up for debate." It was his turn to throw a wink in the redhead's direction. "You need a hand with anything?"

"No. Just sit there and look pretty."

The air suddenly felt warm.

He moved to the dining table where he didn't have to wait for long.

"Okay, I know it's not a meal that looks the best, but I swear it tastes amazing *and* I even made a salad to go with it so that we can pretend it's somewhat healthy." Callum placed a plate down in front of him. Riley looked at the food. Without warning, his chest began to ache from the pounding of his heart. It wasn't the food itself that was causing the reaction. His brain somehow brought up memories based on the delicious cheesy smells that filled his nostrils, but a rancid taste filled his mouth.

With a shaky hand, he picked up the fork, willing himself to eat, but he couldn't bring himself to touch the food.

"Is something wrong?" Callum asked. "You don't like macaroni and cheese? Or is it the bacon? Shit. I should have asked, I—"

"No. No, it's not that." He was hoping for a night away from his past, but like everything, it always came back to haunt him. "I, um…" He put the fork down. "My…*our* mother passed away when we were fifteen."

"Riley…I'm so sorry."

There was never an easy way to have that kind of conversation. No one ever wrote a book on how to talk about dead parents or how to respond.

I'm sorry. It sounds like the right thing to say but it doesn't help. It means jack shit when the person saying it has nothing to be sorry for. Yet there Callum was, apologising, and Riley knew he meant it. That it resonated with the guy sitting across from him.

"Her name was Marlene. She and my dad met when they were seventeen. The 'it' couple in high school, apparently." He began to tell their story, knowing it from all the years it was shared with him by various people in his life. "You know how it was back then, everything moved so fast. They got married at eighteen and by nineteen she had Noelle and I."

The back of his thumb scratched a phantom itch on the tip of his nose. "The ah, the town started callin' em Mac 'n Cheese as a joke. Everywhere we went, I remember people calling them that and was confused at first, until my mother explained it to me." He surprisingly chuckled.

"You ever ask them why that nickname?" Callum asked.

"Nope, just knew my dad, Malcolm, he fuckin' hated it, but ma thought it was cute that they had a nickname."

"Like the older generation of a ship name," Callum joked, which helped the tension in Riley's heart.

"Ha, yeah, exactly…." He adjusted himself in his seat. "Malcolm, he ah, he started to have a hard time at work. There were layoffs, which meant he was working longer, so he became a pain in the ass to deal with at home. Never wanted to do anything, only wanted to spend the weekends sitting around and, in his words, 'Have some time to himself.'"

Riley's palms began to sweat. "Ma finally convinced him to take her out, to have a date night. Noelle and I stayed home, we were old enough at this point so we didn't need a sitter. Anyway, it was getting late…later than usual when I got a call." It was at that moment Riley locked eyes with Callum for the first time since he began his story. "Malcolm was in the hospital and Marlene, Mum, she…she died on the scene. Turns out while my father was having time to himself, he was too lazy to get the tyres on our car checked." He shook his head, the anger inside of him bubbling once again whenever he thought about that night. "It would have taken him a few minutes to check the pressure when he got gas, even the garage down the road that he bought the tyres from offered a free service to have them rotated and checked, but he never bothered."

He leaned his elbows on the table. "The grip had worn down on the two back tyres. The front right one blew out, which caused the car to skid on the wet road. Without the traction, the car swerved and wrapped around a tree." He looked up at the ceiling light to stop the tears from falling. "It was eleven years ago yesterday."

Callum's hand reached out and enveloped his. Warm, soft thumbs rubbed soothing circles into the tops of his hands.

"I've had an aversion to macaroni and cheese since then." He huffed. "So fuckin' weird since the food has no connection to her death besides the fact that it was a nickname for her." Riley sniffed back a tear.

"Thank you for telling me." Tender green eyes stared back at him. "I can't even imagine losing a parent so young."

"I wouldn't recommend it." The comment helped to clear the air as both men softly chuckled. "That's, ah, that's why my dad…they prescribed him fentanyl after the accident. The doctors stopped once they saw he was abusing the drug but by then, he was using it to numb himself rather than for physical pain."

"Grief can make us do things we never thought we'd do."

"Grief. Guilt. He's been using her 401k to fund his addiction. There wasn't much in there, but Noelle and I never saw a cent." Callum gave his hands a comforting squeeze. "We pay for the food, utilities, mortgage. Thankfully there isn't much of that left, but we can barely cover things between us let alone if we were to try and move out on our own."

"Is that what you want? To move out on your own?"

He shrugged. "I've thought about it. Would be nice to come home and not have to worry about what I'm walking into, what mood I'm going to get from him. But it's hard, saving enough money to survive on your own when most of what I make goes towards keeping a place over his head…towards sharing the responsibility with Noelle." Memories of Malcolm unconscious on the floor flooded his mind. "And then, ya know, who takes care of him? Cos he sure as shit won't." He took a calming breath in and out. "Whatever little money I can save, I do. Maybe I'll get that dream though, once I have someone to share it with…" He looked around at Callum's studio, seeing that he was already living the life Riley was striving towards.

There may be moments when he hated his father. He blamed him for the accident and the life they were stuck with, but deep down, Riley knew that if he walked away and learnt later on that Malcolm had passed, OD'd, or possibly starved, he would carry a similar guilt to that which had slowly eaten away at his father.

"Is this why you became a mechanic?"

He nodded. "It was the best I could do to make things right. Try to keep the road safe…" He could have sworn a lightbulb appeared on the top of the ginger's head, illuminating Callum's face as his eyes widened and his mouth gaped open.

"Wait…you didn't…was it because…"

As Callum stumbled for words, Riley couldn't help but laugh at how adorable it was. "Cal, the second I saw the state of your engine, there was no fuckin' way I was letting you drive that Jeep out of the shop until I had it fixed."

"My knight in greasy overalls."

"Ey, at least I scrub up nicely. I swear, the second someone takes on the role of a mechanic, they act like they're destined to have black oily fingers."

"You prefer to have white sticky ones."

Well, that sure made Riley blush. Both men let go simultaneously and leant back in their chairs.

"How 'bout we order like I should have done in the first place?" Callum suggested.

"No. No, it's okay, it's…" The food truly did look amazing, and the smell caused Riley's stomach to grumble and growl. "You put a lot of effort into this…into tonight, so it's time for me to try to move past it."

As though his mother was sitting in Callum's place, offering a nod of encouragement at her son for trying something new, Riley picked up the fork and broke off a large portion of macaroni and cheese. The bacon looked crisp, the melted cheese was stringy and in that moment, Riley made a conscious decision to put this behind him and shoved it in his mouth.

He should have felt embarrassed by the moan that followed, but who in their right mind didn't love a well-cooked macaroni and cheese?

"Holy fuck, this is good." He spoke through a mouth full of food, not caring one bit how it made him look.

Callum followed suit and began to eat as Riley devoured his plate, warming his heart and filling his stomach with the delicious meal. A weight had been lifted in the process. His mother's death wasn't a confession he needed to share with everyone he dated, but it was a deep and personal situation that explained what kind of life Riley lived. Callum could now understand what he dealt with regarding his father and why his passion for fixing cars grew stronger every day.

Following dinner, they moved onto the couch. Two empty beer bottles sat on the coffee table. The Christmas lights above Callum's bed had been turned on for the ambience, only to prove a point to Riley after he refused to believe Callum sat around his apartment with nothing but the festive string of lights to pave a path of light.

"I hope it was okay that I showed up at the hospital the other day." Callum's knee rested against his while he sat with one arm over the back of the couch, a leg bowed on the seat while the other hung over the edge. It felt oddly intimate for something so simple.

"A lot was happening at the time, so if I forgot to say it, thank you. Sometimes people assume because Noelle and I have each other that we don't need the support, but honestly, I probably need it more because of Noelle."

He watched Callum tilt his head like a confused puppy.

"When shit goes down, we don't have the luxury of both being able to break down. One of us always has to be level-headed. So, on Thursday, that was me. I had to be strong because it was me who found him. It was me who had to call 911, which meant I was the one who had to answer the doctor's questions and have the right questions ready to ask." He could feel himself finally letting go of the responsibility he was speaking of. "I was Noelle's support, so when you showed up, you instantly became mine. I hope that's okay?"

"I've got no objections to being your support partner."

Like a siren playing its song, Noelle's words suddenly crept into his head and Riley knew he couldn't avoid it much longer. He was opening up to Callum, sharing his life and, dare he say, his heart.

"Fucking Noelle," he cursed under his breath, though it seemed not low enough.

"What about Noelle?"

He rubbed at the back of his neck.

"She might have said something the other day and now it's playing on my mind and I mean, it's stupid because we've had this talk already but my sister, Jesus, she can be persistent."

"Riley?"

"Hmm?" he answered, like a pet being called by its owner.

"If you're referring to what I think you're referring to, the answer is no."

"No...right. Um—" He tried to hide the disappointment in his voice.

"No," Callum spoke again. "I'm not seeing anybody else."

A smile broke out on Riley's face. The instinct to bow his head to hide how wide it was won the battle. However, the ever-familiar touch of warm dainty fingers gently tilting his chin to rise, is what caused their eyes to reunite.

"We agreed to date, which means…I'm all yours…exclusively."

Riley's eyes closed momentarily. He couldn't remember the last time he had something that was only his.

"Besides," Callum continued. "What's the point of looking, when everything I want is sitting right in front of me?"

Callum's hand moved from his chin to cup the side of his face. His cheek fit perfectly into the palm of Cal's hand and he couldn't help but lean into it.

Riley bit his lip in anticipation, his eyes drifted down to Callum's lush pink lips and when they locked back onto emerald green eyes, he could feel his body leaning forward, the gap growing smaller as Callum did the same.

He had kissed people in the past, but kissing Callum was like nothing he'd ever experienced before. Time froze the second their lips met. The faint taste of beer was still present on Callum's lips, but it was the possessive way that Riley was held in place that, to his surprise, made him feel safe.

The kiss lit a fire within Riley that he could feel deep within his bones. He parted his lips momentarily, so he could fill his lungs with oxygen, and Callum took the opportunity to take ownership of his mouth.

His first kiss with Callum was like his soul had returned to his body. Like the sun was warming him from the inside out. It was in that kiss that Riley felt it all. Powered by an entity that he had no control over, Riley pushed off the couch only so he could land back down on Callum's lap. The kiss never broke, and Callum's hand never pulled away.

"Fuck, Cal." He barely had enough air in his lungs to pant the words against Callum's lips. By that point, his arms had found a place to rest on Callum's shoulders while his hands were finding comfort in running through Callum's short, spiked ginger locks.

Callum used that moment to break away and leave a trail of kisses down his neck. The mix of tender warm pecks, with various nips, and the scratch of Callum's scruff, was a recipe for a sensation overload.

"Want to mark every inch of your body." The confession sent a quiver through Riley's body.

"Don't make promises you can't keep." Callum's large hands gripped his ass and squeezed. Riley felt himself being lifted off of Callum's lap. What he hadn't expected was for the Greek god to carry him towards the king-size bed.

"I never break my promises," Callum's deep, husky voice whispered in his ear, and Riley knew that whatever happened next, he was a thousand per cent ready for it.

Chapter 5

Riley's sitting on the bed; has been for the last fifteen minutes, staring at his sister's contact on his phone. He hasn't spoken to her since the argument, which for them, is the longest they've ever not spoken.

When they were younger, hitting those early teenage years where hormones had them talking constantly and bickering about first-world problems, Malcolm had reached his limit. He convinced them that if they could go twenty-four hours without saying a single word, he'd take them to the cinema and let them watch an R-rated movie, one with as much action and swearing and gut-exploding graphics as possible.

They made the deal. It was easy. They could still write to one another, pass messages, and play games. They simply couldn't speak a word, which Riley used to his advantage.

It was coming up to the twentieth hour, and he and Noelle were sitting on the couch together; she was reading while he played his Gameboy Advance and without any hesitation, he sat up, aimed his ass at his sister and let rip the biggest fart he'd ever done.

Hell broke loose.

Voices were raised and they both blamed each other for losing the bet.

He couldn't remember the last time he reminisced over that memory, yet here he was, chuckling as he recalled how annoyed his dad was. To this day, Riley still thinks his dad agreed to take them to see the movie only to stop the arguing.

Deciding to rip off the band-aid, Riley hits the call button and places the phone next to his ear. The second the line connects, he's speaking before his sister can even say hello.

"I'm not sorry about what I said, but I am sorry for how I reacted," he begins, taking in a deep breath and exhaling before he continues. "You're my sister, Noelle. My twin, which means you're like the other half of me. But holy fuck, we have not lived the same life. At least not in the last year, so please, *please*, back the fuck up and let me process everything on my terms, alright?"

Silence, but he can hear the faint sounds of Noelle breathing in and out while she no doubt marinates over his words.

"The last time I left you to process, I—"

"I know." It's so soft that he clears his throat and repeats himself. "I know, okay? Look, I'm doing the therapy thing or whatever Dr Bech calls it."

"*Which* you're only doing for me." Noelle throws his words back at him.

"It's not for everyone, Noelle. This isn't something I would have chosen to do but you kinda left me no choice."

"*I* left you no choice?"

He rubs the palm of his hand into his eye, realising his mistake. "Stop! I'm not doing this. We're just gonna go around in circles." He takes a deep breath in and slowly lets it go, remembering a few of the techniques Dr Bech had mentioned during their session about panic attacks, not that he felt like he was having one, but he figured it was sure to help him from biting his sister's head off.

"I'm going to the sessions, alright? I'm answering her stupid questions, can't that be enough?"

"You know for it to work you have to dig deep, Ry. You got to tell her what happened."

He scoffs. "Thought you did that for me." His leg begins to bounce on the spot. He gnaws at his lip till he tastes a hint of copper on his tongue. "I, ah, I got to go. I have a session in twenty minutes, so…" He isn't lying.

"If you ever want to talk, ya know, outside of the sessions, I'm here for you."

"Yeah…yeah, I know. And, ah, say…say hi to Joel for me." He hangs up the phone before his sister can hear him sniff back the tears. A photo of himself sitting against Callum's chest as his boyfriend plants a kiss against his head stares back at him, a candid photo his sister took at the beginning of spring.

"You know, for someone reluctant to give me a somewhat decent answer to my questions, you seem to want to arrive on time for every session," Dr Bech points out.

"If you're going to take my money I might as well make you work for it." He throws in a cocky smirk.

"I thought we agreed that we're 'doing this', as you so kindly phrased it in our last session."

"You wanted to open Pandora's box." He phrases it to make it seem like whatever comes next is her fault.

"I've opened many in my time as a psychologist."

He sighs. "Here's the thing, like I told Noelle early today—"

"You spoke with your sister?"

"Course. We fight but I'm not gonna hold a grudge." He gives her a look as if to say, "duh".

"Anyway, this whole talking thing isn't for me. No one has a perfect life, not even the rich and famous who post lies online to sell a fake dream. But we all find our own way to deal with it." He leans forward, resting his elbows on his knees. "Ignore it. Write it in a journal. Fuck it away. Drink it away. Snort it away. Fucking pill pop or inject it if ya have to. Point is, the answer ain't always to talk."

"Riley, you're talking about substance abuse to deal with an issue that someone like myself can help with."

"Not all issues are so big that they need to be talked about; some people simply can't handle when shit doesn't go their way."

"So, your answer is to self-destruct…like your father did."

"Don't." His eyes look up at her with a warning.

"Isn't that what happened? Your father became an addict."

"I'm *nothing* like my father. I'd never do what he did."

Dr Bech gives him a challenging look. "What did he do, Riley?"

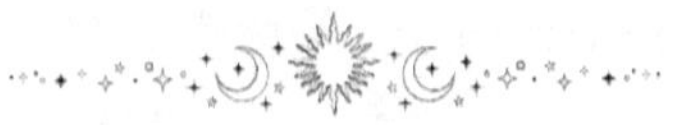

Eight Months Ago

"Noelle is riding my ass to meet you…officially." Riley was looking up at the wooden beams, his head resting on Callum's chest, using him as a pillow. A muscular arm draped over his shoulder, locking him in place while fingers he could recognise in the dark traced patterns on his chest.

"I thought I was the only one riding your ass." Callum nibbled at his earlobe and a wave of heat shot through his body.

The blankets on Callum's bed were lazily tossed over their bodies and the string of Christmas lights—that now suited the month of the year—were turned on, glowing above them. Riley's hand was caressing the arm Callum had resting on his chest, both of them basking in the afterglow of their late-night activities.

"Think that's why she wants to meet you." Riley thought back to the morning he arrived home after his first night with Callum. Noelle looked at him as though he had committed the walk of shame when in fact, he had experienced a night so amazing he needed an ice bath for the pounding his ass took.

Fair to say, Noelle was adamant that she got to have a proper introduction because according to her, the hospital didn't count.

"You tell me when and I'll be there." He turned towards Callum, whose sleepy, content green eyes were cast down at him.

"You sure? I told you; I'd be throwing you to the wolves when it came to my sister."

"I'm sure she's more bark than bite."

Riley scoffed. "Your funeral." He used that moment to roll over, so he lay naked on top of Callum. "We going to keep talking about my sister, or are we going to go for round two?"

He couldn't help but chuckle as Callum rolled them over so he was no longer on top.

Callum smirked as he cocked his well-groomed eyebrow.

"I was ready ten minutes ago, was waiting to make sure you could handle it."

"Oh, look who actually slept in his bed last night." Riley gave his sister the finger, though the smile that he was unable to hide ruined the vibe he was going for.

"Calm down, only been out a couple of nights," he grumbled back.

"It's also only been a couple of weeks since you did the horizontal tango. Looks like someone's making up for lost time when he was trying to be a monk."

"Jesus, you going to act like this when we all have dinner this weekend?"

"Wait. He said yes?"

"Course he said yes. He's technically already met you so why would he say no?"

"Because now I get to interrogate him over the dinner table." Noelle's voice sounded innocent but her expression made her look like a mastermind plotting revenge.

"Do you want me to spend my life alone?" He gave her a deadpan look.

"If my questions are enough to scare him away then he isn't good for you, little brother."

"Twenty minutes, that's how much longer you've been on this earth than me." He spoke like he was cursing the sky.

"And yet I'm much wiser." Noelle flicked her hair over her shoulder.

Riley adjusted his overalls, the extra layer that he wore underneath to keep warm during winter was never comfortable, but a necessity when working in the garage. He was about to shoot off a flirty good-morning text to Callum when the front door banged open, slamming against the wall, as his father stumbled over the threshold.

"Jesus Christ. You serious?" he yelled at his father. "The hell you doing out this early in the morning?" It was rare to see Malcolm awake, let alone leaving the house, which Riley knew his father only did when he needed another hit.

"Dn't worry. Be out ya way in a min-ut." Malcolm's words were slurred.

"Are you drunk?" A belch and stumble as Malcolm fell against the wall answered Riley's question.

"It's about to snow and you're walking around in a thin sweater and sweatpants." Noelle helped their father onto the couch where a winter blanket lived for all the times Malcolm had fallen asleep there.

"'m fine." Malcolm pushed Noelle away as he sunk into the couch. A hiccup escaped their father's lips. "Got no monies left."

"Wait, it's gone?" Riley walked around so he too was facing their father. The irony wasn't lost on him that he and Noelle looked like two parents scolding their child. "Mum's money. You've pissed it all away?" To be fair, Riley was surprised it lasted this long, but he couldn't believe every cent had been used on drugs.

"Why ya think 'm drunk." Malcolm hiccupped again and that was all Riley could handle.

"Fuck it. I'm going to work. Noelle?" He looked back at his sister as he grabbed his to-go mug of coffee. She stood over their father, her face looked as innocent as a child's.

"For the first time in my life, I'm glad Mum's dead. At least now she can't see you like this." His sister's words cut through him deeply. Riley only hoped it had the same effect on their father.

"I'm so borrrrrrred." Clint spun around on the office chair behind the front desk.

"You could pick up that book and, I don't know, read it. Try and learn a thing or two about car engines," Riley called out from the undercarriage of a 1969 Dodge Charger.

"Can't you just show me?"

"No, because whenever I show you, ya space out and forget everything I said."

"That's cos the words you use make no sense."

"Clint, you're not making things any better for yourself."

"How 'bout I help you and learn by doing?"

"Over my dead body." Riley could hear Charlie chuckling as their boss stepped into the garage space.

"Clinton, Riley doesn't let anyone near that car." Charlie kicked at his foot, which was the cue for 'get up'

"Why? It's only a car," Clint commented.

By this point, Riley was standing, wiping the grease from his hands. "*Only* a car? Only a—" He was close to throwing his hands in the air in defeat.

"See, this is why you're not going anywhere near her."

"Son, we all have to start somewhere," Charlie reminded him.

"Not here he won't. I've spent over a thousand hours on her. I've just added the high-flow stainless-steel exhaust system, and sourcing the gauges and controls to keep the authenticity has been a bitch. No way am I letting butterfingers around anything that involves this car."

He turned his attention from Charlie to Clint.

"This car is one of the first great American muscle cars. Its performance and speed are unrivalled." He felt a hand on his shoulder.

"I think what Riley is trying to say is that this is his passion project, kid, so perhaps you need to go find your own and let him finish the Dodge himself."

Clint rolled his eyes and took the book off the desk before walking out back.

"He ain't going to read a damn word in that book." Riley pointed at Clint, though his words were directed at Charlie.

"Probably not." Charlie chuckled as he turned to look over the Dodge himself.

"For a car that was a heap of junk, she sure looks like she's ready to hit the road."

Riley's thumb scratched at his nose. "Not far off. Still, a bit of work to do cosmetically, but engine-wise, she's almost there."

Charlie turned his attention toward Riley and he knew instantly from the look on his boss's face that the topic was about to turn serious.

"How's your dad?" Charlie crossed his arms, but it wasn't menacing. He looked relaxed as he leaned against the car, which Riley allowed.

"Things are about to get worse before they get better." He knew he needed to elaborate. "He's outta money, so my guess is the withdrawal is going to put him back in the hospital or kill him."

"Hmm. Rehab?"

"There's a free one in Baltimore. The program goes for a year, but after I suggested it, the asshole barricaded himself in his bedroom for three days. Besides, they won't take him if he ain't willing."

He watched as Charlie nodded his head, a sign he was processing Riley's words.

"Unfortunately, son, you can't force someone into fixing their life. They are the only ones who can decide that they're ready to heal."

"So what? Noelle and I sit back and watch him kill himself?"

"Isn't that what you've been doing for the last eleven years?"

It felt like a low blow, but Charlie wasn't wrong. He and Noelle could have stopped the pills long ago. Could have found help for their father. But perhaps Riley's grief and anger had fueled his decision to allow Malcolm to self-destruct. Maybe a part of him had hoped that one of those pills would take his father's life.

The bell above the garage door chimed but Riley left it to Clint to deal with, his mind focused on the discussion with Charlie.

"Grieving is the price we pay for love, son. Your father, he isn't perfect, but he's human."

"While he's been grieving, he's lost out on eleven years of our lives. Eleven years of seeing how we became adults."

"The day your mother passed, God rest her soul, was the day you became an adult, son. You stepped up. You made sure you and your sister completed your schooling, and the second you could work, you came here." Charlie placed a hand on his shoulder and gave it a reassuring squeeze.

"You're doing good. Just be sure that no matter what happens, you continue to live your life. Don't let it waste away like Malcolm has."

"My annual Christmas party is this weekend, you comin'?" Jackson asked through the speaker as Riley drove home.

"Sorry, man, got plans."

"Let me guess, does it involve a spicy ginger with washboard abs?"

Riley had a flashback to when he cleaned Callum's abs with his tongue. Lapping up every last drop of cum. He shook the visual from his head but swore he could taste Callum in his mouth.

"Yes and no," he chuckled. "We got dinner with Noelle."

"Oh shit. So, it *is* serious," Jackson said with a smug tone to his voice.

"I don't know if I'd call almost three months serious."

"See, the fact that you said 'almost' proves how serious it is. Your sappy ass is counting the days."

"Fuck off. All I have to do is count from your fuckin' barbecue."

"Aww, I'm touched that my presence will always be a memory of your first date." The sass in his best friend's voice had him chuckling.

"Whatever, Butthead. Don't be jealous that all my spare time no longer goes to hanging out with you."

"You barely had spare time as it was. Besides, how do you know I'm not dicked down and taken?"

Riley almost laughed until the tone in Jackson's voice made him reconsider.

"Wait, for real? You're dating someone?"

"Oh, hell no. Though I *am* getting dicked down."

"Jesus." Riley huffed.

"Don't be a hater, man. You had your chance. Anyway, make sure Noelle doesn't castrate ya man. That would be a shame for everyone." Riley hung up once he heard Jackson make noises he didn't need to have in his head.

The plan was to meet at Cristina Ristorante Italiano, a restaurant not too far from home. Noelle said she'd meet him and Callum there, as she was planning to leave straight from work. That gave Riley a little over an hour to shower and change before Callum would arrive to pick him up.

The fear he once had of his boyfriend visiting the house only to bear witness to a drug-induced Malcolm no longer bothered him. Mostly because nothing could be worse than Callum showing up after that 911 call.

It was a relief to walk into the house and not find his father comatose on the couch. What had surprised Riley, however, were the noises coming from his sister's bedroom, since Noelle wasn't home.

He crept closer; the sound reminded Riley of the times Noelle had thrown a tantrum and scattered everything she had on display onto the floor. As he pushed the door open, the sight of his father rummaging through Noelle's belongings, his hand holding the few pieces of her jewellery, was enough for Riley to accept that the man before him was no longer his father. He was a mere shell of the man he once knew.

"The fuck you think you're doing?" Riley called out, pleased to see his words had caught Malcolm off guard.

"Riley. I—ah, I was thinking of—"

"Of pawning off your daughter's jewellery so you can get a fuckin' fix?" He stepped into the room and grabbed the few pieces from his father's trembling hands. Most of Noelle's jewellery were items that once belonged to their mother; earrings, a necklace, her wedding ring, which Noelle wore daily on her right hand. A few were gifts he had given Noelle over the years, but nothing overly expensive.

Malcolm wiped his hands down his thighs, a streak of sweat changed the colour of his old, faded denim jeans. It was evident that the withdrawal symptoms Riley had read up on had already set in.

"Have you looked at yourself in the mirror lately?" he spat at his father. "You're falling apart."

"I just need a small hit. That's it. Then—then I'll be fine." Malcolm was begging.

"What you need is rehab. What you need is to detox this shit out of your system."

"No. No." Malcolm was shaking his head frantically. "No. I'm not letting you lock me up so they can dry me out."

"As opposed to you locking yourself away so you can shoot up with God knows what."

Hands grabbed at his shirt. For a man who looked as though he was crumbling, Malcolm still had enough strength to knock the wind out of Riley as his back connected with the wall.

"You have no fucking clue what I'm feeling. What I'm going through." Malcolm spat the words in his face. His stale breath and yellowed teeth were enough to give Riley nightmares.

"It's been eleven years. You want to keep using Mum's death as an excuse, be my fuckin' guest. But we all know your pain is a phantom ghost."

Dark eyes bore into his soul. "I hope you never have to know what it's like to lose someone you love. You wouldn't have the strength to survive."

Riley pushed back; his father's grip was now loose enough to let go, or perhaps weak.

"This isn't surviving. This is hiding. This is you living in a world that doesn't exist." His tongue swiped at his bottom lip. "Is that why you do it? Do you go into a fantasy world where she's still alive? Where you have two perfect children and we're as close as the fucking Brady Bunch?" He didn't give his father time to answer.

"See this?" He held up a necklace that had two hearts intertwined. "You gave this to Mum the day Noelle and I were born." He reached for another item. "This bracelet, Mum told me it belonged to her mother and was the 'something old' on your wedding day. You want to hold onto her, and yet you're doing everything in your power to erase whatever we have left of her."

Riley stormed out of his sister's room, surprised yet thankful that his father followed.

"Here, pawn the TV. That'll get you a couple of hundred." He began to unplug the cords.

"Riley," Malcolm whined.

"Ya know what, how 'bout some kitchen appliances, that shit is easy to move, right?" He stopped with the cords and made his way over towards the kitchen, going for the kettle, then the microwave, unplugging and moving them both onto the dining table.

"Not like *you're* using it. Doesn't matter that Noelle and I need it or helped fucking pay for it."

"Enough." Malcolm's voice broke.

"Hell, how 'bout I give you my debit card." He reached out for his wallet, removed the plastic card and threw it at his father's feet. "I'm sure the second I used the shower or fell asleep you would have stolen it anyway. Pin code's my birthday unless you've forgotten when that is."

"I said enough!"

The air was thick. Emotions were high. Riley had his hands balled into fists by his side.

Malcolm's nose was running and his eyes were watery, though Riley knew it had nothing to do with him being saddened by the exchange.

"Everything okay in here?" Callum's voice cut through the tension. "Sorry, I know I'm early but the door was unlocked and then I heard…"

Riley exhaled. His face softened.

"Who the hell are you?" Malcolm spoke first.

Riley turned his attention back towards his father. He stood tall, proud.

"This is Callum. My boyfriend." It was the first time Riley had used that term. It felt right, and the glint he caught in Callum's sparkling green eyes was enough for Riley to know that he agreed.

He watched as the man who had been nothing but kind and supportive since day one held a hand out for his father to shake. To no one's surprise, Malcolm didn't reciprocate. The man stared Callum down until the redhead pulled his hand back and accepted the insult.

"Thought I told you that I don't want any of this shit in my house." Malcolm was looking directly at Riley.

"This shit? That's what you're calling my sexuality now?"

"For God's sake, Riley." Malcolm placed a hand on his hip. To anyone else, it would seem like a power pose, a way to show authority. But Riley knew that it was more likely a way for Malcolm to mask the cramping in his stomach, another side effect.

"I get it. You're gay. But I don't need to see any of that homosexual behaviour in my own house."

"Good thing you didn't walk into my room two nights ago when I was shoving a thick seven-inch dildo up my ass." The way his father's face turned a shade of green was more satisfying than any argument they had exchanged in the past.

He reached down, took his debit card from the floor, placed it in Callum's hands and then took a step toward his father.

"This house might have your name on it, but you'd be on the street if it weren't for Noelle and me." He didn't blink. He didn't cower. "We're going out to dinner with Noelle. But neither of us is coming home tonight. So, while we're gone, if you want to steal from your two children, the only family you have left, this is your chance."

Riley reached out for Callum's hand and pulled him towards his bedroom. The shower was going to have to wait. All he wanted to do now was change, pack a bag, and get the fuck out of there.

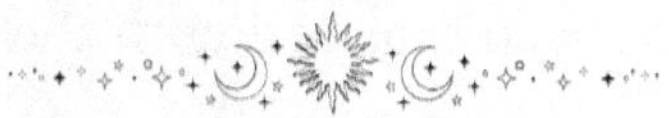

"You okay?" Callum asked once they had turned off his street.

"How much did you hear?"

"Enough."

He gnawed at his bottom lip.

"I didn't mean to—" Riley cut Callum off.

"It's fine. Not like you were ever gonna have a sit-down meal with the guy." A small part of Riley's heart twinged at the thought.

Callum reached over and took his hand, their fingers intertwining. Riley's body calmed instantly from the contact.

"If you ever need to get away…" Callum began. "If things become too much, too dangerous, you can come to my place. Stay as long as you need."

"You asking me to move in, Cal?" he joked. He tried to ease the tension after the seriousness of the conversation, on top of the argument with his father, which had left him feeling drained. "Three months, man. That's a little soon," Riley added.

"I'm not saying today. But I'm not saying that the thought hadn't crossed my mind, either."

Riley would be lying if he denied having the same thought.

"If we move too fast, we'll break. But if we move too slow, we'll miss things," Callum began to explain. "Relationships are built at the speed of trust, so I guess what I'm saying is—"

"I trust you too." Riley interrupted.

They drove the next few minutes in silence, their hands not once letting go. It was at that moment that Riley realised how easily the word trust could have been replaced with the word love.

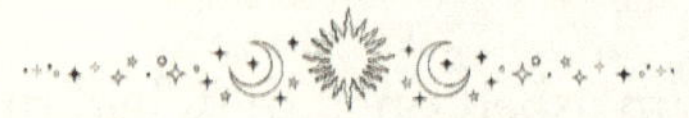

"They had to cut off all my hair. Everything! I was seven years old with this pixie haircut and all the kids at school thought I was a boy!" Noelle exclaimed.

Riley watched as Callum laughed along to the story.

"You asked me to play hairdresser with you, how the fuck was I to know those ball thingies wouldn't come out?" Riley tried to defend himself.

"They were called Bunchems and I wasn't expecting you to put all one hundred and fifty of those spikey ball *thingies* in my hair."

"Oh, I remember those," Callum added.

"Yes!" Noelle got excited that Callum understood what she was talking about. "The more Riley tried to remove them, the worse they got. My hair was a tangled mess." Noelle used her hands to emphasise how her hair looked at the time of the incident.

"Well, instead of playing hairdresser, you got to go to one. See, win-win." Noelle wasn't pissed with him, at least not anymore. But the playful banter was comforting, and a chance for Callum to see how he and his sister behaved around one another.

"At least you had your brother to blame. My parents had to give me a buzzcut when I was sixteen. I was doing a school project at home, an experiment with a slime volcano. The thing erupted and long story short, the ingredients I used to make the slime caused it to dry like glue, so a buzzcut was my only option."

"Hmm, buzzcut, I could work with that." Riley felt flirty, though it could have been from the drinks he had consumed and the way Callum's hand hadn't left his thigh all night.

His boyfriend leaned towards him, initiating a kiss Riley gladly returned.

The questions hadn't been too intrusive, and the ones that were, Callum handled calmly and in a way that had seemed to satisfy Noelle's nosy personality. The few questions that Riley knew his sister asked to put Callum under pressure, were ones that he had already heard the answer to.

So many evenings, they had stayed up talking well into the early morning, and some Sundays, they spent the whole day in bed, talking in between rounds of sex. Those were the times when they'd asked each other those deep questions. The ones where they shared what they wanted out of life, out of their future. Career, marriage, children. They spoke about previous relationships and their fears from the past and the present.

When the cheque was placed on their table, Callum was the first to snatch it away before either he or Noelle could reach for it.

"No way you're paying for this," Riley argued. "We'll each pay our own."

Callum held it high, so it was out of reach for Riley. "Pretty sure the etiquette for meeting my boyfriend's sister is for me to pay for her meal, and of course, I was going to pay for yours, so…" Callum leaned down, pecking his lips before he left the table to pay.

Riley could feel the blush creep up his cheeks. Maybe it was from the alcohol, or perhaps it was from that warm feeling he got whenever Callum was nearby.

"Being in love looks good on you," his sister commented, a happy smile of contentment spread across her face.

"Bit soon to be throwing that word around."

"Never too soon, Ry. When you know, you know. Don't hold it back because you're scared of what it means."

Was he scared?

He leant forward. "I swear I'm going crazy, " he whispered across the table. "He's under my skin, Noelle. Like a tattoo that no one can see, but I can feel it. Spreading. Overtaking every part of my body and I don't want to fight it. I want to let go and give myself over to the feeling…to him."

"So let go." Riley was shocked by his sister's response. "What's the worst that could happen?"

He could think of a few things.

"Ry…baby brother. We only get one life and it's not always as long as we think it will be." Their mother instantly came to mind. "I've spent all night trying to find the skeletons in that man's closet, trying to trip Callum up, but honestly, all I saw was how doe-eyed in love he is with you."

Riley wanted to argue, but Callum returned to the table and Noelle was quick to draw him into conversation so Riley could have a moment to collect his thoughts.

"Where are we going exactly?" Callum asked Riley as they walked hand in hand, thick coats protecting them from the winter chill.

"What's the time?" He avoided the question.

"Almost half past seven."

"Shit." He pulled Callum behind him, his legs taking two steps to Callum's one, the need to get to their destination before seven-thirty was critical.

Once inside, they could finally stop to catch their breath. The cold air filled Riley's lungs, which made him cough once or twice, his body now somewhat overheated in his coat.

"Okay," Callum panted. "Now are you going to tell me why we're at Gaylord National Convention Centre?"

But Riley didn't have to explain, because the second the clock struck seven-thirty, the building lit up with festive cheer.

The large glass panel windows had an electronic Christmas tree hanging from the ceiling. Music began to fill the room as twinkling lights lit the tree and the surrounding area. Carols started playing, the ones that every single person in the room knew the words to. Strobe lights flashed to the beat of the music while a projection was displayed on the windows.

A voice spoke through the speakers once the intro music had faded.

"The spirit of the Christmas season is illuminated year after year by the glow of a candle, the twinkle of a tree, the sparkle of an icicle and most importantly, the light that shines within us all."

The show was spectacular. It was a ten-minute feature that played three times a night, but for Riley, his eyes stayed on the greatest part, the magical sparkle in Callum's eyes. There was a lull between the voice and the next song, which Riley used as his chance.

"You said Christmas was your favourite time of year, so here you go. A magical Christmas wonderland."

The music continued before Callum could respond, but it didn't matter. They stood in the middle of the crowd as the show of lights reflected off their bodies.

Once it ended, the convention centre broke out in applause; the fountain in the middle of the building settled, and the crowd slowly dispersed toward the other seasonal activities.

"That was…" Callum turned toward him. "I can't believe you put this much thought…you're amazing."

Riley loved how he had to tilt his head slightly back so he could look directly into Callum's eyes. He loved how, if he didn't want Callum to bend forward, he needed to stand on his tippy toes to kiss those soft pink lips. And he especially loved how much the twenty-five-year-old would enjoy the Christmas spirit all year round if it were possible.

"In case you're wondering, I didn't drive you thirty minutes *just* for a light show." By that stage, Callum's hands were wrapped securely around his waist. "Your next choice of events are…"

"Oh, I have choices?" He didn't miss Callum's playful tone.

"The sculptures that tell the beloved story of Rudolph the Red-nosed Reindeer, tubing down an ice slope, ice skating, or we can decorate a gingerbread house."

Callum's laugh had to be the best sound he had ever heard. He vowed to spend every day making Callum laugh to the point that his smile reached his eyes. And that's when it dawned on him that he wanted to spend every day with the man standing before him.

"I'm thinking Rudolph and then some gingerbread houses." Callum leaned down so his lips were pressed against Riley's ear. "I don't want anything to bruise that gorgeous ass tonight before I get a chance to leave my mark." Riley couldn't help but moan as teeth grazed his earlobe, a sudden burst of confidence told him now was his chance.

"In that case, best I give you your Christmas gift now then." He had never done this. He had never wanted to do this. And to be fair, he felt a little shitty not putting any money toward his gift, but he hoped the thought behind it outweighed that fact.

He handed over a folded-up piece of paper, and with trepidation, he waited for Callum to read the document.

"Riley…is this what I think it is?" Callum had yet to make eye contact with him.

"Merry Christmas. Clean bill of health and I'm, ah, I'm now taking PrEP." Riley hoped he could blame his red cheeks on the cold air, but being that they were standing inside, he figured it wouldn't be believable.

"This is…"

"Shit." He began to panic. "It's too forward, isn't it?"

"Riley," Callum spoke.

"Fuck, forget what I said." He went to snatch the paper away but Callum pulled it back. "Look, it doesn't mean we have to…I thought if you were wanting to…I figured we should know, ya know."

"Riley."

This was all new to Riley. Safety first, always. But in the few short relationships he'd had, none had Riley wanting to offer every part of himself to his partner. Until now. That in itself was proof that time didn't measure how strong a relationship was. Three months with Callum had already felt longer than the nine months he had with an ex. The connection was deeper, the trust was mutual, and the sex was mind-blowing.

"Riley!"

He snapped out of his thoughts once Callum spoke with authority. *It was kind of sexy.*

"My only issue with this gift is that I didn't have the time to get the same thing for you."

Oh…*Oh.* A lightbulb went off and a warmth spread deep within Riley's body at the magnitude of that statement.

"But, ah, yeah, I'd really, *really* like to do that." Riley was pleased to see a blush appear on Callum's cheeks. It was only fair they matched. "I've never, either…but I want to with you."

The gingerbread had more cinnamon than ginger to the taste, but it had a crunch that made the biscuit moreish. Riley was sad to see they had almost finished the contents of their house, the chocolate and candies the first to be eaten.

"So, I have an idea for your Christmas gift." Callum scuffed his feet as they continued to walk side by side.

"I thought we agreed earlier on what that would be." He bumped into Callum's side playfully.

"Besides that." The smirk Callum offered should have been illegal. He was wearing a black beanie, which contrasted perfectly with his ginger scruff. Riley had given it a tick of approval based on how intoxicating the sensation was against his skin. The complete look had made it hard for Riley to concentrate throughout the night.

"Why do I get the sense that I should be worried?" He spoke through a mouth full of cookies.

"Depends…you once told me that you wanted to learn how to step out of your comfort zone." By this stage, they had stopped walking. "Is that still the case?"

He mulled the question over. He thought back to when his mother passed away, a moment in time that had set him in his ways, a sudden desire to play by the rules. If he followed a routine that kept him safe, then perhaps he also wouldn't be taken from this world too soon, and he wouldn't end up leaving Noelle with no one, since their father was unreliable.

But that night at the garage, he meant it. It wasn't that his life had begun to feel mundane, but he knew there was excitement waiting for him beyond what he knew. An adventure. A romance. Love. Whatever his subconscious was seeking, it wasn't going to be found playing it safe, staying in his comfort zone, and Callum was already proof of that.

"Yeah," he admitted. "That's still the case."

"Good…okay." His hand slipped into Callum's; their pulses lined up as their wrists rested against one another. "I'll set it up."

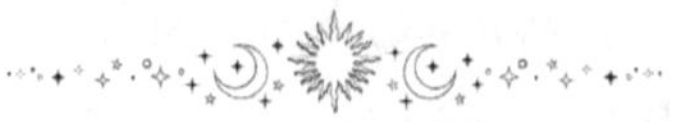

"I can't believe this is how I'm spending Christmas Eve." Riley shook his head in disbelief.

"It's not too late to back out," Callum offered with a sly smirk, as though he was daring Riley to bail.

"Not happening, I'm doing this. The question is, why the hell are you doing it?"

Callum shrugged. "I've always wanted to but never knew what to get." He turned so he was walking backwards. "You said it yourself, you wanted to step out of your comfort zone more, so let's do something crazy. Let's make bad life decisions together."

How could he say no to that? Especially with the soft smile and puppy dog eyes Callum had thrown his way. Riley reached for the door to the little shop and stepped inside. Antiseptic filled his nostrils, the smell giving him a sense of déjà vu from when he had to go to the hospital. He supposed that was a good sign, at least.

"Hi, appointment under Reed," Callum spoke to the young woman behind the counter. She looked down, then made eye contact with them both.

"Which one is first?" Her gum popped, a hint of grape hitting his senses.

"I guess I will." Riley put his hand up like he was back in school. "It's *my* gift after all." He wasn't sure if he volunteered to go first because it was Callum's gift to him, or because he didn't want to sit around and convince himself this was a bad idea.

Riley sat in the chair, with Callum oblivious to what he had in mind. When he told the tattoo artist his idea, the location was the only factor he hadn't taken into account. The tattooist suggested a few areas and Riley picked one, but everything else was a secret and he couldn't wait to share it.

An hour later he walked out, jacket back on, not giving any indication of what had happened behind the curtain. Riley swapped seats with Callum and watched as the light of his life whispered into the ear of the tattoo artist, shifty green eyes looking back at him once or twice before the artist gave a nod and indicated Callum could sit.

Christmas lost its appeal after Malcolm got lost in his pills. Riley and Noelle decided Chinese food and horror movies were the way to go, camped out in the living room while their father was locked away in his bedroom.

This year, however, it felt different. A shift in the tide, a sign of new things ahead, which gave Riley hope. Although he was once again planning to eat his weight in sweet and sour pork with a side of Singapore noodles, Callum's enthusiasm for Christmas was enough for them to both feel the magic around this time of year.

Riley fidgeted with the cuff of his jacket, knowing in his heart that this time next year, he and Callum would be spending Christmas together.

He was surprised with how quickly time passed when Callum walked out from behind the curtain.

"Finished already?"

"Yep. I'll pay and we'll go." A small part of Riley was suspicious and wondered if Callum had decided to back out at the last minute.

He shook the thought away and stood, ready to head back home. *Home.*

Since when did he consider Callum's apartment his?

The bell above the door brought him out of his head as a chivalrous Callum held it open for him while readying himself to head back out into the cold winter night.

"So how are we doing this?" Riley asked once they were in the warmth of Callum's apartment.

"How 'bout we turn around and on the count of three, reveal what we got?"

God, it was like he had teleported back to elementary school.

"Jesus, fine." The grin on his face, however, gave his excitement away. With their backs turned Riley began to remove his jacket and roll the sleeve up his left arm, his wrist still wrapped.

"Alright, you ready?" Callum checked.

"Yeah, start counting." Riley felt nervous.

"One," Callum started.

"Two," Riley breathed

"Three." They spoke simultaneously, both of them spinning to reveal their chosen art.

Riley blinked once, twice, and on the third, he closed his mouth, which gaped like a fish's.

"Holy shit." They spoke simultaneously.

"Did the guy tell you what I got?" Riley asked.

"No! I swear! All I did was ask the location you picked..."

"How did we—" Riley began.

"I had no idea—" Callum offered.

Was this a sign? Is this what couples did when they were connected? Make decisions that subconsciously the other was already deciding to do also? Is this what it was like for his parents?

"I wanted a sun. A reminder of the light and warmth that you've given me every day," Riley finally let out. Their wrists were aligned, though he was still in shock over Callum's tattoo.

"That day on the hayride," Callum began. "I may have said it as a passing joke, but that night, I went home and thought about it. Thought about how you really were like the moon. You've shown me time and time again how you can shine through darkness, even if you're not always whole."

Callum moved his body so they were standing side by side, only to then intertwine their hands, their fingers linked so their sun and moon tattoos touched behind the thin layer of film.

"You know," Callum's voice was soft, "I once read that the sun loved the moon so much, that he died every night to let him breathe."

Instantly, Riley looked up from where their tattoos were linked and made contact with tender green eyes.

"I love you, Riley," Callum confessed. "I do. And, God, I've never—I've never felt this before, with anyone."

Riley looked back down at their hands; the words absorbing into his body.

"You came into my life like some angel of release." He found the courage to look Callum in the eyes, his own damp with unshed tears. "It scared the shit out of me." He sniffed. "But you were my sun and I was the fuckin' sunflower that blossomed and grew the second you were in my orbit."

A hand reached out and cupped the side of his face while a smooth padded thumb brushed away the tear that rolled down his cheek.

"So, in case you couldn't tell, I fuckin' love you too." He was pulled into Callum's space, once again thriving from being close to the man he loved.

He wasn't ashamed of the few extra tears that fell the second their lips touched. The salty liquid added a unique taste to their kiss. Their tongues roamed each other's mouths, and teeth clashed, mixed with the uninhibited sounds they made as they got lost in each other.

Riley moved his hands to Callum's waist and held him closer, so they couldn't part, as his sun walked them back towards the bed.

The removal of their clothes was difficult as neither wanted to break the kiss, though somehow, they found a way, both landing naked on the bed.

Although Riley didn't have vast experiences to compare it with, the one thing he was certain of, regardless of that fact, was that sex had never felt the way it did with Callum. The man beneath him read his body like it was a map, and Callum was the key to working out all of the coordinates.

Since their first time together, their sex had been wild and fierce, hot and intense, slow and sensual, even rough and downright filthy. But that night it was different.

Callum's touch was as soft as a feather, skirting across his body so delicately that goosebumps littered his skin. His body was pulsing from each kiss, nip, touch and squeeze. When Riley eventually pulled back, the hues of red, blue, green and yellow from the Christmas lights cast a shadow over Callum's face.

They were both growing firmer, but neither made a play to reach out and give any attention to their dicks.

"You have no idea what you do to me." Callum's scruff grazed against Riley's skin, and a red tinge appeared within seconds, leaving a trail of all the places his boyfriend's mouth had been.

"Want you," Riley whined, the teasing getting to him.

"I'm all yours." Callum rolled them so he had his back against the mattress. "Always."

Chapter 6

He wakes up sweating, his breathing is laboured and from how quickly his eyes are darting around the room, he begins to feel lightheaded. Riley reaches out beside him, the bed is cold, empty, and panic once again starts to set in.

Within the darkness of his bedroom, it's impossible to escape the dream, or more accurately, nightmare. He leans over, his hand rummaging around till he finds the switch against the wall.

The twinkle of soft-coloured Christmas lights comes to life and illuminates Riley's bedroom, but it's not enough.

Dr Bech said breathing is the best way to ground himself in the present, and if that doesn't help, to make lists in his head or voice them out loud. Riley finds the best list for him is car parts, something he's comfortable and familiar with.

Tyres. Rims. Exhaust. Fan belt. Windshield. Radiator.

His voice is barely a whisper, but his lips are moving, and slowly, his heart rate begins to steady. The feeling of ants crawling under his skin vanishes and once he names at least thirty car parts, he's able to open his eyes and remind himself that he's in bed, safe.

Cautiously, his hand slides back out to the space beside him. Riley closes his eyes as the coldness seeps into his hand. The vibration of his phone has his eyes snapping open, fear threatening to come back since phone calls at three in the morning are never a good sign. But then he sees the name appear on the screen and he instantly feels better than any list can help him feel.

"Hey." The word is dragged out. "What are you doing up this time of night? I was planning on leaving a voicemail for you to listen to once you woke."

Riley couldn't help but smile at the kind gesture.

"Couldn't sleep. Didn't help that you weren't here beside me." He leans back against the headboard.

"Riley?"

How does he always know when he's lying?

He exhales. "...I had another nightmare."

"I'm sorry, baby. Want me to help?"

"Really?" Riley questions. "How?"

"Put me on speaker, you're going to need both your hands for this."

Riley does so without batting an eye, though it may have to do with how exhausted his body is feeling.

"'M Ready."

"I want you to cross your arms over your chest, baby. Wrap yourself in your own embrace, can you do that for me?" The instructions are calm and at a slow pace. It reminds him of being read a bedtime story.

"Let your fingers trail up and down your arms, lightly ghosting over your skin." Riley knows it's his own hands roaming over his body, but subconsciously, it's easy to believe otherwise.

"Now, squeeze yourself. Imagine that your arms are mine, holding you tight, keeping you in a safe, warm hug."

He breathes in, squeezes, and doesn't let go as he exhales.

"You're okay. You're safe. I've got you, Riley…I'm not letting go." Without realising it, his eyes begin to droop, the exhaustion from waking in such a panic takes over now that his body begins to relax.

"I want you to slowly move your right hand up your body, gently feel your way toward your face until your cheek is resting in the palm of your hand."

Riley does as he's told.

"Take your thumb, stroke your cheekbone for me. Feel how well your face fits into the palm of *my* hand."

A sigh of relief falls from his lips.

"Keep that one hand wrapped around you, the other on your cheek, and I want you to slowly lay down for me. I want you to snuggle into those blankets where it's warm…and safe. I want you to keep holding yourself the same way I would be holding you. Protecting you. Caring for you."

He scoots down onto the mattress, settling back under the covers, his left arm still wrapped around his waist while his right hand rests tenderly against his cheek, his arms crisscrossed over his chest.

"That's it, Riley. Feel how soft the blankets are? How warm *we* are? I'm right here, I've got all your fears, your worries. I'll hold them for a while, you just rest and I'll keep watch."

Riley sniffs back a tear.

"Sleep. Rest. Everything will be okay in the morning. I've got you."

He doesn't have any recollection of falling asleep or the phone disconnecting. But he did sleep peacefully for the remainder of the night.

For the last couple of months, Riley hasn't once woken up feeling this rejuvenated. It's refreshing, and the first person he wants to tell is Dr Bech.

This is a sign. Proof that he doesn't need therapy. That other people, other ways, are all he needs to kickstart his day.

He slept later than usual but thankfully has plenty of time to shower, eat and head over to his appointment.

"How was your night?" Dr Bech asks. A question she's asked at every appointment thus far.

"About that. I don't think I'm goin' t' need to keep coming here." His hands are rubbing up and down his thighs as his legs bounce nervously.

Why is he nervous?
Isn't this what he wants?

"Oh?" Dr Bech puts her pen down, giving him all of her attention.

"Yeah. I mean," he leans forward, resting his elbows on his knees to hopefully settle himself, "look, I get that the occasional panic attack or whatever might happen and maybe some trouble with sleeping. I mean, who doesn't? But Doc, I'm good."

"You're good?"

"Yep."

"Riley, what happened last night?"

"I had, whaddya call it, one of those breakthrough thingies which, makes no fuckin' sense cos nothing's actually wrong with me. This is all for Noelle but ya see, I did what you said and then I tried something else and whaddya know, all good." He took a deep breath after the long sentence winded him.

"And when you say you tried something else, you…?"

"I didn't snort coke if that's what you're asking." He sits back against the couch cushion. "I spoke to Callum."

"To Callum." Dr Bech looks shocked.

"Yeah. Ya know, the guy who's been in all my stories since day one."

"No, I know who Callum is, I'm just surprised."

"Why?" He couldn't help but feel defensive.

"You know what, no reason." Dr Bech writes something down. "What did he say?"

"It wasn't so much what he said. I mean, it was, but like…" He gnaws on his bottom lip. "Okay, so I woke up from this nightmare or whatever and I did the whole list thing and I don't know, I guess it helped, kinda."

"Good. That's good, Riley." He waits, curious to see if she writes more notes.

"Anyway, I was still feeling a little on edge, and then Callum called. He was going to leave me a message for the morning, but when I answered, he kinda, I don't know, calmed me down and lulled me back to sleep, I guess."

That's when Dr Bech takes notes.

"That's interesting, Riley. I mean, that's great for you that this technique was able to help you when you were feeling…unsettled."

"Yeah…right…so, we good?" Riley goes to stand.

"Well," Dr Bech's words cause him to stop, "since this session is already in motion, I'd have to charge you, so why don't we make the most of it?"

He slumps back down with an exaggerated sigh and scratches at his eyebrow.

"Why don't you tell me more about Callum?" Dr Bech prompts.

"Callum?"

"Mhm. He sounds like a very important person in your life."

Riley looks down at his left wrist, the sun still as bright and vibrant as the day he got it inked into his skin.

"He is my sun."

Seven Months Ago

Everyone was standing around, the point of the whole night finally coming to a close as voices began to countdown.

"Ten. Nine. Eight. Seven. Six. Five. Four. Three. Two. One. Happy New Year!" Riley and Callum cheered with the crowd as fireworks filled the night sky, streamers popped and whistles were blown. The embarrassing party hat was knocked off his head when someone drunkenly threw their arms in the air, but he didn't care.

Time stopped. The crowd froze. The music was merely a low hum.

In that moment, the only thing that mattered to Riley was the look of devotion and adoration in Callum's soft, dreamy eyes. The man Riley loved gave him a smile that was a mix of flirtation and affection.

There wasn't much space between them during the countdown, with more bodies crammed into Jackson's house than there was room for, so neither of them had to move for their lips to meet.

Riley's chest exploded, much like the fireworks that Billy was setting off, each bang in rhythm with his beating heart. He felt like he was floating.

"Guess our bond is unbreakable," Callum spoke against his ear, the only way he was going to hear his boyfriend over the screams.

"You had doubts?" Riley joked.

"Never. But the superstition is if a couple doesn't kiss at midnight, then their bond is not as strong and the relationship could fail in the year to come."

"We better cover all our bases then." Riley pulled Callum in, perched on his tippy toes to prevent the ginger giant from having to bend down as he devoured Callum's mouth.

He wasn't one for superstitions, but he wasn't going to say no to the opportunity to get lost in Callum. Besides, he couldn't think of a better way to start the new year.

"What are you doing this weekend?" Callum called out from the bathroom as Riley lay in the wet patch. Cum seeped out of him, an additional sensation to his already overstimulated body.

"Noelle wants me to help her get a safety deposit box." He shivered. The heat left his body. Unprotected sex was a first for them both, an experience they wanted to share only with each other, and Riley couldn't deny that he loved the feeling of being filled and claimed from the inside out.

Rather than attempting to stand and clean himself up, he decided to reach for the duvet and snuggle a little longer in their filth.

"Everything okay?" Callum leaned against the doorframe, arms crossed over his naked chest, which caused Riley's dick to stir. The hope of round two came to mind until he remembered that Callum had asked a question.

"Hmm?"

The smirk on Callum's face told Riley that he was busted.

"Oh, yeah…she wants to store some things away. Nothing has gone missing, but the paranoia is there."

"Your dad still using?" Callum began to walk towards the bed.

"Honestly, no fucking clue. Been avoiding him as much as I can, and when I'm home, he's MIA or holed up in his room." He licked his lips.

"Well, what I was going to ask is," Callum began to crawl up the bed, "if you're free…" He kissed Riley's thigh. "My parents invited you to dinner."

Riley looked down his body, his eyes landing on a hopeful-looking Callum. He'd never been asked to meet the parents before, but he'd also never wanted to.

"Sure. I think I can squeeze that into my calendar." He tried to play it off with a cocky smirk, but the excitement behind what that step meant for their relationship was too hard to hide.

"I mean, if your schedule is *that* busy, maybe we need to create some free time for you." Callum began to sit up, but Riley was quick to follow.

"If you think cutting out sex will help, you're sadly mistaken." He wrapped his legs around Callum, clawing onto him like a koala.

"Seems to me that it does take up a lot of your spare time." Callum smirked.

"I don't see you complaining. But if you think I'm giving up sex now that I finally have it back in my life, you've got another think coming."

"That so?" Riley could see Callum holding back laughter.

"You've unleashed the beast. It was lying dormant, waiting for the right dick to come along and—"

"A sex beast?" Callum began to laugh. "I thought I was the dork in this relationship?"

"Whatever. You going to fuck me or should I get the toy box?"

"Didn't realise the beast I was unleashing was so bossy…" Callum's mouth found its way back to Riley's body. "So needy…" Teeth nipped, tongue lapped, lips sucked.

Riley squeezed his legs tightly around Callum's waist, a silent approval of what was to come. He knew he'd be covered in markings by the time he was finished. Riley trembled at the thought of his body becoming a canvas for Callum's desires.

"Fuck. Shit. Cal…get in me already," Riley panted. His legs quivered when a finger massaged and teased around his rim.

"Ask nicely," Callum tantalised.

Riley knew the game Callum wanted to play. "*Please…*" he whined a little. "Need to feel you stretch me open." He bit his lip and threw the bottle of lube at Callum once he laid back onto the mattress. He gasped when two fingers breached him; the cum that hadn't yet seeped out was being finger-fucked back inside of him. The swift flicks of his prostate distracted him from Callum lining himself up.

"Think you can take it?" Callum asked, and it took a moment for Riley to understand what his boyfriend was referring to.

Callum was a decent seven to eight inches, but it was his girth that made the size queen within Riley preen. It offered a satisfying stretch to both his mouth and his hole on many occasions. Taking the extra width from Callum's fingers was going to be a challenge he desperately wanted to try.

"Fuck yes."

At a pace that was slow enough for Riley to adjust to, he breathed through the slight burn as Callum gradually pushed inside. That glorious stretch of his asshole felt incredible.

"Holy shit. Talk about feeling full." He looked down in the hopes that he could see for himself, but the angle made it impossible. Leaving him to envision what Callum must be seeing.

"Fucking sexy seeing you stretch open for me, taking my dick and fingers…" Callum sounded wrecked, looked intoxicated, and felt otherworldly.

Riley hadn't waited for Callum to move. Instead, he took control and began to slide himself up and down his boyfriend's glorious dick, basking in the long, drawn-out drag against his rim.

"That's it," Callum moaned. "*Fuck.* Nice and slow. Want you to feel yourself opening up for me."

"Touch me, Cal," Riley begged. "*Please.*"

He gasped when Callum's free hand clawed down his chest, his blunt nails leaving trails of pleasure. His thighs trembled from the various sensations, his body not knowing which one to react to. With no warning, Callum extracted his fingers, and a whine fell from Riley's lips. Muscular arms pulled at his body, forcing Riley to sit on Callum's toned thighs, their heaving chests pressed firmly together, the new position allowing him to sink further and take Callum deeper.

His arms clung to Callum as though his life depended on it. His fingers dug into pale, freckled flesh.

"I love the way your ass is made for me," Callum growled in his ear. "The way your body fits against mine." The steady pounding continued. "You have no idea what you do to me. The second I saw you," Callum panted, "I knew I wanted you." Teeth sunk into his neck, and Riley willed Callum to bite down. The constant thrusting against his prostate had Riley leaking between them.

"Cal…can't…fuck, needa come." Sweat rolled down his spine. His thighs burned from the workout he was giving them.

"Not. Yet."

He whined. His cock screamed for release.

"I know you can hold it. You're doing so good, only a little longer."

Riley buried his face into the crook of Callum's neck, taking in a lungful of his scent that had begun to mix with his own and fill the room around them. Callum increased the speed, and the abuse his hole was receiving from the jackhammered force made Riley pliant in Callum's embrace.

"Shit…*please*, Cal."

"Now."

He was sure he blacked out when Callum shot thick white loads of warm cum inside of him. He was not afraid to admit to himself that this new sensation was one he would find himself becoming addicted to.

On some level, his subconscious must have known that barebacking was an intimacy only meant to be shared with Callum. With the one person he has connected to mentally and physically, as though they were made for one another. The sun to his moon.

The universe had aligned and whenever he was in Callum's presence, he felt whole.

He panted as his vision finally returned and his heartbeat steadied. The cum painted on their stomachs had them stuck together.

"I love you," Riley whispered into the air. "So fucking much."

Tender lips placed kitten kisses on his shoulder blade.

"Love you more."

"You've been smiling like a kid at Disneyland lately. What's going on?" Charlie asked him as they sat around the table in the breakroom.

He blushed and licked his dry lips.

"Ahh, that's the look of young love." Charlie sat back, his hands behind his head as though he had solved a mystery.

"His name's Callum."

"Wait, is this the young man with the Jeep?"

He took a bite of his BLT, using his mouth full of food as an excuse to avoid the question.

"Well, well. The Reeds are nice folk; I didn't realise Callum was their son until after he picked up his Jeep."

"Hold on." He quickly swallowed. "You know the family?"

"Son, I know everyone in this town. Why you ask?"

"I'm meant to be meeting them this weekend."

"I see." Charlie leant forward, elbows on the table, hands clasped together. "You nervous?"

"That's an understatement."

"Never known you to meet anyone's parents before. This Callum must be something special."

"He is." It seemed his answer wasn't enough for dear old nosy Charlie. "Mum used to tell me stories about how she knew Malcolm was the one. How everything around her would seep into the background, and all that was in focus was him." The sleeve of his shirt hitched up, revealing a portion of the sun's rays. "Never understood what she meant until Callum came along."

"Does he make you happy, son?"

He broke out in a smile. Charlie chuckled, satisfied with that as an answer.

"I sometimes worry it's too good to be true. Ya know?" Riley continued. "Took twenty-five years and now it seems way too easy. Like it shouldn't be this perfect."

"Why not?"

"Huh?" He wasn't sure what Charlie meant with his reply.

"Why can't it be easy?"

"Because since when does easy end well?"

"Kid, just because you and Callum didn't have to fight for your relationship, don't mean it's doomed. You tellin' me if the world was against you and not a single person supported your relationship it would be easier? Stronger?"

"No. Course not." There was a but at the tip of his tongue.

"Spit it out, son. I'm not getting any younger."

"*But* maybe then it would feel like we earnt it. That we deserved to be as happy as everyone else."

"Oh, boy. I don't know what kool aid you've been drinkin' but I can promise you this, you deserve happiness and then some. You deserve to have something easy for a change, and I sure as hell don't think you need to worry about it not being real. I've known you for seven years and not once have you looked as happy as you've been in the last few months."

Riley knew that. He did. He knew the love and happiness he felt with Callum was real. But hearing someone else confirm it helped settle the small voice in the back of his mind that was adamant he'd ruin the sunshine that was Callum. Or maybe he was trying to sabotage it all before he embarrassed himself in front of Callum's parents.

"They'll love you," Charlie added. "His parents...don't overthink it. Besides, they can't be as bad as Noelle."

He laughed. The tension eased and he felt calmer.

"Thanks, Charlie."

"Anytime." Charlie slapped his hands on the table and then rose. "Now, be sure to bring that young man around for me to meet properly. Don't think you can hide him forever."

"Wasn't planning to." He reached out to grab his can of soda.

"Well, what do we have here?" Charlie pointed at his wrist where his sun tattoo had become visible.

He chuckled. "Christmas gift from Callum."

Charlie's eyebrows rose.

"Noelle's face looked exactly like yours when she saw it too. Especially when I said Callum got a moon tattoo on his right wrist."

Charlie walked away, shaking his head, a hint of a smile on his face as he left the room.

"Whaddya mean gone?" Riley was getting dressed for dinner.

"I mean three days ago, Dad walked out the front door and he hasn't been home since," Noelle explained as she leant against the doorframe.

"You sure he hasn't been coming home late and leaving again before you wake?"

"Yes, because after the first night, I made his bed and it's still untouched. And before you say it, he hadn't crashed on the couch either because the cushions and blanket were in the same place."

"OCD much?"

"Riley, this isn't funny, it's serious."

He looked himself over again, his dark denim jeans, white V-neck T-shirt and black blazer gave him the semi-casual look he was aiming for. He turned to his sister once he fluffed the front of his hair.

"Look, Noelle. He has nowhere else to go. So, unless he's sleeping on the streets in the middle of January, I'm sure he's fine and will be home soon."

He squeezed past his sister to grab his phone and keys from his bedside table.

"So that's it? You get a boyfriend and suddenly you don't care if our father is dead on the street?"

He froze. His hand clenched around his mobile.

"I-I'm sorry," Noelle mumbled. "I didn't mean—"

Riley turned to face his sister; shame was written on her face.

"Eleven years, Noelle." His voice was low, but the hurt and frustration in his words were evident. "Eleven fucking years we have been using the excuse that he's our father to let him get away with his shitty behaviour, and I'm done. So no, this isn't because of Callum. This is because Malcolm's reached the point of no return and I've reached the point of not giving a shit about what happens to him."

"What if I give a shit?" His sister's voice was on the verge of breaking.

"Then maybe you're the one who can convince him to get help. Because he sure as hell won't listen to me." He turned back around and made his way out the door. The last thing he wanted was to be late.

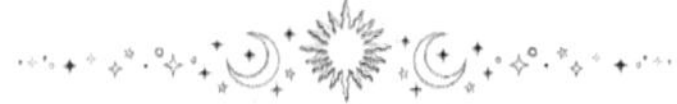

When the front door opened, Riley wasn't sure who was more relieved, himself or Callum.

"Thank God, I swear they were this close to believing that I made you up." Callum pulled him inside and planted a kiss on his lips, which Riley took willingly, not at all phased that Callum was shoving his tongue down his throat in the middle of his parent's house.

"Wow." Riley pulled away. He wiped at his lips where their sloppy eagerness had left a trace. "Had a few drinks already, have you?" Callum tasted strong enough that Riley felt like he was the one who had taken a sip of whiskey.

"Needed to take the edge off."

If Callum was this nervous, he was doomed.

"Callum, is that him?" A woman's voice sang from within the house.

"Don't hog him to yourself, son, bring him in." A male voice, just as chipper, followed.

"If you need me to fake a medical emergency, now is your chance," Riley whispered. It seemed to take the edge off, but he still saw the tension in Callum's shoulders.

"Better to get this over with," Callum admitted. "Oh, before I forget, you look incredible." He leaned in to place a kiss on the pulse point of his neck.

Callum's hand interlinked with his. Through the fabric of their clothing, the sun and moon were connected. It fed Riley strength, which he suspected did the same for Callum. He followed Callum's lead while his eyes roamed the décor of what looked to be a very modern, well-kept family home.

They left the empty sitting room where they had shared their kiss and walked through the kitchen and dining area until they were standing in the living room, the back wall covered with bookshelves from ceiling to floor.

Nothing in their relationship had ever made him feel as though they weren't equals, but this small glimpse into Callum's life confirmed that they were from different worlds. Not greatly, but enough to once again have Riley doubting that he was right for Callum.

The woman screeched, which made Riley jump. Callum squeezed his hand before he was suddenly embraced in a hug tighter than he thought possible for a woman her size. When she pulled back, a male hand was being shoved at him to shake and Riley did so willingly. It was a strong, sturdy handshake, not weak and lacklustre like his own father's.

"Alright, alright. You don't have to smother him," Callum ordered. Riley had a chance to breathe as Callum's parents sat back in their chairs. There was a small couch across from them, a clear sign it was meant for him and Callum to sit in.

"Drink?" the older gentleman asked.

"Whatever you're having, sir," Riley replied.

"Sir? I like this one, Callum. Already more polite than the others."

A groan fell from his boyfriend's lips.

"Oh, I promise I'm nothing like Spencer or, what was that other guy's name again? The one that had his whole life planned out and said you could only date if *you* fit into *his* plan?"

"Ugh, Elliot."

"That's right." Riley returned his attention to Callum's parents, who seemed surprised that he knew of Callum's dating history. Riley may have used it as a tactic to prove how well they knew and trusted each other.

"I suppose I should introduce everyone," Callum offered. "Riley this is my mother, Marilyn, and my father, Bradley."

"Oh, please. You can call me Lyn."

Bradley handed him a glass of amber liquid. "Brad is fine. I feel old every time someone calls me Bradley."

Riley smiled and gave a polite nod.

Straight off the bat, it was clear that Marilyn had been the one to gift Callum his fiery red hair. Her scarlet shade was much more subtle, courtesy of hair dye and natural regrowth, Riley guessed. But the freckles that sat across her nose and spread onto her cheeks were a giveaway, especially since Bradley was a brunette with hazel eyes. Riley had a sneaking suspicion he was a jock back in his day.

"Now, Callum here has kept you to himself for far too long, including how you two met. So, while we're waiting for the pot roast to finish, I want details." Marilyn took her martini glass, crossed her legs, and waited.

"Really? Nothing?" Riley was somewhat surprised as he directed the question at Callum.

"I was enjoying our bubble, didn't want to burst it. Is that a crime?"

"Honestly, if we hadn't seen your message pop up on his phone over family dinner, he probably would have kept you away from us longer."

Was Callum hiding him?

"Mum, please."

From the tone of his boyfriend's voice, Riley realised Callum wasn't hiding so much as protecting him from Marilyn and Bradley. He squeezed the hand that had not left his since he arrived, and put forward his most charming self.

"We met through my work. I'm a mechanic at Rising Sun."

"Oh, you hear that honey? Maybe Riley can look at our car and tell us why it does that jerky motion thingy."

"Honey, I told you, you need to remember to release the handbrake and stop putting your handbag on top of it."

Riley used his thumb to scratch at his lip so that Marilyn and Bradley didn't catch him laughing at them.

"Sure, because it never happens when you drive." Marilyn rolled her eyes.

"Actually—" Bradley stopped abruptly and looked at Callum with wide eyes. Riley caught it and looked directly at Callum who had his eyes closed as he shook his head.

"Anyway, continue Riley," Marilyn instructed.

"Ri-right. As, ah, as I was saying, Cal brought—"

"Ooh, look, they already have nicknames for each other. Isn't that sweet, Brad?"

"Mum!"

"Sorry, sorry." Marilyn used her hand to zip her mouth, only to unzip it again so she could sip her martini.

Riley wasn't sure if it was safe to continue his story so he took his cue from Callum, who squeezed his hand.

"So, he brought his Jeep in for a service and I guess, as they say, the rest is history."

"Oh, it was a lot more than that," Callum quickly added. "My Jeep was on the brink of dying and costing me triple, had I left it. And he didn't rip me off like that other mechanic, remember?"

Was he blushing? It felt like he was blushing.

"That's so sweet. Like a modern-day Romeo and Juliet, except gay." Marilyn took another sip of her martini only to realise it was empty. She handed her glass to Bradley who instantly rose to make another.

"Mum, Romeo and Juliet both died at the end."

"They did? Oh. I never finished it, too complicated with all the jargon."

Callum groaned, though it was only loud enough for Riley to hear.

A ding from the kitchen broke the awkwardness, and Bradley and Marilyn both jumped up to attend to the food.

"…is this why you were so nervous about me meeting your family?" Riley kept his voice low as the room went from four bodies to two.

"They're so…" Callum gave an exhausted sigh. "Mum still has the prom queen act and it's not as cute as she thinks it is; it's embarrassing, simple as that. And Dad, well, he tries to act more like my best friend than my dad ever since I told him I was gay." Callum gulped his drink. "Don't get me wrong," another gulp, "I love them both and they are so supportive, but they don't know how to act in front of my boyfriends."

"Good thing I'll be the last one you'll need to introduce them to then."

Was it too soon to make such a remark? Probably. Did it scare Callum off? Not at all.

If anything, the moment Riley said it, a calmness washed over Callum. Riley could see in his stunningly green eyes that he felt the same.

"The moon and sun." Callum leant forward, his forehead resting against Riley's.

"Okay, dinner is ready you two so—Oh! I'm sorry. Am I interrupting?" Marilyn rambled away. "Don't mind me. Young love, I get it. Just…don't be too long sweetie, you know how your father is when food is served cold."

Riley was desperately trying not to laugh while Callum shook his head. Marilyn flew out of the room before Riley had a chance to explain that they weren't doing anything that she had to leave the room for.

"Ready to do this?" Callum questioned.

"Hell yeah."

They were sitting at a table of empty dishes. The alcohol was flowing through everyone's bloodstream, which had lightened the tension in Callum and Riley. Once the awkward questions had passed, the traditional ones came up.

"Tell us about your family."

"Where did you go to school?"

"I didn't take you for a bottom." Oh yes, Marilyn found a way to throw that comment in the mix. Riley almost choked on the pot roast and Callum gave her a firm scolding.

Nevertheless, with Callum's arm draped over Riley's shoulders, and his hand placed comfortably on Callum's knee, the atmosphere was much more relaxed. Riley couldn't remember why he was so nervous in the first place. That was until Bradley spoke up.

"Riley. How do you feel about kids?" The water he had sipped got stuck in his throat, and he hacked it back into the glass, causing a fit of coughs.

"Dad? Seriously?"

"It's an honest question, dear." Marilyn picked up her third martini, though Riley suspected she had downed a few before his arrival. "You're twenty-five and we'd like grandbabies."

This woman had an alcohol tolerance stronger than his.

"Riley, don't answer that."

He was still focused on getting the oxygen back in his lungs to settle down the coughing.

"Honey. You always told us you wanted a wedding, kids and a husband by the time you were thirty."

"Yes, and I also told you I wanted to be in a band and have a record deal with a solo album by twenty-eight."

"So…you don't want kids?" Bradley clarified.

"No, that isn't what I s—"

"Then your father's question for Riley was justified," Marilyn cut in.

"What I'm saying is life changes your plans, and sometimes things have to be pushed back." Callum had moved his arm from around Riley at this point, both arms firmly on the table.

"You and Elliot had spoken about kids after two months together."

"And Elliot was also a control freak that was trying to manipulate me and trap me into a loveless relationship."

That seemed to be a detail Callum's parents hadn't known, but Riley did.

"Look," Riley coughed one last time after he used his voice again, "Mr and Mrs Reed. This," he motioned his hand back and forth between himself and them, "is all new to me. The whole meeting-the-parents thing. Never done it before, never been asked to, and frankly, I have never been with someone where I wanted our relationship to progress to the stage of meeting the family."

Marilyn and Bradley looked at him as though they were trying to understand his point.

"I love your son, so fucking much." He hadn't meant to swear, but Callum's chuckle helped ease the panic that had begun to rise from his slip-up.

"Can I see myself spending forever with him? Yes, without any hesitation." He swallowed. "Will we get married? I hope so. Are kids in our future? Maybe. The point is, with no disrespect, that is for Callum and I to decide, together. And although we have spoken briefly about it, the final decision is ultimately up to us, not you."

The room was silent.

Oh shit.

Marilyn was clutching her necklace and Bradley adjusted the glasses that were perched perfectly on his nose.

He had overstepped. Fucked up. Ruined everything, he thought. But then Callum gripped his face, and his warm palms pulled him in to kiss him.

Whatever anxiety had arisen from being seen as the rude boyfriend who spoke out of line, faded.

"I fucking love you too and yes, to all of that." Callum was still holding his face but he was facing his parents so he could address them directly.

"When we're ready, *if ever*, for any of those things, then we'll let you know."

Callum stood and gave Riley a look that made him rise quickly and place his cloth napkin on the table.

"Mum. Dad. Thank you for dinner, but I think it's time for us to leave."

"Bu—I— what about dessert? I made brandy snaps!"

"Maybe next time." Callum began to leave, and although Riley felt like walking out without helping to clean could be a dealbreaker for getting parental approval, he did offer a quick, "Thank you for dinner" before Callum dragged him out of the house.

The door closed behind them and Riley watched as his boyfriend breathed easily for the first time that evening. Their winter jackets protected them from the soft flutter of snow that was sprinkling down on them. The cold January air was still and crisp, which allowed them to not freeze the second they took a step outside.

"That felt…incredible!" Callum barked. "God. Wow." Callum had his fingers intertwined, his hands resting on the top of his head, similar to when athletes try to catch their breath after a race.

"I just…They are so overbearing sometimes. Being an only child, all their attention fell on me and I love them, I do, but fuck, it felt suffocating when they tried to meddle in my love life."

Riley watched in awe as Callum looked…free.

"You did this." Callum picked Riley up and spun him around in his arms, the street lights casting a glow.

"What?" He chuckled, trying not to get dizzy and lightheaded.

"My moon," Callum purred. "You give me this strength and power, similar to how the moon can control the tides of the water."

His feet were back on solid ground. "You saying I controlled what happened back there?" He pointed his thumb over his shoulder.

"No. No. I'm saying that, like the moon in the sun's shadow, I've wanted to speak up to them for years and tonight—similar to the power of an eclipse, where the moon and sun finally sync up and shine at the same time—I finally told them to mind their own fucking business. After you stood up for yourself and didn't let their intimidation scare you. Your bravery encouraged me." Callum ran his fingers through his hair.

"Okay, Cal. Think it's best I drive you home." He knew his boyfriend was on an adrenaline high since neither of them had drunk more than two glasses, but still, he had never seen Callum behave this way before.

"Wait, my car."

"We can pick it up tomorrow," Riley offered.

Callum enveloped him in a hug from behind, his chin resting on Riley's shoulder as they walked as one toward Riley's car.

"How 'bout tonight, I go back to your place," Callum whispered suggestively in Riley's ear.

They had yet to spend a night at Riley's home. It could have been because he enjoyed the peace that came with being in Callum's apartment or the fact that they didn't have to share the space with anyone but each other.

Malcolm, the main reason why Riley had been avoiding his house like the plague, was no longer an excuse, not when Callum had met the drug addict several times and knew the truth. Regardless, his father was also becoming less present at home, for reasons Riley couldn't care less about.

He turned around in Callum's arms so their eyes locked. "Sure. Probably time we christened my bed." He had to quickly calculate the last time he changed his sheets and whether he had left his room clean or if they'd get there only to find discarded clothes all over his floor.

"I promise to sit in the car for ten minutes so you can quickly check over your room," Callum offered. Riley looked down, blushing from being called out as they both laughed. His head pressed against Callum's chest, amazed yet again at how well Callum could read him, something that took other couples years to perfect.

"Deal."

The scenario Riley planned in his head on the drive home, the one that involved him riding Callum into the mattress after his boyfriend opened him up with his tongue, was short-lived when he saw his sister sitting on their front step.

"Noelle?" He rushed from the car. It was dark out and the snow had begun to thicken on the drive home. He could see an outline of his sister's body on the step, a sign she had been sitting there for a while as the snow fell around her.

"What's wrong?" He knelt in front of Noelle as his eyes scanned her body for injury.

"It's…it's gone." Noelle broke, tears fell once again, her stained and blotchy face proof that she had been crying earlier. She shivered uncontrollably.

"What's gone?" Riley pushed, needing to understand, as he took off his jacket and wrapped it around her quaking body.

"I only took it off to wash the dishes. But—but then my phone rang and it was Joel, and when I came back, it was gone."

Riley looked up at Callum, trying to see if he could make sense of his sister's riddle.

"Mum's ring, Ry." Noelle looked at him for the first time. "Dad took it! It's gone."

"He came back?" He knew the point was moot, but he was trying to get all the facts.

Noelle was shaking her head. "I didn't see him. I—I heard the front door, which is why I ended the call with Joel. I knew it had to be him and I wanted to make sure he was okay." Noelle used the sleeve of her thick hoodie to wipe at her eyes. "By the time I walked back into the kitchen, he was gone, along with Mum's wedding ring that I always put on the windowsill above the sink."

All he could do was take his sister's cold hand and hold it for as long as she needed. Riley cast his eyes down so Noelle didn't think the fury on his face was directed at her.

How they moved from the front step to back inside the house, Riley couldn't recall. But what he did remember was the way Callum helped Noelle onto the couch with the same care a vet would use with a wounded animal.

Riley recalled how his boyfriend made hot chocolate for all three of them, then fetched the blanket from his bed and seated himself in the middle. Riley leaned his body into Callum's side, his boyfriend's arm tightly wrapped around his chest, while Noelle laid her head in his lap so he could run his fingers through her hair and coax her to sleep. A Hallmark movie that featured a special needs boy and the bond he formed with a dog over Christmas played in the background.

"Thank you," he whispered so as not to disturb his sister.

"She's your family…which makes her *my* family," Callum whispered against Riley's temple before placing a kiss in its place.

His mind momentarily travelled back to the discussion from dinner. The one about marriage and children. With nothing but the low hum of the television, Riley allowed himself to daydream about what that might be like in the not-so-distant future.

Moments like this, full of tenderness and care, were setting an example of the type of father Callum would be. A kind, patient one, at that. With the way he always put Riley first, and now Noelle, there was no denying that starting a family with Callum would only enrich their lives.

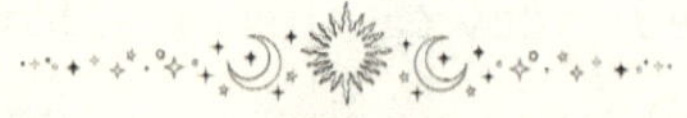

The morning welcomed Riley with a stiff neck and an ache in his lower back that he didn't get from riding Callum reverse cowboy, as he had hoped. He did, however, wake to the smell of coffee after he'd used his boyfriend's chest as a pillow. Callum's head was still buried in a cushion that was leaning against the couch armrest.

Thankfully, Callum was a heavy sleeper, which allowed Riley to extract himself from his arms and shuffle into the kitchen where he found Noelle leaning against the dining table, sipping away at her coffee.

"Hey, how'd you sleep?" He reached for the biggest mug he could find and filled it with the hot liquid.

Noelle shrugged. "Woke around one, snuck off to my room and left you two love birds to spoon on the couch."

"Thanks," he said sarcastically. "My back appreciates you being so courteous."

They stood on opposite sides of the kitchen in silence until they both tried to break it.

"How'd it go with his parents—"

"Look, about last night—"

It at least brought a smile to Noelle's face to see their twinning hadn't faded away.

"What about last night?" Noelle encouraged.

"I'll visit the local pawn shops. Tell 'em what happened, leave a photo of the ring. If we have to buy it back, so be it. But I'm not going to let him get away with this."

His sister sighed. "If he's stealing, Ry, then he's still using."

"Honestly, even after he told us the money was gone, I knew that wouldn't have stopped him." He gripped his mug tightly. "This drug, down…scares the shit outta me."

They each sipped at their coffee while soft snores filtered in from the living room.

"I'm sorry about what I said yesterday. I really am happy for you, Ry. Callum seems perfect."

He smiled. "Yeah…yeah he is."

"So…do his parents approve?"

With a heavy exhale, Riley filled his sister in on the sitcom drama that was Marilyn and Bradley Reed. When he got to the moment where he had stood his ground on his and Callum's relationship being their business, especially regarding marriage and children, Riley noticed the glimmer of unshed tears in his sister's eyes. He went to ask Noelle what he had said but she beat him to the punch.

"I always wanted this for you." She sniffed back tears. "A partner. Someone you could see a future with. Whenever I tried to bring it up, you made it seem like that wasn't the life you wanted."

"No, Noelle. It wasn't that. It was a life I wasn't looking for, at least not at the time. With the shit going on with Malcolm…sure, I had been in relationships, but I wasn't looking for a partner. The guys in the past…eventually it felt like more work than it was worth. So I stopped altogether till I was ready, and until I knew the guy was worth it.

"And Callum is worth it?"

He didn't have to answer. Twin or not, his sister knew that in his heart, Callum was the guy Riley saw himself ready to settle down with.

"Charlie! Remember I'm finishing up early today," Riley yelled loud enough that his boss could hear him in the back, from where he stood behind the front desk.

"I don't remember saying yes to that." Charlie's voice grew louder as he walked closer to Riley.

"Come on, man. Don't go pulling that poor memory shit on me. Besides, it's like an hour early."

Charlie chuckled. "Alight, alright. Don't go getting all dramatic on me. Of course, I remember, though I don't recall why you're leaving early."

"Callum booked some restaurant in Baltimore that has a huge ass waiting list. Apparently, the only way we could get in was if we took the early seating."

"Hmm, fancy restaurant, hey?"

Riley gave his boss and long-time mentor a look.

"Ain't like that."

"Ya know, son. Back in my day, kids could have been together for only a month or so before they were getting engaged and married. Most of the time it was because someone was knocked up but sometimes, it was because they knew they didn't need to keep looking."

"No one's proposing tonight." At least he didn't think they were.

"I'm just saying, no shame if someone did. The older we get, the less time we need to know if we're dating *the one*."

At that moment, the shop door opened, the signature bell chimed and in walked Callum, dressed in fitted black jeans, a soft grey T-shirt and a denim jacket that had wool lining on the inside. His hair looked freshly cut, the fade on the side trimmed down with his fluffy red hair on top. And of course, the mouth-watering, neatly trimmed scruff that had left more marks on Riley's thighs than he could count.

For a split second, Riley's heart stopped beating. The sight of his boyfriend took his breath away, and at times he had to pinch himself to remember that this was all real. That he belonged to him.

"Hey," Callum spoke up. "I know the plan was for me to pick you up from your place but Deja said her car had been stalling recently, so I wanted to come in and see if you could fit her in. I told her I'd ask you, so I thought…"

Callum was rambling. He was nervous and Riley couldn't understand why.

It was only after he drew his eyes away from the gorgeous man before him that he noticed Charlie staring Callum down like he was about to be caught shoplifting.

"Oh, for Christ's sake," Riley huffed. "Charlie, this is Callum, my boyfriend. Callum, this is Charlie, my overbearing boss."

Callum was the first to hold his hand out and Charlie moved closer to shake it. As the men shook hands, Riley sighed in relief.

"And, ah, what're your intentions with Riley, young man?"

If Riley was drinking, he would have spat it out.

"For fuck—are you serious?" Riley noticed that Charlie still had a grip on Callum's hand.

"I'm sorry, sir?" Callum seemed confused by the exchange.

"Cal, don't answer—"

"This fine man is like a son to me, you understand? I knew his parents and I gave him his first job. Now, if you're afraid of a couple of questions then may—"

"No, sir. I'm not afraid, I was simply caught off guard." Callum held his own while Charlie tried to shake him down.

"I intend to treat Riley with the love and respect that he deserves, sir. I want to spend as much time with him as he'll allow because whenever I'm in his company, my day is instantly better. And if I can make him even the slightest bit happier than how he makes me feel, then anything and everything I do will be worth it."

Riley wanted to leap over the counter and kiss the fuck out of Callum. He wanted to tell Callum that simply breathing the same air as him made everything in his life clearer.

"Good answer, kid." Charlie finally let go of Callum's hand. "Why don't you head on back and collect your things, Riley? I'll check the books for Callum's friend."

Riley followed Charlie's instructions, though he made sure to act fast.

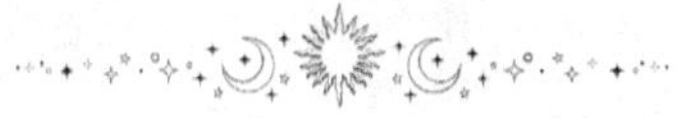

The waiter poured them a glass of wine that was tailored to their dinner selection. The restaurant decor was dark, the tones a mix of mahogany, maroon, black and white. The lighting was warm and dimmed, which allowed Riley to see only Callum sitting across from him, everyone else fading into the dark, moody surroundings. It reminded him of a 1950s mobster restaurant, especially since eighty per cent of the menu was some form of red meat.

"Sorry about before," Riley started, gulping his wine to help ease the tension.

"I think I was owed such behaviour after I made you endure my parents."

"Still. He had no right. So…sorry about that." He took another gulp before he placed the glass back down.

"I think he had every right," Callum spoke truthfully. "He said you were like a son to him, so he merely asked questions a father would ask."

"Yeah, but, he's my boss…"

"Who I'm guessing steps in when Malcolm can't."

Riley would be lying if he didn't admit that the thought had crossed his mind at one time or another, with how the lines had sometimes blurred between employer and father figure. Charlie was always around to listen, give advice, and, when needed, offer small touches of physical affection, like a supportive hand on Riley's shoulder. All the qualities that Malcolm sadly lacked.

"I've been working at that garage since I was eighteen," Riley began to explain. "I was still holding my graduation cap when I walked in, nervous as fuck to ask him for a job." His hand fumbled with the three forks situated on the left side of his plate.

"Charlie didn't ask if I had any experience with cars. He didn't ask why I wanted the job. He just told me to be at the garage at six on Monday morning. I was on an apprentice wage and he taught me everything. He gave me the books I had to study, he showed me every issue that came into that garage and then told me to study and come back the next day with the knowledge on how to fix it."

"You didn't go to school?"

He shook his head. "These days, most places want employees to have that knowledge, but Charlie's shop is old school. None of those computerised chips and shit."

What he also knew, deep in his heart, was that Charlie understood he didn't have the time or money for further education. With his mother gone, both he and Noelle had set out to find jobs they could start straight away so they had a reliable source of income.

"And you've been there ever since," Callum pointed out.

"And I've been there ever since." Riley smiled. "Honestly, it's all I know. Can't picture working anywhere else."

"Not even if you moved?"

He tilted his head at the question.

"I'm just saying, do you see yourself living in Maryland, ya know, forever?"

He opened his mouth to say yes but then stopped. When he thought about it, the only people keeping him here were Malcolm and Noelle. One of which was killing himself slowly and the other, well, Noelle was going steady with Joel, and he was sure any day now the guy would be asking Noelle to move in. Then marriage, followed by two point five kids.

So, what was keeping him here?

"I guess I never thought about it."

Callum held his hand out, palm up. Riley immediately slipped in hand into the offering.

"I always wanted to travel. The United States is a big place and I've never been outside of our state. I'd love to walk the shores of Mexico. See the snowy mountains of Canada. Surf in the waves of the Australian beaches."

"You surf?" Riley cut Callum off.

"No," Callum chuckled. "But there is always time to learn."

That got them both laughing.

"My point is," Callum continued, "I always wanted to do those things, and I could have, but I wanted to set myself up first. Get a good job, earn money and put some savings behind me. But maybe," Callum's thumb began to caress Riley's hand, "I was also waiting for someone to share those things with."

It didn't take a genius for Riley to know what Callum was getting at.

"I think anything is possible." He bit his lip, eyes cast down as a warm heat spread across his cheeks.

"Did you mean it?" Callum quickly asked. "What you said about kids…about marriage? I know we've spoken a little about it before but…" Callum stopped, perhaps nervous or scared to continue.

After they left Callum's parent's house, they both avoided the conversation and then, neither found the right time to bring it up. It seemed this was the time.

"Yes…and no." He felt Callum begin to retract his hand but Riley held on, giving his boyfriend's hand a reassuring squeeze. "I have always liked the idea of marriage. The commitment it represents. The undevoted love and bond between two people."

Under the table Riley hooked his foot around Callum's, the simple touch of their hands not enough.

"I didn't care if I was married by thirty or fifty-two, I just wanted to know that the person I was promising forever to was going to love me up until the end. But in the last few years, the idea itself had completely left my mind. Though, if I'm being honest, recently it has begun to creep back in." He smirked, a reassurance that what they were building together was leading to something bigger than boyfriend status.

The moment was interrupted by a 10oz Filet Mignon steak being placed in front of each of them, both with a side of chargrilled vegetables and a mushroom sauce. All Riley had to do was look at the meal to know he wasn't going to be bottoming tonight; Callum might have to settle for mutual blowjobs at best.

"I always pictured a big wedding," Callum spoke up. "Not so much with guests but with the whole ceremony in one location, reception in another."

Riley took a bite of his food when his boyfriend did the same, silently moaning at the flavours that mixed with the wine on his tongue.

"But I always wanted kids," Callum continued. "At least two, so that they had one another. Only child syndrome kicking in there, I'm sure, but I knew that none of those dreams were going to change just because I was gay, so…"

He waited a minute. Not because of what Callum had said, but because he wanted to remember everything about that moment. The way Callum looked and smelled. The way Callum smiled softly at his memories while his eyes crinkled at the corners. And once he had it all burned into his mind, then and only then did Riley speak from the heart.

"I'm sure one day we could find a stray or two that need a place to call home."

Chapter 7

It's been three nights of restless sleep, his mind on a constant loop, replaying memories that have seeped out of the box he had them locked and chained in. Some are worse than others, and then there are the ones that cause him to jolt upright in bed, a cold sweat perspiring from his forehead. Those are the ones that make it impossible to fall back to sleep, and Riley eventually makes himself a cup of coffee at two in the morning and watches reruns of some random 90s sitcom on the TV in the living room.

It's now Friday and his colleagues have planned for a night out to celebrate the few staff birthdays that are coming up on the weekend. He's declined, unable to think of anything worse than pretending to smile, laugh, and follow along with pointless conversations with people he barely knows. He settles for a night in, alone, instead.

Earlier in the week, Jackson called. Riley had let it go to voicemail, waiting till he had the strength to listen.

"Yo, Riley. Just checking in, brother, feels like a lifetime ago since I saw you."

Funny, feels like lifetimes have passed.

"Don't be a stranger." The message continued. "Come on over. Billy and Kimberley miss you and Rihanna is driving me nuts." There's a chuckle on Jackson's end.

"You know you're the only one who can handle all that. Must be because you're both blondes." There's a pause, then a sniff, and Riley almost thinks the voicemail is finished until he hears a less confident voice. "I'm here if you need me, Riley. Always."

If anything, the message only makes him less inclined to see his friends. The anxiety of what they'd expect from him if he were to show up has his heart pounding hard enough for him to hear it.

Noelle sends him a series of text messages, his phone constantly vibrating against the coffee table to the point that it buzzes right off the edge, landing face down on the floor. For a split-second, Riley panics that his screen is cracked and he's broken his phone, that's until the damn thing buzzes again.

Whenever he looks in the mirror, a brain-dead zombie looks back at him; bloodshot eyes and purple bags beneath from his inability to obtain a solid eight hours of sleep.

Riley hasn't mentioned his issues to anyone, especially Noelle. She'd force him to go back to Dr Bech and after how well that conversation went, he isn't looking forward to another one.

Gnawing at his cuticles, Riley stares at Jackson's number. The contact open on his phone, the screen staring at him like a game, the first to blink is the loser. With a deep exhale, he brings his hand to hover over his phone and as he goes to press *call*, the loud, screeching sound of a ringtone pierces his ears.

Saved by the bell.

No.

He doesn't need saving.

It's fine.

He'll call once he hangs up from whoever has called him.

Oh shit, it's still ringing.

"Hello?" he answers uncertainly, as the caller ID says it's a private number.

"Riley? It's Dr Bech."

Fuck. He should have let it go to voicemail.

"Ah, yeah…Hi."

"Sorry to disturb you, I wanted to check in and see how you're doing since this was our first week without an appointment."

"I'm doing great." *Except for the inability to sleep.* "I was about to call Jackson when you called. He wanted to catch up and since I had some free time, well…"

"Oh, that's wonderful."

"Mhm." He isn't sure what else he is meant to say.

"Have you experienced any panic attacks since we last spoke? Moments of anxiety that you'd like to talk about?"

Does the sweat-inducing fear of picking up his phone only minutes before count?

"N-no, no, not really…"

There is a pause. Riley thinks the line may have disconnected, so he checks his screen to see that the numbers are still ticking away, recording how long the call has been connected.

"Riley," Dr Bech's voice seems hesitant, it almost scares him…almost. "In my professional opinion, I think it would be best if we continue our sessions."

"Oh, here we fucking go." He stands, pacing the length of his coffee table where his phone still sits on loudspeaker.

"There is still so much to discuss that I believe has affected you in ways that you may not be aware of," Dr Bech informs him.

"No. No! See, this is what you wanted, isn't it? To sit me down and be all, 'Poor fuckin', Riley. His father destroyed his life,' and then you'll dope me up so you can get some kickback on whatever drug you prescribe or institution you lock me up in." The anger that rises within him is so strong he can taste it.

"Riley, of course no—"

"Malcolm was an addict. So, what? He did the shit addicts do but guess what, Doc, I ain't the only kid that had to deal with fucked-up parents." His hands curl into fists; his nails dig into his skin.

"No, you're not the only—"

"You know, I was fine until Noelle forced me to see you. *You're* the problem here."

"Riley, I think—"

"You opened Pandora's box, which was fine being locked up, chained and buried deep in the fucking ocean, lost in the Bermuda Triangle." His chest is heaving as he finally stops to catch his breath. He collapses onto the couch, his body suddenly weak from his outburst.

Time passes. How long, he isn't sure. But when Riley checks his phone, Dr Bech is still connected on the line, waiting patiently, silently.

"I didn't mean…" He stops himself before he admits to another lie.

"It's okay, Riley. What happened turned your life upside down."

He's done talking. This isn't a session. This isn't mandatory. This is *his* choice.

"Thanks for the call, Doc. But Jackson's expecting my call."

"Of course. If you need anything I'm—"

"Yeah. I got it." Riley hangs up.

Thirteen minutes and fifty-four seconds; the length of the phone call.

Although Riley knows deep in his heart that he was one hundred per cent going to call Jackson before Dr Bech interrupted, now, not an ounce of him is interested in socialising with his friends after the conversation he just had.

Thanks, Doc.

Riley stands from the couch, rushing towards the kitchen for a cold beer.

Maybe something stronger will help him sleep.

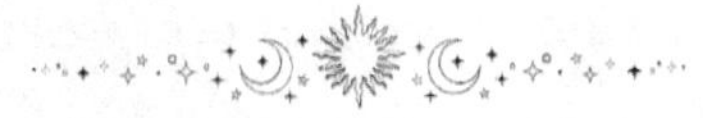

Six Months Ago

"You seriously doin' nothin' for Valentine's Day?" Jackson asked as Riley brought the Chinese food to the table after collecting it from the delivery driver.

"This is your house, why am I getting the food?"

"I ghosted the delivery guy from the restaurant. Safer for me that he doesn't know where I live."

All Riley could do was shake his head, not even surprised by his friend's behaviour.

"And stop avoiding the question," Jackson bit back.

"Callum has to work. Being an EMT means someone has to be rostered on during the holidays, and Valentine's Day fell on him after he got New Year's Eve off so we could go to your party."

"The party where you left ten minutes after it hit midnight because you were about to get it on in the middle of my mumma's living room?"

Riley's eyebrows said it all while he shoved some beef and black bean into his mouth.

"There should be a rule that states couples in their first year of a relationship get Valentine's Day off," Jackson spoke as though he were president.

He shrugged. "I'm sure we can celebrate next year."

"Well, well, well," Jackson cooed. "Already planning twelve months into the future I see."

"Isn't that the point?" he questioned through a mouth full of food. "Why date someone if you can't see forever with them?"

"Because it's reliable dick."

Riley threw a fortune cookie at his best friend, who opened his mouth to catch it. Jackson missed and was hit in the eye by the sugary treat, which in Riley's mind was a win.

They sat in comfortable silence while they ate. Jackson's mother was out playing bingo with her church friends. The nostalgia of sitting at his friend's dinner table had Riley deciding he was long overdue for a sit-down meal with Jackson and his mother, like he did when he was younger.

"Ya know, you're allowed to be disappointed that Callum has to work," Jackson stated.

Riley nodded along to show that he heard, though he felt too vulnerable to speak up.

He didn't have to let Jackson know that on some level, he was disappointed. Jackson would know because of their years of friendship. Riley had never shared a Valentine's Day with someone, and as cheesy and overrated as the holiday was, it still felt like this year was different considering his and Callum's relationship was deeper than any he had before. But he had no right asking Callum to change his shift again, especially when he was still the rookie.

"Guessin' Noelle is busy?" Jackson changed the subject.

"Joel's booked a whole weekend away. Wouldn't be surprised if he proposes."

"Shit. Think she'd say yes?"

"Fuck if I know. This is the longest she's ever been committed to someone. I was worried she was going to follow in your footsteps, to be honest, bounce from dick to dick." A hand shoved Riley, almost knocking him over and his food with it.

"Ay, watch it. If I leave a stain, I'm telling your mumma that it was your food, not mine."

"Shit, she'd believe you too," Jackson agreed.

Since Malcolm had stolen, and no doubt pawned off their mother's wedding ring, the man had become a ghost. Riley had casually begun asking around if anyone had seen his father when he was out buying groceries or stopping by the pharmacy. Nothing.

Finding his mother's ring was also a dead end. No one had it and he had yet to receive a phone call to state that it had been brought in, though he suspected no one would call on account of having to admit they had purchased a somewhat stolen item. Technically, it was Malcolm's. After all, it belonged to his dead wife.

As time passed and Malcolm remained on the missing list, Riley would move around the house as though it were his. Noelle spent more and more time at Joel's and in her absence, Riley would daydream of ways he could improve the property with a fresh coat of paint and less outdated furniture. Still, he should have known the quiet was too good to be true as his father finally reared his head out from the gutters, literally.

"Jesus Christ!" Riley yelped as he turned a corner to find his father hovering by the entryway. For a split second, he thought it might be an intruder, the man's body unrecognisable until Riley caught sight of his father's face partially hidden by the hood of his jacket.

He was going to make a half-assed comment about it being nice to see his father alive, but the air was off, and not because Malcolm smelt as though he hadn't showered in weeks, which he suspected was true. It was because, for the first time in Riley's life, Malcolm Maddox looked frightened.

"Yo, everything alright there, Pops?" Riley hesitated to take a step closer. "Noelle's been worried. I even started asking around since we had no idea where you went." There was no point lying, Riley hadn't cared about where his father might have been, not anymore.

It was eerie to watch Malcolm stand stock still. If not for the laboured breathing, Riley would have mistaken his father for dead. Or a hallucination.

"Ey, Pops. You gonna tell me where you've been?"

Malcolm's head slowly rose from where his eyes were cast down to the floor. Riley gasped. His father's face looked like one huge hematoma. He could barely distinguish facial features from the swelling, all shades of black, blue, and purple.

"Hey, son," Malcolm choked out; his voice weak.

"The fuck happened to you?" It may have been shock, fear, or even guilt, but at that moment, Riley forgot about showing compassion and skipped straight to wanting an explanation.

"I fucked up, son."

Riley's blood ran cold.

He kicked into motion and reached out for his father's arm. Malcolm winced, and a hiss fell from his lips as Riley dragged him further into the house so he could sit. This seemed to aggravate Malcolm's body further.

"Ah, fuck!" Malcolm bellowed.

"Easy, Pops." Riley looked over his father's body for any signs of further damage.

"Relax, nothin's bleeding," Malcolm let out, "…anymore."

With a huff, Malcolm fell back onto the couch and all Riley could do was take a step back and hold out for the answers he felt desperate for.

"I owe some people a bit of money and they got tired of waiting, I guess."

Riley dragged his hands down his face. He wanted to rewind the last fifteen minutes, to give him time to run out the backdoor so that he didn't have to come face-to-face with his beaten-to-a-pulp father. Malcolm lifted the hem of his hoodie; more bruises could be seen, but it was the square patch that Riley watched his father peel off his ribcage like a Band-Aid that caught his attention.

"You'd think I wouldn't feel a damn thing usin' one of these, but guess their punches are stronger than whatever shit they sold me."

"And what the fuck are those?" Riley questioned.

"Fentanyl patch." Malcolm threw it on the floor after he held it up like proof. "With the price I was charged, figured I was getting at least a hundred micrograms, but I've had to swap them over quicker than the forty-eight hours I was promised."

Riley wanted to pull at his hair and scream into the void.

"Are you trying to tell me the whole fucking time you've been gone, you've been hiding out somewhere using? With what money?"

"Would I look this way if I had money?"

He clenched his fists. "How much?"

Malcolm sighed. "Ten grand."

A vase that sat on the coffee table, with flowers Joel had given to Noelle, was in Riley's hand only briefly enough for him to throw it at the wall. The sound of the glass shattering while the water dripped down the paint mimicked how he was feeling inside. Broken.

"You're so fucking selfish, you know that?" Riley couldn't look at his father. "You think we have that kinda money?" His voice rose along with his anger. "Would we still be living here with you if we did?" By this point, he spat the words at his father like venom.

"I know, son. I know."

Who was Malcolm kidding? The word *son* had no effect on Riley, not anymore. The only thing connecting them was their bloodline, but to Riley, family was more than shared DNA.

"Did they follow you? Do they know you're here? Is Noelle in danger?"

"No. No, they were all asleep when I left."

He huffed. "Sneaking out sure is your MO."

"I had no other option!"

"You had rehab!" Riley fought back. "You had the choice of getting clean. Getting your life back."

"What life?" Malcolm stood. "My wife is dead! My children can't stand to be around me, and everyone in this town looks at me like I'm a waste of oxygen."

"But we stayed!" Riley sniffed back the tears he could feel threatening to fall. "Maybe we couldn't stand you, but we stayed…we stayed because we still loved you. Because you were still our father."

Malcolm sunk back into the couch; his head fell into his hands as a dam of tears broke free. The last time Riley heard his father sob that loud was the night of their mother's funeral. And if he wasn't mistaken, he could hear his mother's name in between sobs.

He knelt on the ground, bringing himself to eye level with Malcolm, though he didn't offer any consolatory touches. He took a deep breath and, perhaps he'd regret it, but he knew on some level, that he wouldn't be able to live with himself if he didn't at least try.

"I could maybe give you half, that's all I've got. Everything I've saved since I was eighteen."

The sobs lessened. The tears slowed. The broken older man Riley once looked up to now looked up at him. A glimmer of hope in his eyes for the first time, through the bruises and pain.

"I'll try and find a way to get the rest, but at least it will give you some time…right?"

"Right. 'M sure they'd be okay with that."

He searched his father's eyes for a slither of the man he once knew.

"Only on one condition." *Surely it was obvious.* "I need you to go to rehab, Pops. I need you to get clean. *Noelle* needs you to stop. *Please.* Because, if you don't…then don't bother coming back. Ever."

There was a hitch in his father's throat.

"We can't keep living our lives wondering if you're dead or alive." He let the words sink in, pausing to see if Malcolm would reject the suggestion. "We can't worry about coming home to find everything gone because you've pawned it." He saw the shame in his father's eyes. "And we can't have your mistakes land on us." This one was especially important.

"I get it." Malcolm yielded. "I'm sorry, son. Really. I-I never should have let it get this far."

Whether it was the tone of his father's voice or the look of love and guilt in his blue eyes, Riley believed him.

"Give me a few days and I'll have the money for you. Lay low until then, just to be safe."

It was February 14th and that morning, Riley had given his father the five thousand he had been saving for the day he could get out on his own, or what he recently had been daydreaming about, using it towards a new start with Callum. Malcolm was back to living in the house, though Riley had told him to avoid Noelle until his face had healed. His sister had worried enough over the last few months to last her a lifetime, and Riley didn't want her to have a visual of their father's beaten face.

Malcolm offered a kind smile, which Riley read as a thank you. His father walked out the door, with the money hidden away and a twinkle in his barely healed eye that Riley hadn't seen in years, perhaps a sign that this was the beginning of a new chapter.

He set off to work. Noelle had left the night before for her weekend away, and for a Friday, the roads were surprisingly quiet.

The snow had temporarily stopped. The wind was still, and if not for the chill in the air, it would have been a beautiful day for the last month of winter.

By lunch, Riley was ready to head home. February had the locals bringing in their cars that they hadn't correctly cared for throughout winter. It made no sense how in the span of nine months, the same customers couldn't follow the instructions that Riley, Charlie and Clint had given them, even if it meant avoiding coming back the following year.

The snow had begun to ease earlier in the year than normal, which is why the influx of cars hit mid-February compared to the usual first day of spring drop-off.

"There should be a second part to getting your license," Riley grumbled as he walked into the breakroom. He grabbed a Coke from the refrigerator and downed half the can before he continued. "How to care for a car's engine. It can be multiple choice."

Charlie was flicking through a magazine that looked as old as the shop. He offered a chuckle at Riley's frustration.

"Kid, if we had to rely on people being able to care for their cars just to drive on the road, we'd be out of business."

"Because everyone wouldn't need us?"

"Because everyone would be taking the bus." That caused them both to laugh, a welcome relief from the frustration of stupid customers.

"You seem on edge. Don't you and Callum have plans for this evening?"

"Ah, 'fraid not." He rubbed at the back of his neck. "He's gotta work."

"I see. You okay?"

"Why is everyone acting like it's a big deal that I'm not spending Valentine's Day with my boyfriend?" Riley was surprised by how much hostility was in his voice.

"Maybe because you've never spent it with *anyone*."

He forgot how well Charlie knew him sometimes. With a sigh, he sat his ass down in one of the chairs and spoke from the heart.

"It's like any other day, right? I don't need to sit down in some overcrowded restaurant, accepting flowers Callum paid double for that will die the next day, and be given some Hallmark card that was no doubt written for a straight couple."

"You'd actually want to be given flowers?" Charlie joked, his tone behind the question light and playful.

"Shut up," Riley laughed as the blush crept up his skin. "You know what I mean."

Charlie was nodding along. "I do, I do." His boss turned in his chair so he could rest his arms against the table. "But have you heard from Callum today? At all?"

"I mean, I got a good morning message."

"Ya see," Charlie began, "before all the hoo-ha and the Hallmark mumbo-jumbo that made Valentine's Day what it is today, it used to be as simple as a day to send messages. To show love and affection toward the people we couldn't say it to in person."

He waited for the point.

"So, did you get a message of love and affection, ya know, since you aren't seeing your man today?"

No.

No, he didn't.

The fuck.

"Guess that explains the attitude." Charlie went back to reading his magazine.

"Man, attitude my ass. People are just dickheads."

"Mhm."

Riley fiddled with the cuff of his overalls, his teeth gnawed away on his bottom lip until finally he came out and said it.

"Malcolm's back."

The magazine was forgotten. Riley had Charlie's full attention.

"You okay?" It was the same question, but a different tone. Riley knew he wouldn't be able to bluff his way through the answer.

"He rocked up, beaten pretty badly. His eye was as swollen as his cheek and I could've sworn he had a broken nose, but he was still walking upright." He shrugged to help play it off.

"Shit, I'm sorry, son. No one should ever have to see their parents like that."

"No one should ever have to pay their parent's debt either." He couldn't look Charlie in the eye.

"Please tell me you didn't."

"And have his death on my conscience?" He looked up at this point, only to find Charlie looking down, shaking his head.

"Look, I don't know who he owed money to, but if they were willing to do that to him, who knows how far they'd go. I was looking out for Noelle."

"I get it, kid. I do." For the first time since Malcolm stepped foot through the front door, Riley's hands had begun to shake. He hadn't told Callum, knowing that if the man he loved and trusted more than anyone had told him not to hand over his entire savings account to his father, Riley would have listened.

"How much he owe?"

"Ten thousand, but I couldn't pay it all."

"Jesus, Riley. I know for a fact you don't have that kinda money. I'm the one that bloody pays you." Charlie shook his head. "You shouldn't have had to pay any of it. It's not your responsibility."

He bit his lip. "Done now. Gave him the money this morning and in exchange, he said he'd go to rehab."

"And he agreed?" Charlie seemed surprised.

"Mhm. Got him booked in for the end of the month."

"Well, I'll be damned." Charlie sat back in his chair. "I'm sorry it took giving up everything you had for him to finally go."

"Small price to pay for the bigger picture though, right?"

"…Right." Charlie took longer to agree with him than Riley would have liked.

"If, ah, if you need me to do some extra hours or something, just tell me when. The answer is gonna be yes." Riley stood. He didn't want to see the look in Charlie's eyes. The one that he was sure showed pity and sadness.

He turned around and walked back out onto the garage floor, to the cars that called his name.

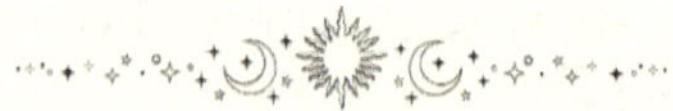

When Riley got home, he was emotionally and physically exhausted. Charlie had kept his distance for the remainder of the day, and every time Clint opened his mouth, he wanted to punch it, so that left Riley alone with the cars. Typically, he would have no issue with that, only this time, it left him alone with his thoughts.

Malcolm was, of course, front and centre. Sparks of regret would swoop in and overshadow the joyous possibility of the man their father used to be, his biggest supporter, who'd cheer him on in life and encourage him when the pressure got too much to bear.

The what-ifs of the situation were endless. What if the five thousand wasn't enough? What if the money hadn't gone to the dealer? What if Malcolm never returned home? What if rehab didn't work? What if. What if. What if.

But he couldn't control the what-ifs.

As he approached the front door, the what-ifs disappeared when he noticed it was unlocked, slightly ajar. Riley knew that he had locked the door behind him that morning.

He pushed the door open at a snail's pace, preventing the creaking sound that only came from opening it quickly. He couldn't hear anyone moving around inside, and although there was a glow of light, it wasn't coming from the ceiling lights, which were switched off.

Riley reached for the baseball bat that had lived beside their front door since the day he was born and held it above his head, ready to swing.

Only to drop it.

Callum stood there in his living room with flowers in his hands. The room was covered in an array of variously sized lit candles, and beside Callum was a small table covered in delicious-looking food and wine. He instantly forgot about the possibility of a threat.

"Happy Valentine's Day, Riley." Callum was wearing a white button-up shirt, the cuffs rolled to his elbows, and a few buttons already undone to reveal the gorgeous slither of chest hair that Riley had run his fingers through more times than he could count. The shirt was tucked into black slacks and it was intimidating how gorgeous the redhead looked while Riley stood in his dirty overalls, grease still on his hands.

"I–I thought you had to work." It was the first thing that came to Riley's mind.

"I did. But I took the morning shift. One of the guys at work got dumped last week and was happy to switch."

Riley was speechless. He looked around the room and took in all the details Callum had put into the evening. His favourite meal from the Italian restaurant they had visited with Noelle was sitting on the coffee table. The excessive number of candles created a warm glow that electrified Callum's hair. And then there were the long-stemmed sunflowers in his boyfriend's hand, much like the ones he laid at his mother's grave each year, which were the icing on the cake.

"Callum, this is…"

"Too much?" The ginger took a step closer. "Noelle gave me her key when I told her I was able to get my shift changed. Hope you don't mind. I needed enough time to set it up."

"No, no it's…fuck, it's perfect." They weren't in a crowded restaurant. They weren't eating overpriced food that had to be selected from a set menu. And most of all, Riley knew exactly where Callum had purchased those flowers and that the store wouldn't have overcharged because of the day's date.

"I—Jesus, I'm a mess." He looked down at his work clothes.

"You're beautiful," Callum spoke truthfully. "But if you'd like to shower, I'll happily wait."

Riley rushed off towards the bathroom, but he circled back so he could lay a deep, passionate kiss on his boyfriend's lips. He smiled into the kiss, letting Callum know how happy he truly was at that moment.

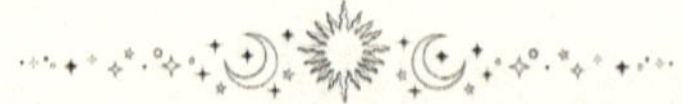

Dressed in a white T-shirt with an open maroon button-up shirt over the top, Riley raced back into the living room to see Callum waiting for him on the couch, a relaxed smile on his face and his arm slung over the back of it. Riley joined him, and they ate dinner straight from the box while they shared stories of past Valentine's Days. Riley admitted he had no memories to offer, not even a card slipped into his locker at school, or a failed attempt at asking someone out. To this, Callum placed his hand on Riley's cheek and whispered how he was honoured to be Riley's first. Then he placed a soft kiss on his lips.

Callum on the other hand, had experiences with Elliot and Spencer, both horrible and memorable all for the wrong reasons. He also shared a story of how he slipped a Valentine's Day card into the wrong locker in high school, which led to a girl named Amber batting her eyes at him for six months before he had the heart and courage to let her know the card was meant for Alex, her brother.

Riley laughed so hard he was worried he was going to choke on his pasta and have it come out of his nose.

"Stop laughing," Callum ordered, though he too was chuckling. "Our lockers were alphabetical by last name. It was an easy mistake since they were side by side."

"You didn't think Al for Alex came before Am for Amber."

"I do now." Callum twirled the fork in his pasta. "I was sixteen, about to out myself at school, can you blame me for being a little nervous and screwing up?"

The laughter settled. "No, no I don't blame you. If anything, I think it's really brave." Riley waited. "What happened, anyway? Did you get a shot with Alex?"

"Oh, God no. Straighter than an arrow. He almost punched me when he found out, but by then, Amber was a close friend and convinced him not to."

Everything was going perfectly. It wasn't over the top, there were no gifts, which meant Riley had no guilt about not organising one for Callum. The food lay discarded on the coffee table and the two of them snuggled into one another on the couch when the door opened. On the other side was a reminder that, outside of Riley's bubble, reality rudely awaited.

When Riley saw Malcolm, he froze; a hesitation brought on by fear, unsure of which version of his father would walk through the door.

"I didn't mean to intrude," Malcolm spoke first. "I'll hide away in my bedroom, give you two some privacy."

Malcolm's appearance didn't look dishevelled. And there were no signs that he had used. Unless he stripped his father down to check for a patch, though, he couldn't be certain. However, perhaps it was the way his father showed kindness within that moment—a sight he had not seen in years—that gave Riley the hope that this time *would* be different.

Riley sunk back into the warmth of his boyfriend. He watched as his father walked past them to get to his room, only to stop near the end of the couch.

"I apologise for how I behaved in the past." Malcolm held his hand out, and it meant the world to Riley when Callum shook it instantly. "Take good care of my son. You won't find anyone like him."

"I will, sir. He's more special than he realises."

They spoke as though he wasn't in the room, but as Riley watched the two exchange pleasantries, it unlocked something inside of him. What, he wasn't sure. But when his father walked away and closed the bedroom door behind him, Riley felt free.

He felt warm, secure arms wrap around him, his body held tight, and Callum nuzzled into his neck.

"You didn't tell me your father was back." Callum didn't sound upset by the fact.

"It's only been a little over a week. Wasn't sure what to make of it myself, but Noelle doesn't know. Been hiding him from her."

"Why?"

He spun so that his eyes met Callum's. "Story for another day, let's not ruin tonight."

Callum offered a tender kiss, a sealed agreement that the discussion could wait till tomorrow. What started as soft pecks turned into longer, meaningful, lingering kisses. It reminded Riley of two teenagers making out on the couch because they weren't allowed to be alone in the bedroom, only he wasn't a teenager, and he was more than allowed.

"Maybe we should move this into my room." He kept his eyes closed. They exchanged Eskimo kisses since their lips were occupied with talking rather than kissing. "Though I can only promise heavy petting after how much food we ate."

Callum chuckled. "Just because it's Valentine's Day, doesn't mean we have to have sex."

"You sure? I swear that's in the fine print." Riley cocked an eyebrow.

With a grin that could light up the night sky, Callum nodded. "I'm sure. Would be happy just to hold you. Preferably naked."

Riley shoved Callum enough for his tight grip to lessen, which gave him a chance to get up and make a run for his bedroom. Callum's laugh and hastened footsteps followed after him.

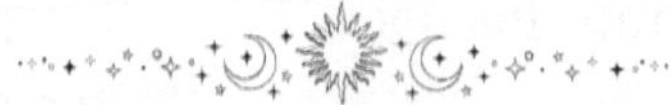

When Noelle learnt of Malcolm's return, the first thing his sister did was slap their father across the face, which shocked both men. Riley stepped forward in case he needed to interfere, but Noelle's arms quickly wrapped around the shoulders of their last remaining parent and they both wept in each other's embrace. Riley almost felt as though he was intruding, but this was what needed to happen so his sister could heal, so they all could.

It would take time for Noelle to forgive Malcolm for their mother's wedding ring, how much time, he wasn't sure. But there was a glimmer back in his sister's eyes that had been missing for the last few months.

"You're really doing it? You're going to rehab?" Noelle asked. The three of them were seated at the dining table, sipping away at coffees with an assortment of cookies placed in the middle, a leftover treat from Callum.

"I am. Your brother has organised it and it's time. I need to do this. For you both, for myself…for your mother."

Noelle's hand landed on top of Malcolm's, her other was placed palm up, waiting for Riley to slip his hand into her grasp, till the three of them were all holding each other's hands. A circle formed, making it look like they were about to chant some spell to awaken the dead. Instead, they each squeezed the other person's hand, and it was the most connected Riley had felt to his family since their mother's passing.

"Riley…" His father began. "I want you to know that I was never against you being gay." Malcolm's words shocked him, especially since it wasn't a topic he was expecting to discuss. "Whatever I've said in the past, I hope you know it wasn't me…it was the drugs."

He wanted to believe him, but didn't drugs lessen a person's inhibitions, allowing inner thoughts and emotions free reign?

"I'm happy you've found someone. And from what I saw and heard from him the other night, he cares deeply for you."

What had he seen?

"I'm sorry if you ever felt outcasted or disowned by my actions. Gay, straight, I don't care, as long as you're safe and loved and treated correctly."

Riley had never allowed himself to think hard enough about his father's words whenever the topic arose. It could be why he made sure to never bring it up when Malcolm was coherent. But this apology had left Riley feeling a vulnerability he had tried to suppress in the past. He gave his father's hand a squeeze, the three of them still connected, and with a shaky voice, Riley thanked his father for owning his mistakes.

It was a quiet afternoon, the plans for that night were to drive Malcolm to rehab and check him in, but before that, Riley still had to work. When Callum entered the garage, it was a random surprise, which brought a smile to Riley's face.

He rubbed the oil from his hands as his handsome EMT strutted towards him with a smirk.

"Better watch it. You keep walking around here in that uniform, people are gonna think Charlie is on the way to an early grave."

"Ain't nothin' gonna kill me, boy," Charlie called from the backroom; impressive hearing for a man of his age. "Well, except maybe this bookwork. This is why half of America avoids payin' their damn taxes."

Riley chuckled at his boss's grumbled complaint, the smile on his face widening further. "What brings you by?"

"Can't a man stop in to say hello to his boyfriend?" Riley wasn't buying it. He cocked an eyebrow. "Fine, we got a flat on the rig and *someone* forgot to replace the old spare."

"You know I'm a mechanic, and this is not a tyre shop?"

"Isn't that the same thing?"

Riley shook his head, laughter falling from his mouth. "No, smartass. Thankfully though, we do keep a small collection on hand, though I can't promise we have what you're after."

Callum handed over a folded-up note. Riley opened it and saw the details of the tyre that was needed.

"Knew I'd forget once I got here." Callum winked.

"Smooth…" Riley began to walk away. "Lemme check," he called behind him.

When Riley returned empty-handed, he noticed that Callum had spent the time getting a little too close to the car he was working on, and by close, Riley meant the man's hands were leaving prints on the paintwork.

"Ey, what d'ya think you're doing?" He had a strong urge to slam down the bonnet of the car like a parent would smack away the hands of a child attempting to steal candy. Instead, Riley took the more mature approach and pushed Callum away.

"Woah! Alright, alright. No need to get testy."

"Sorry," Riley mumbled. "I don't let anyone near her. Not even Charlie unless I really need his help."

"Her?" Callum cocked an eyebrow.

"Callum," Charlie announced his presence in the room. "I see you've met the other love in Riley's life, you know, besides yourself."

His boss stood with both hands in the pockets of his overalls.

"Wow, Charlie, that's a strong scent of bullshit you got rolling off of you right now." Riley deflected his embarrassment.

"Oh, I see. Callum doesn't know about her." Charlie winked at Callum to stir the pot.

"Charlie, go back into your cave." He turned back towards his car.

There were only a few moments of silence. Riley assumed the other two men were exchanging looks or reading lips so he couldn't hear whatever they wanted to share behind his back.

"I guess I'll leave you both," Charlie eventually stated. "Just be aware, Callum, wherever you two decide to live, unless it has a garage to store this beauty, Riley ain't gonna move there."

Without turning around, Riley threw up his middle finger, the distant chuckles proof that Charlie had gotten his message.

"Didn't know I was competing for your love," Callum joked.

"Ha. Ha. Laugh it up. You came here for a tyre, remember? Or did you forget between all the teasing?"

"Who's teasing?" Callum said sincerely. "You just never mentioned…her."

He gave Callum an amused look at the way he struggled to give an inanimate object a gender.

"She's a passion project," Riley offered. "About two years ago, there was this estate sale. Not many people showed up since the house was nothing special, so I guess people figured everything was junk. Even the house was a shit hole. But still," Riley pulled the rag from his back pocket and began to shine her sleek black paint, "it was just my luck that I was driving past, so I stopped, and right before they were getting ready to finish up, they pulled the sheet back on, well, her." He stood back to admire the car.

"She was practically a shell. The engine had to be gutted, the exhaust was rusted, the paint was battered and scratched to shit and the interior, I don't even know how it got as bad as it was, but I had to have her." He smiled at the fond memory. "Got it for a steal. Charlie let me store her here and when I have a little extra money or some time on my hands, I help bring her back to life."

Riley thought back to the hours he spent getting lost in his car, his mind would wander off as he would lose track of time, focused purely on the task at hand.

"She was calling to you," Callum offered.

He shrugged. "Maybe. I mean, isn't it every kid's dream to own a Dodge?" From the look on his boyfriend's face, Riley assumed not. "Okay, maybe not *every* kid, but at least the car enthusiast ones."

"Eh…" Callum scrunched up his face.

"Man, shut up." He pushed at Callum's arm playfully.

"No, I think it's great. Really. Everyone deserves a hobby."

"Then what's yours?"

"Oh…nope, not going there. We're not at that level in our relationship yet."

"You can eat cum outta my ass but you can't tell me what your hobby is?" Riley's eyebrows were up to his hairline, he wasn't going to back down.

"Pretty much." Callum shrugged.

"I've met your parents, yelled at them about marriage and children, but you're keeping your lips sealed about your hobby."

"That is correct."

"Okay." Riley went back to work, though he made sure to speak loud enough so Callum could hear what he said over his shoulder. "Just so you know, if you want to get laid again, like, ever, you're gonna tell me." Riley spoke so calmly, as though it was a simple fact, much like 'we need milk.'

The grunts and choked-out words as Callum tried to fight against Riley's statement had him laughing.

"Ugh, *fine*." Callum caved.

Riley spun around, a proud, cocky smirk on his face. He crossed his arms, making his biceps pop against the fabric of his overalls. It was his power move.

"But you have to promise not to laugh."

All Riley did was nod his head, encouraging Callum to get on with it.

"I, ah…" Callum rubbed the back of his neck. "I—" There was a cough.

"I—I ah, collect copiesofthebookthenightbeforechristmas."

Did Callum expect him to suddenly speak fluent gibberish?

"What's that, Mumbles?"

Callum sighed. "I collect different editions of the book *The Night Before Christmas*. My parents read it to me every year on Christmas Eve and each year it was a new copy." Callum looked embarrassed as he continued. "Once I got older, I decided to keep the tradition alive, so, every year I buy a new edition, and look at the different illustrations. Sometimes, I *might* buy a copy during the year if I find one in a second-hand bookstore or something. So there."

Riley thought it was the most adorable hobby he had ever heard.

"How many copies do you own?"

There was a pause. "Forty-eight."

He took a step toward Callum and placed his hand on his warm, freckled cheek.

"I think I just fell in love with you a little more…if that's even possible." Riley pushed up on his tippy toes so he could plant a comforting kiss on his boyfriend's lips.

"You don't think it's childish?" Callum asked with their foreheads still touching.

"I think we all deserve to hold onto a piece of our childhood as we get older. Remind us that the world can be a magical place if we allow it to be."

"You know, if I stay any longer, Deja's gonna think we're up to no good."

"You'll have to come back when Charlie isn't around. You can be the first to fuck me in the back seat." He motioned his head towards the car behind him.

The groan Callum let out was enough to get Riley twitching in his pants. Nevertheless, with restraint he never knew he had, Riley pushed his boyfriend away, giving them the space they needed to cool off.

"Go, get outta here before she comes lookin' for ya."

Callum backed away; their eyes still locked as he continued putting distance between them. The door opened and as Callum was about to walk out, he called back, "Wait, what about the tyre?"

"Told ya, we aren't a tyre shop. Got nothing in the back that can help, but thanks for the visit." Riley winked and then turned back to his car with a smile on his face, a warmth in his chest, and butterflies fluttering in his stomach.

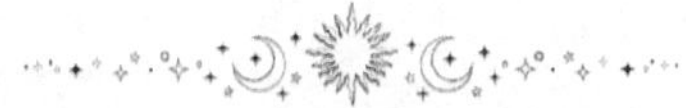

"Ay, Pops. I'm home. You ready to go?" Riley called out as he stepped into the house. The lights were on and the heat was running, which was a welcome relief to the cold darkness he had stepped out of.

"I figured we could get something to eat on the road." He opened the refrigerator to see if there was something he could snack on, but no one had visited the grocery store in a while.

It was only as he closed the refrigerator door that he noticed the complete silence.

"Dad?" He walked towards his father's bedroom. The room was clean, too clean, and the bed had been stripped and made up with fresh bedding.

"Hey, this ain't funny." Riley walked out. He went to check the second bathroom, knowing his father wouldn't be there when he had his own, but he had to see with his own eyes. He even popped his head into his and Noelle's bedrooms on the way.

"Dad!" He was back in the living room, the pain in his chest had him clutching at his heart while he took deep, drawn-out breaths.

That's when he saw it. On a simple piece of hotel stationery that had lived beside the house phone for as long as Riley could remember, was a note in his father's scribbled handwriting.

Son,

I can't do it. It's too late for me and I know rehab will be an experience worse than death.

I know what the deal was and for that, I'll be sure to stay away.

You and your sister deserve a life and you can't have that if you're worrying about your old man. This way you can both move on and forget about me.

I'm sorry. I hope you will someday thank me for what I did instead of blaming me.

Always,

Your Father

"No," Riley whispered. "No. No. No. No. No. No. No!"

His father promised. His father swore. His father...his father...his father lied. Again. His father took *everything* he had. Everything he had worked hard to save so he could make a future for himself.

And now it was gone.

The money.

His father.

Everything.

He felt lightheaded.

He could feel the tears pushing behind his eyes, wanting to blind him. He could hear a high-pitched ringing in his ears, but he fought it.

Riley picked up his keys and got back into his car.

Did he lock the house? He couldn't remember.

His foot was on the gas and his eyes were focused on the road because it was all he could do. If he stopped for even a split second, he would break, and no one would be around to put him back together.

In record time, Riley was parking his car. Again, he may have left it unlocked, his mind was too distracted to remember. All he could do was follow his feet as they led him inside the building thanks to someone else walking out.

Banging on the door with his fists, he probably sounded like a madman. They were abrupt and loud and didn't stop until the door was flung open. Callum was standing on the other side of it, his face morphing from annoyance to confusion, then to worry.

"I needed to see you." His voice broke. "I didn't know where else to go." Riley was unable to hold back the tears.

"What happened?" Callum asked, concerned.

"He—he's gone. Dad. He took everything I had and left…for good." Whether he fell into Callum's arms or it was Callum who pulled Riley into them, he didn't know. But he found himself being wrapped in a tight, warm embrace as he broke down, unashamed at being seen that way.

"Shhh, it's okay. Everything's going to be okay," Callum cooed into his ear.

And for the first time, Riley wasn't sure if everything *was* going to be okay. Not anymore.

Chapter 8

Riley's walking back from the corner store near his apartment when his phone rings. Noelle is calling, again. She called three times when he was in the store but he didn't have the energy to deal with her in a crowded space. However, he knows that there is no escaping her and that if he doesn't answer then she'll keep on ringing, or worse, decide to show up at his apartment.

The beginnings of the cool fall evening are already bringing a chill to his bones. He immediately regrets not dressing for the weather; his only protection from the cold is his thin, long-sleeved Henley. He balances the bags in one hand so he can yank his phone from his front pocket, cursing the tight jeans that he used to love wearing.

"Hey," he answers. Riley sniffs back, the wind suddenly causing his nose to run.

"Hey, where are you?"

"Walking back from the store." He says it as though it's obvious, even though Noelle would have no idea of his plan.

"Did you forget I was coming over tonight?"

Shit. That was tonight?

Guess he was right about her showing up.

He stops walking and looks around as though it will help give him a sense of what day it is or perhaps a faster way to get back home, regardless that he's only two blocks away.

"Jesus, Riley. I messaged you this morning."

"Look, I forgot okay?"

"You forgot? You're always forgetting."

"Then you can't hold it against me then, can you?"

"I can if you're doing it on purpose."

"On purpose? You fuckin' serious right now?"

"Not like—I meant—"

Without warning, Riley hears loud, explosive sounds coming from the alleyway ahead of him and suddenly, he is thrown into a state of panic.

"Hello? Ry?" He distantly hears the echo of Noelle's voice through the phone speaker, but to Riley, it's white noise.

His back is up against the wall, how he got there he can't remember, but he finds the cold solid brick comforting as he uses it as a shield for his blind spot.

Bang! Bang! Bang!

The shots come one after another in fast hits.

Riley's breathing is rapid.

His vision is clouded.

This isn't what you want to do.

Past and present are beginning to blur.

Get the fuck out.

Somewhere between freezing in utter panic and moving to safety against a nearby wall, Riley had dropped his food. When his vision clears, he recognises the scenery of his local streets, with cars passing by and streetlights offering a glow to the neighbourhood. He can see the discarded brown bags abandoned in the middle of the sidewalk. Milk glugging out of the bottle and eggs cracked.

Through the sound of blood rushing to his ears; his laboured breathing echoes in his mind. Eventually, a familiar voice snaps him back to the present.

"Riley! God damn it! Answer me!" his sister's panicked voice screeches through his phone, which he's still holding onto with an iron grip. With shaking hands, Riley brings the phone up to his ear, the sound of his deep shuddering breaths enough to calm Noelle down.

"Oh, thank god." Noelle's voice settles, but not before he hears a hitch in her voice, as though she'd been crying in his absence.

"Noelle?" He can't trust what he hears, needing to confirm that his sister is truly on the phone with him, grounding him.

"Yes. Yes, Ry, I'm right here…I'm here."

Riley nods. With his eyes closed, he listens to his sister's voice as he tells himself he's safe.

When he opens them, he spots a mother pulling her son out of the alleyway he heard the shots being fired from. The boy has a mischievous smile on his face, his hand clutching onto something that Riley can't quite make out.

"I told you not to waste your money on those stupid firecrackers," the mother berates her son as she drags the boy past Riley.

Firecrackers.

Not a gun.

Just firecrackers.

His back slides down the brick wall. Riley brings his knees up to his chest, his arms wrap around them to keep them in place.

"Ry, please. You're scaring me." Noelle's voice breaks through the void. He had his phone against his ear the whole time, though his sister's voice wasn't registering. Until now.

"I…I need help, sis." He doesn't recognise his voice. It's fragile and faint and affected by everything Riley is feeling in that moment.

"Where are you?"

Riley looks around, but he can't find any clear street names.

"It's fine, I'll use Find My Phone," Noelle explains.

Find my…when did he have that switched on?

It doesn't matter. What does is the fact that his sister is on her way. That soon, he won't be alone.

"Stay on the phone, please." He brings his legs closer to his body and buries his face into his knees so he's hidden away from the world. A human ball in the shadows, ignored and abandoned like so many others.

He can hear the sound of footsteps through the phone. His sister's breathing comes through in huffs of air as she no doubt jogs the few blocks to get to him quicker. By the time Noelle finds him on the street, he's rocking himself back and forth, an old habit from when he was young that he thought he had grown out of.

"Ry?" Noelle is soft-spoken, but even through the street traffic, he can hear how concerned his sister is.

When he feels a gentle hand on his shoulder, Riley trusts his instinct to look up and make eye contact with his twin.

"How 'bout we get you home, hmm?" He's thankful that his sister, his other half, automatically knows to bypass asking if he's okay, and skips straight to what he needs; to get home.

His body is still trembling, and as he reaches out to accept Noelle's hand, it's only then that he realises how weak he is; how much energy the incident has drained from his body.

On jelly legs, Riley drapes his arm over his sister's shoulder while Noelle places her arm around his waist. To passersby, it looks like another intoxicated idiot being escorted off the streets. But to Riley, it's confirmation that he can no longer pretend that he's okay. As much as he wants to, what just happened isn't normal.

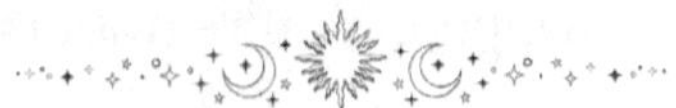

Back in his apartment, Noelle sits Riley on his couch where he waits till she returns with a bottle of water.

"At least you had that in the refrigerator. Everything else is bare," Noelle points out.

"In case you forgot, you did find me on the way back from the store." He reaches out for the bottle of water, hands shaking as he takes a small sip, enough to wet his lips.

Noelle takes a seat on the coffee table so they are face to face, but Riley can't bring himself to look up at her.

"If you're going to say I told you so, don't."

"Do you think I'm that cruel?" Noelle asks.

"You're not cruel, but you're persistent."

Noelle sinks to the floor and places her small, tender hands on his knees.

"Talk to me, Ry. It's me. We used to tell each other everything."

"What do you want me to say? That I'm not sleeping? That when I close my eyes all I see is what happened? How about the fact that I feel hollow inside? Is that what you want to hear?"

"No. Of course not. But if that's how you're feeling then let me help. Let *someone* help," Noelle begs.

"Who? Dr Bech?"

"Well, for one. She is trained in these things, Riley."

He scoffs.

"What if she tells me that I'm crazy and need to be put under psychiatric care? You going to believe in her then?"

"That's not going to happen. You're not crazy."

"No? Then what am I?"

"You're grieving."

He sits back against his couch and lets the tears fall. He doesn't have the strength to hold them back any longer.

"Oh, baby brother." Noelle leaps onto the couch to sit beside him, but she doesn't go to touch him. For this, he is thankful. Any touch right now would feel suffocating.

He pushes the palms of his hands into his eyes in the hopes that it'll stop the tears from falling. If anything, it only makes it worse.

"I just want to forget," Riley chokes out.

"Only time will heal, Ry."

"No…" He moves his hands away from his face and sniffs back the tears and snot till everything has slowed down to a near stop. "No," he says again, turning to his sister so their matching blue eyes are connected. "I want to forget everything."

He's back in Dr Bech's office, reluctantly, but after what happened the other night, Riley knows there is no longer a point in fighting it. He needs help, even if the reason he's been so adamant about not attending the sessions is because deep down he's afraid of admitting that he isn't okay.

Nothing has changed. To be fair, it's only been a little under two weeks since he last sat in Dr Bech's office, but there are still twelve plants in the room. Some seem to have grown a little fuller, and the bookshelf looks to have one or two additions sitting among the rest.

"It's nice to see you again, Riley." Dr Bech sits across from him, her notebook in hand, her pen at the ready. It's sickening while simultaneously comforting, which confuses Riley greatly.

"Suppose my sister told you why I'm back?"

"No. I can promise you nothing was shared."

Shame. Would have made things easier for him.

His knee begins to bounce on the spot. His eyes wander around the room, perhaps looking for danger, or an exit. But eventually, he lands back on Dr Bech's relaxed face. No sign of frustration or boredom, or the desire to rush things along.

Riley takes a deep breath in and as he slowly exhales, he brings up the reason he has found himself back in this room.

"The other night, Noelle had to come find me in the middle of the street. It was dark and I had a panic attack that caused me to forget where I was and how to get home."

"I'm sorry that happened. I'm sure it would have been troubling to find yourself in that situation."

"Troubling? That's a nice way of putting it." He huffs, his sweaty palms rub up and down his jeans while Dr Bech writes her first note of the session.

"I thought…I thought by now it wouldn't hit me like that. So hard, and… out of nowhere, ya know?"

"Unfortunately, that's how panic attacks work. Sometimes we are lucky enough to see the signs before they become too severe, giving us a chance to calm ourselves with breathing techniques or mantras to remind us that we are safe and in the present. Other times, they hit us like a freight train."

"Who doesn't love a good splatter on the train tracks?"

Dr Bech once again takes notes.

"That's not—" He reaches his hand out as though to stop the psychologist from writing. "That's not what I meant. I wasn't referring to, you know, *that*."

"It's okay. I'm just writing notes, Riley."

He coughs to clear his throat and perhaps his thoughts.

"So, anyway. Here I am. After Noelle found me and got me home, it was pretty clear I'm not okay like I th—*hoped* I was."

"So, you had a panic attack," Dr Bech clarifies. "Do you know what may have triggered this attack?"

"Can we not fuckin' call it that?" His voice is suddenly loud and aggressive. Riley closes his eyes and exhales to bring his emotions back into check. "…Please." He lowers his voice to a more acceptable level.

Perhaps his body is still on alert.

"Sorry. I didn't mean…sorry." He leans forward, resting his elbows on his knees as he drags his hands down his face, inhaling and exhaling to steady his nerves.

"I'm the one person you don't have to say sorry to, Riley. It's my job to listen, analyse, and assess, and part of that means taking the hits in whichever way you wish to throw them. Well, verbally, of course."

Peeking through the slits of his fingers, Riley catches the slight smirk on the doc's face. Nice to know his psychologist finds this amusing.

"What if we now refer to them as stressors?" Dr Bech suggests. "Would that make you feel more at ease?"

Stressor does seem less intrusive.

Riley nods in approval and waits for Dr Bech's prompt.

"As we were discussing, what *stressor* do you think may have caused your panic attack?"

The question seems much less accusing now that the phrase has changed. He doesn't get the sense that whatever answer he gives, the doctor will somehow relate it to being his fault.

"Kids were playing with firecrackers in an alleyway."

"I see..."

He waits for a beat before he speaks again. "You were right, you know. About my dad."

Dr Bech crosses her legs and then calmly interlocks her fingers before resting her hands on top of her knees.

"What he did...it was fucked up."

"Perhaps. But as you said yourself, Riley. He was an addict. And addicts can be separated from the person if we choose to accept it."

"What d'ya mean?"

"I mean, you can decide to see your father as who he was before the accident. Before your mother died and he turned to drugs to cope, and perhaps in your mind, you could choose to see it as the day you lost both parents. Therefore, forgetting everything that followed. Or you can see him as the addict he is, and choose to blame his addiction for the person he became, but not remember him for it. You can look at his addiction like a demon that possessed his body. It made him do things he wouldn't have done, but it doesn't mean that's who he is."

He thinks back to their first session, to the way he made Dr Bech earn his answers. He hated every second that he had to spend sitting in this room. He hated how he felt judged and yet here he is, seeking out deeper explanations from the small pieces of advice she is offering to him.

"Do you want to talk about what happened?"

Riley opens his mouth as though he's ready to go down nightmare lane, but the words get stuck in his throat and his eyes begin to glisten with tears.

"That's okay. It's okay." Dr Bech's encouragement is soothing. "How about we talk about something else? Hmm? What if, instead, you tell me about Charlie, will that help?"

"Y-yeah, yeah. I can tell you about Charlie."

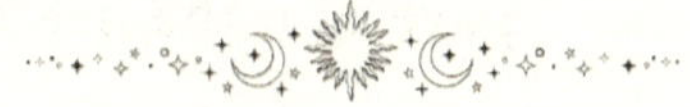

Five Months Ago

The bedframe still had Christmas lights hanging from it, the calm array of colours cast a glow around Riley and Callum while the remainder of the studio apartment sat in pitch black. Riley had told Callum to keep them up, not needing a holiday as a reason to display decorations when they could bring happiness to his boyfriend all year round. Riley was nestled into Callum's side; his hand gripped the back of Callum's neck, while his legs were curled up, placed over his boyfriend's torso. Callum had his arm wrapped under Riley's knees, the other held him close from the way it was draped over Riley's shoulders, pulling him into Callum's embrace. He couldn't help but think how it looked like Callum was holding him bridal style as they lay peacefully on the bed.

Maybe one day Callum would hold him like this while walking through the door.

He hadn't wanted to leave the safety of Callum's bed. But when his stomach growled, or his bladder screamed, he trudged his way to the location his body was demanding it be led to, only to complete the task and find himself back in the warmth of his boyfriend's loving embrace.

It took some time after arriving at Callum's for Riley to feel settled enough to explain what had happened. He shared the cliff notes after Valentine's Day, but with Malcolm lost to the wind, the whole story needed to bear its wings.

"So that's what I did. I gave him the five grand, emptied my account, and now he's gone and so is my money." He hadn't been able to look at Callum while he shared the story. Riley's eyes stayed focused on the loose thread of Callum's green T-shirt as his finger repeatedly twirled it around.

"I don't even know if he paid the guy he owed the money to. Maybe he stashed it or spent it on his next hit." Riley thought back to how he didn't blink an eye at how level-headed Malcolm had been the whole time he was at home. No itch that needed to be scratched. No jittery legs, nervous twitch. No stomach cramps or vomiting or sweating.

None of the signs he had seen in the past when his father was going through withdrawals.

Nada.

Zilch.

How could he be so blind?

Perhaps it was the promise of change. The promise of Malcolm wanting to fix himself had fooled Riley into believing that this time would be different. Or was it perhaps that this time, he wasn't focused? In the past, it had been himself, Noelle, and Malcolm. Now, he had Callum. Could it have been his love for the man who was holding him tight that blinded him from seeing the whole picture?

"I'm not mad," Callum chimed in, an interruption to Riley's thoughts. "But why didn't you tell me?"

"Honestly," Riley took a deep breath in and exhaled before he answered, "because I knew you'd tell me not to do it…and I knew that if you had, I would have listened."

Callum responded with a kiss on Riley's forehead. "You're not wrong," Callum whispered against his skin. "But I still would have supported you had that been what you wanted."

Tears once again began to fall. "I just wanted my father back," Riley sobbed. "Seeing him weak and beaten…"

"Shhh, I know." Callum enveloped him in such a way that he felt like a small child being protected from the monsters under the bed.

Time passed in silence while Riley wept, and only when his tear-stained face felt dry and tight did Callum then speak.

"I know you asked him not to return. But if a part of you wants to find him, I'll help you look." Riley pulled away just enough so he could look up into Callum's green eyes. "I can ask around at work, get everyone to keep a lookout when they get called out to crack houses and such. Places addicts like to hide out in. That's got to be where he is, no?"

"It's his only option. We have no family in the area and Malcolm lost any friends he had years ago. So, he's either hiding out there or with the dealer," Riley explained.

"My guess is, if he owes money, he wouldn't be buddying up with the dealer."

"… probably right."

His body was beginning to protest the position he was lying in, his limbs ached to be stretched out. Riley groaned as he pulled away and twisted his body while his arms and legs extended.

"You need to tell Noelle." The relief from his stretch vanished at the mention of his sister. Callum had messaged Noelle to let her know that Riley was staying at his for a few days, but that was all.

He sighed. "I know."

"Do you want me there when you do?"

Yes.

"No. No, it's okay. I've taken enough of your time as it is."

"You haven't taken anything that I didn't want to give," Callum explained.

"Still, this is between us." Riley sat up, Callum not far behind him, leaning closer to run his hand through Riley's bedridden hair, and curling a strand behind his right ear. Riley felt as though his troubles had been washed away within the confines of this cosy, tender moment. But he knew that the moment his feet touched the cold floor, he'd no longer be able to hide away from what was ahead of him.

"I love you," Riley let out. "In case I don't tell you enough, I want you to know that I do."

"I know. Even when you don't say it, I know. I feel it in the way you look at me, in the way you smile, and how you touch me."

Riley bowed his head to hide his blush, but Callum gently tilted his face up with two fingers under his chin. Riley's eyes locked with kind, soulful ones, as Callum whispered, "As long as you know, Riley, that my love for you is endless."

And he did. With all that he was, Riley knew that Callum's love for him went beyond this life.

When he stepped into the empty house, Riley decided then and there that the best way to move forward was to stop living in the past. This house had them trapped in a constant shadow of what was. He grabbed garbage bags from the kitchen, and though it may have been the anger that was fuelling his energy, it was the boost he needed.

Riley started with the master bedroom. They had rid themselves of their mother's belongings a few years back after one of their father's rages from a come-down led to her clothes being thrown on the front lawn. While the night sky masked their faces, Riley and Noelle had crept outside to bag everything up so they could donate it the next day. After all, whatever remnants of their mother's belongings they had wanted to keep for themselves, they had already taken shortly after her death.

He started with his father's clothing. It didn't look as though any had been taken when Malcolm decided to leave a few nights back, which begged the question yet again of how he was surviving. Next, he cleared out the bathroom. There was water rust all around the taps, the shower drain had soap scum buildup, and the toilet had made Riley gag. He scrubbed the toilet, shower, and sink to the point where he'd feel safe enough to lick it if he was dared to.

An hour and a half later, he pulled the bedroom blinds open to let in sunlight and fresh air. He breathed in the sweet, dewy smell from the start of spring melting the snow on the grass. It was surprisingly warm, with spring arriving earlier than it normally would.

He threw the pill bottles on the bedside table into the garbage bag, along with whatever was found in the drawers. On his mother's side, there was a picture frame of Marlene holding Noelle and Riley on their fifth birthday. He couldn't remember if it was Noelle's birthday or his, being that they were lucky enough to have separate days. The sentiment had still pulled at his heart. The photo had been long forgotten, along with the memories. He was unable to recollect the last time he stepped foot in this bedroom.

He picked up the frame. "I'm sorry, Mum. We tried." Riley sniffed back the emotions that the photo had brought up. He removed the picture from the frame, slid it into the back pocket of his jeans, and then continued to shed the room of all things Marlene and Malcolm.

Another hour passed before he finally stood at the doorframe, looking at a bare room with nothing but a bed and side tables. All bedding had been removed, including the clean sheets Malcolm had put on before he vanished into the night.

Riley didn't sit on it for long, he simply turned and did the same to the living area, taking down photos that hurt more to look at than they were worth. He stripped the couch cushions and loaded the covers into the washing machine. He shoved his hand down each crevasse in the couch to ensure that whatever stash Malcolm had hidden was gone.

Although he knew the kitchen wasn't an issue, he still felt like it needed to be cleaned of 'what was' to make room for 'what is.'

Old food in the fridge was thrown out along with expired cans in the cupboard. Seasonings that had dried and turned to rock were chucked away in the process.

"Ah, what's going on?" The sound of Noelle's voice was the only indication of how much time had passed. The first Saturday of each month was when Noelle was shifted on to open the rental properties for inspection, which is why she was never home till mid-afternoon.

"Dad's gone." Riley didn't even look at Noelle. "This time for good." His busy hands lifted each item so he could search for a date while he continued to explain. "He owed ten thousand dollars to drug dealers that had beaten and threatened him, so I gave him everything I had to cover some of the debt." He stopped, hands resting on the counter where his arms took the weight of his tired body. "That's why Dad agreed to rehab and that's how I ended up with everything gone, including Malcolm." Riley turned to look at his sister.

"He took the money and left. Promised to never return and although the man has never kept a promise, kinda feel like this one might fucking stick." His chest was heaving, air struggled to get into his lungs as his body finally had a moment to rest and catch up from the ferocious cleaning spree.

Noelle stepped toward him. Her heels clicked on the tiles, her pencil skirt too tight for her strides to be more than a few inches. As Riley waited for his sister's tears, anger, and resentment, all Noelle did was take the garbage bag from his hand and ask him how she could help.

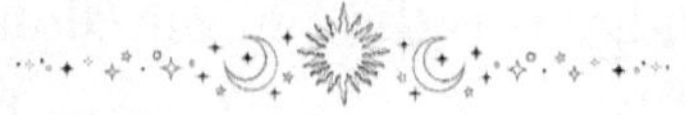

Riley had completed most of the work before Noelle had arrived home, but they had both put themselves in a zone that led to them cleaning out their bedrooms and ridding their closet of clothes that were no longer their style or size. Old memorabilia from his high school days were discarded along with items Riley had kept for a reminder of the better days between himself and his parents.

There were six garbage bags piled up in the front yard by the time they were finished. The cushion covers were dry and back in place, and when Riley and Noelle finally sat, for the first time ever, the house felt like it was theirs.

"It looks so much bigger," Noelle spoke softly. It matched the stillness of the quiet house.

"Feels too big for two people." Riley looked around the living room, ghosts of memories in each corner.

"That's because it was always meant for the four of us." Noelle reached over; her hand sought out his. Their fingers intertwined and they gave each other an encouraging squeeze.

"I would have done the same, you know."

Riley looked over at his sister.

"The money. Had I been the one who found him like that, I would have given him everything I have."

There was no denying they were twins.

He gave his sister's hand another squeeze, words evading him, and the soft smile Noelle offered in return was enough for Riley to know she understood.

They were going to be okay.

They had each other.

They had their partners.

They were going to be okay.

For the next week at work, as much as Riley tried to act like everything was peachy keen, Charlie noticed the minute he walked through the shop door Monday morning that something was wrong. Hell, Riley could never get anything past Charlie, it was a trait that he loved and hated about the older man.

However, it wasn't until Friday afternoon, after Charlie ordered Clint to go home early because Riley had snapped at the kid so many times it looked as though the younger boy was about to cry, that Charlie spoke up.

"Alright, son. Either you're gonna start talking or Imma take a key to the paintwork of your Dodge and draw a nice long line from front to back. Up to you."

Riley linked his hands together and laid them upon his head. He pressed down, the compression felt like a release of tension had been expelled from his body.

"Nothing," he mumbled. "Nothin's wrong." He continued to walk up and back behind the counter, relishing in the way his hands felt like dead weight on his head.

"Horse shit. I've seen Clint do far more stupid shit than he did today, and yet, not once have you bit his head off like you did today."

He was right. Riley already felt shame in how he treated the guy.

"Is this about Malcolm? He already skipped out on rehab or somethin'?"

His arms fell down like limp noodles on either side of his body. The feeling of the blood rushing back into them provided a tingling sensation.

"He would've had to have gone in order to skip out."

"Oh, Jesus." Charlie sighed.

"I mean, who knows? He came crawling back after two months, so he might very well break his promise again, and return home begging for help." He felt emotionally exhausted. Callum was back on night shift, so all they'd been able to manage was quick morning phone calls and text messages before he went off to work and Callum to bed.

"Come over to my house tonight. I'll cook us some steaks, we can talk, or not…but I think it might do you some good."

The offer was appealing. Noelle had been staying at Joel's from Friday to Monday, which left Riley in the house alone while Callum was working. He could call up Jackson and Billy, but he wasn't in the mood for their wild, crazy antics.

"That'd be nice. Thanks."

Dinner felt like a typical man's meal. Charlie served steak like he promised, with a mushroom sauce and a side of garlic potatoes. Riley joked about there being no greens. If looks could kill, Riley would have dropped dead at that moment.

"Boy, doctors have been telling me for years to eat more vegetables and then they do a physical and I'm fitter than the age on my birth certificate. So don't be telling me I need greens, ya hear me?"

Riley laughed, shut his mouth, and enjoyed the hearty meal that was cooked for him.

It was only after the clean-up was done and the two of them were enjoying a beer in the backyard, with a small fire pit keeping them both warm, that Charlie used the opportunity to have the discussion Riley suspected was inevitable.

"First thing tomorrow, I want you to change the locks."

Riley stopped mid-sip of his beer.

"You got to make sure Malcolm doesn't come back for anything valuable and you need to protect yourself from anyone he may be upsettin' out there."

He swallowed. "You think we're in danger?"

"Can never be too careful, kid. I'm sure you'll be fine. But I'll sleep better at night knowing you've at least done that."

Riley took another sip of his beer. The condensation allowed for his thumbnail to pick at the paper label, avoiding Charlie's gaze.

"Did I ever tell you about the time your father used to work for me?"

"What?" He looked up. "No way!" Riley couldn't believe he had never heard about this.

Charlie chuckled. "He lasted a week before he quit. That boy was good with cars but he hated getting his hands dirty, literally."

"Bullshit."

"I swear. He wanted to make money, and was happy to do the work, but said his girl only deserved to be held with soft and tender care. The grease and process to clean it off, well, you know it can start to make ya hands as rough as sandpaper, so, guess he wanted to stop before it was too late." Charlie laughed once again.

"Holy shit."

"See, from day one, he only wanted the best for your mother and he did that up until the end."

"Where you going with this, man?" He wasn't in the mood to go down memory lane.

"I'm telling you because *it* reminds me of you. Or more specifically, you and Callum."

If Riley had any liquid in his mouth, he's sure he would have spat it out.

"That's a visual I don't fuckin' need."

"Not like that." Charlie shook his head. "Mind's always in the gutter, I swear." The older man adjusted himself in the chair so his body turned towards Riley.

"I've seen it, and maybe not with my two eyes but from the conversations I overhear, the way you speak about Callum or how you smile when you talk about him…it's like déjà vu with your parents."

Holy shit, Charlie was serious.

"You've heard it all before, the way this town spoke about them, Mac 'n Cheese. Marlene and Malcolm. Couldn't have one without the other being around." Charlie huffed like he was thinking of a fond memory. "The town labelled them as soulmates."

"Look, Charlie, I know all this. What's it got to do with—"

"Because of what the definition of a soulmate is, kid."

Riley shrugged. "Means we're suited for each other. Fuckin' born to be together or whatever."

"To an extent. But a soulmate is someone who we carry with us forever. They love us and accept us for all that we are and all that we do."

Riley thought he understood where this conversation was heading but suddenly, he wasn't so sure.

"Your mother, God bless her soul, although she'd be disappointed in your father, she'd still love him. And because your father knew this, deep in his heart, he understood that leaving was the only way he'd stop disappointing and hurting his kids. Was the only way he'd be able to live with himself. We carry our soulmates with us forever. Malcolm's been carrying his love for Marlene for eleven years without having her by his side."

Like a wise Yoda, Charlie's words started to make sense.

"I know Malcolm hurt you, kid. I know he fucked up; I know he set you back in life by taking your money, but it's time now to let him go. You've found your soulmate and he loves you the way the earth loves the rain after a heatwave." Charlie rested back in his chair. "The earth knows the rain's there, even if it hasn't been seen in a while and then suddenly, when it hits, everything the rain touches is instantly better. The lakes fill up, the flowers grow taller, and their colours more vibrant. The grass is no longer wilted, and even the air has a smell to it, like new life. That's what Callum does to you, son. That's his power as your soulmate."

"You believe that?" It's not that Riley didn't, but it was interesting to see that others around him believed it too.

"Like I said, ain't got to believe it, I can see it with my own goddamn eyes." Charlie smiled.

A blush on Riley's cheeks had him looking down at his beer.

"My point is, it's time to move on and go live your life. You don't gotta be in the shadow of your father no more, and I don't want you hanging around for the day he might return. You've had your life on pause since you started working for me, son, and maybe that was the universe's way of making you wait for your soulmate to arrive, I don't know. But now's your chance to do things for you."

"What about Noelle?"

"Something tells me she's already got someone looking out for her. Maybe not a soulmate, but a love that is kind enough to keep around." Charlie was talking about Joel, and Riley had to admit, he saw how smitten his sister was with the guy who he'd only had the chance to meet a couple of times.

But Charlie was right. From the moment he turned eighteen and graduated, Riley had been doing everything he could to keep things afloat at home. He worked to help cover the expenses of the house and utilities. He had forgone college and partying with his friends to pick up extra shifts, and to study the textbooks Charlie had lent him.

He spent years being the parent, and now it was time to do things not because he had to, but because he wanted to.

"Anyone ever told you to write self-help books?" Riley joked to help clear the air and move on to a lighter topic of conversation.

"Once you start offering help in exchange for profit, the advice no longer helps each individual, it just turns into bullshit that not even the author believes." Charlie raised his beer, a cheers to his advice, to which Riley offered one back. Both men chuckled away.

It felt nice. It felt as though these moments should be the kind he shared with his father, but he had the next best thing, a father figure by choice, not by blood.

When Riley saw Callum's name appear on his phone, a huge smile spread across his face, like that of a child who'd just walked into the Wonka Factory.

"Hey, Cal. Was just thinkin' bout ya." Riley's voice oozed with seduction.

"You're on speaker with Deja," Callum quickly offered.

"Hey, Riley. Oomph, that voice could do things to a girl. You sure you're gay, honey? Maybe you just need the right—"

"Okay, okay. Stop trying to steal my man. You got your own," Callum scolded her playfully.

"A queen can always have more than one boy toy." Riley heard the clicking of fingers. He wasn't even embarrassed by what had happened earlier, the entertainment between his boyfriend and work partner overshadowed it all.

"Anyway, the reason I was calling," Callum got back on track, "was because I was wondering what your plans are next Thursday."

Next Thursday was Riley's birthday. *Callum knew that, right?*

"Thursday? The 25th?" He mentioned the date to see if it jogged Callum's memory. "Of March?" Hell, best to throw the month in too.

"*Yes,* of March."

"Right. Um, nope. Nothing comes to mind. I mean, besides work and then work again Friday." Riley covered his face with his hand, the pure stupidity of his comment felt awkward even for him.

"Good, there is this charity event being held at The Royal Sonesta Harbor Court Hotel. EMTs, paramedics, firefighters, they're all invited, well, except for those working, but that's beside the point."

His boyfriend was rambling and Riley was sure he heard Deja cough, as though she was reminding Callum to focus and get back on the topic.

"Right, anyway, I was invited and I was hoping you'd be my plus one."

What was he going say? "No thanks, it's my birthday, but since you're busy, I'll spend it alone?"

Riley had heard wonderful things about the hotel. It was prestigious, romantic, and had beautiful views of the harbour, but was it how he wanted to spend his first birthday with his boyfriend? He pinched the bridge of his nose.

"Sure. Free booze. Who can say no to that?"

Deja whooped and Callum laughed. "It's semi-formal. I'll pick you up at seven and I can drive us over."

"Sounds good."

The radio in the rig started talking random numbers and giving off a location that was too fast for Riley to piece together.

"Getting called out! Gotta go," Callum spoke fast.

"Right. Be safe, Cal. B—" The line was cut before he could say bye.

Like every year, Riley woke his sister up with an air horn blaring in her room minutes before the sun was due to rise, and then he shot a confetti cannon over her bed once the sound had shocked Noelle into jolting upright.

Each year, he laughed hysterically, and each year, his sister forgot to go to bed with earplugs.

"You fucker. I swear you're going to give me a heart attack if you keep up with that."

"Please, you're twenty-six. I'll stop when you reach peak 'risk of heart attack' age." He crawled onto the bed next to his sister, the paper confetti littered around them, a mess he at least helped his sister clean each year—he wasn't that much of an asshole.

"So, you want your gift now or later?"

Noelle answered by holding her hands out, palms up, and closing her eyes. Riley placed the small box on his sister's hands and ordered Noelle to open her eyes.

"A matchbox? What the hell, Ry?"

"Open it before you bitch about the wrapping."

With an eye roll and a huff, Noelle slid open the matchbox and gasped at the contents inside.

"Is that...?" His sister took the ring off its bed of tissue paper and out of the box.

"I got the call a week ago. It was a store just outside of town, but a local store owner had seen it and mentioned that I was looking for it."

Noelle slipped their mother's wedding ring back onto her right hand. He hadn't necessarily had the money to buy it, but to see it back where it belonged, to see the joy on his sister's face, it was worth the sacrifice and small debt.

"It's perfect." Noelle wrapped her arms around Riley's neck, his arms enveloped her in return, holding her tightly as they took the moment as a win after the last few months.

"So, you got plans with Joel later?" Riley pulled away, sniffing back the tears he didn't want to shed.

"Mhm. He's picking me up after work. I'll come back here to change and shower, but probably won't be home tonight."

He playfully shoved his sister's shoulder. "Look at you, sleeping over on a weeknight."

"Not like I haven't before." Another eye-roll. His sister was the queen of them. It hadn't gone unnoticed that once Callum had entered the scene, Noelle began to break her own rule of not staying at her boyfriend's place.

"No, but you haven't since dad left..." He hated having to bring Malcolm up, but he needed to get this off his chest. "You know I'm okay, right? That I can sleep here alone and not go into a panic or I don't know, whatever you think will happen if I'm by myself."

Noelle played with their mother's ring, a habit of hers when she was nervous.

"I guess I liked the idea of knowing you were with Callum rather than being alone in this house. It's why I've stayed."

"Stayed?"

With a sigh, Noelle's body deflated. "Joel asked me to move in with him."

"And you said?"

"I said not yet."

This time the shove Riley gave his sister was less playful.

"Ow! Watch it! It's my birthday, remember? You're supposed to be nice."

"And you're supposed to tell me everything."

"Oh, like you did with Dad?"

That was a low blow.

"Sorry," Noelle said as she rubbed her shoulder.

"Me too," Riley grumbled.

"I'm not saying no, I just need some more time. With everything that's happened recently, I wouldn't feel right leaving you here alone, but—"

Riley went to interject but his sister wouldn't allow it.

"*But,* I'm also not comfortable leaving yet myself." That caught his attention. "Things haven't been exactly stable, and you'd still need help paying for things here, so I wanna stay."

"Noelle."

"No, Ry. I'm serious. I wanna stay, at least a little longer till we're both ready."

If that was the only gift his sister gave him this year, he'd be happy. Once again, he held onto Noelle tight, silently thanking her for the sacrifice she had made so that they could work things out together.

"Besides," Noelle began as she kept her head buried in Riley's neck, "with me at Joel's, you and Callum have the place to yourself for birthday sex."

It was his turn to pull away first. "I'm spending tomorrow at a charity event for firefighters and paramedics, so…not sure how much sex will take place."

"Wait, seriously?"

Riley shrugged. "Callum asked me to be his plus one, not like I was going to say no."

"Want me to call him and yell a little?"

His big sister was always going to be his protector.

"No," he chuckled. "It's fine. We'll celebrate while we're there."

He hoped.

At seven o'clock, there was a knock at the door. Riley was in a shitty mood because just as he'd feared, Callum had one hundred per cent forgotten his birthday. Not a single message or call and the one text he did receive was a reminder that Callum would pick him up at seven.

So, when Riley opened the door, ready to bite his boyfriend's head off, he was shocked into silence when he saw the literal man of his dreams standing in a light grey suit jacket that looked like it was made for his body. Callum wore a white button-up shirt underneath, the collar unbuttoned, with black jeans, and the sight alone was enough to make Riley forget he was angry.

"Happy Birthday, Riley." Callum gave him a tender smile. The front porch light shone down and turned his boyfriend's hair a beautiful shade of honey orange. "I promise I didn't forget; I just didn't want to wish you a happy birthday until I could see you and say it in person."

Callum took a step toward him and Riley melted into his arms as they wrapped around his waist and pulled him in close.

"You mad?" Callum asked.

Riley swallowed. "I mean…" He tried to collect his thoughts. It was as though one look and somewhat of an apology from Callum had made him forget how he felt before he opened the front door. "Honestly, I was ready to make you go stag to this event tonight but—wait, hold up, the charity event, is that happening still?"

Callum chuckled. "Doesn't even exist."

That warranted a shove from Riley, only for it to heighten Callum's laughter.

"I'm sorry," he begged, though it was hard to believe through the giggles. "I wanted—" Callum settled down, his face serious, though still smiling. "I wanted to surprise you, and I figured the only way I could do that was to pretend I had other plans."

"You're an asshole, you know that?" With Riley's smile, he was sure Callum didn't believe him. "Could've said you made plans but it's a surprise."

"True, but make-up sex is so much better." Callum was once again surrounding him. It was intoxicating.

"Better than birthday sex?"

"Hmm, guess we'll have to go two rounds so we can compare." Finally, Callum leaned in so Riley could press their lips together. He loved the mix between the soft tenderness and the rough texture of Callum's stubble that grazed his skin when they kissed.

"You look perfect, by the way."

Riley looked down at his black blazer, with a black V-neck shirt underneath and skinny-leg jeans. It was black on black on black, but it was a fashion choice that represented the slight annoyance of having to spend his birthday at the event.

He coughed. "I, ah, I may have been rebelling a little."

Callum was nodding along. "You don't say," he chuckled. "You can change if you want, but I think you're sexy as fuck the way you are."

Suddenly, Riley had an urge to spend his birthday in the house, but he pushed that impulse down, ready to enjoy whatever Callum had planned for them.

It was late by the time they left the Senator Theatre in Baltimore. It was a historical landmark, the oldest working theatre to still be in operation. Walking hand in hand, the moon and sun connected at their wrists, Riley and Callum set out for a night's walk around town.

"It's been years since I've been to the Senator Theatre," Riley explained with a smile on his face from what a wonderful surprise it had been.

"Would you believe me if I told you that I had never been?"

"Seriously?" Riley was surprised. Almost everyone at some point visited the theatre, whether it be with family, friends or the cliché first date.

"I'm serious. My parents came here all the time; it held a lot of sentimental value to their relationship and I guess I didn't want to come here for the first time with just anybody."

A warmth in Riley's heart spread through his body.

"Not even your past relationships?" He was surprised. "It's not like they were short-lived."

"Some should have been shorter than they were, that's for sure. But I don't know," Callum shrugged, his hand still intertwined with Riley's, "guess a part of me knew they were relationships of convenience, not love. Like, regardless of how long we had been together, my heart knew they weren't the one. They weren't the person I wanted to share this place with."

Riley heard Charlie's voice in his head and the discussion they had about soulmates by the fire pit.

Could this have been the work of the universe?

They weren't walking anywhere in particular. It was too dark to stroll through the nearby park, and the restaurants seemed crowded for a random Thursday night in March. Suddenly, Callum stopped walking and turned so Riley was facing him.

"There was one part of tonight that I didn't completely lie about."

"Oh?" Riley was intrigued.

"I booked us a room at The Royal Sonesta Harbor Court Hotel. Charlie has given you tomorrow off work so, if you'd like to continue the evening back in our room, I believe I promised at least two rounds."

"You really thought this through, didn't you?"

"Well, I know it's your birthday and all, but tonight is also kind of a big deal."

Riley frowned; his mind stumped.

"We've been dating for six months." Callum acted nonchalant, but Riley could see through the façade. He caught on to how proud Callum was of that fact, and that it meant a big deal to him. Truth be told, it meant the same to Riley.

"W—six? No. No, that can't be." Riley was sure he'd remember such a detail. "I took you to the barbecue in October."

"But the pizza we shared was in September."

"You're counting *that* as our first date?" Riley asked with sincerity in his voice, the thought heart-warming.

"Of course. I know you've been counting since the barbecue, but I paid for the pizza. We shared a meal while talking about ourselves, and by definition, that's a date." Callum pulled Riley in by the hips. "Besides, the second I saw you, I was hooked. Couldn't get you out of my head, just needed an in so I could ask you out."

"So, what you're saying is, you stalked me and then lured me in with pizza," Riley joked.

"Don't tell anyone." Callum winked. Both smiling, they leant in and kissed on the sidewalk. Patrons walked past as they blocked the path, but neither of them cared.

Riley pulled away first, but only enough so he could speak. Their foreheads and lips still connected.

"You gonna show me this room you got, or what?"

Riley had never partaken in make-up sex, but it sure was an experience he hoped to enjoy again in the future. Even though the thought of arguing with Callum to the point of needing to make up did unsettle him, if the promise of mind-blowing, sweat-inducing, ass-pounding sex was sure to follow, he could potentially live with it.

Callum's naked body covered Riley like a blanket. Their legs tangled around white linen sheets as they looked out the window that offered a view of the harbour. They kept the room dark, using the city lights to illuminate the space, taking their time to explore each other's bodies through touch rather than sight.

"It's almost midnight," Callum mumbled against Riley's neck.

"I kinda like that I get a whole day. Perks of being born just after midnight. I sometimes give Noelle shit by saying her birthday isn't technically till 11.52."

"That sounds like something you'd do."

"One year, I refused to give Noelle her gift until the exact time she was born." He laughed at the memory but stopped when he felt the cool air against his back after Callum moved away.

"Noooo, get back, it's cold," Riley whined playfully. A side lamp was turned on and the brightness blinded him momentarily.

In record time, Callum was back in place, his chest pressed against Riley's back, and his chin resting on Riley's shoulder.

"Here. Happy birthday, Riley." Callum placed a medium-sized square box in front of him on the mattress.

He wiggled around so he had use of both hands, but in no way wanted to disturb the comfort of their position. When Riley lifted off the top of the box, he was mesmerized by the item inside.

A black, stainless steel box chain necklace that had a small 10-millimetre pendant of a crescent moon.

"There is this website that tells you what the shape of the moon was for any given date, in any location in the world. So, for us," Callum removed the necklace from the box and placed it around Riley's neck, "on the night of our pizza date, it was a waning crescent moon, which is the last quarter of light before the moon disappears into the darkness of a new moon."

Riley's hand clasped around the pendant.

"I figured that was kinda fitting since we were both on a path to new adventures for ourselves." Callum snaked his hands around Riley's torso, chin back to resting on his shoulder. "But what stood out to me was how love under this moon usually occurs after someone has turned over a new leaf. That even through hard times, couples know how to console each other."

Riley thought back to September, about the black eye he was nursing when he saw Callum outside the pizza shop. He was thankful that throughout the night, the gorgeous redhead he was interested in hadn't brought it up.

"And here I thought I had gotten away with it," Riley whispered into the quiet of the room.

"It wasn't my place to ask, at least not yet. I figured if you had wanted me to know what had happened, you would have said something."

"Guess you pieced it all together, huh?"

"I suspected it had to do with Malcolm. Not right away, but after we had gotten to know each other a little more, the pieces fell into place." Callum planted a kiss on Riley's temple. "All I wanted was to be enough so that I could hopefully be a distraction."

"You're more than enough." Riley twisted in Callum's arms so that he was lying on his back. His left hand cupped his boyfriend's face while the sun tattoo on his wrist caught his eye.

"Tell me this is real." His eyes pleaded with Callum. "I swear, half the time it's like this is all too good to be true and then I realise that if it's not, then I don't want to wake up."

Callum was hovering above him, his muscular arms on either side of Riley's face. Riley moved his hand from his cheek and gently scraped his blunt nails through Callum's coarse hair.

"This is real," Callum purred. "This has never felt more real and I know..." Callum paused, then leaned down so their foreheads touched and simultaneously, their eyes closed. "I know without a single doubt that we were written in the stars. We're forever, Riley. The sun and moon. Together."

A deep, firey passion burned through Riley as his lips attacked Callum's. He ached to be claimed, for their bodies to be one, and the only way that was going to happen was if Callum filled him. "I want you," Riley panted. "Need you inside of me."

Callum was pulling away and Riley felt himself lifting off the mattress so he could chase his departing lips.

"Hey, shhh, hey." Callum's voice eased the hunger, but only temporarily.

"We're in no rush." Callum looked deep into his eyes. Riley felt the tips of his boyfriend's fingertips begin to trail down his body, leaving invisible marks that he wished would appear to the world. So everyone could see every inch of his body that Callum had claimed.

"Slow down." Riley's body began to tremble, and he opened his legs wider to make room for Callum to lie in between them. "We only get so many moments like this…I want to make sure we savour it."

Chapter 9

"Charlie sounds like a wonderful man," Dr Bech calmly offers.

Riley looks around the room, emotions high from reliving moments from his past that greatly impacted his life.

"It's funny," he begins, eyes still focused on the frames hanging on the wall, "it's like the universe knew I was going to have a shitty father so they put Charlie in my life to compensate." He sniffs.

"Sometimes when we need something in our lives that is missing, we find ways to fill that void. If we're not careful, we can go down a dark path, much like your father did, to compensate for what he had lost. But in your case, you found it in someone you could trust and rely on."

"Guess we can't have the good without the bad, right? Yin and Yang. Sun and Moon. All that shit."

"Is that what you believe?"

"It's obvious, isn't it? The second something good comes my way, the universe has to throw me in the fire."

"I don't think that's the case at all," Dr Bech clarifies.

"You must be on better terms with the universe than I am then," he grumbles under his breath.

"You know, Riley. I hear you talk about the universe a lot. About fate and soulmates. You seem to have a lot of faith in something that we not only have no control over but also have no proof of its existence."

"So? How is that any different to the people out there that believe in God? And there are a fuck tonne of Gods too, apparently. Selfish assholes can't just have one, they all need their own version."

Dr Bech nods along.

"What? You going to tell me that wanting to believe in something like fate and how the universe has plans for us is crazy?"

"Not at all. If anything, I want to understand what part of it gives you comfort."

Riley settles back into the couch, his aggression simmers after his mind confirms that Dr Bech isn't attacking him.

"What I like," he exhales slowly, "is the hope it gives me."

"Hope?"

"Yeah, hope. That belief that when life is shit, something good gets to come from it. That there is always a plan as to why something so horrible and cruel and unjust was thrown my way when there are evil, horrible, corrupt people in this world, and nothing so much as a splinter ever happens to them."

"So, you believe that our path is already written for us?"

"I mean, I got to, right? Because if I don't then—" Riley lowers his voice. "If I don't then it means everything that's happened is my fault."

He reaches for the glass of water sitting on the small table in front of him. It's the first time he's ever taken a sip from the drink Dr Bech provides in every session. Regardless of how thirsty he's been, by refusing, Riley felt like he was rebelling. Proving to Dr Bech, yet again, that he was in control of the situation.

"Under normal circumstances, I'd say that we will continue this in the next session but right now, after what happened and the fact that this was somewhat of an emergency session, I'd like to continue, if you're up for it?"

"Continue how?"

"Well, we could talk a little more about why you blame yourself, or if you're ready, maybe we should talk about what caused the panic attack that brought you back to my office."

A cold sweat breaks out at the thought.

Is he ready to head down this road?

Is he ready to re-live such a memory?

Will he ever be ready?

He told Noelle that he wants to forget, not just the bad but all the good that is connected to it. How will trudging up the past help him move forward, though?

His thumb rubs at the yellow, red, and orange ink that's dyed into his skin.

"It was a week or so into April…"

Four Months Ago

Clint had called in sick, so it was only him and Charlie at the garage. The street was quiet. The shop was dead and so it gave Riley a chance to work on his car while Charlie tended to matters in the back office.

The cherry blossom trees had begun to bloom, the sun was making the days warm enough to wear a T-shirt and nights only required a light sweater. He and Callum had plans to go out for dinner with Noelle and Joel that evening. It was long overdue, and to be honest, Riley was looking forward to it. He had nothing against Noelle's boyfriend, the guy was nice enough, cared for his sister, and wasn't some douchebag that was going to leech off all her hard work. But Joel had yet to meet Callum, and if he and his sister planned to settle down with these two men, it would be nice to know whether they got along, too.

"Alright, son. Time to close up. Imma make room out back for the delivery that's coming on Monday. You close everything down out front and then lock up behind you."

"Can do," he called out from the hood of his car.

When he stood up, his back ached from where he had been bending over for a few too many hours, but Riley was pleased to see his progress as he admired his car from afar. He was sure it would be ready by the end of the month and his first stop was going to be Callum's apartment. Then, with his boyfriend in the passenger seat, a road trip to God knows where. All Riley wanted was to get out of this town for a while.

It was something they had agreed upon the night of his birthday. Whispers in the dark about what they wanted in the future, for themselves and as a couple. Callum had suggested that when his lease expired, he could move in with him, that way it would allow Noelle to move out with Joel and not put the pressure on Riley to cover the costs of the house.

"You'd do that? Move into my old family home when you have a nice, modern apartment?"

Callum had been drawing invisible patterns with his fingertip up and down Riley's back.

"Home isn't a place, not for me," Callum spoke. "It's a person. And in case tonight hadn't proved that to you, you're my home, Riley."

He wiped the tear that had fallen down his face discreetly so that Callum wouldn't notice. After a few moments and a kiss or two, they both then spoke about travelling, and places they wanted to visit. That was when the plan for a road trip had been decided as the first of their many plans.

Riley walked out back to scrub the grease off his hands. Charlie always kept a supply of Fast Orange available to mix with the hand soap so they didn't leave a trail of grime behind them when they left work.

He heard the chime of the shop door ring throughout the garage.

He called out, "With you in a sec!" Riley reached for the hand towel and walked back out onto the floor, drying his hands in the process.

Looking at the four men before him, Riley's instincts kicked in and he knew something was off. His stomach churned, but he played it cool.

"Hey, how can I help?" He gave a nod to the guy in front, the one in a black T-shirt, with a gold chain and loose-fitted jeans. The one Riley could tell was the leader since the three minions had fanned off behind him. Had Riley walked past this guy on the street, he wouldn't have thought anything of it, but when put in a room where he felt caged in, it raised the hairs on the back of his neck.

"My boys and I are looking at gettin' our car modified. Ya know, rims, new paint job, that kinda shit. Word on the street says this is the place."

Riley smirked. "Appreciate the flattery, but the streets are wrong. Only thing we do here is fix engines, maybe change a tyre if we have it in stock."

"Ah, gee, that's…that's a real shame." The guy rubbed his mouth while he looked around the garage.

"I don't know, Johnny, this looks like the place to me," one of the guys behind this so-called Johnny spoke up.

"Hmm. I'm assuming you're Riley?" Johnny asked the question.

He tried not to panic. Small town, everyone knew his name, especially since he'd had the same job for eight years.

"You assume correct." The room felt smaller as the three minions stepped a little closer towards Johnny.

"Then, in that case, you tryin' to tell me ya father's a liar? Cos, from what he said, you're the best in the business."

Oh, fuck.

He couldn't run.

He couldn't call for help.

He couldn't get to the exit.

He couldn't breathe.

"Ahhh, there it is." The man who looked to be in his mid-thirties smirked. "I love that look. The one that says: 'Oh shit, I've been caught.'" Riley was lost for words. This Johnny character was acting more like the class clown than someone threatening, but when Riley saw him remove a gun from the waistband of his jeans, he became catatonic.

"You see, Riley. Your old man stole something of mine." The barrel of the gun was aimed right at him, though Johnny seemed to be acting as though the weapon was a toy, loosely flinging his hand around to accentuate his words.

"Product, with a street value of 100k, to be exact. You wouldn't happen to know anything about that now, do you?"

Riley's mouth opened then closed, then opened again as he blinked a few times at the gun before him.

"Do you?!" The dealer screamed, the friendly banter gone. Johnny's aggression fuelled him as the man stepped forward, the gun now held with conviction and promise while it was aimed at Riley's head.

"N-no. No. I don't know anything about it." Riley felt beads of sweat form on his forehead as he stuttered out his words.

"That so? Cos Daddy dearest said you were the one that gave him the money he owed me, and then a week later, Daddy disappeared along with *my* drugs." Riley flinched when the barrel of the gun was pressed into his forehead. Cocked, the safety off, and ready to be used.

"You better tell me where he is, motherfucker, or Imma shoot you and wait for that lying cockroach to return to town so he can attend his son's funeral." Without warning, Riley was pistol-whipped, the impact causing him to buckle to his knees.

The room was spinning. Riley's vision was fuzzy with a few stars clouding his sight. A warm liquid ran down his face. A firm grip clenched at his hair, and his head was yanked back, forcing him to make eye contact with his father's enemy.

"Better yet, maybe we should go visit that sister of yours. She wasn't too bad on the eyes either, was she, boys? Petite blonde with an ass *that* fine. Man can do *a lot* to a girl like that."

A chorus of cheers, snide remarks, and crotch-grabbing filled the room.

"You leave her out of this," Riley spat out. It seemed his attitude aggravated Johnny further as the man stopped his chuckling and decided to use Riley's face as a punching bag.

The blow was ten times stronger than any hit Malcolm had landed on him. Riley felt his body hit the floor before he could work out how he got there.

"This one has a mouth." Johnny still had the gun aimed at him. "What do we do with people like that, Vin?"

"Word around town, his mouth has some talents," Vin offered up to his boss.

"Well, well, well. Guess a little roughhousing will only get this one going then, won't it?"

Riley spat blood onto the concrete floor. "Trust me guys, you ain't my type." Before he could blink, the barrel of the gun was shoved deep inside his mouth.

"I'm everyone's fucking type. Now you're either gonna tell me where your scumbag of a father is, or you're going to put that cocksucking mouth to work. We can tell everyone that your talents are what caused a bullet to shoot down the back of your throat."

The only way Riley was going to make it out alive was to lie. Lie and hope that it gave him enough time to pack some clothes, pick up Noelle, and get the hell out of town. This is what his life had come to; going on the run because of his father's mistakes.

"Riley? Boy, what you still doin' h—?" Riley strained his eyes to see Charlie, who had walked in from the storage room out back.

No. Charlie. Get out of here!

"Well, seems I've interrupted a party." Even with a gun in Riley's mouth, Charlie had to crack a joke.

Vin extracted a gun from behind his back. "The fuck are you?"

"I'd be the owner of this garage that you fine gentleman have taken the liberty of turning into a fighting ring."

He wanted to tell Charlie to get out of there. That this wasn't his fight.

"That so?" Johnny spoke up. "In that case, how do we know you're not in on this, too?" The gun was yanked from Riley's mouth. It hit a few of his teeth on the way out, and the vibration added to the ache in his jaw.

"Man my age, hell, I don't even know where I put my keys some days, let alone help organise whatever it is you think young Riley is capable of."

"He knows nothing," Riley spat out. "Let him go. This is between you and me."

"No, no, I think this is between me and anyone who is connected to that piece of shit, Malcolm."

The tension was thick, but the silence allowed for the sound of sirens in the near distance to fill the echoing walls of the garage.

"The fuck did you do, old man?" Johnny asked.

"I did what anyone would do if they found four criminals assaulting one of their employees." It was eerie how calmly Charlie was behaving.

Johnny reached down and yanked Riley off the floor. A muscular arm gripped his throat, and the gun was pointed at his temple, the exact spot where Callum had placed a kiss many times in the past.

"This isn't what you want to do." Charlie had his hands held up in self-defence, and all Riley could do was claw at the arm that was cutting off his oxygen.

"You have no idea the things I want to do, old man. Pulling this trigger is easy compared to the other things on my list."

The sirens were getting closer.

Riley's vision was fading in and out as he struggled to breathe.

"You probably have a minute, at most," Charlie offered.

He was surprised that the threat of police didn't cause any of these men to flinch.

"That's enough time to shoot you both and run out the back door."

"Get the fuck out and I'll tell them you ran in the opposite direction."

"Come on boss, they ain't worth it," Vin said.

"You're right," Johnny confirmed. "But I don't like a snitch."

It happened so fast.

The pressure from the barrel moved from his temple.

A gasp of oxygen entered his lungs.

Riley crashed onto the cold hard floor, his body thrown to the ground. The sound of a gun firing three times, and the echoed ringing that followed, made him cover his ears.

Hurried commands and chaotic feet rushed around him. All Riley could do was curl up into a ball in the hopes that the four men would forget his presence.

Loud voices of authority screamed from outside the shop. There were threats of some kind, but Riley couldn't make out the words. He peeked open his eyes to watch the four men make a run for it through the back. It was then that Riley saw the target of those three bullets.

"No. No, no, no, no, no, no, no." Riley scrambled towards Charlie. The man was clutching a hand over his chest, another over his lower abdomen. Blood seeped out regardless of the pressure Charlie had on the wounds. It pooled on the concrete beneath the older man, staining it instantly.

"Lous...lousy shot," Charlie coughed out. "First one...missed me." Blood leaked from Charlie's mouth, and although Riley knew nothing about gunshot wounds, he figured that wasn't a good sign.

"You-you're gonna be okay, alright? This is, this is nothing. This is, this can be fixed." Riley choked out the words while he tried to find an ounce of truth in them, his hands trying to hold the blood within Charlie.

"HELP! PLEASE! SOMEBODY HELP!" he screamed at the top of his lungs. The police barged into the garage and began to sweep the area.

"OVER HERE! PLEASE! WE NEED AN AMBULANCE!" Riley kept his eyes on Charlie the whole time. Even when a police officer knelt beside them, calling for an ambulance on his radio. Riley held his hands over the wounds to help with the pressure.

"Don't you die on me, Charlie. I swear to fucking God." Tears were falling.

"Not a...not a bad way to go though, right?" Charlie's voice was hoarse, his eyes struggled to stay open. "Protecting my son...I'd say that's worthy of any death."

In all the years Charlie had referred to Riley as his son, it was only then that he felt the power behind the title. He felt the love, guidance, and protection that a son was meant to feel from his father, and in a cruel twist of fate, the man he had chosen as a father was now being taken away from him.

"No," Riley sobbed. "No, Charlie." He moved his hands away from the wounds so he could hold Charlie close. "I'm sorry. I'm so sorry." Riley rocked back and forth; Charlie's limp body hung in his arms. "This is my fault, Charlie. I'm so sorry."

Arms were pulling at him. Voices were begging for him to let go, but he wouldn't listen.

"Sir, the paramedics need to call the time of death."

It took three officers to finally extract Riley from Charlie's body, and he screamed and cried and shouted in protest as they did so.

It happened so fast. One minute Charlie was alive, trying to save Riley's life. The next, Riley was holding Charlie in his arms, watching the older man bleed out before him, unable to stop it, to take it away. To fix it. With a gunshot wound to his abdomen and chest, Charlie had begun to choke on the blood filling his lungs while his abdomen bled internally.

In the movies, they made it seem like people have longer to live after such wounds. Some even crawl to cover so they can spit out instructions for their partner to get to safety.

What bullshit.

The reality of it was cruel.

Minutes, barely.

That's all it took for Charlie's wounds to take his life.

It felt like an out-of-body experience when hands pulled him from the garage and pushed him into the back of an ambulance where EMTs looked him over. Riley couldn't recall a single thing they did or any questions that they asked. He had winced when they touched the wound on his head and groaned when they applied pressure to test if his nose was broken. But to Riley, it felt like he was watching everything from a distance.

When the police began to question him, Riley's eyes glazed over and the sounds around him were muffled, as though his head was underwater. He wasn't even sure if what was happening was real. If he even gave the correct answers.

Were the police standing before him actually there?

Were the stitches in his hairline real?

Was Charlie really dead?

"Riley!" That voice. He knew that voice. "Oh my god! Riley?!" He blinked repeatedly, allowing his vision to clear. Riley's mind switched back on, the mechanisms began to turn, and his body was once again in functioning order. Riley took in the chaos around him, a way to get his bearings, and only then did he allow himself to zone in on Callum, who was running toward him.

Tender hands encompassed his face. He hissed, but when Callum went to pull away, Riley placed his hand over his boyfriend's, keeping him there. He sighed at the realness of the touch, not wanting the man he loved to let go.

"I heard the address over the radio. Our rig was too far out to respond but...Jesus, what happened?" There was fear and sadness in Callum's voice. His green eyes swam with concern and sorrow.

"He—" Riley's voice broke the second he tried to speak. It hurt from his screams, and after the shock had caused him to go radio silent, Riley feared that perhaps he had lost his voice altogether.

"Sir?" A police officer interrupted Riley's attempt to explain things. "We'll be taking Mr Lawson's body to the morgue. Do you know of any family or friends we need to contact?"

Riley shook his head. The only family Charlie had left was him; *the cause of his death*. He watched as the body bag was wheeled out of the garage, into the street, and pushed into the back of an ambulance. Charlie's blood still soaked his hands and the metallic smell lingered on his clothes.

"We should get you home," Callum offered.

"Wait." His voice was surprisingly firm. "Where's Noelle? She's not safe."

Back at the house, Riley sat on the toilet seat lid while Callum turned the shower on, adjusting the taps to get the perfect temperature.

"Do you need help getting undressed?"

Funny how words that were, in the past, sexy and enticing suddenly sounded mechanical and dry. Riley stood and because his boyfriend knew him better than he sometimes knew himself, Callum took that as a sign that assistance was needed; and he wasn't wrong.

Hands untied the sleeves of his overalls that had been tied around his waist. It was a relief when his legs were slipped out of the fabric, taking with it all remnants of Charlie's death. That was until Riley looked down, his tank top was no longer white, but a pale pink, with some areas showcasing a deeper red.

Where his hands were generally black, the grease leaving a stain on his skin, they were now crimson.

"Lift your arms for me."

Riley followed the order without too much thought. His top was removed and then he found himself being led into the shower where the spray of warm water attacked his skin. The jolt brought him back from the memories that were replaying in his mind.

He stepped under the showerhead, his eyes closed tight as he gulped and spat at the water that was filling his mouth. Riley couldn't understand how the taste of blood found its way onto his tongue but he was doing everything in his power not to vomit.

When his hands went to rub away the filth on his face, Riley froze, remembering his hands were not clean. No. They held the blood of the man who supported him when his father did not. The man who guided him and encouraged him and helped Riley believe in having a future for himself.

With the nail brush and body wash, Riley began to scrub his hands. The water at his feet changed colour, and remnants of Charlie were soon washed down the drain.

"What happened, Riley?" Callum's soft voice broke through. Riley hadn't even realised that his boyfriend was still standing near the shower door, a watchful eye protecting him.

"Not till Noelle gets here." He didn't recognise the tone of his voice. "I don't think I have it in me to say this more than once."

Who was he kidding? Callum had seen the body bag. Had heard the radio call about a gunshot wound. The only information that was missing was the knowledge of how it came to be—that Charlie died to save his life.

Tears began to fall but with the spray of the water, they were washed away before they could leave a stain. Riley felt Callum envelope him from behind. The redhead was still in his uniform, though Callum didn't seem to care as the water soaked them both.

His chest ached.

The wounds on his body throbbed.

His lungs burned from the lack of oxygen while he tried to gasp for air between each sob.

"Breathe, Riley. Everything's going to be okay, but you need to breathe."

Callum's hold on him loosened but it was still firm.

Riley wasn't sure how long they stayed in the shower, but it was long enough for his sister to arrive and for his fingers to prune.

The silent room was ghostly. Between the three of them, they were a lively group, which proved that the information Riley had shared was serious beyond anything they had dealt with.

"So, what do we do?" Noelle was the first to speak after the reality of it all seeped in, inconspicuously wiping the tears away.

"First, you both have to leave."

"What?" they both shouted simultaneously.

"It's too dangerous for you, Noelle. They fucking know your name and what you look like. Who knows what else Dad told them?" Riley sat up. "And you," he addressed Callum. "I love you with all that I am, you know that. But you didn't sign up for this, Cal. You didn't agree to my drug addict father pissing off dangerous dealers who aren't afraid to kill in the name of revenge."

"No. No, I didn't."

Why did a part of Riley break when he heard Callum agree?

"But in case you forgot, I told you we were forever. Written in the stars. So, if this is the path we have to take, then we take it together. You and me."

Once again, tears glistened in his eyes.

"I-I don't even know what path this is, Cal."

"You're not alone in this, Ry. Malcolm did this to *us*, not to you." Noelle moved off the couch and took a seat beside him where he sat on the coffee table, her arms hugging him from the side.

"What did the police say?" Callum asked.

"Honestly, I don't remember much," he admitted. "Turns out they're aware of who these guys are but, where to find 'em…how to catch 'em…"

"And Malcolm stole from them," Callum confirmed.

"Yep, because he's a selfish fuckhead."

"I'm staying," Noelle declared.

"Noelle…" Riley exhaled out of frustration.

"No. You had a gun held to your head, Riley. *A fucking gun!*" Tears welled in his sister's eyes. "You were beaten and threatened and almost killed. I'm not running away in fear, not knowing if you're safe or alive."

"So what? We're meant to go about our days while we look over our shoulder from here till eternity?"

"If that's our only option, then yes," Callum cut in. "Running is going to get us nowhere if these guys are willing to kill an innocent bystander." Riley winced at Callum's words. "What's to say they don't start going after others in the hopes that it draws you back into town? They were willing to kill you to draw Malcolm back, so what if they go after Jackson, Billy or Joel?" Callum listed all the important people in their lives.

"He's right, Ry." He hated that they had a point. "We have to leave this up to the police."

A thought came to mind.

"Charlie's funeral." He looked to the ground; those two words threatened to open the wounds that had barely closed inside of him. "I bet they'll be there, watching. If we get the police to, I don't know, go undercover or something, hide in the background, maybe they can help. Maybe they can catch 'em."

How did this become his life?

It felt like a TV show where the actors were mediocre cops and yet somehow always found a way to crack the case. When in reality, Riley had no idea how this case was going to end. Would another life be taken or would they get justice for Charlie's death?

"I can't—I can't think about this anymore." Riley pulled out of his sister's arms and, without a second glance at Noelle or Callum, began the short walk to his bedroom. A wave of relief washed over him when his body hit the mattress and only seconds later, he felt a dip in the space beside him.

He could see the night sky out his window, the blinds open, but he had no inclination or energy to get up and close them.

Something he would regret come morning. Their breathing was in sync, which gave Riley a sense of calmness as his mind tried to take that away.

"It keeps playing in my head," Riley whispered. "I barely remember being beaten, my body is so numb I can't even feel the pain but Charlie…Charlie, I can see over and over and over again. My hands feel wet as though blood is oozing out onto them."

"I promise it will pass," Callum offered.

"How can you be so sure?"

"Because the same thing happened to me when I lost my first patient."

Riley turned around in Callum's arms so they were facing one another.

"It was a day or two after I had left my Jeep with you to get looked at. The patient was a victim of a robbery and even though I followed all the procedures and I was focused, she still didn't make it."

It never dawned on him how taxing Callum's job was. Although they spoke about it, the ending to each story had always resulted in a successful save. But life isn't a fairy tale. Not everyone can get their happily ever after.

"How do you cope?"

"By saving the next one. And the next one. And the one after that. As I said, I did everything right, the universe simply decided that it was her time to go."

"No. I may believe that the universe has our paths planned to some degree, but death? Death shouldn't be prewritten. I refuse to believe our time on this earth is already decided for us."

"How else can you look at it? How else can I explain why a mother gives birth to a healthy child, only for it to suddenly die in its sleep? How a little boy on his bike gets hit by a car or how a marathon runner wakes up with stage four cancer? We can't explain it. It makes no sense and it infuriates me, but this is life. And I suppose somewhere along the line, by accepting that these horrible, unjust deaths are the universe's choice, then it's not so hard to wake up in the morning and believe that my job isn't for nothing. When I save a patient, I'm saving the person whose time isn't up, but still needs the assistance so they can keep writing their story."

In all his years, though he had never admitted it out loud to himself or those around him, Riley knew out of all the fears and phobias of this world, death was his.

"How can I accept that his death was the universe's plan and not because he was protecting me? That had he not intervened in the mess Malcolm made, he'd still be here?"

"You don't have to accept it. But believing it will prevent you from falling apart."

Riley pushed his body into Callum's, seeking out his boyfriend's warmth and touch. His eyes stayed focused on the night sky. The clouds rolled by, and with how long they lay silently together, Riley was sure Callum had fallen asleep.

"Do you want to talk about him?" Callum asked out of the blue. "I know how much he meant to you."

One thing Riley had learnt after losing his mother at such a young age was that the best way to honour the dead was to always talk about them. He could never understand the people who closed up and claimed it was too painful to talk about the loved one they had lost. Talking about the memories shared, tears cried in joy or sadness, and the moments of laughter—that's what eases the pain and puts a smile on a mournful face.

So that's what Riley did in his moment of pain; he spoke about the dead.

"He called you my soulmate." Protective arms tightened around his waist; it was comforting. "What we have, it reminded him of my parents, how deeply they loved each other." He recalled holding back the tears during his discussion with Charlie, but in the privacy of his bedroom, he allowed the tears to fall freely as he lived the memory.

"Something must be wrong with me," Riley choked out. "Charlie is dead and yet here I am wishing my mum was alive so I could turn to her for help. So that she could meet you and tell me I've picked a good one." He buried his face into the pillow, not at all ashamed that Callum was seeing him in this way.

"Nothing is wrong with you." Callum rubbed his hand up and down Riley's arm. "Charlie was your family. I can't—" Callum took a moment. "I can't imagine what you're going through, but it makes sense that your grief for Charlie has opened up the grief you feel for your mum."

"There's no one left now," Riley confessed.

"That's not true. You've still got Noelle…you've still got me."

The cherry blossoms were in full bloom on the day of Charlie's funeral. The sun was hidden behind the clouds as though it was being respectful and knew its place. Looking around, Riley could have sworn the whole town had shown up. He knew that was unlikely, but he had never seen a cemetery as crowded as it was that day.

When the priest invited him up to speak, Riley gave Callum's hand a firm squeeze, taking with it the energy from his boyfriend's tattoo. Their wrists and tattoos had sat lined up on Callum's thigh while the eulogy took place.

Riley spoke. He was able to hold in the tears that threatened to spill and even earned a chuckle from the crowd as he shared a fond memory that made the people say, "That's Charlie." He read from the notes he made, and when he glanced up, the only person he could lock eyes with was Callum; green sparkly eyes fed him the strength to finish what he had to say about the man he lost. He knelt to grasp a handful of dirt to throw on the coffin before he walked back to his seat.

As Charlie was lowered into the ground beside his late wife, the crowd began to drift off. There was no wake, no house for everyone to go to afterwards, but Riley was in no rush to leave. Callum stood to his left, and Noelle to his right, and in his mind was a silent prayer that the people who did this got what was coming to them.

It only took a week for the garage to no longer be declared a crime scene. When Riley arrived to open the shop, Clint was already waiting. They nodded at each other but offered no pleasantries.

They walked inside and everything felt off. The smell was no longer welcoming, the air felt thick, and even with the sun shining in and the lights turned on, there was a dullness to the garage that had never been there before.

Charlie's blood was still stained into the concrete. A colour more brown than red, which allowed Riley to pretend it was an oil stain until he Googled how to scrub the area clean.

"Where do we start, Boss?"

Riley spun around. *Boss?* No. No, this place would forever be Charlie's.

"Don't call me that." There was no heat behind his request, but Riley caught the way Clint seized up.

He walked a few steps toward Clint and pulled him into a hug, his hand holding the kid's neck as he drew the younger boy into his shoulder. Riley's other hand wrapped tightly around Clint's back.

"He was proud of you. You did good. Don't ever doubt that." It dawned on Riley that it was the first time he had ever complimented Clint, and although he said it because he knew that's what the apprentice needed to hear, he had meant every word.

They eventually separated. Both men sniffed and wiped at their faces, not acknowledging the emotions they had revealed to one another.

"Right. So, I guess we—" A cough from the front entrance interrupted Riley's orders. He watched as some Ivy League kid in a suit walked towards him.

"Hello, my name is Duncan. I'm from the Bank of America." He held his hand out, which Riley shook.

"I'm so sorry for your loss, gentleman." Duncan was still shaking Riley's hand.

"Ah, thanks." Riley pulled his hand away. "I'm sorry, but we're not taking on any new customers at the moment so if y—"

"Oh, no. No. Sorry." Duncan motioned to a document in his hand. "As I mentioned, I'm from the Bank of America. Upon learning of Mr Lawson's passing, I came here to inform you that Rising Sun Motors is now no longer in operation."

"I'm sorry, what?" Riley may have been shorter than Duncan, but he stood taller from the way he held his head high and pushed his chest out.

Duncan coughed. "Um, you see…Mr Lawson's business is now part of the deceased's estate and as Mr Lawson had no will, or living family or relatives to distribute ownership to, Bank America will be liquidating the business to cover the remaining debt that Mr Lawson owed."

His head was spinning.

This couldn't be happening.

And although everything this Duncan guy had said sounded accurate, Riley wanted to fight it.

"So, what you're saying is, if someone were to pay off Charlie's debt, then they could own this garage?"

"Well, typically it's more complicated than that but, I suppose logistically, yes, that is correct."

"Okay, great. How much he owe? Shouldn't be too bad since he's had this business for over thirty years."

"A hundred and fifty thousand."

Impossible.

"Bullshit. No way. That's—"

"I'm afraid so. Mr Lawson took out a loan on his business five years ago to help with," Duncan opened the document in his hand to do a quick read-through, "renovations on his house, it seems."

Riley cursed. The renovations from when his insurance wouldn't cover the damage to his basement. It had flooded during the storm they endured many moons ago. Charlie needed an additional cover that he hadn't taken out or updated his policy with.

"Fuck." Riley ran his hand down his face.

There was no way he could make that repayment. A loan of that size wouldn't be approved considering he had no money in his account. Or knowledge of whether he'd be able to make the repayments because Riley had no idea what profit margin the shop was pulling in.

Fighting this seemed like a losing battle, one he did not have the energy for.

"How long we got?"

"Thirty days from the day Mr Lawson passed. Then whatever is left inside this building will be the property of the estate."

The paper that Duncan handed to him was Riley's official notice. He looked at it as though it was a life sentence. This place was all he knew. All he'd ever wanted to know. And in the blink of an eye, it was disappearing from under him.

This wasn't Charlie's fault. He hadn't planned on being a victim of the fucked-up Maddox family drama, but Riley was positive that had Charlie known it was his last day on Earth, the wise man wouldn't have let his legacy to this town be buried along with him.

A chime indicated that Duncan had opened the door and left. Typical. Banks take what they want but never care about the lives they were tipping upside down. Riley walked toward the counter where he took a seat behind the desk, papers still left in their place, post-it notes in Charlie's handwriting regarding calls to be made or stock to be checked.

"So that's it? We can't fight it?" Clint asked.

"Not unless you got that sorta money lying around." There was silence. "Didn't think so."

Riley deflated. "Go home, Clint. I'll check the books, see if there's any way I can pay you, but good chance the bank has frozen the accounts, so, best you start looking around for another job."

"What about you?"

Good question.

What about him?

Chapter 10

"Riley?"

"Hmm?" His gaze shifts from the bird sitting outside on the window ledge, back to Dr Bech.

"Where'd you go just then?"

"Go?"

"Well, I asked you a question three times before you acknowledged my presence." Dr Bech didn't sound annoyed, more so curious, concerned even.

"Sorry. Guess I wasn't listening."

"Wasn't listening or lost in a memory?"

He shrugs. "Both."

"How did you cope after our last session? I can't imagine it would have been easy reliving Charlie's accident."

He tries not to scoff at her use of the word accident. Instead, Riley picks at his cuticles, taking his time.

"It sometimes doesn't feel real." He can hear the scratching of the pen against Dr Bech's notebook, glaringly loud within the small space. "I have moments where I wake up and get confused when

I don't see overalls in my wardrobe. And then instead of my mind reminding me that I now work at a grocery store, it attacks me with flashes of Charlie's death."

"Does this happen regularly?"

He shrugs. "Once, maybe twice a week."

"Huh." Dr Bech takes a few more notes.

"Is there supposed to be an expiry date on grief, Doc?" Riley picks up on the aggression in his tone and dials it back.

"Of course not."

Riley can sense a but.

"But…"

There it is.

"Considering everything else, I'm not surprised that you're constantly at battle with your mind and your memories."

He watches as the doctor interlinks her fingers and rests her hands on the top of her knee.

"Riley, this is now our eighth session together…I think it's time we talk about why you're here."

"What do you mean, why 'm here? I told you. Or haven't you been listenin'?"

"I've been listening, and I understand things a lot clearer than I did when you first walked through my door, desperate not to share a single word with me."

Riley gives her a look as though to say, "So what the fuck are you talking about?"

"We need to discuss the reason Noelle called me."

He began to shake his head.

"Riley…"

"No. No, we're not talking about that."

"It's time, Riley."

"You can't make me."

"No…no, I can't. But it's the only way you're going to be able to move forward."

He leans forward, the palms of his hands pressing firmly into his eyes. The tears are threatening to fall, and the memory is making its way to the surface, but he refuses to let it invade his mind.

Still shaking his head, he says, "If I don't talk about it then it never happened."

"And if you don't talk about it, then next, it might be Noelle sitting where you are, crying over the guilt of what more she could have done to help you."

"Fuck," he gasps the word, aware his lungs are tight and restricting his airway.

"I promise we'll stop if you need to, but it's time, Riley."

He sniffs, then wipes his nose with the sleeve of his jumper. Snot leaves a trail on the fabric, but he doesn't care.

"Take your time…"

Riley nods at her encouragement. "Okay, let's talk about the time Malcolm came back."

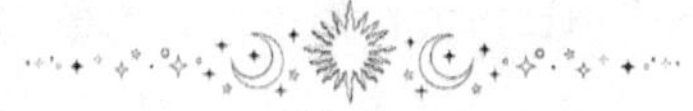

Three Months Ago

"Do we really need to do this?" Callum groaned.

"They're your parents. You agreed to this," Riley shot back, chuckling at his boyfriend's childish tantrum.

"Have you not learnt anything? Saying no is worse than saying yes, especially if you want me to get off the phone so I can worship that sexy ass of yours." Callum made grabby hands as he tried to pull Riley into his personal space. He stepped aside so Callum embraced nothing but air, knowing that any cheeky behaviour would only delay them further.

"Come on, I'm sure we can survive it." Riley took his boyfriend's hand and began the walk from his car a few houses down from Callum's parent's house. "After the interrogation I got last time, this should be a walk in the park."

They didn't have to knock on the front door because Marilyn had already swung it open and lept onto Riley, squeezing him tighter than he felt comfortable with.

"Okay, Mum. Let him go." Callum's words hadn't seemed to register. "Jesus Christ, Mum, you're suffocating him."

Riley gasped when Callum finally yanked the tightly gripped arms from around his neck, but he did so silently so as not to make a scene.

"I'm sorry, but maybe if you brought my one day hopefully soon son-in-law over more often, then I wouldn't have to memorise his scent." Marilyn turned her attention to Riley. "That cologne by the way; I love it. So earthy, like rain on a summer day."

He felt somewhat embarrassed and disturbed because he wasn't wearing any cologne.

"I swear to God." Callum pinched the bridge of his nose. "If you make one more comment about marriage or children or whatever, we're leaving."

Marilyn rolled her eyes. "Ugh, fine. But I'm not getting any younger." She turned to walk back into the house but stopped halfway to look back over her shoulder and said, "However, I have been told I don't look a day over thirty," before winking, turning her back to them and sauntering off. She did love a dramatic exit, it seemed.

Riley and Callum began their descent into the house, following Marilyn's retreating form. Riley made sure not to react when Callum leaned in close and whispered in his ear, "Any chance Noelle can call to bail us out?"

"She's at an awards night for real estate agents. Something about her being in the running for the top property manager of Maryland," he whispered back.

"No shit? She kept that one quiet."

"She likes to gloat *after* shit's confirmed."

"Now, now. All this whispering. Share with the class, boys," Marilyn cut in.

"Just talking about my sister, Marilyn. Promise to share if it becomes worthy of sharing." It was cooler inside the house, a relief from the beating sun that prickled their skin. It made Callum's freckles pop and Riley beat red.

"Refreshments, boys?" Bradley was standing in the front room with two glasses of what Riley could only assume was homemade lemonade. With a nod of thanks, he took both glasses and handed one to Callum before drinking his own and, yep, homemade.

"Dinner is ready. Let me go dish it up. I was expecting you two sooner."

"Sorry, Mum. Had a call out right before my shift was due to end, needed to work a little overtime." Marilyn gave Callum a look that screamed, "I don't care who is dying, you were due for dinner an hour ago."

"Don't mind her. She just hates that she doesn't get to see you as often," Bradley explained once his wife had left the room.

"Dad, I'm here two nights a month and I call every Sunday." Callum sighed in defeat.

"I know. But you're also our only child and if your mother doesn't have you to meddle with, then she turns to me, so buck up and help out your old man. I've got to live with her, remember?" Bradley put his arm around Callum's shoulder and they both chuckled before making their way into the dining room.

Everyone sat in the same spots they were in last time, the table lined with enough food to feed at least ten people.

"Are we expecting more guests, Mum?"

"No? Why? Is it not enough?" Marilyn turned toward Bradley. "I told you I should have also made the paella. Who doesn't like rice?"

"Dear, I'm sure everyone would have loved it, but I do think we have enough."

"Your son doesn't think so."

"Actually, I do. That was kinda the whole point of my question." Callum looked around. "Is everything okay? You're not stuffing me with food and then springing me with news of a divorce or cancer or something, are you?"

"What?! Can't a mother take care of her child?" Marilyn began to dish up everyone's plates, a heaping so high that Riley was glad he had forgotten to eat lunch.

There was silence for only a minute as everyone took their first mouthful, and then Marilyn was back to playing twenty questions.

"So, Riley. How are you? Every time Callum visits, I've been begging him to bring you but he says you're always busy."

Riley didn't miss the way Marilyn looked at Callum like she was about to catch her son in a lie.

"He's not wrong. I am sorry I haven't been able to join, there's been…a situation with my family that needed my attention and, I guess, looking for a new job has taken precedence."

The gasp that fell from the woman's mouth caused Riley to jump.

"Oh my, of course. How could I forget, you poor thing." Marilyn stood and rushed over towards him.

"No, no that's alri—" Riley was once again having the life hugged out of him, unable to finish his sentence, and also curious where Marilyn hid her strength.

"That must have been so terrifying. I couldn't believe it when Callum told me someone tried to rob Rising Sun Motors. I mean, does this town not have any dignity left?"

"Okay, let's sit back down so we can all eat," Bradley requested as he peeled Marilyn away. Riley quickly looked over at Callum.

A wink from his boyfriend told him that he'd hidden the truth from his family intentionally, whether to protect Riley or to avoid making him feel embarrassed or guilty. Either way, he loved Callum even more for it.

"Police know who did it, but they're having trouble finding the guys." He shoved a forkful of potato salad in his mouth.

"You're so brave. I couldn't imagine being held hostage. When Callum told us, the poor baby broke down. He was so scared of losing you."

It's not that they hadn't spoken about what Riley had been through. Once the pain of Charlie's passing had simmered, it gave him a chance to process what had gone down and opened up another influx of emotions Riley hadn't even taken into account, which gave Callum a chance to voice his own fears.

They worked through it together, slowly, the fear of death knocking at the door after being faced with it. However, hearing Marilyn voice how distraught Callum was, to the point that his boyfriend turned to his mother for support, caused a tightening around his chest.

"And Charlie." Marilyn placed a hand over her heart, and another over her mouth. "He didn't deserve to go like that. Ugh, so sad."

Honestly, Riley couldn't make out if Callum's mum was genuinely sorry or acting the role, but the mere mention of Charlie had Riley's throat closing up and tears springing to his eyes.

"I thought I said not to bring it up," Callum bit back.

"Cal, no, it's fine." Riley tried to calm his boyfriend.

"It's not fine." Callum had reached for his hand and gripped it tightly while giving Marilyn a look Riley had never seen on his boyfriend's face before; a line had been crossed.

"Riley, I'm sorry. I didn't mean to upset you. I simply wanted to show my deepest sympathies for your employer."

"Family," Riley corrected.

"I'm sorry?" Marilyn asked.

"Charlie is…*was* family. Not just my boss." He sniffed, using his thumb to scratch at his nose to mask his emotions, but it was too late. "Excuse me." He stood and made his way to the bathroom.

Locking the door behind him, Riley walked over to the basin and ran the cold water for a few seconds. He cupped his hands under the tap and allowed the water to pool in his hands, watching with fascination as the liquid flowed over the top and ran down his skin, creating a waterfall. It was so freeing, the way water could move however it wanted with no consequences.

Riley pulled his hands apart and the liquid seeped through the smallest of gaps and gushed down the drain. He wasn't sure what possessed him to bend down and place his head under the faucet, but the instant rush of cold water sent a shiver through his body and cooled every part of him that had heated up during the conversation he escaped from.

With the slightest movement, the water dribbled down his forehead, along his nose and then into the drain. It was calm. Refreshing. Perhaps if he put a plug in the sink and then allowed the bowl to fill, he could—

A knock at the door startled him.

"Riley?" Callum's voice eased the rapid thumping of his heart. He turned off the tap and looked up. Remnants of the water trickled down his back and onto the collar of his shirt.

Another knock filtered through the silence.

"You okay in there?"

He grabbed for the hand towel and scrubbed his hair dry, attempting to style it with whatever gel was left. When a third, anxious knock filled the room, Riley swung the door open and deflated from the concerned look on Callum's face.

"Say the word and we'll leave." Callum's hand cupped the side of his face, fingers playing with the strands of hair tucked behind his ear. The sudden confusion on Callum's face was enough for Riley to know that his hair was still damp.

"She doesn't know when to keep her mouth shut. Or when to mind her own business." Callum spoke of Marilyn as though she wasn't his mother.

"She's also your mother, who was no doubt concerned about your safety. What if you had been in the shop when it happened? What if that gun had been pointed at you? She would have blamed me. *I* would be blaming me, just like I do for Charlie."

The hand on his cheek moved to the back of his neck, where Callum gripped Riley and pulled him so their bodies clashed together. Their arms clutching each other, seeking comfort.

"I wasn't there. So don't blame yourself for a situation that doesn't exist."

What Riley heard was, "Don't blame yourself," and holy fuck was he trying.

He exhaled. "As much as I want to leave, we don't need her holding something else over our heads so, come on, let's finish dinner," Riley offered.

"You sure? I feel like this is the perfect excuse to bail."

"And then we'll be asked to come back next week instead of next month."

"Oh, she'll be asking us back next week even if we do stay." Callum's little eye roll and smirk brought Riley out of his slump, a light chuckle breaking out between them both.

"I promise I'm not going to push," Callum dropped his voice as he leaned in to rest their foreheads together, "but do I need to be worried about you?"

Riley had to think it over before he felt confident enough to give his answer.

"You don't need to be worried," Riley whispered back. "But I need you to help bring me back sometimes, remind me that I'm here, that we're here."

"Don't you remember?" Callum paused. "The sun loved the moon so much that he died every night to let him breathe." He pressed a kiss to Riley's forehead. "Let me help you breathe."

Riley took in a deep breath and felt his lungs expand in a way they hadn't for over a month. He no longer felt as though he was drowning.

"Come on, you can watch my mum squirm after I bit her head off while you were in here." Callum took his hand but waited till Riley was ready to take the first step out of the bathroom and back into the role of socialising boyfriend.

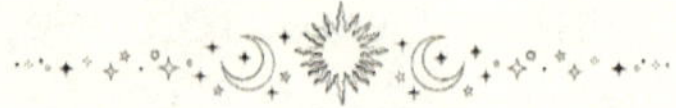

"Will you still love me if I never get a job and I start mooching off o' ya?" Riley looked up at the wooden beams of Callum's ceiling while his head rested on his boyfriend's lap.

"So, I'd be like your sugar daddy?"

"I mean, only if you can start buying me fancy things and taking me out on lavish dates and luxury holidays."

"Hmm, guess I better put in for more overtime."

They both laughed, hands swatted at each other to make up for the playful banter.

"You know I'll help, but I'm sure you'll find a job soon."

"It's almost summer break, all the jobs have been filled by the school kids who are a lot cheaper to pay than someone my age."

"What about another garage?"

"No." His voice was stern. "No," he said it again, softer. "I don't think I'm ready for that. Wouldn't feel right, ya know? Charlie taught me everything I know and working for someone else, most of the time they have their own way of doing things and I just…I can't."

Long slender fingers began to massage his scalp as they ran through his hair. On reflex, Riley closed his eyes and took in the sensation.

"I get it." Riley knew in his heart that Callum did. "Give it some time. Put the word out. This town knows you; they love you. I'm sure you'll find something."

He appreciated Callum's positivity, but that didn't stop the small voice in the back of his mind from telling him that one day, those words wouldn't be true.

"Worse case, I could sell the Dodge." Just saying the words made him nauseous.

"I'd rather sell photos of my feet before you're forced to sell your car," Callum assured him.

"You'd do that for me?"

"Course." Callum shrugged. "I'm sure someone out there will get off on my big, freckled feet. Maybe they'd like an unwashed sock or two that I wore during a workout."

Riley scrunched up his nose at the thought. To each their own, he supposed, but he hoped it wouldn't come to that. The storage unit he had rented out to store his baby was where she'd stay, and if it came to him needing to start an OnlyFans to survive, so be it.

"Hey, you never told me, how did Noelle go?"

"Hmm?" His mind was brought back from the thought of webcams and stage names.

"With the award?"

"Oh. Right. Turns out the chick that's banging the boss got it. Noelle was furious. Everyone knew that she should have taken the award home."

"Shit. Is that legal?"

"Doubt it, but would you be the one to jeopardise your job to prove a point."

"No, probably not."

"Maybe I need to start screwing the boss of some corporate job. Get myself a nice, cushioned office." Callum was on top of him before Riley could smile and wink at him. The redhead had his wrists gripped tightly and pinned above his head.

"Only person you bend over for is me." Teeth began to gnaw at his neck, nips and licks made him hiss and moan from the mix of pleasure and pain.

"You saying you want me to become an EMT?" Riley could barely get the words out as his mind was focused on the serotonin boost. "Become the new rookie you train and then fuck in the back of the ambulance on lunch breaks?" He was surprised that the idea was getting him going, though more surprised by the desire that seeped off of Callum.

His boyfriend's grip tightened to the point that Riley was sure there'd be imprints on his skin. He gasped at the way Callum's body gyrated on top of him, the friction of their pants only increasing the pleasure.

No way was Riley going back to school to become an EMT, but he was happy to pretend for the next hour or so.

"I feel like it's the calm before a storm," Noelle spoke out, sitting beside him on the couch with only the reflection of the TV lighting the room.

"We are watching Twister so, kinda how it works."

Her hand smacked his shoulder. He flinched though it barely hurt. "I'm talking about in real life, you moron, not some 90s thriller movie."

He felt the same, though, unlike his sister, Riley was afraid to voice it, sure that he'd jinx himself if he did. So instead, he changed the subject.

"Callum's birthday is two months away, early July." That got his sister bouncing on the couch cushion, her body turned toward him and the movie forgotten.

"Oooh, whatcha got in mind? Another matching tattoo?" He gave his sister the finger. "I still can't believe you did that. Had known the guy for a few months and there you were, getting matching ink."

"It's not matching," he argued back.

"Fine, not *matching*, matching, but it's still, ya know, connected or whatever."

"You done?" He rolled his eyes, but couldn't hide the smile that formed on his face, inevitable whenever he thought of the symbolism behind their tattoos.

"Yes, fine, bore me with your birthday gift idea."

"Well, that's the thing, I don't have any."

"For real?"

Riley rolled his eyes again to shield his embarrassment. "There's so much pressure. Look at all the amazing things he's surprised me with and all I've given him was a Christmas festival and test results."

"Test results?" Noelle looked confused and slightly worried.

"Don't ask." It took a mere two point four seconds for his sister to scrunch up her face in disgust.

"Ewwww. Gross. I did not need that visual."

"Why the fuck would you visualise it?" Riley began to laugh.

"Because I was trying to work it out and then my mind went there." Picking up a pillow, Noelle threw it at him, and the two siblings began to laugh and play fight like they did when they were younger.

"Alright, alright. Truce." He held his hands up to prove he meant it. "Can we get back to the issue here?"

"I don't see the problem. You're great at giving gifts. Case in point." Noelle held up her right hand, their mother's ring still firmly placed on her finger.

"Gifts for my sister are completely different to gifts for my boyfriend."

"Ugh, men. Fine, break it down, what has he given you?"

Riley crossed his legs and leant forward so his elbows were resting on his thighs. As he listed off each gift, he held a finger up to count along.

"Tattoo. Moon necklace. A night at The Royal Sonesta Harbor Court Hotel. Then there was the Valentine's Day surprise." He watched his sister sit before him with a thoughtful look on her face.

"So, he's a romantic, is sentimental…"

"Holy shit, I'm an idiot." To prove his point, Riley slapped his forehead. The answer to his question was right there all along.

"Care to share with the class?"

"*The Night Before Christmas.*"

Noelle looked at him, confused. "Hate to break it to you little brother, but it's May."

"N—" He scoffed. "The book. Callum collects different print editions of *The Night Before Christmas*." Riley gave up explaining any further and instead took out his phone as he looked for copies of the book that would have been printed around important dates of Callum's life. Meanwhile, Noelle went back to watching the movie, no longer needed.

"Oh fuck, right there," Riley moaned into the couch cushion as Callum railed him from behind.

They had come home from dinner, crashing through the front door, the hunger between them too strong for them to care about removing their clothes completely. Especially when a quick slide of their pants would be enough to give them access to what was needed; his ass and Callum's dick.

"Harder, Cal. Fuck me like your life depends on it." He pushed his ass back against Callum's pelvis, sinking himself deeper onto his boyfriend's delicious dick, craving to be stretched and marked from the inside out. A slap landed on his right ass cheek and he moaned into the fabric of the couch.

"Such a slut for my cock," Callum purred in his ear. The sudden weight of his lover's body draped over his back changed the angle of each thrust. "You're mine." Callum's teeth nibbled at Riley's earlobe. "Every inch of you was made to be mine." Callum's hand gripped his dick firmly. "Can feel it in the way you clench around me."

Riley couldn't hold it any longer. The pleasure was too intense. The friction from Callum's hand working his shaft and thumbing over the tip each time his foreskin was rolled down was mind-blowing.

"Cal—" He was panting. "Callum, I-I'm—"

The front door crashed against the wall. The bang frightened Riley and Callum, their bodies instantly pulled apart, jolting their systems. The sight of Malcolm slamming the door closed put Riley on alert.

"Jesus Christ, Malcolm, what the fuck?" The man before him no longer deserved the title of father. He was quick to pull his jeans up to his waist, his dick soft, though his ass ached from the quick withdrawal and sudden emptiness.

"I think they found me," Malcolm spoke fast. What should have been a sentence sounded like one word spoken in a singular breath. It was only when Malcolm's frantic hands pulled at his hair that Riley noticed the gun in his hand.

"Jesus. Put that fucking thing away." He stood in front of Callum on instinct. His arms stretched out to block as much of him as possible. He had hoped he'd never have to see another gun in his lifetime, but perhaps that was wishful thinking.

Malcolm brought his hand down, bloodshot eyes focused on the weapon, and Riley could have sworn the man had no idea he was carrying a gun until Riley pointed it out.

"Malcolm, tell us what's going on," Callum spoke calmly from behind him, and Riley wished more than anything that the redhead wasn't in the room with them.

"They found me," Malcolm stated yet again, legs pacing the small walkway.

"Who?" they both asked.

"Johnny and his boys." Malcolm was using his hands too freely, which was making Riley nervous.

"Fuck." Riley ran a hand down his face. "Cal, call the cops." His boyfriend was already doing it.

"You're a selfish fucking asshole," Riley began to rant. "Why the fuck would you lead them here?"

"I had nowhere else to go, that's why."

"And who's fault is that? You destroy everything you touch, including the relationship with your kids."

"Getting railed by your boyfriend in the house I bought doesn't seem like you're that disheartened by my actions."

What nerve.

Riley could have swung his fist and happily continued to use Malcolm's face as stress relief.

"You may have bought it, but Noelle and I are paying the bills. Keeping a roof over our heads, yours included."

"Good for you. Glad I was able to teach you how to take care of yourself so you didn't end up like one of those brats that mooch off their parents till they're thirty."

"Police said they're fifteen minutes out," Callum interrupted.

"You called the fuckin' cops?" Malcolm brought his hands back up toward his face, fingers pulled at his hair, but all Riley could focus on was the gun that he hoped had the safety on.

"Just give them the drugs back," he begged Malcolm.

"I can't." Malcolm used the barrel of the gun to scratch at his temple.

"And why not?"

"Because they're gone."

"Gone?" The air started to feel thick. "The fuck you mean gone?"

"They're gone, Riley! Okay. Fucking gone. I don't have them anymore and I can't get them back."

Heavy fists began to pound on the front door.

"Open the fuckin' door, Malcolm, or Imma start shooting my way inside." The sound of Johnny's voice took Riley back to the day in the garage. His body froze for a split second as he tried to remember how long had passed since Callum said the police were due to arrive.

Malcolm held his index finger to his lips, ordering everyone to be silent.

It was late at night. The streets were quiet. Surely one of their neighbours could hear what was going down and call for help. Get them the backup Riley feared they may need.

"Open the fuck up!" The sound of a body being slammed into the door echoed throughout the house. "Give me the fucking drugs or I'll use your kids as target practice."

In the blink of an eye, gunshots had Riley crouching to the ground, and Callum's body covered his like a blanket as they hid from the gunfire.

Glass shattered around them.

Bullets landed in the TV, which caused loud cracks and sparks to fill the room. They could still hear the angry voices of Johnny's men. There was another loud shot as the front door swung open. Riley assumed the lock had been shot off as the men rushed in.

Riley had never seen Malcolm hold a gun before and, to be honest, he had no idea where the drug-crazed man had got one, but it seemed he knew how to shoot it. Riley watched stunned as Malcolm shot round after round at the men who tried to invade their home. If it weren't for Callum, who dragged his body off toward the side, out of the line of fire, he was sure a few of those poorly aimed bullets would have landed in him.

The sound of sirens was a relief, though it had seemed to only anger Johnny further in his vengeful rage.

"Fuckin, snake. Called the police on us like some rat."

"Come on, we need to get the hell out of here," Callum screamed over the chaos. They were crouched down behind the wall that separated the kitchen and the living room; plaster fell on them like snow as bullets struck.

Riley knew of a safe exit and to his relief, the sirens were loud enough to be heard over the gunshots. As he motioned for Callum to follow him while they both crawled on their hands and knees, a hiss and groan from Malcolm stopped him in his tracks.

Malcolm had been hit.

"Maryland State Police! Put the guns down!" Their announcement meant Johnny and his gang had turned their guns onto the police, who were using their cars as shields, giving Riley a chance to run toward Malcolm.

"Dad." His eyes scanned for damage.

"'m fine, flesh wound at best," Malcolm croaked. The gun was still in his right hand while his left pushed into his thigh, which was bleeding profusely onto the floor.

"C'mon, we need to get you outta here," Riley ordered. Callum was already on the other side of Malcolm, the both of them putting one of Malcolm's arms around their shoulders to help the older man walk out the backdoor, the only safe exit from the house.

"It wasn't meant to happen like this," Malcolm groaned as they hobbled out back.

Riley could see the door to the laundry, their escape to freedom only a few steps inside that room.

"Hey, Malcolm." They froze. Johnny's voice, as clear as day, halted them in their steps. Riley heard the gun cock, he felt the air around them shift, and as the three of them stood stock still in the hallway, Riley knew there was no escape. "I'll see you in hell."

The two quick bangs caused Riley to flinch.

His eyes closed reflexively and when they opened, Malcolm was still standing, supported by himself and Callum. But the sight of blood seeping from his father's stomach brought him out of his shock.

The sound of a body hitting the ground had Riley confused, and his eyes left Malcolm's wound long enough to spin around and see Johnny's body on the floor. A gunshot to the head, an instant kill, though not quick enough before Johnny had pulled the trigger. It was the sound of coughing and wheezing that brought his attention back to Malcolm. Riley's eyes travelled slowly over his father's bloodied hand, clutching the wound on his stomach. He lowered his gaze to the blood that seeped through the fingers of that hand, the same one that once held him with such love and care. That time felt so long ago, and so far removed from the here and now.

An officer stepped into view and rushed to assist.

Riley's ears were ringing.

Hands were everywhere as other officers stepped in; Riley was unsure of where they had come from.

He watched in slow motion as his father was carried out by paramedics.

Callum's arms wrapped around his shoulder; his body numb while his father's life was hanging on by a thread.

Outside the house, his nosy neighbours were on the front porch of their homes, watching as dead bodies got zipped up and wheeled away. He and Callum were being looked over by paramedics and, once again, he was interrogated with question after question to find out who was at fault. A few of Johnny's boys had survived, their wounds were what had saved them, or they surrendered before they lost their lives to a fight that wasn't even theirs.

Callum was sitting protectively beside Riley, despite the paramedics trying to separate them so they could be examined properly. Eventually, the paramedics gave up the fight and gave them the all-clear to go home; though there wasn't much left of it.

"Mr Maddox?" An officer who looked as though they'd just graduated from the academy stepped forward. Riley blinked a few times before he had the energy to look up and meet the eyes of the officer. "Your father is currently in surgery, we'll have some questions for him when he wakes, but until then, is there anyone we can contact for you?"

It took far too long for his brain to process that he needed to call his sister. Relief at the fact that she had once again been safe during the mayhem.

"Why don't you call Noelle, and we can meet her at the hospital?" Callum suggested gently.

"I-I can't see her looking like this." Dry blood clung to his skin and his clothes weren't any better. But he wanted to get to the hospital sooner rather than later. A street light shined down on them, illuminating the blood that had stained Callum's clothes. Recently, it seemed Riley was a beacon of death, putting the people he loved in harm's way and subjecting them to violence.

"They have showers at the hospital," Callum noted, as though he could read Riley's mind. "I'll go to my apartment, get us something to change into, and then meet you there."

"I can give you a ride if you'd like, Mr Maddox?" the officer offered.

Mr Maddox? That was his father. The name sounded too formal to be associated with Riley.

"Y-Yeah. Yeah, okay." He could call Noelle from the car, though she'd probably arrive before Callum did. All he knew was that his house was a crime scene and the last place he wanted to step foot in.

"I'll wait by the car." The officer pointed to his vehicle and then stepped away, giving Riley and Callum their first moment alone together.

"Talk to me," Callum said. "Are you okay?"

Physically, he supposed so, mentally, who the fuck knew?

"He'll pull through. This will all get sorted out and then we can go back—"

"Go back to how things were?" Riley cut in. "I don't even know what the fuck that looks like, Cal." He pulled the blanket that the paramedics provided them tighter around his body.

"We can work it out together." Callum opened his arms, only to wrap them around Riley, two blankets now warming him. Although it was summer, the extra heat was necessary after the adrenaline had worn off and his body had begun to shake.

"You're my world, Riley. I revolve around you. And after what just happened, if we can survive a shooting from vengeful drug dealers, then we can survive anything, as long as we're together." Callum kissed him gently on the forehead.

"What did I do in a past life to deserve someone like you?" he mumbled against Callum's chest.

"Funny, I ask myself the same question. We must have sacrificed ourselves to some God."

He could hear the humorous tone in Callum's voice. It helped ease the tension in his body.

"Come on, quicker I go, quicker I can get back to you."

As much as he didn't want to, Riley let go of his boyfriend, but not before he laid a kiss on his rosy lips.

People would one day write sonnets about that kiss. They'd write about the way it spoke the words that Riley and Callum couldn't express or comprehend at that moment. How a new world was born through the love and devotion these two men shared for one another. How the heat and passion of that kiss on the front lawn of Riley's shot-up house was scientific evidence of why acts of crime could be an aphrodisiac.

Their lips were red and swollen, their pupils blown, and appendages hardening. All that was needed was a smirk between them to both know that the kiss didn't just say, "I love you"— it was a reminder that they were each other's lifelines.

Riley reached into his pocket, surprised and relieved that through the interrupted sex and show-down, the keys to his car had firmly stayed in place.

He threw the keys at Callum and watched as the man who had kept him going throughout the madness that was his life sashayed away. It was only once the car had turned the corner that Riley put himself in the back of the police car and made his way towards the hospital.

Within the first hour of his arrival, Noelle had busted through the doors as though she was in labour. He had showered and was wearing some spare blue scrubs, and together they held one another's hands in the waiting room.

After two hours, Riley approached a nurse for an update. She told him that they were unaware family had arrived for his father and that they'd have someone there shortly to speak with him. At this point, he had left three voice messages on Callum's phone.

It was close to three hours since he had stepped foot inside the hospital when a doctor approached himself and Noelle, along with the same police officer who had given him a ride.

His heart sank.

He knew something had gone wrong.

As much as he didn't want to believe it, he knew in his heart that the universe wasn't finished with its destruction.

Noelle began to speak with the doctor but Riley stepped away, not able to register what they were saying. The blood rushed from his head, his ears started ringing, and he felt as though his body was floating towards the police officer, on a path that he could not control.

When he stopped in front of the young officer, who held his hat against his chest with a look of remorse in his eyes, Riley's mouth was drier than a kitchen sponge left out on a hot summer day.

"Mr Mad—" He held his hand up to stop the officer from continuing.

"Just tell me if he's okay," he choked out the words. "Just tell me if Callum's alive."

Three words.

"I'm sorry, sir."

That's all it took for Riley's legs to give way and for his world to be covered in darkness.

Chapter 11

Two Months Ago

People say everyone deals with grief differently. Some swallow the pain down and get on with their lives since the world doesn't stop spinning when life does. Those people tend to put on a fake smile and accept everyone's condolences, then break down at night in the privacy of their own homes so that no one can see how much pain they are in.

Riley wasn't like those people. Callum's death consumed him. How was he expected to function like a human being when a part of him died the night Callum did?

The officer informed him it was a car bomb—homemade with a timber that was poorly configured—attached to Riley's vehicle by Johnny's men before the shooting. Callum's body was unrecognisable. A neighbour had called it in when the vehicle exploded out the front of Callum's apartment.

He couldn't remember what followed. Blood had rushed to his ears, making the voices around him muffled, like his head was underwater, or perhaps he was drowning. The room began to spin and his breathing felt laboured. The air was thick; he swore he was choking, and when his legs buckled from under him, knees crashing to the floor, people swarmed around him. Immediately, Riley felt claustrophobic.

"NO ONE FUCKING TOUCH ME!" He screamed so loud the patients behind the heavy swinging doors no doubt heard him.

His vision was clouded. Thick tears fell down his face.

"Riley," Noelle's soft voice echoed through the deafening white noise. "Ry."

He had curled into himself at some point, praying he could shield himself from the world that was collapsing in on him. His head was cradled in his hands, fingers clenched at his hair as he pulled. He pulled with so much force he was sure he'd yanked his hair out, yet the pain didn't compare to what his heart was feeling.

"Ry…" Noelle's voice once again tried to break through. He could hear the hitch in her voice, the sniff of tears.

Was his sister crying?

When he felt a hand on his shoulder, Riley pulled his body away. It didn't feel right. It wasn't *his* hand…it wasn't Callum's.

"Sir, I'm going to need you to stand." A deeper, unfamiliar voice broke through the void.

"Would you just give him some space?!" Noelle barked back, breaking Riley from the fog.

It was his sister's face that he saw first, matching blue eyes; red and puffy, no doubt like his own.

"We're going to get through this." His sister's voice trembled.

Riley shook his head, more tears threatened to fall as he struggled to get the words out.

"I can't…" His voice was barely a whisper. "I ca—" He looked to the floor, wishing more than anything that he could vanish. "I can't do this without him."

"I know, baby brother…but you're going to have to try." Hands that no longer felt foreign helped lift him. Somehow, he had the strength to stand and from there, the rest was a blur.

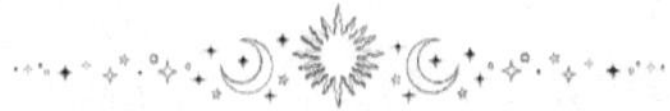

Riley had been holed up in the darkness of the spare room at Joel's house for a week, unable to move. Unwilling to speak. Resisting the urge to shower, even. On top of the gut-wrenching news that the man Riley had planned to spend the rest of his life with was gone, it turned out that Malcolm had died on the operating table.

He wondered if it was humanly possible to only process one death at a time or if he was merely different. Noelle would walk into the room and begin to talk about funeral arrangements for their father, but he didn't care. He couldn't. Not when he saw the sun rise outside the bedroom window each morning, knowing it was another day that Callum wasn't beside him.

"The sun loved the moon so much that he died every night to let him breathe."

When he heard Callum's voice in his ear, saying those exact words that used to sound waxed poetic, another influx of tears would trickle down his cheek.

"I don't want to breathe anymore," Riley whispered into the room. "You can come back now…" He begged. "Please, Cal…the moon is nothing without his sun." His hand found its way to the chain that still hung around his neck, his fingers clutched the moon pendant for strength, but without the sunshine to light his path, Riley knew he would live forever in the dark shadows.

They skipped out on a funeral for Malcolm. His body was buried beside their mother with no service or wake. It saved them money they didn't have. It also kept them from receiving looks from friends and townsfolk that Riley knew they were getting behind their backs. Most importantly, it meant he didn't have to fake being the grieving son.

When the police granted Riley and Noelle access to their home, it took almost an hour before he found the courage to step inside.

Ironically, despite the summer sun beating down on him, Riley felt cold. Not a drop of sweat perspired from his body; dried out from crying perhaps. He looked on and analysed what was left of their family home.

The windows were shattered.

The front door was off its hinges.

The weatherboards were chipped and cracked from where bullets had hit the wood.

He could only imagine what it looked like internally. But before he stepped inside, Riley turned to the driveway. The last place his Toyota Corolla sat before Callum drove off in the death trap.

Riley could listen to logic:

'It wasn't your fault.'

'Neither of you could have known.'

'It was Johnny and his men who did this, not you.'

'Malcolm brought this on us.'

However, none of that mattered when Riley was the one who pulled the keys from his pocket and told Callum to leave.

Why hadn't he insisted on them going to the hospital together?

Why did he need clean clothes so badly?

His mother died in a car accident and his boyfriend, his sun, his soulmate, died in a car explosion.

The universe was cruel.

"Riley, you coming inside?" Noelle asked from the front porch. His eyes were still locked on the driveway.

"I don't know if I can." He blinked, his eyes squinted, and eventually turned back towards his sister who hadn't moved.

"I think it might help."

It might help? The only people who said that were the ones who had no idea how much a person was hurting.

"How?"

"Closure, maybe."

He scoffed.

They hadn't allowed him to see the body. Perhaps it was better that way. He hadn't wanted the last image he had of Callum to be his body, burnt to a crisp. But in Riley's mind, that was the only way he was going to be able to get closure. He needed to see Callum one last time and tell him all the things he had yet to share, afraid that it had been too soon in their relationship, or not the right time to say them.

With trepidation, he began to walk towards the front door.

Who was it that decided how long a person should wait before they said, "I love you"? Before it was acceptable to propose or move in together or have children? Life seemed to have these rules that everyone was automatically supposed to know, and breaking them was cause for being labelled 'too forward' or 'too rushed' or 'too clingy'. But no one knows when their time is going to be up. No one knows when the universe is going to stop writing their story, and Riley had so much he wished he had said and done, but instead, he was left with a gaping hole in his heart

It was muscle memory that got Riley to his bedroom. He ignored the chaos of the living room and kitchen that Noelle seemed to be sorting through. The inside of their house looked like a pile of hard rubbish dumped on the sidewalk for people to sift through.

When he opened his bedroom door, the room smelt musty. It had been closed up for weeks, but under the stale smell was a hint of forest breeze after it rained. Callum.

He picked up a sweater near the floor of his bed and brought the fabric up to his nose. He inhaled and the smell of his lover lined the inside of his nostrils and soothed the ache in his body.

It was as though Callum was standing in front of him.

The scent was so strong, it caused Riley to tremble as a fresh wave of tears formed in the corner of his eyes.

"I don't know what to do without you," he whispered into the sweater. "It should have been me..." his voice broke.

"IT SHOULD HAVE BEEN ME!"

His body spun to face the mirror in his room and as he caught his reflection, Riley's fist connected with the glass; it cracked much like his heart had. He punched his reflection again and again. His view of himself, broken beyond repair, was covered in blood, and he didn't stop until fragments of glass shattered and fell to the floor.

Heaving in deep lungfuls of oxygen, his anger eased momentarily, only for the pain and sorrow to seep back into its place.

Riley had no idea where his life would take him now that everything had changed, now that Callum wasn't standing beside him, going on life's journey as his partner. His equal. His soulmate.

Pushing the palms of his hands into the socket of his eyes, he begged for the tears to stop.

"Ry?" Noelle's voice had him looking up from where he found himself sitting at the edge of his bed. "Do I need to be worried about you?"

Like déjà vu, Noelle's words took him back to Callum's parent's bathroom, where his boyfriend had asked him the same question.

"I can't imagine what you're going through right now, but I've also never seen you act like this...not even when Mum died."

Riley turned his hand around so he could see the damage to his knuckles. He could see cuts, with a few small shards of glass in between each knuckle. Blood dripped down his arm, leaving a trail.

He sniffed. "It was an accident." His sister stepped into the room.

"You could never lie to me, so no point trying now." Noelle sat beside him and took his hand in hers to examine.

Callum was the air that he breathed. It was no coincidence that now, as he sat in the room with remnants of his scent, Riley finally had the strength to open up to his sister for the first time in weeks.

"I haven't even reached out to his parents," Riley confessed. "I-I don't know what to say. How do you look someone in the eye and say sorry for taking away your only child? Sorry that he got involved in my fucked-up family drama and died in a car bombing that was meant for me."

"Sometimes being there are all the words that need to be said."

"They don't want to see me, Noelle."

"And how would you know? You said it yourself, Marilyn practically called you her son-in-law."

"She's probably relieved that the title never became official."

"Then maybe you should look at it from another viewpoint."

He looked up at his sister.

"Don't see it as what you or Marilyn would want, look at it as what Callum would want you to do."

He felt the knife that had seemed to be stuck in his heart since the night of Callum's death twist tighter yet again, it was unbearable. He took a deep breath in and said, "Sell the house."

"What?"

"Sell it. Get one of the guys from your work to do whatever the fuck he has to do, but get rid of it. We'll split whatever we get, but I can't be in this house anymore. It's filled with too many ghosts that will haunt me if I stay any longer."

Not caring about his hand, Riley stood and bagged up whatever clothes he could, not sure what was his or Callum's. He grabbed a photo or two and then left. He wasn't in the right headspace to look at anything else.

His hands were sweaty and shook with nerves. He knew the second he stood outside the house with a bouquet of lilies that he should have gone with his gut and bought the sunflowers.

With his knuckles bandaged, Riley rapped at the door and took a step down so there was space between everyone. He could hear rustling from the other side of the door as locks were turned and chains were slid off. When he came face to face with Bradley, Riley knew in his heart he should have come sooner.

"Hello, Mr Reed." He sniffed; *this was even harder than he imagined.* Before he could continue, Marilyn reared herself behind Callum's father. The woman he remembered as bubbly and well-put together was now a crumpled piece of paper, clenching a tissue that kept dabbing at her swollen eyes as they zeroed in on him.

"I, ah, I know I should have reached out sooner, and for that, I'm sorry. I have no excuse, but I-I needed time before I could find the strength to come see you and give my condolences." He was still holding the flowers. He needed something in his hand to hide how much he was shaking.

"How dare you even step foot here," Marilyn spat. "Our baby boy is gone…and it's…it's all your fault." She brought her tissue up to her green eyes that reminded Riley of Callum. Tears were wiped away only for new ones to replace them.

"I told Callum to leave." Why Riley was trying to defend himself, he wasn't sure. He deserved all the blame and more. "I wanted him safe. I wanted him gone."

"Bullshit. If you truly loved him, you would have pushed him away so he was nowhere near your family's gang violence and drugs." Gone were the pleasantries, open arms, and well wishes that had greeted Riley many times before.

Honestly, Riley wasn't sure what the police had told Marilyn and Bradley, whether they knew all the details or only the cliff notes. But he stood on the doorstep and took the hate because it was what he deserved. There was no point fighting it or trying to explain the situation because, at the end of the day, the narrative wouldn't change.

Callum was dead because he fell in love with someone who had a dark cloud hovering over him since he was a teenager. Callum was the light, and now he was gone.

Riley outstretched his hand to offer the lilies to Mr and Mrs Reed. Marilyn walked out from behind Bradley and took a step down so they were at eye level. He held his breath in anticipation until Marilyn finally accepted the flowers from his hand, though that relief was replaced with a searing hot pain as a hand smacked him across the face, the force powerful enough for his head to turn to the side.

"Our Callum may be in heaven, but when your time comes, you'll be going to hell. Not in this life or the afterlife will you two ever be together, and that's all on you." Marilyn threw the flowers onto the ground and marched back inside, leaving Riley stunned and aching as that invisible knife dug further and further into his heart.

When Bradley walked down and stopped on the same step as Marilyn had, Riley was prepared to be punched in the face. He knew he would deserve it. Instead, he watched as Bradley kept his hands in the pocket of his pants, his face lacking any sign of emotion.

"I don't necessarily agree with my wife's choice of words, but I do hold you accountable for our son's death."

He opened his mouth but stopped when Bradley held a hand up.

"Callum's funeral is tomorrow. Took some time to organise it with how things happened but…even after everything, it wouldn't seem right for you not to be there."

All he could do was nod.

"Eleven a.m. It's the cemetery not far from here."

Riley knew the one.

"Thank you, sir. I'll be there."

"I know you'll be." And with that, Bradley turned around, walked inside, and closed the door behind him.

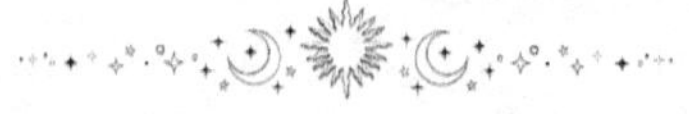

Riley wasn't going to hide. He took his place at the front of the crowd so he could look at the casket while the priest spoke. When he felt Marilyn's eyes on him, Riley kept his own on the stained oak timber. He wondered whether the casket was big enough for him to crawl in and be buried along with Callum.

When the crowd began to disperse, Riley realised he had zoned out and missed the entire service. He'd blocked out the stories and memories shared about the man who was supposed to be his forever. Whatever they said wouldn't have compared to the memories he had created with Callum.

A faint smile, the first he had shown since that horrible fateful night, appeared on his face when he thought of the memories he had to look back on. Their time together had been short, but special because no one got to see Callum the way Riley had. No one truly knew that doe-eyed redhead like he did, and that was something he got to hold on to in his moments of sadness.

Now alone, Riley took a step toward the casket. His hand dragged against the silky-smooth wood and it took all his strength not to open it and look inside.

"I don't think I'm ready to say goodbye to you," Riley began to speak. "I still don't believe that you're gone sometimes. I like to pretend you're working when I can't talk to you, or I tell myself you're on night shift when I roll over to find the bed beside me cold."

His index finger rubbed under his nose as he sniffed.

"Noelle helped me find an apartment. Nothing special. A little run down, but I don't have a lot to spare. Even with the sale of the house, we won't have much left."

Why was he bothering with the topic of living arrangements when this was his last chance to say what he needed without six feet of dirt between them?

"You changed me, you know that? You took me out of my comfort zone and opened up this world of possibilities I was sure would never be available to me." He placed his left hand on top of the casket, his sun tattoo pressed into the wood. Riley closed his eyes and swore he could feel Callum's lips ghost over his tattoo. He was overcome with memories of all the times Callum would kiss it gently, feeding him energy that no drug or aphrodisiac could ever compare to.

"I'm going to wait for you," Riley choked out through the new set of tears. "I'm going to wait until the universe is ready for us to be together again." He removed his hand. "I'm going to see you again, Cal."

When he stepped back, Riley turned toward the workers who were lurking. He gave a nod but didn't turn away as he watched them lower the casket into the ground. It was only when it hit the bottom that he stepped forward so he could look down at Callum's final resting place.

Under his black suit, shirt and tie, much like what he wore the night of his birthday, Riley reached for the necklace around his neck and lifted the chain over his head. With a final squeeze of the pendant, he threw the moon necklace on top of the casket, making sure a piece of him was with Callum until all of him could be.

Whatever he had left at Callum's apartment was lost. It was already July by the time he dared to visit, a little over a month since the shooting. The landlord had already changed the locks and informed Riley that Mr Reed's parents had emptied the studio.

He stepped inside his family home once more before it was emptied. He took the remainder of his clothes, put his bed in the storage unit with his car, and grabbed the small box that was filled with his mother's belongings which, over time, was joined with mementos from his relationship with Callum.

On the day of Callum's birthday, he got the keys to his apartment. Riley spent the day in bed at Joel's, locked away from him and Noelle. Boxes of his belongings were on a truck that delivery drivers were waiting to unload on the other side of town.

But none of that mattered as he lay in bed, shutting himself out from the world and leaving Noelle to deal with the movers. Was it selfish of him? Probably, but today was supposed to involve the celebration of Callum being brought into this world, and all that was left was a tombstone.

He managed to send a message to Callum's parents; a simple 'I'm sorry' was all he could bring himself to write.

He never received a reply.

It was minutes before the clock was due to strike midnight, ending this reminder of what should have been. Using the glow of his lamp, Riley unwrapped Callum's birthday gift. He found an edition of *The Night Before Christmas* that was printed in the year of Callum's birth. A hardcover that had pop-up images on each page. He read the story to himself, closing the book as the clock struck 12.01.

It was the first week of August when he found the courage to move into his apartment, which was not too far from the grocery store he had started working at. Although Noelle was looking at him like he was moving forward, Riley was becoming more numb as the days went on.

He hadn't spoken with his friends since before Malcolm and Callum's death, let alone Charlie's. If not for the reporters, they wouldn't have known what had happened, but a shooting in the middle of White Oak, followed by a car explosion, was sure to hit the news come six a.m.

Riley didn't see a problem with his new way of living, though. He had suffered too many losses.

His mother.

Charlie.

Malcolm.

Callum.

He had begun to feel on guard. At first, the grief clouded his thinking, but once time had passed, it was clear that Malcolm's actions could still have repercussions. So, he avoided leaving the house unless necessary.

Sudden noises startled him and it was around this time that the nightmares started. Noelle had noticed the darkness under his eyes within his first week of living alone. When his sister tried to offer words of advice, he'd snap at her, knowing there was nothing she could say or do that could help. Noelle still had Joel. Noelle didn't suffer the way he did, and although Riley wouldn't want to wish that on anyone, at times he thought it might make his sister understand better had Noelle gone through that loss as well.

After a bloodcurdling nightmare where Callum was screaming from a burning car, begging Riley to help as he watched frozen in place while his boyfriend burned alive, Riley found himself sitting on the toilet seat lid. He held a razor above his wrist, where the brightly inked sun reflected in his eyes. A part of him no longer wanted to wait and see what the universe had in store for him, he was ready to skip the line and get to the end so he could see Callum again.

"RILEY! NO!" Noelle was suddenly swatting the blade from his hand. He heard the sound of metal clink on the bathroom floor, but it was nowhere to be seen.

His sister was crying, tears heavier than when their father had died. But Riley still felt numb, unsure why his sister was so upset.

"Noelle?" *Was he so lost in thought that he didn't even hear his sister enter the apartment?*

"How could you be so selfish?" Noelle sobbed. "You wanted to leave me here with no one?"

The thought never crossed his mind because he knew he wouldn't have gone ahead with it. Putting the metal against his skin involved a drive he no longer possessed.

"I wasn't going to," he admitted, though the lack of emotion in his voice hadn't seemed to convince her.

"Wow, that makes me feel a whole lot better, Ry." Noelle sounded angry. "I can't live like this anymore."

"Live like what?" he spat.

"Like a lone twin," his sister choked out. "Callum died, Riley. I get that, I really, truly do." Noelle had her hands on his knees, her blue eyes peered into his. "But you need help because this isn't normal."

Riley stood up and stormed out of the bathroom, his sister hot on his heels.

"I'm fine."

"How can you say that when I just walked in on you holding a razor to your wrist?"

"You sayin' you never had a moment of weakness where you considered what something might be like?"

"A moment of weakness is when you kiss the guy that's flirting with you when you're out for drinks with your friends, not suicide."

Riley reached for a beer in his fridge.

"Whatever. It didn't happen, so you can relax. I ain't leaving you twinless or whatever the fuck you called it."

"I want you to see someone."

"In case you didn't get the memo, I'm not planning on fucking dating."

"No, I mean professionally."

"What, like a shrink?"

"She's more of a psychologist."

"She? Wow, guess you already had this planned out then, huh? No checking to see what I wanted to do?"

"If I allowed you to decide, you'd be buried six feet under."

"Fuck you. It wasn't even touching my skin." He held his wrist up. "See? Clean."

"If you honestly think there's nothing wrong, then you won't have an issue sitting down with her. If she gives you the all-clear, you can rub it in my face."

"You're not my mother."

"Then stop acting like I need to be." That shut him up.

He didn't want to die, not really. Like he told his sister, it was a moment of weakness after he woke from a nightmare that shook him to his core.

But he was fine. He was working. He was going through the motions. He had lost a lot of people in his life and, because of that, it was only natural for his mind to need a moment to shut down and give him a chance to breathe again.

Who was he kidding, though? Noelle was relentless, and there was nothing he'd love more than to shove this back in her face and prove her wrong.

"I'll go. But doesn't mean I'm going to fucking talk."

Chapter 12

Riley takes a tissue from the table and wipes the tears from his eyes.

"And that brings us to where we are now," Dr Bech speaks calmly. "You sitting on my couch. Your first appointment was at the end of August and I just want to say, Riley, I'm so proud of how far you've come since then."

"Don't have to be so smug about it, Doc."

"Who's being smug?"

Riley scoffs. "You won, okay? You got me to talk, to open up and spill all my deep dark secrets."

"Does that make you feel uncomfortable?"

"Don't like being judged, is all."

"No one is judging you, Riley. What you have gone through in the last twelve months is more than some people go through in a lifetime."

He sniffs.

"Now that you're here, *not* being judged…what were you really thinking the day Noelle found you in the bathroom?"

"Wow, come out swinging why don't ya?"

"You know this is a safe space, Riley."

He exhales and thinks back. "Two things were running through my head that day." Riley flips his wrist so he can look at the sun tattoo, remembering how it felt to hold the cold blade in his hand. His chest tightens.

"I was thinking how desperately I wanted to see Callum again, knowing that it would be impossible except in death." The fingertips of his right hand begin to trail along the tattoo's outline.

"And then I thought about removing the sun tattoo. Cutting it off and ridding myself of the last thing that was connecting me to him." The tears threaten to fall, but he's quick to hold them at bay.

"A cover-up tattoo may have been a safer choice," Dr Bech states, and Riley isn't sure if that's humour he detects or sarcasm.

"Probably, but as you can see, it's still here. As I told Noelle that day, it was a moment of weakness. I haven't thought that way since, not even about removing the tattoo. I couldn't survive him being completely gone." He knows it's only somewhat of a lie. He still thinks about seeing Callum, but in no way does he plan on cashing in his ticket early.

"Do you think you would have gone along with it had Noelle not shown up? Had she not stopped you?"

Riley is shaking his head before Dr Bech finishes the question.

"I would rather live a miserable life alone than know the last thing I did on this earth was destroy my sister." His thumb presses into the sun on his wrist. He can feel his pulse, an even *thump-thump* under his skin. Riley takes a deep breath in and knows Callum is with him, that his sun is proud of him and loves him.

"Our house is gone," he begins to explain, "or maybe it's still there, but it will be gone." He looks up from his wrist, at Dr Bech. "Developers bought it. It's how we were able to sell it so quickly, and not have to worry about fixing it up…probably just land by now."

"You don't seem too troubled by that fact."

"That house hadn't been a home for years. It was a place to sleep. To shower and eat and store my belongings at best…Callum was my home." Memories of the redhead whispering those words to him in the darkness of a hotel room spring to mind.

"Where Callum was, that's where I felt the safest. The most loved. I could have lived in the back of my car with him and I would have been happy because I was with *him*."

Dr Bech puts the notepad and pen on the coffee table between them, something she has never done before, and Riley watches her face turn serious.

"The thing is, Riley, when Noelle called me, the only thing I knew about your situation was that your boyfriend, Callum, had died."

He figures, considering Noelle pushed for him to get help after she caught him with a blade to his wrist.

"Which is why, when you mentioned the phone calls, I began to worry."

Riley tenses.

"Have you heard of auditory hallucinations before, Riley?" Dr Bech continues, to his relief, giving him a chance to process her question.

"Hallucina—are you calling me crazy?" He goes on the defence.

"No, Riley. I'd never call any of my patients crazy."

The use of the word patient isn't helping the doc's case.

"When you first began to share your story, I was leaning towards survivor's guilt."

"What the fuck is that?"

"It's exactly what it sounds like. It's a mental condition that occurs when a person believes they have done something wrong by surviving a traumatic or tragic event when others did not."

The diagnosis doesn't seem too far-fetched. After all, Charlie never should have died, it was simply the wrong place at the wrong time for his beloved friend. And Callum, well, Riley will always believe it should have been him who died that day, not Callum. But as he has unwillingly learnt to accept, the universe, for some reason, has decided that it wasn't his time to go.

"Some signs of survivor's guilt can consist of nightmares and flashbacks. Constantly having the event play over in your mind while you try and determine how you could have fixed it or changed it. And of course, anger."

Check, check and check.

"So?"

"So, let's circle back to the phone calls."

He'd rather not.

"It's rare, but in some cases of PTSD, auditory hallucinations are when an individual may hallucinate tinnitus, a constant ringing or in your case, may hear a voice that isn't physically present."

"Which is it, Doc, you saying I have survivor's guilt or PTSD?"

"Both. The two aren't mutually exclusive, and when you spoke about your mother's death, there were already some signs; panic attacks, anxiety. It was only after the loss of Charlie, Malcolm and Callum that all the other pieces came together."

Riley's leg begins to bounce on the spot, a typical reaction in the doctor's office that he has picked up on. His fingers twist and rub at the digits of his other hand while his eyes look out the side window.

"Riley? Are you okay?"

"Hmm?"

"Were you aware that when a person is mentally exhausted, they zone out to recharge and allow their brain to mentally rest from the overload of information and cognitive tasks it's endured? I notice that when we get to a difficult topic of discussion, you look outside the window, or at my bookshelf."

His thumb rubs at his nose, a trait Riley knows he does when nervous.

"Alright, so I zone out, who doesn't?"

"All I'm doing is helping you understand why you might find yourself zoning out."

He sighs, allowing himself to calm down and continue to hear what Dr Bech has to say.

"You began to guard yourself, Riley. Pushed away your co-workers, Noelle, friends, even. Trying to cope through self-destructive behaviours such as drinking. When we factor these in with your nightmares, trouble sleeping, feeling emotionally numb with no thoughts of the future, they're all signs of Post Traumatic Stress Disorder."

"You sound like I went to war."

"In a way, you did. War is merely a conflict between different countries or groups. You were at war with Malcolm and his addiction. You were at war in the conflict he caused between his dealer, having to be on alert and constantly watching over your shoulder. And, you were at war with yourself when Callum died, a fight between life and death…*your* life or death."

"And now I'm crazy."

"No. Now you're trying to live in a world after the war has ended."

He sinks back onto the couch

"You don't have to be on guard anymore, Riley. There is no one left to fight with, including yourself." Dr Bech pauses. "Including Callum."

His eyes lock on the psychologist's.

"Callum never called you, Riley." Dr Bech's voice is soft, and weary, like a parent telling their child that Santa Claus isn't real, preparing for a backlash of anger. "When you were at your weakest; when your mind and body couldn't take anymore and it needed a release, a chance to zone out, if you will…you hallucinated the phone calls with Callum."

"I-I know that," he chokes out.

Does he, though?

He thinks back to the times he thought Callum had called; always alone. Always in need. The first was when Billy kept calling and he tried to push down a panic attack, back when he had no idea that's what was happening. He remembers thinking how much Callum's voice used to calm him and then out of the blue, he swore his phone was ringing. That Callum was on the other end. It felt so real. He was sure it was.

After the fight he had with Noelle when he burnt his hand, the voice of a well-educated EMT speaking through his phone helped him through the best treatment for his burns. And of course, the night after he woke from his nightmare, only to have a severe panic attack, it was the tone of Callum's voice in his ear that coaxed him back to sleep. It was Callum's soothing murmur, instructing him to hold on tightly and relax into his arms, envisioning they were his, that brought him the most comfort.

When the phone calls were happening, he didn't question it. He didn't end the call or consider why he was having conversations with the dead. Perhaps it was because he didn't want someone ruining that small glimpse of happiness, or perhaps, it was because he was taking comfort in believing it *was* Callum, even if he knew in his heart that it wasn't.

If that were so, why did he tell Dr Bech about the phone call? Was it so she could label him insane? Dope him with drugs and help him escape the pain without leaving this world entirely? Without leaving Noelle?

He feels like a detective who has finally pieced together the puzzle, his mind yelling, "Ah ha!" after working out what all the clues had been pointing at.

"Callum never called." He voices in one breath. He knows this, he's sure of it, but perhaps the happiness that came from hearing his lover's voice one more time outshone the truth; that it was never real.

"Judy Blume once said that our fingerprints don't fade from the lives we touch." Dr Bech's voice breaks through his thoughts. "Callum has left a mark on you that you will carry with you forever, it doesn't have to be a heavy weight now that he's gone. It can be a treasure that only you get to keep a hold of."

A single tear rolls down his cheek. "His fingerprints are burned into my heart. No one, not a single fucking soul will ever be able to wash that away."

"I'm not saying they will. Soulmates, that's what you believed you were, correct?"

He nods as he bows his head to catch a glimpse of his tattoo.

"A soulmate's love isn't the same as falling in love with a person. Your connection with Callum was stronger, perhaps cosmically spiritual, in a way. Your soulmate, as you said, owns your heart. When you described your relationship, it was intense and pure and, at times, it overwhelmed you with how quickly you were falling in love. But you never slowed it down because you believed in the magic that was forming between you both. You believed in your love." Dr Bech pauses. "Is it not better to have one great love for a short time than to live with an average love for the rest of your life; or perhaps no love at all?"

Riley never understood the word *love* until Callum entered his life, that much he knew.

"There is no rule that says you need to love again," Dr Bech continues. "There is no rule that says you have to move on and replace Callum or forget what you two shared. Honour his memory, Riley.”

“How?”

“By living.”

He rubs his hands down his face, pulling at his tight skin from where the tears had dried.

“The road trip,” he whispers.

“Road trip?”

Riley didn’t realise he said it out loud, but now that Dr Bech has questioned him on it, he continues.

“We were planning a road trip after the mess with Malcolm had cleared up.”

Dr Bech smiles. “Where were you planning to go?”

“Anywhere.” He huffs. “We had no idea, just knew there was a world out there to explore and we wanted to see it together.”

“Okay, so do it.”

“You make it sound simple.”

“It is, Riley. Get in your car and go. See where the road takes you and know wherever you end up, Callum is beside you.”

His heart begins to ache.

“I–I don’t know if I can.”

Dr Bech leans forward. “You can. You have that strength inside you and it’s what Callum would want you to do. It’s what Noelle would want, to see her brother living again and not waking each morning with guilt and shame and heartbreak weighing him down.”

"So, your professional opinion is to send me away, with all the fucked-up versions of myself; the panic attacks and anxiety and fucking hallucinations and shit."

"I can prescribe you an antidepressant, perhaps a mood stabilizer, or an antianxiety medication. But many people with PTSD learn to live with it drug-free."

"No, no. I don't want to take anything. I don't want to risk—"

One look at Dr Bech and he knows the psychologist understands.

"Then how about we keep up with our meetings? You can call me. Facetime, Zoom, or whatever works from where you are. You can even look at attending meetings and support groups for people like yourself."

"I came here wanting to run away from you and now the thought of getting away has me wanting to chain myself to your chair." He makes a joke of it, but the sentiment is true.

"I've become your crutch. The thought of it being taken out from under you has your heart racing and your body unstable."

Ding, ding, ding!

"Tell me what you're thinking. Right now. No bullshit." Dr Bech quizzes him, and Riley delivers.

"Maryland is full of ghosts. My mother's memory is everywhere, even when going on dates, a lot of the things Callum and I did together reminded me of her." He crosses his legs by balancing his ankle on his knee.

"Then Charlie died and the one thing I loved doing in the world was taken away from me. I couldn't be a mechanic anymore, at least not here. Not in the town that whispered about the real reason my boss died. Maybe if I opened my own store, sure, but...no way could I afford that."

He licks his bottom lip, "And now...now with Callum gone, the only place I'm not feeling like I'm surrounded by ghosts is in my shitty apartment where, ironically, I'm having conversations with ghosts."

Dr Bech chuckles. "I promise you're not talking to ghosts."

"Maybe we should pretend I am. Sounds cooler than PTSD and survivor's guilt." He tries for a joke; it seems to make Dr Bech smile.

"You're going to be okay, Riley. I wouldn't say it unless I meant it. Will it be easy? No. But will it get easier? Yes."

And for the first time in the last three months, he believes it.

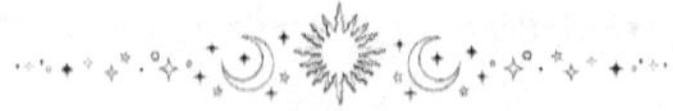

Noelle is waiting for him when he steps outside the building. The sun is peeking through the gloomy October clouds. Riley closes his eyes while he tilts his head up towards the largest star in the sky and soaks in the warmth like a cat on the windowsill.

"Hello, my sun," he whispers into the sky.

When he gets into the car, they begin to drive back to his apartment. Neither of them speaks, and Noelle doesn't ask how the appointment went. As his sister pulls up to the curb, Riley puts his hand on the door handle and turns to his twin.

"I'm leaving." His mouth suddenly feels dry as he swallows and waits.

Tears form in his sister's eyes, but he's surprised to see a smile appear on her face.

"It's okay. I knew you would," Noelle chokes out.

"I can't be here anymore. I can't…"

Noelle nods her head in understanding.

"I promise I'll visit." It doesn't go unnoticed that he chose the word visit over return, the decision already made that Maryland will never be a place he can find himself living in ever again.

Noelle reaches over, enveloping him in a hug that consumes his entire being.

"You better call. Or text. Or send a photo so I know where you are."

Riley can't trust his voice so he nods in agreement. If he waits any longer, he may back out. He'll convince himself that he has to stay for his sister, that even as a shell of a man, he's still needed to make sure his twin is okay.

Silently, he pulls away and exits the car, walking up towards his apartment without turning back.

It takes one day to pack up what he owns and donate it to a local thrift store. Noelle lets him know that she'll sort out his apartment. He takes his duffle bag and shoves in every piece of clothing he has. He plans to work side jobs on the road to help with extra cash until he eventually finds a place where he feels settled. In the meantime, the money from selling the house will be his only source of income.

He calls Billy and Jackson, and a smile appears on his face when he hears their voices. After a few moments of awkward silence, Riley apologises for ignoring them and then shares his plan with them. They support Riley and tell him that they'll miss him, but he can hear it in their voices that his two best friends since high school understand why he has to do this. Why it's what's best for him.

Three days after he walked out of Dr Bech's office, Riley's getting ready to step outside the door and embark on what he knows is going to be a challenging adventure when his phone rings. Hands full, he answers.

"You were just planning on leaving without saying goodbye?" Callum's voice comes through the phone.

Riley looks around his apartment and then at his phone. The timer is counting, seconds and then minutes being added to the call. He puts the phone back to his ear.

"Still here," Callum states.

"No, no you're not real." But Riley wants it to be real. Callum sounds gentle and caring. The sweet honeydew of his voice calms him and takes Riley to a place where he feels safe.

"How do you know?" the voice, Callum's voice, asks on the other end.

"Because you're dead," Riley chokes out. "You died five months ago. I went to your funeral. I mourned you. You're a-a hallucination."

There is a moment of silence and for a split second, Riley thinks that he's back in control of the situation. Reminding himself of what's reality

"I want to see you again, Riley. If you want to see me too, I'll be waiting."

The phone call ends.

He can feel the onset of a panic attack but he settles himself down with deep breaths, in and out. Dr Bech's voice in his head guides him along.

"It's okay," Riley whispers to himself. "You're about to make a big change and your mind is using Callum as a way to cope with that." His words work to some extent, but in the back of his mind, a little voice is screaming how badly he wants to see Callum.

He unlocks his phone and checks his call logs.

There it is, an unknown number with a two-minute and thirteen-second call time. He takes a screenshot but then decides to address the craziness of his mind later. Today is the day he leaves, and he doesn't want to have Noelle worrying about him already. He'll question it when he gets to his first stop.

With an Uber booked to take him to his storage unit, Riley gets downstairs and is frozen by what he sees.

His Dodge.

Parked, with the engine purring. The sunlight glints off its shiny, black paint.

Did Noelle get him his car from storage?

Had he asked her to?

Confused, and yet again questioning if he should reconsider taking medication, Riley cautiously steps towards the car, the black tinted windows making it impossible for him to see inside.

The street is quiet. At six in the morning on a Sunday, no one is willing to get out of bed.

When he stops in front of the passenger side window, it automatically rolls down and Riley gasps.

"I promise to answer every question, but right now, my only question is whether or not you still trust me enough to get in the car and leave this place for good?"

Callum.

Callum is alive?

No. No, he can't be.

Callum's dead.

Well, the police *told* him Callum was dead.

He never saw the body.

His mind races through every heartbreaking moment. He relives every memory of the suffering he endured at the unbearable loss of Callum, trying to pinpoint a moment that can confirm that this isn't real. But his pain was never connected to a solid confirmation.

He never saw the body.

"Tell me I'm not crazy," Riley sobs, tears cascading down his face involuntarily, the vision too unreal to accept. Was this something the doctor had forgotten to inform him of, visual hallucinations?

"Would you believe me even if I did?"

"Y-you're really here?" He puts his hands on the car windowsill. It's then he notices what used to be bright orange-red hair is now black. And the scruff, the scruff he still has dreams about, which in the past had left marks on his body for days, is now gone, leaving behind a clean-shaven, baby-faced Cal.

"So, what's it going to be? You going to tell me goodbye, or are we going on that road trip we promised each other?"

He looks at the empty road ahead of them, wiping his dripping nose. *What the actual fuck is happening?* No car in sight, not a single person in the streets. He pinches himself to be sure he's awake.

"I don't understand…"

"As I said, I'll explain on the road," Callum offers gently, as Riley looks up at the emerald green eyes he has missed looking into. "But before you hate me, just know that this was all Malcolm's idea."

When they finally stop, it's at a run-down motel in a town Riley can't remember the name of, but he remembers the sign reading *population of a thousand*. He and Callum are sitting on the lumpy mattress with questionable stains on the sheets, staring at one another, soaking in the sight of the other.

The car ride had been silent. Riley was still in shock and questioning his sanity. He couldn't even bring himself to reach over and hold Callum's hand like he had in the past. They just drove and kept their focus on the road.

"Why didn't you tell me?" Riley finally breathes.

"Malcolm made me swear not to."

"Since when did you start listening to what Malcolm said, let alone lie to me?"

"I know…"

Riley takes a moment. "How? Make me understand, Cal."

"It was all Malcolm. After Charlie's death, well…he knew you weren't safe, neither of you were, and so he came to my apartment one night after he'd sold the drugs. We talked, and honestly, when he told me the plan, I thought he was crazy, or high, or both. But as he kept talking, I could understand his reasoning behind it, what he was trying to do for you. Before he left, he gave me the money to then pass onto you, when it was time."

"I still don't understand."

"The police officer, the one who drove you to the hospital and told you about the explosion…he owed me a favour. It was easy to get him on board, especially once money was involved. Turns out their wage isn't the best."

"The car?"

"Really did explode. I just wasn't in it."

"The funeral?"

"All real. The state has declared Callum Reed dead."

"Why did you have to fake your death?" Riley is asking questions quicker than Callum can answer them.

"Malcolm had a lot of regrets. A lot to make up for. But he still knew you. He knew you would have eventually left town, whether it be with or without me. This way, a grieving boyfriend looking for a fresh start; he figured it would be less suspicious. Especially if Johnny or his men had tried to sell Malcolm out, make some deal. The missing money was still in question, as well as who he had sold to. Had you and Noelle come into money, well…"

"Your parents?"

"I've made peace with that part of my life. I know it's selfish, the pain they would be feeling, but I have you, Riley. The only thing in my life that has truly ever had an ounce of meaning. If doing this meant you were safe, that *we* could be together without looking over our shoulders, surely you can understand why I agreed?"

Riley sees a hint of sadness appear on Callum's face. He reaches forward and lays his hand over Callum's. It's warm. It has actual life pumping through it, and a spark of electricity travels down his spine, igniting the flame deep within him that had died that day with Callum.

"I can't believe Malcolm did all this, for us…his family." He can't remember the last time he associated Malcolm with being family. "Wait, his death?"

Callum squeezes his hand. "That was never the plan…but he knew there was a chance he wasn't going to survive. If the drugs hadn't killed him, the target he had put on his back with how deep he got in with Johnny would have. He knew that, and this plan was his redemption. The money was to make up for the last ten years and he was willing to risk his life so that you and Noelle could live yours in safety."

Riley notices how Callum doesn't apologise or offer condolences, his relationship with Malcolm had long ago passed that point.

Callum waits before continuing. "The officer supplied the car bomb. I was keeping it at my apartment. All I knew was Malcolm had a plan to lure Johnny out after tipping the police off since they were on the hunt for him. I don't think he meant for you or me to get in the middle of a showdown. But regardless, everything went down the way it did and I knew that was when I had to use it."

"I still have so many questions."

"And I'll answer them. But too much too fast might be a little overwhelming." Riley nods his head in agreement. "This was his way of making it up to you. Setting you up for life. We even discussed a way to send money to Noelle at a later date without it being suspicious."

Riley's head spins.

"Lie down with me?" Callum asks, and of course he does.

Their heads lay on separate pillows, hands tucked underneath as they look into each other's eyes. Their bodies are practically touching even with the gap between them. The heat radiating off of Callum has Riley vibrating with the realisation that this is real, Callum is breathing and alive and right here with him. But he still reaches out to touch Callum's cheek. He brushes his fingers against soft skin.

"I'm sorry I put you through that," Callum whispers into the room.

"You have no idea what I went through." Riley wants to be angry with the man staring back at him, but every molecule in his body fights the urge, too consumed with his physical presence.

"No, I don't. But I'm willing to listen if you want to tell me."

"…not today, but someday." Riley keeps his hand on Callum's face, a small gasp falling from his mouth as the warmth spreads under his palm.

"How…how did you know I was leaving?" he spoke in a whisper. The vulnerability from old wounds being ripped open again had stripped away any confidence he had built back up.

"The officer was keeping tabs. He'd call Noelle, act like he was checking in and he'd ask her about you. I was told to lay low until the heat died down, but you wanting to leave brought my timeline forward." Callum breaks eye contact. "The first night I called, I was planning to tell you everything. I couldn't stand knowing how much pain you were in but then when you answered the phone, not even questioning how someone who was supposed to be dead could be calling, I knew the damage was done. That the pain had gone deeper and it was shortly after that I found out about Dr Bech."

Callum's eyes meet his, regret clear on his face. "Whatever pain you went through, know that I would have gone through the same if the roles were reversed." Callum turns his head just enough so his lips can lay a kiss on the palm of Riley's hand.

The sun loved that moon so much that he died every night to let him breathe, and in return, the moon reflected the sun's love.

But what is more beautiful? How the moon lets the sun shine through the day or how the sun lets the moon glimmer at night?

The universe isn't cruel like Riley had thought.

The universe isn't finished with his story yet, either.

There are decades of stories ahead of them, and Riley is ready to live them all with the love of his life; his soulmate, his sun, his Callum.

About the author

Rachel O'Rourke is a rising star in the MM romance genre, celebrated for her ability to craft heartfelt stories that delve into deep, emotional narratives. Her works tackle complex themes such as mental health, trauma, addiction, and the intricacies of relationships, all framed through the lens of male/male (MM) romance. Rachel's storytelling transcends traditional love stories, offering her readers tales of healing, hope, and resilience.

Other Titles Written by Rachel:
Be My Saving Grace

Find Rachel Below:
Website: www.rachelorourke.com.au
Newsletter subscription: www.rachelorourke.com.au
Instagram: @rachelo.rourke
TikTok: @authorrachelo

Also on Facebook Pages, Amazon & Goodreads

Thank you so much for reading See You Again.
If you enjoyed the book, please leave a review.
Your support is deeply appreciated.